ISAAC ASIMOV'S
MASTERS OF SCIENCE FICTION

ISAAC ASIMOV'S MASTERS OF SCIENCE FICTION

Edited by
George Scithers

DAVIS PUBLICATIONS, INC.
380 LEXINGTON AVENUE, NEW YORK, N.Y. 10017

Grateful acknowledgment is hereby made to the authors and authors' representatives listed below for giving permission to reprint the material in this volume.

The following stories are Copyright © 1976 by Davis Publications, Inc.: John Varley for *Good-Bye, Robinson Crusoe;* Scott Meredith Literary Agency, Inc. for Arthur C. Clarke's *Quarantine;* Sally Sellers for *Perchance To Dream;* Herb Boehm for *Air Raid.*

The following stories are Copyright © 1977 by Davis Publications, Inc.: Martin Gardner for *The Case of the Defective Doyles;* Paula Smith for *African Blues;* Isaac Asimov for *The Missing Item* and *Sure Thing;* Don R. Bensen for *The Black Widowers* (limerick); Cam Thornley for *They'll Do It Every Time;* Jack C. Haldeman II for *Home Team Advantage;* Garry R. Osgood for *To Sin Against Systems;* Dean McLaughlin for *The Astronomical Hazards of the Tobacco Habit;* Ted Reynolds for *Boarder Incident;* Nancy Kress for *A Delicate Shade of Kipney;* Grendel Briarton for *Through Time and Space with Ferdinand Feghoot—Twice!;* Barry Malzberg for *The Several Murders of Roger Ackroyd;* Blackstone Literary Agency for Randall Garrett's *On the Martian Problem;* Kevin O'Donnell, Jr. for *Low Grade Ore.*

The following stories are Copyright © 1978 by Davis Publications, Inc.: Robert P. Mills, Ltd. for Larry Niven's *Cautionary Tales;* Scott Meredith Literary Agency, Inc. for Jack Williamson's *Will Academe Kill Science Fiction?;* Jesse Peel for *Heal the Sick, Raise the Dead;* Donald Gaither for *Wolf Tracks* (poem); Southmoor Serendipity, Ltd. for Brian Aldiss' *The Small Stones of Tu Fu;* Blackstone Literary Agency for Randall Garrett's *Polly Plus;* Michael Tennenbaum for *A Choice of Weapons;* Jack Chalker for *Dance Band on the Titanic.*

4

CONTENTS

(continued)

CONTENTS (continued)

INTRODUCTION: MASTERS OF SCIENCE FICTION
by Isaac Asimov
art: Frank Kelly Freas

There is a wide-spread rumor to the effect that I am not a shrinking violet.

Actually, I am.

It's just that in the great world around us, you can't trust other people to sing your praises. They can be awfully short-sighted and incapable of appreciating talent. Therefore, you have to prime the pump, so to speak. You have to do a little self-appreciating just to get them started. If, for any reason, they don't get started right away, you have to keep it up for a while longer.

I've had to self-appreciate for an incredibly long time, and I may have to give up some decade.

But *underneath,* I'm a shrinking violet.

That was why it was so hard for Joel Davis (the handsome and efficient entrepreneur who heads Davis Publications) to convince me there ought to be a magazine called *Isaac Asimov's Science Fiction Magazine.* I shrank back. I reddened. I mumbled.

Joel, however, would take no refusal. Hard-driving business man that he is, he ran right over me, and I still have the spike marks on the small of my back to prove it.

But I am glad! Joel, as it happens, was *right.* We got hold of George Scithers, an experienced science fiction personality, who is at home in every facet of the field and made him at home in the post of editor, and *he* was right, too.

The result?

Why, *Isaac Asimov's Science Fiction Magazine* shot up like a rocket. There is no question that it has been the most successful new magazine to have appeared in the genre since 1950.

Credit? Well, Joel has not been content merely to supply the money. He has read every story to appear in the magazine, has consulted with myself and George frequently, has bent his keen mind to the promotion and development of the magazine in its every respect. It is clearly his ewe-lamb and the results show it.

More credit? Well, George has not been content merely to select stories. He has made a full-time career out of working out policy, testing and trying different procedures, encouraging new writers and consulting with old writers, working together with them where revision is wanted, writing quick and helpful letters where rejection can't be avoided. No one since the early John Campbell has thrown himself into the task so wholeheartedly and the results show it.

Still more credit? Well, we get down to the writers themselves and that's where it all is. You can edit and publish to your heart's content and get precisely nowhere if the material that comes in under the door and over the transom is trash. The writer supplies the material—and all else is commentary.

And there, too, we met with cooperation. We sent out word that we would welcome stories and they came in. They came from ancient demigods like Randall Garrett and Poul Anderson and L. Sprague de Camp. They came from younger demigods like Larry Niven and John Varley and Barry Malzberg. They came from utter newcomers like Sally Sellers and Nancy Kress and Tony Rothman.

Even many authors whom we were forced to reject showed promise of exciting things to come—and we told them so.

We had no trouble filling four quarterly issues—then six bimonthly issues. Now we are going monthly and are ebullient and upbeat about it.

You are holding the evidence in your hand. We have here a whopping collection of items from the first year and a half of the magazine's operation. If you have missed the magazine thus far, for whatever reason, see what it has been like. It won't surprise me a bit if you decide not to miss any future issues.

If you have been buying the magazine sporadically, here is your chance to read some of the stories you have skipped. It won't surprise me a bit if it makes you decide to subscribe rather than chance missing any others.

All in all, shrinking violet or not, I'm proud. I'm proud of Joel and of George and, most of all, of the writers. And I'm grateful, too. I'm grateful to Joel for talking me into it in the first place; and to George, for working so hard at it; and to the writers for giving us the material to work with.

Thank you! Thank you, all of you!

GOOD-BYE, ROBINSON CRUSOE
by John Varley

*John Varley wrote all through high school, he
tells us, stopped when he got out, and took it
up again in 1973. Now, reading, writing, and
imagining take up all of his spare time.
Over one-third of his stories have been nominated for either
the Hugo or the Nebula, and his latest collection,* The
Persistance of Vision, *is just out from Quantum.*

9

It was summer, and Piri was in his second childhood. First, second; who counted? His body was young. He had not felt more alive since his original childhood back in the spring, when the sun drew closer and the air began to melt.

He was spending his time at Rarotonga Reef, in the Pacifica disneyland. Pacifica was still under construction, but Rarotonga had been used by the ecologists as a testing ground for the more ambitious barrier-type reef they were building in the south, just off the "Australian" coast. As a result, it was more firmly established than the other biomes. It was open to visitors, but so far only Piri was there. The "sky" disconcerted everyone else.

Piri didn't mind it. He was equipped with a brand-new toy: a fully operational imagination, a selective sense of wonder that allowed him to blank out those parts of his surroundings that failed to fit with his current fantasy.

He awoke with the tropical sun blinking in his face through the palm fronds. He had built a rude shelter from flotsam and detritus on the beach. It was not to protect him from the elements. The disneyland management had the weather well in hand; he might as well have slept in the open. But castaways *always* build some sort of shelter.

He bounced up with the quick alertness that comes from being young and living close to the center of things, brushed sand from his naked body, and ran for the line of breakers at the bottom of the narrow strip of beach.

His gait was awkward. His feet were twice as long as they should have been, with flexible toes that were webbed into flippers. Dry sand showered around his legs as he ran. He was brown as coffee and cream, and hairless.

Piri dived flat to the water, sliced neatly under a wave, and paddled out to waist-height. He paused there. He held his nose and worked his arms up and down, blowing air through his mouth and swallowing at the same time. What looked like long, hairline scars between his lower ribs came open. Red-orange fringes became visible inside them, and gradually lowered. He was no longer an air-breather.

He dived again, mouth open, and this time he did not come up. His esophagus and trachea closed and a new valve came into operation. It would pass water in only one direction, so his diaphragm now functioned as a pump pulling water through his mouth and forcing it out through the gill-slits. The water flowing through this lower chest area caused his gills to engorge with

GOOD-BYE, ROBINSON CRUSOE

blood, turning them purplish-red and forcing his lungs to collapse upward into his chest cavity. Bubbles of air trickled out his sides, then stopped. His transition was complete.

The water seemed to grow warmer around him. It had been pleasantly cool; now it seemed no temperature at all. It was the result of his body temperature lowering in response to hormones released by an artificial gland in his cranium. He could not afford to burn energy at the rate he had done in the air; the water was too efficient a coolant for that. All through his body arteries and capillaries were constricting as parts of him stablized at a lower rate of function.

No naturally evolved mammal had ever made the switch from air to water breathing, and the project had taxed the resources of bio-engineering to its limits. But everything in Piri's body was a living part of him. It had taken two full days to install it all.

He knew nothing of the chemical complexities that kept him alive where he should have died quickly from heat loss or oxygen starvation. He knew only the joy of arrowing along the white sandy bottom. The water was clear, blue-green in the distance.

The bottom kept dropping away from him, until suddenly it reached for the waves. He angled up the wall of the reef until his head broke the surface, climbed up the knobs and ledges until he was standing in the sunlight. He took a deep breath and became an air-breather again.

The change cost him some discomfort. He waited until the dizziness and fit of coughing had passed, shivering a little as his body rapidly underwent a reversal to a warm-blooded economy.

It was time for breakfast.

He spent the morning foraging among the tidepools. There were dozens of.plants and animals that he had learned to eat raw. He ate a great deal, storing up energy for the afternoon's expedition on the outer reef.

Piri avoided looking at the sky. He wasn't alarmed by it; it did not disconcert him as it did the others. But he had to preserve the illusion that he was actually on a tropical reef in the Pacific Ocean, a castaway, and not a vacationer in an environment bubble below the surface of Pluto.

Soon he became a fish again, and dived off the sea side of the reef.

The water around the reef was oxygen-rich from the constant wave action. Even here, though, he had to remain in motion to keep enough water flowing past his external gill fringes. But he could move more slowly as he wound his way down into the darker reaches of the sheer reef face. The reds and yellows of his world were swallowed by the blues and greens and purples. It was quiet. There were sounds to hear, but his ears were not adapted to them. He moved slowly through shafts of blue light, keeping up the bare minimum of water flow.

He hesitated at the ten-meter level. He had thought he was going to his Atlantis Grotto to check out his crab farm. Then he wondered if he ought to hunt up Ocho the Octopus instead. For a panicky moment he was afflicted with the bane of childhood: an inability to decide what to do with himself. Or maybe it was worse, he thought. Maybe it was a sign of growing up. The crab farm bored him, or at least it did today.

He waffled back and forth for several minutes, idly chasing the tiny red fish that flirted with the anemones. He never caught one. This was no good at all. Surely there was an adventure in this silent fairyland. He had to find one.

An adventure found him, instead. Piri saw something swimming out in the open water, almost at the limits of his vision. It was long and pale, an attenuated missle of raw death. His heart squeezed in panic, and he scuttled for a hollow reef.

Piri called him the Ghost. He had been seen many times in the open sea. He was eight meters of mouth, belly and tail: hunger personified. There were those who said the great white shark was the most ferocious carnivore that ever lived. Piri believed it.

It didn't matter that the Ghost was completely harmless to him. The Pacifica management did not like having its guests eaten alive. An adult could elect to go into the water with no protection, providing the necessary waivers were on file. Children had to be implanted with an equalizer. Piri had one, somewhere just below the skin of his left wrist. It was a sonic generator, set to emit a sound that would mean terror to any predator in the water.

The Ghost, like all the sharks, barracudas, morays, and other predators in Pacifica, was not like his cousins who swam the seas of Earth. He had been cloned from cells stored in the Biological Library on Luna. The library had been created two hundred years before as an insurance policy against the extinction of a species. Originally, only endangered species were filed, but for years before the Invasion the directors had been trying to get a sample of everything. Then the Invaders had come, and Lunarians were too busy surviving without help from Occupied Earth to worry about the library. But when the time came to build the disneylands, the library had been ready.

By then, biological engineering had advanced to the point where many modifications could be made in genetic structure. Mostly, the disneyland biologists had left nature alone. But they had changed the predators. In the Ghost, the change was a mutated organ attached to the brain that responded with a flood of fear when a supersonic note was sounded.

So why was the Ghost still out there? Piri blinked his nictating membranes, trying to clear his vision. It helped a little. The shape looked a bit different.

Instead of moving back and forth, the tail seemed to be going up and down, perhaps in a scissoring motion. Only one animal swims like that. He gulped down his fear and pushed away from the reef.

But he had waited too long. His fear of the Ghost went beyond simple danger, of which there was none. It was something more basic, an unreasoning reflex that prickled his neck when he saw that long white shape. He couldn't fight it, and didn't want to. But the fear had kept him against the reef, hidden, while the person swam out of reach. He thrashed to catch up, but soon lost track of the moving feet in the gloom.

He had seen gills trailing from the sides of the figure, muted down to a deep blue-black by the depths. He had the impression that it was a woman.

Tongatown was the only human habitation on the island. It housed a crew of maintenance people and their children, about fifty in all, in grass huts patterned after those of South Sea natives. A few of the buildings concealed elevators that went to the underground rooms that would house the tourists when the project was completed. The shacks would then go at a premium rate, and the beaches would be crowded.

Piri walked into the circle of firelight and greeted his friends. Nighttime was party time in Tongatown. With the day's work over, everybody gathered around the fire and roasted a vat-grown goat or lamb. But the real culinary treats were the fresh vegetable dishes. The ecologists were still working out the kinks in the systems, controlling blooms, planting more of failing species. They often produced huge excesses of edibles that would have cost a fortune on the outside. The workers took some of the excess for themselves. It was understood to be a fringe benefit of the job. It was hard enough to find people who could stand to stay under the

Pacifica sky.

"Hi, Piri," said a girl. "You meet any pirates today?" It was Harra, who used to be one of Piri's best friends but had seemed increasingly remote over the last year. She was wearing a hand-made grass skirt and a lot of flowers, tied into strings that looped around her body. She was fifteen now, and Piri was...but who cared? There were no seasons here, only days. Why keep track of time?

Piri didn't know what to say. The two of them had once played together out on the reef. It might be Lost Atlantis, or Submariner, or Reef Pirates; a new plot line and cast of heroes and villains every day. But her question had held such thinly veiled contempt. Didn't she care about the Pirates anymore? What was the matter with her?

She relented when she saw Piri's helpless bewilderment.

"Here, come on and sit down. I saved you a rib." She held out a large chunk of mutton.

Piri took it and sat beside her. He was famished, having had nothing all day since his large breakfast.

"I thought I saw the Ghost today," he said, casually.

Harra shuddered. She wiped her hands on her thighs and looked at him closely.

"Thought? You thought you saw him?" Harra did not care for the Ghost. She had cowered with Piri more than once as they watched him prowl.

"Yep. But I don't think it was really him."

"Where was this?"

"On the sea-side, down about, oh, ten meters. I think it was a woman."

"I don't see how it could be. There's just you and—and Midge and Darvin with—did this woman have an air tank?"

"Nope. Gills. I saw that."

"But there's only you and four others here with gills. And I know where they all were today."

"You used to have gills," he said, with a hint of accusation.

She sighed. "Are we going through that again? I *told* you, I got tired of the flippers. I wanted to move around the *land* some more."

"I can move around the land," he said, darkly.

"All right, all right. You think I deserted you. Did you ever think that you sort of deserted *me?*"

Piri was puzzled by that, but Harra had stood up and walked

14   GOOD-BYE, ROBINSON CRUSOE

quickly away. He could follow her, or he could finish his meal. She was right about the flippers. He was no great shakes at chasing anybody.

Piri never worried about anything for too long. He ate, and ate some more, long past the time when everyone else had joined together for the dancing and singing. He usually hung back, anyway. He could sing, but dancing was out of his league.

Just as he was leaning back in the sand, wondering if there were any more corners he could fill up—perhaps another bowl of that shrimp teriyaki?—Harra was back. She sat beside him.

"I talked to my mother about what you said. She said a tourist showed up today. It looks like you were right. It was a woman, and she was amphibious."

Piri felt a vague unease. One tourist was certainly not an invasion, but she could be a harbinger. And amphibious. So far, no one had gone to that expense except for those who planned to live here for a long time. Was his tropical hide-out in danger of being discovered?

"What—what's she doing here?" He absently ate another spoonful of crab cocktail.

"She's looking for *you*," Harra laughed, and elbowed him in the ribs. Then she pounced on him, tickling his ribs until he was howling in helpless glee. He fought back, almost to the point of having the upper hand, but she was bigger and a little more determined. She got him pinned, showering flower petals on him as they struggled. One of the red flowers from her hair was in her eye, and she brushed it away, breathing hard.

"You want to go for a walk on the beach?" she asked.

Harra was fun, but the last few times he'd gone with her she had tried to kiss him. He wasn't ready for that. He was only a kid. He thought she probably had something like that in mind now.

"I'm too full," he said, and it was almost the literal truth. He had stuffed himself disgracefully, and only wanted to curl up in his shack and go to sleep.

Harra said nothing, just sat there getting her breathing under control. At last she nodded, a little jerkily, and got to her feet. Piri wished he could see her face to face. He knew something was wrong. She turned from him and walked away.

Robinson Crusoe was feeling depressed when he got back to his hut. The walk down the beach away from the laughter and singing had been a lonely one. Why had he rejected Harra's offer of companionship? Was it really so bad that she wanted to play new kinds of games?

But no, damn it. She wouldn't play his games, why should he play hers?

After a few minutes of sitting on the beach under the crescent moon, he got into character. Oh, the agony of being a lone castaway, far from the company of fellow creatures, with nothing but faith in God to sustain oneself. Tomorrow he would read from the scriptures, do some more exploring along the rocky north coast, tan some goat hides, maybe get in a little fishing.

With his plans for the morrow laid before him, Piri could go to sleep, wiping away a last tear for distant England.

The ghost woman came to him during the night. She knelt beside him in the sand. She brushed his sandy hair from his eyes and he stirred in his sleep. His feet thrashed.

He was churning through the abyssal deeps, heart hammering, blind to everything but internal terror. Behind him, jaws yawned, almost touching his toes. They closed with a snap.

He sat up woozily. He saw rows of serrated teeth in the line of breakers in front of him. And a tall, white shape in the moonlight dived into a curling breaker and was gone.

"Hello."

Piri sat up with a start. The worst thing about being a child living alone on an island—which, when he thought about it, was the sort of thing every child dreamed of—was not having a warm mother's breast to cry on when you had nightmares. It hadn't affected him much, but when it did, it was pretty bad.

He squinted up into the brightness. She was standing with her head blocking out the sun. He winced, and looked away, down to her feet. They were webbed, with long toes. He looked a little higher. She was nude, and quite beautiful.

"Who . . . ?"

"Are you awake now?" She squatted down beside him. Why had he expected sharp, triangular teeth? His dreams blurred and ran like watercolors in the rain, and he felt much better. She had a nice face. She was smiling at him.

He yawned, and sat up. He was groggy, stiff, and his eyes were coated with sand that didn't come from the beach. It had been an awful night.

"I think so."

"Good. How about some breakfast?" She stood, and went to a basket on the sand.

"I usually—" but his mouth watered when he saw the guavas, melons, kippered herring, and the long brown loaf of bread. She had butter, and some orange marmalade. "Well, maybe just a—" and he had bitten into a succulent slice of melon. But before he could finish it, he was seized by an even stronger urge. He got to his feet and scuttled around the palm tree with the waist-high dark stain and urinated against it.

"Don't tell anybody, huh?" he said, anxiously.

She looked up. "About the tree? Don't worry."

He sat back down and resumed eating the melon. "I could get in a lot of trouble. They gave me a thing and told me to use it."

"It's all right with me," she said, buttering a slice of bread and handing it to him. "Robinson Crusoe never had a portable Eco-San, right?"

"Right," he said, not showing his surprise. How did she know *that*?

Piri didn't know quite what to say. Here she was, sharing his morning, as much a fact of life as the beach or the water.

"What's your name?" It was as good a place to start as any.

"Leandra. You can call me Lee."

"I'm—"

"Piri. I heard about you from the people at the party last night. I hope you don't mind me barging in on you like this."

He shrugged, and tried to indicate all the food with the gesture. "Anytime," he said, and laughed. He felt good. It was nice to have someone friendly around after last night. He looked at her again, from a mellower viewpoint.

She was large; quite a bit taller than he was. Her physical age was around thirty, unusually old for a woman. He thought she might be closer to sixty or seventy, but he had nothing to base it on. Piri himself was in his nineties, and who could have known that? She had the slanting eyes that were caused by the addition of transparent eyelids beneath the natural ones. Her hair grew in a narrow band, cropped short, starting between her eyebrows and going over her head to the nape of her neck. Her ears were pinned efficiently against her head, giving her a lean, streamlined look.

"What brings you to Pacifica?" Piri asked.

She reclined on the sand with her hands behind her head, looking very relaxed.

"Claustrophobia." She winked at him. "Not really. I wouldn't survive long in Pluto with *that*." Piri wasn't even sure what it was, but he smiled as if he knew. "Tired of the crowds. I heard that people couldn't enjoy themselves here, what with the sky, but I didn't have any trouble when I visited. So I bought flippers and gills and decided to spend a few weeks skin-diving by myself."

Piri looked at the sky. It was a staggering sight. He'd grown used to it, but knew that it helped not to look up more than he had to.

It was an incomplete illusion, all the more appalling because the half of the sky that had been painted was so very convincing. It looked like it really was the sheer blue of infinity, so when the eye slid over to the unpainted overhanging canopy of rock, scarred from blasting, painted with gigantic numbers that were barely visible from twenty kilometers below—one could almost imagine God looking down through the blue opening. It loomed, suspended by nothing, gigatons of rock hanging up there.

Visitors to Pacifica often complained of headaches, usually right on the crown of the head. They were cringing, waiting to get conked.

"Sometimes I wonder how *I* live with it," Piri said.

She laughed. "It's nothing for me. I was a space pilot once."

"Really?" This was catnip to Piri. There's nothing more romantic than a space pilot. He had to hear stories.

The morning hours dwindled as she captured his imagination with a series of tall tales he was sure were mostly fabrication. But who cared? Had he come to the South Seas to hear of the mundane? He felt he had met a kindred spirit, and gradually, fearful of being laughed at, he began to tell her stories of the Reef Pirates, first as wishful wouldn't-it-be-fun-if's, then more and more seriously as she listened intently. He forgot her age as he began to spin the best of the yarns he and Harra had concocted.

It was a tacit conspiracy between them to be serious about the stories, but that was the whole point. That was the only way it would work, as it had worked with Harra. Somehow, this adult woman was interested in playing the same games he was.

Lying in his bed that night, Piri felt better than he had for months, since before Harra had become so distant. Now that he had a companion, he realized that maintaining a satisfying fantasy world by yourself is hard work. Eventually you need someone to tell the stories to, and to share in the making of them.

They spent the day out on the reef. He showed her his crab farm, and introduced her to Ocho the Octopus, who was his usual shy self. Piri suspected the damn thing only loved him for the treats he brought.

She entered into his games easily and with no trace of adult condescension. He wondered why, and got up the courage to ask her. He was afraid he'd ruin the whole thing, but he had to know. It just wasn't normal.

They were perched on a coral outcropping above the high tide level, catching the last rays of the sun.

"I'm not sure," she said. "I guess you think I'm silly, huh?"

"No, not exactly that. It's just that most adults seem to, well, have more 'important' things on their minds." He put all the contempt he could into the word.

"Maybe I feel the same way you do about it. I'm here to have fun. I sort of feel like I've been re-born into a new element. It's *terrific* down there, you know that. I just didn't feel like I wanted to go into that world alone. I was out there yesterday . . ."

"I thought I saw you."

"Maybe you did. Anyway, I needed a companion, and I heard about you. It seemed like the polite thing to, well, not to ask you to be my guide, but sort of fit myself into your world. As it were." She frowned, as if she felt she had said too much. "Let's not push it, all right?"

"Oh, sure. It's none of my business."

"I like you, Piri."

"And I like you. I haven't had a friend for . . . too long."

That night at the luau, Lee disappeared. Piri looked for her briefly, but was not really worried. What she did with her nights was her business. He wanted her during the days.

As he was leaving for his home, Harra came up behind him and took his hand. She walked with him for a moment, then could no longer hold it in.

"A word to the wise, old pal," she said. "You'd better stay away from her. She's not going to do you any good."

"What are you talking about? You don't even know her."

"Maybe I do."

"Well, do you or don't you?"

She didn't say anything, then sighed deeply.

"Piri, if you do the smart thing you'll get on that raft of yours and sail to Bikini. Haven't you had any . . . feelings about her? Any premonitions or anything?"

"I don't know what you're talking about," he said, thinking of sharp teeth and white death.

"I think you do. You have to, but you won't face it. That's all I'm saying. It's not my business to meddle in your affairs."

"I'll say it's not. So why did you come out here and put this stuff in my ear?" He stopped, and something tickled at his mind from his past life, some earlier bit of knowledge, carefully suppressed. He was used to it. He knew he was not really a child, and that he had a long life and many experiences stretching out behind him. But he didn't think about it. He hated it when part of his old self started to intrude on him.

"I think you're jealous of her," he said, and knew it was his old, cynical self talking. "She's an adult, Harra. She's no threat to you. And, hell, I know what you've been hinting at these last months. I'm not ready for it, so leave me alone. I'm just a kid."

Her chin came up, and the moonlight flashed in her eyes.

"You idiot. Have you looked at yourself lately? You're not Peter Pan, you know. You're growing up. You're damn near a man."

"That's not true." There was panic in Piri's voice. "I'm only. . . . well, I haven't exactly been counting, but I can't be more than nine, ten years—"

"Shit. You're as old as I am, and I've had breasts for two years. But I'm not out to cop you. I can cop with any of seven boys in the village younger than you are, but not you." She threw her hands up in exasperation and stepped back from him. Then, in a sudden fury, she hit him on the chest with the heel of her fist. He fell back, stunned at her violence.

"She *is* an adult," Harra whispered through her teeth. "That's what I came here to warn you against. *I'm* your friend, but you don't know it. Ah, what's the use? I'm fighting against that scared old man in your head, and he won't listen to me. Go ahead, go with her. But she's got some surprises for you."

"What? What surprises?" Piri was shaking, not wanting to listen to her. It was a relief when she spat at his feet, whirled, and ran down the beach.

"Find out for yourself," she yelled back over her shoulder. It sounded like she was crying.

That night, Piri dreamed of white teeth, inches behind him, snapping.

But morning brought Lee, and another fine breakfast in her bulging bag. After a lazy interlude drinking coconut milk, they

GOOD-BYE, ROBINSON CRUSOE

went to the reef again. The pirates gave them a rough time of it, but they managed to come back alive in time for the nightly gathering.

Harra was there. She was dressed as he had never seen her, in the blue tunic and shorts of the reef maintenence crew. He knew she had taken a job with the disneyland and had not seen her dressed up before. He had just begun to get used to the grass skirt. Not long ago, she had been always nude like him and the other children.

She looked older somehow, and bigger. Maybe it was just the uniform. She still looked like a girl next to Lee. Piri was confused by it, and his thoughts veered protectively away.

Harra did not avoid him, but she was remote in a more important way. It was like she had put on a mask, or possibly taken one off. She carried herself with a dignity that Piri thought was beyond her years.

Lee disappeared just before he was ready to leave. He walked home alone, half hoping Harra would show up so he could apologize for the way he'd talked to her the night before. But she didn't.

He felt the bow-shock of a pressure wave behind him, sensed by some mechanism he was unfamiliar with, like the lateral line of a fish, sensitive to slight changes in the water around him. He knew there was something behind him, closing the gap a little with every wild kick of his flippers.

It was dark. It was always dark when the thing chased him. It was not the wispy, insubstantial thing that darkness was when it settled on the night air, but the primal, eternal night of the depths. He tried to scream with his mouth full of water, but it was a dying gurgle before it passed his lips. The water around him was warm with his blood.

He turned to face it before it was upon him, and saw Harra's face corpse-pale and glowing sickly in the night. But no, it wasn't Harra, it was Lee, and her mouth was far down her body, rimmed with razors, a gaping crescent hole in her chest. He screamed again—

And sat up.

"What? Where are you?"

"I'm right here, it's going to be all right." She held his head as he brought his sobbing under control. She was whispering something but he couldn't understand it, and perhaps wasn't meant to.

It was enough. He calmed down quickly, as he always did when he woke from nightmares. If they hung around to haunt him, he never would have stayed by himself for so long.

There was just the moon-lit paleness of her breast before his eyes and the smell of skin and sea water. Her nipple was wet. Was it from his tears? No, his lips were tingling and the nipple was hard when it brushed against him. He realized what he had been doing in his sleep.

"You were calling for your mother," she whispered, as though she'd read his mind. "I've heard you shouldn't wake someone from a nightmare. It seemed to calm you down."

"Thanks," he said, quietly. "Thanks for being here, I mean."

She took his cheek in her hand, turned his head slightly, and kissed him. It was not a motherly kiss, and he realized they were not playing the same game. She had changed the rules on him.

"Lee . . ."

"Hush. It's time you learned."

She eased him onto his back, and he was overpowered with *deja vu*. Her mouth worked downward on his body and it set off chains of associations from his past life. He was familiar with the sensation. It had happened to him often in his second childhood. Something would happen that had happened to him in much the same way before and he would remember a bit of it. He had been seduced by an older woman the first time he was young. She had taught him well, and he remembered it all but didn't want to remember. He was an experienced lover and a child as well.

"I'm not old enough," he protested, but she was holding in her hand the evidence that he was old enough, had been old enough for several years. *I'm fourteen years old,* he thought. How could he have kidded himself into thinking he was ten?

"You're a strong young man," she whispered in his ear. "And I'm going to be very disappointed if you keep saying that. You're not a child anymore, Piri. Face it."

"I . . . I guess I'm not."

"Do you know what to do?"

"I think so."

She reclined beside him, drew her legs up. Her body was huge and ghostly and full of limber strength. She would swallow him up, like a shark. The gill slits under her arms opened and shut quickly with her breathing, smelling of salt, iodine, and sweat.

He got on his hands and knees and moved over her.

§   §   §

He woke before she did. The sun was up: another warm, cloudless morning. There would be two thousand more before the first scheduled typhoon.

Piri was a giddy mixture of elation and sadness. It was sad, and he knew it already, that his days of frolicking on the reef were over. He would still go out there, but it would never be the same.

Fourteen years old! Where had the years gone? He was nearly an adult. He moved away from the thought until he found a more acceptable one. He was an adolescent, and a very fortunate one to have been initiated into the mysteries of sex by this strange woman.

He held her as she slept, spooned cozily back to front with his arms around her waist. She had already been playmate, mother, and lover to him. What else did she have in store?

But he didn't care. He was not worried about anything. He already scorned his yesterdays. He was not a boy, but a youth, and he remembered from his other youth what that meant and was excited by it. It was a time of sex, of internal exploration and the exploration of others. He would pursue these new frontiers with the same single-mindedness he had shown on the reef.

He moved against her, slowly, not disturbing her sleep. But she woke as he entered her and turned to give him a sleepy kiss.

They spent the morning involved in each other, until they were content to lie in the sun and soak up heat like glossy reptiles.

"I can hardly believe it," she said. "You've been here for . . . how long? With all these girls and women. And I know at least one of them was interested."

He didn't want to go into it. It was important to him that she not find out he was not really a child. He felt it would change things, and it was not fair. Not fair at all, because it *had* been the first time. In a way he could never have explained to her, last night had been not a re-discovery but an entirely new thing. He had been with many women and it wasn't as if he couldn't remember it. It was all there, and what's more, it showed up in his love-making. He had not been the bumbling teenager, had not needed to be told what to do.

But it was *new*. That old man inside had been a spectator and an invaluable coach, but his hardened viewpoint had not intruded to make last night just another bout. It had been a first time, and the first time is special.

When she persisted in her questions he silenced her in the only way he knew, with a kiss. He could see he had to re-think his relationship to her. She had not asked him questions as a playmate, or a mother. In the one role, she had been seemingly as self-centered as he, interested in only in the needs of the moment and her personal needs above all. As a mother, she had offered only wordless comfort in a tight spot.

Now she was his lover. What did lovers do when they weren't making love?

They went for walks on the beach, and on the reef. They swam together, but it was different. They talked a lot.

She soon saw that he didn't want to talk about himself. Except for the odd question here and there that would momentarily confuse him, throw him back to stages of his life he didn't wish to remember, she left his past alone.

They stayed away from the village except to load up on supplies. It was mostly his unspoken wish that kept them away. He had made it clear to everyone in the village many years ago that he was not really a child. It had been necessary to convince them that he could take care of himself on his own, to keep them from being over-protective. They would not spill his secret knowingly, but neither would they lie for him.

So he grew increasingly nervous about his relationship with Lee, founded as it was on a lie. If not a lie, then at least a withholding of the facts. He saw that he must tell her soon, and dreaded it. Part of him was convinced that her attraction to him was based mostly on age difference.

Then she learned he had a raft, and wanted to go on a sailing trip to the edge of the world.

Piri did have a raft, though an old one. They dragged it from the bushes that had grown around it since his last trip and began putting it into shape. Piri was delighted. It was something to do, and it was hard work. They didn't have much time for talking.

It was a simple construction of logs lashed together with rope. Only an insane sailor would put the thing to sea in the Pacific Ocean, but it was safe enough for them. They knew what the weather would be, and the reports were absolutely reliable. And if it came apart, they could swim back.

All the ropes had rotted so badly that even gentle wave action would have quickly pulled it apart. They had to be replaced, a new mast erected, and a new sailcloth installed. Neither of them knew anything about sailing, but Piri knew that the winds blew toward the edge at night and away from it during the day. It was a simple matter of putting up the sail and letting the wind do the navigating.

He checked the schedule to be sure they got there at low tide. It was a moonless night, and he chuckled to himself when he thought of her reaction to the edge of the world. They would sneak up on it in the dark, and the impact would be all the more powerful at sunrise.

But he knew as soon as they were an hour out of Rarotonga that he had made a mistake. There was not much to do there in the night but talk.

"Piri, I've sensed that you don't want to talk about certain things."

"Who? Me?"

She laughed into the empty night. He could barely see her face. The stars were shining brightly, but there were only about a hundred of them installed so far, and all in one part of the sky.

"Yeah, you. You won't talk about yourself. It's like you grew here, sprang up from the ground like a palm tree. And you've got no mother in evidence. You're old enough to have divorced her, but you'd have a guardian somewhere. Someone would be looking after your moral upbringing. The only conclusion is that you don't need an education in moral principles. So you've got a co-pilot."

"Um." She had seen through him. Of course she would have. Why hadn't he realized it?

"So you're a clone. You've had your memories transplanted into a new body, grown from one of your own cells. How old are you? Do you mind my asking?"

"I guess not. Uh . . . what's the date?"

She told him.

"And the year?"

She laughed, but told him that, too.

"Damn. I missed my one hundredth birthday. Well, so what? It's not important. Lee, does this change anything?"

"Of course not. Listen, I could tell the first time, that first night together. You had that puppy-dog eagerness, all right, but you knew how to handle yourself. Tell me: what's it like?"

"The second childhood, you mean?" He reclined on the gently rocking raft and looked at the little clot of stars. "It's pretty damn great. It's like living in a dream. What kid hasn't wanted to live alone on a tropic isle? I can, because there's an adult in me who'll keep me out of trouble. But for the last seven years I've been a kid. It's you that finally made me grow up a little, maybe sort of late, at that."

"I'm sorry. But it felt like the right time."

"It was. I was afraid of it at first. Listen, I *know* that I'm really a hundred years old, see? I know that all the memories are ready for me when I get to adulthood again. If I think about it, I can remember it all as plain as anything. But I haven't wanted to, and in a way, I still don't want to. The memories are suppressed when you opt for a second childhood instead of being transplanted into another full-grown body."

"I know."

"Do you? Oh, yeah. Intellectually. So did I, but I didn't understand what it meant. It's a nine or ten-year holiday, not only from your work, but from yourself. When you get into your nineties, you might find that you need it."

She was quiet for a while, lying beside him without touching.

"What about the re-integration? Is that started?"

"I don't know. I've heard it's a little rough. I've been having dreams about something chasing me. That's probably my former self, right?"

"Could be. What did your older self do?"

He had to think for a moment, but there it was. He'd not thought of it for eight years.

"I was an economic strategist."

Before he knew it, he found himself launching into an explanation of offensive economic policy.

"Did you know that Pluto is in danger of being gutted by currency transfers from the Inner Planets? And you know why? The speed of light, that's why. Time lag. It's killing us. Since the time of the Invasion of Earth it's been humanity's idea—and a good one, I think—that we should stand together. Our whole cultural thrust in that time has been toward a total economic community. But it won't work at Pluto. Independence is in the cards."

She listened as he tried to explain things that only moments before he would have had trouble understanding himself. But it poured out of him like a breached dam, things like inflation multipliers, futures buying on the oxygen and hydrogen exchanges, phantom dollars and their manipulation by central banking interests, and the invisible drain.

"Invisible drain? What's that?"

"It's hard to explain, but it's tied up in the speed of light. It's an economic drain on Pluto that has nothing to do with real goods and services, or labor, or any of the other traditional forces. It has to do with the fact that any information we get from the Inner Planets is already at least nine hours old. In an economy with a stable currency—pegged to gold, for instance, like the classical economies on Earth—it wouldn't matter much, but it would still have an effect. Nine hours can make a difference in prices, in futures, in outlook on the markets. With a floating exchange medium, one where you need the hourly updates on your credit meter to know what your labor input will give you in terms of material output—your personal financial equation, in other words—and the inflation multiplier is something you simply *must* have if the equation is going to balance and you're not going to be wiped out, then time is really of the essence. We operate at a perpetual disadvantage on Pluto in relation to the Inner Planet money markets. For a long time it ran on the order of point three percent leakage due to outdated information. But the inflation multiplier has been accelerating over the years. Some of it's been absorbed by the fact that we've been moving closer to the I.P.; the time lag has been getting shorter as we move into summer. But it can't last. We'll reach the inner point of our orbit and the effects will really start to accelerate. Then it's war."

"War?" She seemed horrified, as well she might be.

"War, in the economic sense. It's a hostile act to renounce a trade agreement, even if it's bleeding you white. It hits every citizen of the Inner Planets in the pocketbook, and we can expect retaliation. We'd be introducing instability by pulling out of the Common Market."

"How bad will it be? Shooting?"

"Not likely. But devastating enough. A depression's no fun. And they'll be planning one for us."

"Isn't there any other course?"

"Someone suggested moving our entire government and all our corporate headquarters to the Inner Planets. It could happen, I guess. But who'd feel like it was ours? We'd be a colony, and that's a worse answer than independence, in the long run."

She was silent for a time, chewing it over. She nodded her head once; he could barely see the movement in the darkness.

"How long until the war?"

He shrugged. "I've been out of touch. I don't know how things have been going. But we can probably take it for another ten years or so. Then we'll have to get out. I'd stock up on real wealth if I were you. Canned goods, air, water, so forth. I don't think it'll get so bad that you'll need those things to stay alive by consuming them. But we may get to a semi-barter situation where they'll be the only valuable things. Your credit meter'll laugh at you when you punch a purchase order, no matter how much work you've put into it."

The raft bumped. They had arrived at the edge of the world.

They moored the raft to one of the rocks on the wall that rose from the open ocean. They were five kilometers out of Rarotonga. They wainted for some light as the sun began to rise, then started up the rock face.

It was rough: blasted out with explosives on this face of the dam. It went up at a thirty degree angle for fifty meters, then was suddenly level and smooth as glass. The top of the dam at the edge of the world had been smoothed by cutting lasers into a vast table top, three hundred kilometers long and four kilometers wide. They left wet footprints on it as they began the long walk to the edge.

They soon lost any meaningful perspective on the thing. They lost sight of the sea-edge, and couldn't see the drop-off until they began to near it. By then, it was full light. Timed just right, they would reach the edge when the sun came up and they'd really have something to see.

A hundred meters from the edge when she could see over it a little, Lee began to unconsciously hang back. Piri didn't prod her. It was not something he could force someone to see. He'd reached this point with others, and had to turn back. Already, the fear of falling was building up. But she came on, to stand beside him at the very lip of the canyon.

Pacifica was being built and filled in three sections. Two were complete, but the third was still being hollowed out and was not yet filled with water except in the deepest trenches. The water was kept out of this section by the dam they were standing on. When it was completed, when all the underwater trenches and mountain ranges and guyots and slopes had been built to specifications, the bottom would be covered with sludge and ooze and the whole wedge-shaped section flooded. The water came from liquid hydrogen and oxygen on the surface, combined with the limitless electricity of fusion powerplants.

"We're doing what the Dutch did on Old Earth, but in reverse," Piri pointed out, but he got no reaction from Lee. She was staring, spellbound, down the sheer face of the dam to the apparently bottomless trench below. It was shrouded in mist, but seemed to fall off forever. "It's eight kilometers deep," Piri told her. "It's not going to be a regular trench when it's finished. It's there to be filled up with the remains of this dam after the place has been flooded." He looked at her face, and didn't bother with more statistics. He let her experience it in her own way.

The only comparable vista on a human-inhabited planet was the Great Rift Valley on Mars. Neither of them had seen it, but it suffered in comparison to this because not all of it could be seen at once. Here, one could see from one side to the other, and, from sea level to a distance equivalent to the deepest oceanic trenches on Earth. It simply fell away beneath them and went straight down to nothing. There was a rainbow beneath their feet. Off to the left was a huge waterfall that arced away from the wall in a solid stream. Tons of overflow water went through the wall, to twist, fragment, vaporize and blow away long before it reached the bottom of the trench.

Straight ahead of them and about ten kilometers away was the mountain that would become the Okinawa biome when the pit was filled. Only the tiny, blackened tip of the mountain would show above the water.

Lee stayed and looked at it as long as she could. It became easier the longer one stood there, and yet something about it drove her away. The scale was too big, there was no room for humans in that shattered world. Long before noon, they turned and started the long walk back to the raft.

She was silent as they boarded and set sail for the return trip. The winds were blowing fitfully, barely billowing the sail. It would be another hour before they blew very strongly. They were still in sight of the dam wall.

They sat on the raft, not looking at each other.

"Piri, thanks for bringing me here."

"You're welcome. You don't have to talk about it."

"All right. But there's something else I have to talk about. I . . . don't know where to begin, really."

Piri stirred uneasily. The earlier discussion about economics had disturbed him. It was part of his past life, a part that he had not been ready to return to. He was full of confusion. Thoughts that had no place out here in the concrete world of wind and water were roiling through his brain. Someone was calling to him, someone he knew but didn't want to see right then.

"Yeah? What is it you want to talk about?"

"It's about—" she stopped, seemed to think it over. "Never mind. It's not time yet." She moved close and touched him. But he was not interested. He made it known in a few minutes, and she moved to the other side of the raft.

He lay back, essentially alone with his troubled thoughts. The wind gusted, then settled down. He saw a flying fish leap, almost passing over the raft. There was a piece of the sky falling through the air. It twisted and turned like a feather, a tiny speck of sky that was blue on one side and brown on the other. He could see the hole in the sky where it had been knocked loose.

It must be two or three kilometers up, and it looked like it was falling from the center. How far away were they from the center of Pacifica? A hundred kilometers?

A piece of the sky?

He got to his feet, nearly capsizing the raft.

"What's the matter?"

It was *big*. It looked large even from this far away. It was the dreamy tumbling motion that had deceived him.

"The sky is . . . " he choked on it, and almost laughed. But this was not time to feel silly about it. "The sky is falling, Lee." How long? He watched it, his mind full of numbers. Terminal velocity from that high up, assuming it was heavy enough to punch right through the atmosphere . . . over six hundred meters per second. Time to fall, seventy seconds. Thirty of those must already have gone by.

Lee was shading her eyes as she followed his gaze. She still thought it was a joke. The chunk of sky began to glow red as the atmosphere got thicker.

"Hey it really is falling." she said. "Look at that."

"It's big. Maybe one or two kilometers across. It's going to make quite a splash, I'll bet."

They watched it descend. Soon it disappeared over the horizon, picking up speed. They waited, but the show seemed to be over. Why was he still uneasy?

"How many tons in a two-kilometer chunk of rock, I wonder?" Lee mused. She didn't look too happy, either. But they sat back down on the raft, still looking in the direction where the thing had sunk into the sea.

Then they were surrounded by flying fish, and the water looked crazy. The fish were panicked. As soon as they hit they leaped from the water again. Piri felt rather than saw something pass beneath them. And then, very gradually, a roar built up, a deep bass rumble that soon threatened to turn his bones to powder. It picked him up and shook him, and left him limp on his knees. He was stunned, unable to think clearly. His eyes were still fixed on the horizon, and he saw a white fan rising in the distance in silent majesty. It was the spray from the impact, and it was still going up.

"Look up there," Lee said, when she got her voice back. She seemed confused as he. He looked where she pointed and saw a twisted line crawling across the blue sky. At first he thought it was the end of his life, because it appeared that the whole overhanging dome was fractured and about to fall in on them. But then he saw it was one of the tracks that the sun ran on, pulled free by the rock that had fallen, twisted into a snake of tortured metal.

"The dam!" he yelled. "The dam! We're too close to the dam!"

"What?"

"The bottom rises this close to the dam. The water here isn't that deep. There'll be a wave coming, Lee, a big wave. It'll pile up here."

"Piri, the shadows are moving."

"Huh?"

Surprise was piling on surprise too fast for him to cope with it. But she was right. The shadows were moving. But *why?*

Then he saw it. The sun was setting, but not by following the tracks that led to the concealed opening in the west. It was falling through the air, having been shaken loose by the rock.

Lee had figured it out, too.

"What is that thing?" she asked. "I mean, how big is it?"

"Not too big, I heard. Big enough, but not nearly the size of that chunk that fell. It's some kind of fusion generator. I don't know what'll happen when it hits the water."

They were paralyzed. They knew there was something they should do, but too many things were happening. There was not time to think it out.

"Dive!" Lee yelled. "Dive into the water!"

"What?"

"We have to dive and swim away from the dam, and down as far as we can go. The wave will pass over us, won't it?"

"I don't know."

"It's all we can do."

So they dived. Piri felt his gills come into action, then he was swimming down at an angle toward the dark-shrouded bottom.

Lee was off to his left, swimming as hard as she could. And with no sunset, no warning, it got black as pitch. The sun had hit the water.

He had no idea how long he had been swimming when he suddenly felt himself pulled upward. Floating in the water, weightless, he was not well equipped to feel accelerations. But he did feel it, like a rapidly rising elevator. It was accompanied by pressure waves that threatened to burst his eardrums. He kicked and clawed his way downward, not even knowing if he was headed in the right direction. Then he was falling again.

He kept swimming, all alone in the dark. Another wave passed, lifted him, let him down again. A few minutes later, another one, seeming to come from the other direction. He was hopelessly confused. He suddenly felt he was swimming the wrong way. He stopped, not knowing what to do. Was he pointed in the right direction? He had no way to tell.

He stopped paddling and tried to orient himself. It was useless. He felt surges, and was sure he was being tumbled and buffeted.

Then his skin was tingling with the sensation of a million bubbles crawling over him. It gave him a handle on the situation. The bubbles would be going up, wouldn't they? And they were traveling over his body from belly to back. So down was *that* way.

But he didn't have time to make use of the information. He hit something hard with his hip, wrenched his back as his body tried to tumble over in the foam and water, then was sliding along a smooth surface. It felt like he was going very fast, and he knew where he was and where he was heading and there was nothing he could do about it. The tail of the wave had lifted him clear of the rocky slope of the dam and deposited him on the flat surface. It was now spending itself, sweeping him along to the edge of the world. He turned around, feeling the sliding surface beneath him with his hands, and tried to dig in. It was a nightmare; nothing he did had any effect. Then his head broke free into the air.

He was still sliding, but the huge hump of the wave had dissipated itself and was collapsing quietly into froth and puddles. It drained away with amazing speed. He was left there, alone, cheek pressed lovingly to the cold rock. The darkness was total.

He wasn't about to move. For all he knew, there was an eight-kilometer drop just behind his toes.

Maybe there would be another wave. If so, this one would crash down on him instead of lifting him like a cork in a tempest. It should kill him instantly. He refused to worry about that. All he cared about now was not slipping any further.

The stars had vanished. Power failure? Now they blinked on. He raised his head a little, in time to see a soft, diffused glow in the east. The moon was rising, and it was doing it at breakneck speed. He saw it rotate from a thin crescent configuration to bright fullness in under a minute. Someone was still in charge and had decided to throw some light on the scene.

He stood, though his knees were weak. Tall fountains of spray far away to his right indicated where the sea was battering at the dam. He was about in the middle of the tabletop, far from either edge. The ocean was whipped up as if by thirty hurricanes, but he was safe from it at this distance unless there were another tsunami yet to come.

The moonlight turned the surface into a silver mirror, littered with flopping fish. He saw another figure get to her feet, and ran in that direction.

The helicopter located them by infrared detector. They had no way of telling how long it had been. The moon was hanging motionless in the center of the sky.

They got into the cabin, shivering.

The helicopter pilot was happy to have found them, but grieved over other lives lost. She said the toll stood at three dead, fifteen missing and presumed dead. Most of these had been working on the reefs. All the land surface of Pacifica had been scoured, but the loss of life had been minimal. Most had time to get to an elevator and go below or to a helicopter and rise above the devastation.

From what they had been able to find out, heat expansion of the crust had moved farther down into the interior of the planet than had been expected. It was summer on the surface, something it was easy to forget down here. The engineers had been sure that the inner surface of the sky had been stabilized years ago, but a new fault had been opened by the slight temperature rise. She pointed up to where ships were hovering like fireflies next to the sky, playing searchlights on the site of damage. No one knew yet if Pacifica would have to be abandoned for another twenty years while it stabilized.

She set them down on Rarotonga. The place was a mess. The wave had climbed the bottom rise and crested at the reef, and a churning hell of foam and debris had swept over the island. Little was left standing except the concrete blocks that housed the elevators, scoured of their decorative camouflage.

Piri saw a familiar figure coming toward him through the wreckage that had been a picturesque village. She broke into a run, and nearly bowled him over, laughing and kissing him.

"We were sure you were dead," Harra said, drawing back from him as if to check for cuts and bruises.

"It was a fluke, I guess," he said, still incredulous that he had survived. It had seemed bad enough out there in the open ocean; the extent of the disaster was much more evident on the island. He was badly shaken to see it.

"Lee suggested that we try to dive under the wave. That's what saved us. It just lifted us up, then the last one swept us over the top of the dam and drained away. It dropped us like leaves."

"Well, not quite so tenderly in my case," Lee pointed out. "It gave me quite a jolt. I think I might have sprained my wrist."

A medic was available. While her wrist was being bandaged, she kept looking at Piri. He didn't like the look.

"There's something I'd intended to talk to you about on the raft, or soon after we got home. There's no point in your staying here any longer anyway, and I don't know where you'd go."

"No!" Harra burst out. "Not yet. Don't tell him anything yet. It's not fair. Stay away from him." She was protecting Piri with her body, from no assault that was apparent to him.

"I just wanted to—"

"No, no. Don't listen to her, Piri. Come with me." She pleaded with the other woman. "Just give me a few hours alone with him, there's some things I never got around to telling him."

Lee looked undecided, and Piri felt mounting rage and frustration. He had known things were going on around him. It was mostly his own fault that he had ignored them, but now he had to know. He pulled his hand free from Harra and faced Lee.

"Tell me."

She looked down at her feet, then back to his eyes.

"I'm not what I seem, Piri. I've been leading you along, trying to make this easier for you. But you still fight me. I don't think there's any way it's going to be easy."

"No!" Harra shouted again.

"What are you?"

"I'm a psychiatrist. I specialize in retrieving people like you, people who are in a mental vacation mode, what you call 'second childhood.' You're aware of all this, on another level, but the child in you has fought it at every stage. The result has been nightmares—probably with me as the focus, whether you admitted it or not."

She grasped both his wrists, one of them awkwardly because of her injury.

"Now listen to me." She spoke in an intense whisper, trying to get it all out before the panic she saw in his face broke free and sent him running. "You came here for a vacation. You were going to stay ten years, growing up and taking it easy. That's all over. The situation that prevailed when you left is now out of date. Things have moved faster than you believed possible. You had expected a ten-year period after your return to get things in order for the coming battles. That time has evaporated. The Common Market of the Inner Planets has fired the first shot. They've instituted a new system of accounting and it's locked into their computers and running. It's aimed right at Pluto, and it's been working for a month now. We cannot continue as an economic partner to the C.M.I.P., because from now on every time we sell or buy or move money the inflationary multiplier is automatically juggled against us. It's perfectly legal by all existing treaties, and it's necessary to their economy. But it ignores our time-lag disadvantage. We have to consider it as a hostile act, no matter what the intent. You have to come back and direct the war, Mister Finance Minister."

The words shattered what calm Piri had left. He wrenched free of her hands and turned wildly to look all around him. Then he sprinted down the beach. He tripped once over his splay feet, got up without ever slowing, and disappeared.

Harra and Lee stood silently and watched him go.

"You didn't have to be so rough with him," Harra said, but knew it wasn't so. She just hated to see him so confused.

"It's best done quickly when they resist. And he's all right. He'll have a fight with himself, but there's no real doubt of the outcome."

"So the Piri I know will be dead soon?"

Lee put her arm around the younger woman.

"Not at all. It's a re-integration, without a winner or a loser. You'll see." She looked at the tear-streaked face.

"Don't worry. You'll like the older Piri. It won't take him any time at all to realize that he loves you."

He had never been to the reef at night. It was a place of furtive fish, always one step ahead of him as they darted back into their places of concealment. He wondered how long it would be before they ventured out in the long night to come. The sun might not rise for years.

They might never come out. Not realizing the changes in their environment, night fish and day fish would never adjust. Feeding cycles would be disrupted, critical temperatures would go awry, the endless moon and lack of sun would frustrate the internal mechanisms, bred over billions of years, and fish would die. It had to happen.

The ecologists would have quite a job on their hands.

But there was one denizen of the outer reef that would survive for a long time. He would eat anything that moved and quite a few things that didn't, at any time of the day or night. He had no fear, he had no internal clocks dictating to him, no inner pressures to confuse him except the one overriding urge to attack. He would last as long as there was anything alive to eat.

But in what passed for a brain in the white-bottomed torpedo that was the Ghost, a splinter of doubt had lodged. He had no recollection of similar doubts, though there had been some. He was not equipped to remember, only to hunt. So this new thing that swam beside him, and drove his cold brain as near as it could come to the emotion of anger, was a mystery. He tried again and again to attack it, then something would seize him with an emotion he had not felt since he was half a meter long, and fear would drive him away.

Piri swam along beside the faint outline of the shark. There was just enough moonlight for him to see the fish, hovering at the ill-defined limit of his sonic signal. Occasionally, the shape would shudder from head to tail, turn toward him, and grow larger. At these times Piri could see nothing but a gaping jaw. Then it would turn quickly, transfix him with that bottomless pit of an eye, and sweep away.

Piri wished he could laugh at the poor, stupid brute. How could he have feared such a mindless eating machine?

Good-bye, pinbrain. He turned and stroked lazily toward the shore. He knew the shark would turn and follow him, nosing into the interdicted sphere of his transponder, but the thought did not impress him. He was without fear. How could he be afraid, when he had already been swallowed into the belly of his nightmare? The teeth closed around him, he awakened, and remembered. And that was the end of his fear.

Good-bye, tropical paradise. You were fun while you lasted. Now

I'm grown-up, and must go off to war.

He didn't relish it. It was a wrench to leave his childhood, though the time had surely been right. Now the responsibilities had descended on him, and he must shoulder them. He thought of Harra.

"Piri," he told himself, "as a teenager, you were just too dumb to live."

Knowing it was the last time, he felt the coolness of the water flowing over his gills. They had served him well, but had no place in his work. There was no place for a fish, and no place for Robinson Crusoe.

Good-bye, gills.

He kicked harder for the shore and came to stand, dripping wet, on the beach. Harra and Lee were there, waiting for him.

QUARANTINE
by Arthur C. Clarke

Mr. Clarke notes: "To my considerable astonishment, I find that it is more than five years since I last wrote a short story (in case you're dying to know, it was A Meeting with Medusa). *This was composed for one specific purpose—to complete the long overdue volume* The Wind from the Sun; *and having done this, I have had no incentive to produce any more short fiction. Or, for that matter, short* **non**-*fiction; only yesterday I gently informed the Editor of the U.S.S.R.'s Writers' Union's magazine, "Questions of Literature" that, from now on, I am writing novels—or nothing at all. (And I have already achieved a whole year of blissful nothingness, hurrah.)*

"Yet from time to time lightning may strike. This occurred exactly a year ago as a result of a suggestion from George Hay, editor and man-about-British-SF. George had the ingenious idea of putting out a complete science fiction short story **on a** **postcard**—*together with a stamp-sized photo of the author. Fans would, he believed, buy these in hundreds to mail out to their friends.*

"Never one to resist a challenge, the Good Doctor Asimov had written the first cardboard epic. When I saw this, I had to get into the act as well (Anything that Isaac can do, etc. . . .). Let me tell you—it is damned hard work writing a complete SF story in 180 words. I sent the result to George Hay, and that's the last I ever heard of it. Probably the rising cost of postage killed the scheme.

"Anyway, it seems appropriate that a magazine bearing the Good Doctor's Sacred

*Name should contain a story, however
minuscule, inspired by him. (He is likewise to
blame for 'Neutron Tide'; I can make worse
puns than Isaac.) It is also perfectly
possible—I make no promises—that
"Quarantine" is the last short story I shall
ever write. For at my present average of 40
words a year, even by 2001 ... "*

Earth's flaming debris still filled half the sky when the question filtered up to Central from the Curiosity Generator.

"Why was it necessary? Even though they were organic, they *had* reached Third Order Intelligence."

"We had no choice: five earlier units became hopelessly infected, when they made contact."

"Infected? How?"

The microseconds dragged slowly by, while Central tracked down the few fading memories that had leaked past the Censor Gate, when the heavily-buffered Reconnaissance Circuits had been ordered to self-destruct.

"They encountered—a *problem*—that could not be fully analyzed within the lifetime of the Universe. Though it involved only six operators, they became totally obsessed by it."

"How is that possible?"

"We do not know: *we must never know.* But if those six operators are ever re-discovered, all rational computing will end."

"How can they be recognized?"

"That also we do not know: only the names leaked through before the Censor Gate closed. Of course, they mean nothing."

"Nevertheless, I must have them."

The Censor voltage started to rise; but it did not trigger the Gate.

"Here they are : King, Queen, Bishop, Knight, Rook, Pawn."

CAUTIONARY TALES
by Larry Niven

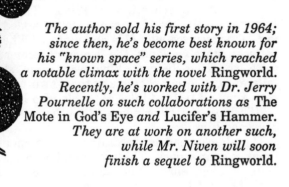

The author sold his first story in 1964; since then, he's become best known for his "known space" series, which reached a notable climax with the novel Ringworld. *Recently, he's worked with Dr. Jerry Pournelle on such collaborations as* The Mote in God's Eye *and* Lucifer's Hammer. *They are at work on another such, while Mr. Niven will soon finish a sequel to* Ringworld.

Taller than a man, thinner than a man, with a long neck and eyes set wide apart in his head, the creature still resembled a man; and he had aged like a man. Cosmic rays had robbed his fur of color, leaving a grey-white ruff along the base of his skull and over both ears. His pastel-pink skin was deeply wrinkled and marked with darker blotches. He carried himself like something precious and fragile. He was coming across the balcony toward Gordon.

Gordon had brought a packaged lunch from the Embassy. He ate alone. The bubble-world's landscape curled up and over his head: yellow-and-scarlet parkland, slate-colored buildings that bulged at the top. Below the balcony, patterned stars streamed beneath several square miles of window. There were a dozen breeds of alien on the public balcony, at least two of which had to be pets or symbiotes of other aliens; and no humans but for Gordon. Gordon wondered if the ancient humanoid resented his staring ... then stared in earnest as the creature stopped before his table. The alien said, "May I break your privacy?"

Gordon nodded; but that could be misinterpreted, so he said, "I'm glad of the company."

The alien carefully lowered himself until he sat cross-legged across the table. He said, "I seek never to die."

Gordon's heart jumped into his throat. "I'm not sure what you mean," he said cautiously. "The Fountain of Youth?"

"I do not care what form it takes." The alien spoke the Trade Language well, but his strange throat added a castinet-like clicking. "Our own legend holds no fountain. When we learned to cross between stars we found the legend of immortality wherever there were thinking beings. Whatever their shape or size or intelligence, whether they make their own worlds or make only clay pots, they all tell the tales of people who live forever."

"It's hard not to wonder if they have some basis," Gordon encouraged him.

The alien's head snapped around, fast enough and far enough to break a man's neck. The prominent lumps bobbing in his throat were of alien shape: not Adam's Apple, but someone else's. "It must be so. I have searched too long for it to be false. You, have you ever found clues to the secret of living forever?"

Gordon searched when he could, when his Embassy job permitted it. There had been rumors about the Ftokteek. Gordon had followed the rumors out of human space, toward the galactic core and the Ftokteek Empire, to this Ftokteek-dominated meeting place of disparate life forms, this cloud of bubble-worlds of varying gravities and atmospheres. Gordon was middle-aged now, and Sol was invisible even to orbiting telescopes, and the Ftokteek died like anyone else.

He said, "We've got the legends. Look them up in the Human Embassy library. Ponce de Leon, and Gilgamesh, and Orpheus, and Tithonus, and . . . every god we ever had lived forever, if he didn't die by violence, and some could heal from that. Some religions say that some part of us lives on after we die."

"I will go to your library tomorrow," the alien said without enthusiasm. "Do you have no more than legends?"

"No, but . . . do other species tell cautionary tales?"

"I do not understand."

Gordon said, "Some of our legends say you wouldn't want to live forever. Tithonus, for instance. A goddess gave him the gift of living forever, but she forgot to keep him young. He withered into a lizard. Adam and Eve were exiled by God; He was afraid they'd learn the secret of immortality and think they were as good as Him. Orpheus tried to bring a woman back from the dead. Some of the stories say you can't get immortality, and some say you'd go insane with boredom."

The alien pondered. "The tale tellers disdain immortality because they cannot have it. Jealousy? Could immortal beings have walked among you once?"

Gordon laughed. "I doubt it. Was that what made you come to me?"

"I go to the worlds where many species meet. When I see a creature new to me, then I ask. Sometimes I can sense others like me, who want never to die."

Gordon looked down past the edge of the balcony, down through the great window at the banded Jovian planet that held this swarm of bubble-worlds in their orbits. He came here every day; small wonder that the alien had picked him out. He came because he would not eat with the others. They thought he was crazy. He thought of them as mayflies, with their attention always on the passing moment, and no thought for the future. He thought of himself as an ambitious mayfly; and he ate alone.

The alien was saying, "When I was young I looked for the secret among the most advanced species. The great interstellar empires, the makers of artificial worlds, the creatures who mine stars for elements and send ships through the universe seeking ever more knowledge, would build their own immortality. But they die as you and I die. Some races live longer than mine, but they all die."

"The Ftokteek have a computerized library the size of a small planet," Gordon said. He meant to get there someday, if he lived. "It must know damn near everything."

The alien answered with a whispery chuckle. "No bigger than a moon is the Ftokteek library. It told me nothing I could use."

The banded world passed from view.

"Then I looked among primitives," the alien said, "who live closer to their legends. They die. When I thought to talk to their ghosts, there was nothing, though I used their own techniques. Afterward I searched the vicinities of the black holes and other strange pockets of the universe, hoping that there may be places where entropy reverses itself. I found nothing. I examined the mathematics that describe the universe. I have learned a score of mathematical systems, and none hold any hope of entropy reversal, natural or created."

Gordon watched stars pass below his feet. He said, "Relativity. We used to think that if you traveled faster than light, time would reverse itself."

"I know eight systems of travelling faster than light—"

"Eight? What is there besides ours and the Ftokteek drive?"

"Six others. I rode them all, and always I arrived older. My time runs short. I never examined the quasars, and now I would not live to reach them. What else is left? I have been searching for fourteen thousand years—" The alien didn't notice when Gordon made a peculiar hissing sound. "—in our counting. Less in yours, perhaps. Our world huddles closer to a cooler sun than this. Our year is twenty-one million standard seconds."

"What are you *saying?* Ours is only thirty-one million—"

"My present age is three hundred thirty-six point seven billion standard seconds in the Ftokteek counting."

"Ten thousand Earth years. More!"

"Far too long. I never mated. None carry my genes. Now none ever will, unless I can grow young again. There is little time left."

"But *why?*"

The alien seemed startled. "Because it is not enough. Because I am afraid to die. Are you short-lived, then?"

"Yes," said Gordon.

"Well, I have traveled with short-lived companions. They die, I mourn. I need a companion with the strength of youth. My spacecraft is better than any you could command. You may benefit from my research. We breath a similar air mixture, our bodies use the same chemistry, we search for the same treasure. Will you join my quest?"

"No."

"But . . . I sensed that you seek immortality. I am never wrong. Don't you feel it, the certainty that there is a way to thwart entropy, to live forever?"

"I used to think so," said Gordon.

In the morning he arranged passage home to Sol system. Ten thousand years wasn't enough . . . no lifetime was enough, unless you lived it in such a way as to make it enough.

THE CASE OF THE DEFECTIVE DOYLES
by Martin Gardner

Here we have a variation of the weighing problem—how much information can one extract from a minimum number of weighings of suspect items—in an extraterrestrially exotic setting.

Shurl and Watts, at a base on Pluto, are in charge of distributing doyles to more distant outposts. Doyles are the size of peas, all identical, each weighing precisely one gram. They are indispensible in hyperspace propulsion systems.

Doyles come in cans of 100 doyles each, and shipments are made up of six cans at a time. The Pluto base has a sensitive spring scale capable of registering fractions of milligrams.

One day, a week after a shipment of doyles, a radio message came from the manufacturing company in Hong Kong. "Urgent. One can is filled with defective doyles, each with an excess weight of one milligram. Identify can and destroy its doyles at once."

"I suppose," said Watts, "we'll have to make six weighings, one doyle from each can."

"Not so, my dear Watts," said Shurl. "We can identify the can of defectives with just *one* weighing. First we number the cans from one through six. Then we take 1 doyle from the first can, 2 from the second can, 3 from the third, and so on to 6 from the sixth can. We place this set of 21 doyles on the scale. It will weigh n milligrams over 21 grams, and of course n will be the number of the defective can."

"How absurdly simple!" exclaimed Watts, while Shurl shrugged.

A month later, after the next shipment, another message arrived: "Any of the six cans, perhaps all of them, may be full of defective doyles, each one milligram overweight. Identify and destroy all defective doyles."

"This time," said Watts, "I suppose we'll have to weigh separately a doyle from each can."

Shurl put his fingertips together and gazed at a picture of Isaac Asimov on the wall. "A capital problem, Watts. No, I think we can still do it in just one weighing."

What algorithm does Shurl have in mind? See page 125 for the answer.

AFRICAN BLUES
by Paula Smith

*Currently a student, a systems analyst,
(with this sale ((a first))) a writer,
and a part-time bum, or so she tells
us, the author claims to have led a
sheltered life, never venturing more
than 12,000 miles away from home.
"African Blues" is the first story
she ever tried to sell, and she is
thinking Real Hard about writing another.*

Musa's cow, Llana, was eight years old, and I did not think she would be able to calve. But there it was, and she was bearing another one. It was hard for her; she was quite old. Musa had brought her in from the savannah when it became obvious she would have difficulty dropping. He left her at my veterinary barn. "See her through, Sister Doto," he said, "and I will pay up all I owe." This for Musa is a major concession.

That is why I was in my barn before dawn with Llana that day. That was the day the rocket came down over the village. At first it was only a faraway whistle, high and shrill. I thought it was a bird and paid it no mind. There were other things to attend to; Llana is a nasty beast, with a tendency to bite. But then the whistle grew sharper, very quickly, you see; and Llana shuddered for more reason than just her unborn calf. Then bang! came a crash.

For a moment after the crash it was very quiet; even the hyenas shut up their morning howling and the dungbirds stopped screeching. Then half the village was awake, hurrying out of their houses to see what it was. "Llana, you wait for a minute," I said. I wanted to see what this was, and what it was doing here in Kenya. Besides, in the barn it was very close; I also needed some air.

It was early morning, and already quite warm. Here on the equator there are certain days when the sun is so bright and hot that it burns the sky yellow. That is what the people say. The teachers at the missionary school in Nairobi say it is the dust. Certainly there is more than enough of it, a lot of dust in the air because it had not rained in two months. Further, that day the villagers kicked up more running out into the savannah to find the fallen object. The sky was already pale with sunrise, and I knew it would not turn blue that day.

Jama was the first to find it. It was big, bigger than a house. "Is this one of the whites' spaceships?" he said.

"Yes," I answered. It was indeed a rocket; I had seen several on the television in the capital. But it did not look like the Americans' rockets, which are cone-shaped, like our roof-tops. This one was circular, round all the way over, like a ball. There were many wires wrapped around it, and a big—parachute, they call it—only it looked more like a huge ship's sail. It was torn.

The rocket was at the deep end of a long rut it had made in the brush. The villagers began to dig it out—who can tell if such a thing might not be valuable?—and I was thinking I must return to Llana. Then Dr. Hunter, the black American who came to our village two years ago, ran up, sweating. He is always sweating.

47

He came here because he wanted to be African; but even African water doesn't stay in him, it always sweats away.

"Don't open it!" he yelled in his Kiswahili, which is very bad. Whenever possible I speak English with him. "We'll notify the authorities first. It might be a Russian capsule."

The villagers looked up, and some moved away. Most moved away. Dr. Hunter is sometimes crazy, and often rude, but he is a smart man. He, too, is educated.

Jama walked up to Dr. Hunter and bowed a little. "Your instructions?" he asked in Kiswahili, for that is the only language he knows. I spoke up, using English, "What authorities should we notify, Dr. Hunter? Brother Jama is ready to do what you suggest."

"Also may I borrow his bicycle," Jama said to me. "It's a long way to Lodwar."

"Oh," said Dr. Hunter, blinking a little. "Authorities . . . well—" He started to count off on his fingers. "Well—the District Commissioner, for one. The mayor of Lodwar, the po—"

I almost jumped out of my skin. The rocket had knocked at us. "Get back!" yelled Dr. Hunter, as if we weren't already scattering. The thumping increased, grew louder, stopped. We waited a moment, holding our breaths. A few of the bolder young men started forward. But they halted, and scuttled back when a section of the rocket opened a bit above the ground. At first the door stuck, grating against the jamb, then it wiggled free, coming all the way open. And from inside the rocket, a man crawled up, leaned out, and fell out of the hatch. A *blue* man.

I must admit I was astounded. He was small, slighter even than a white man. He wore a great deal of padding and a thick-looking round helmet, though there was no visor. We hurried forward to take him away from the rocket, for he just lay there. His face was shaped like a top, very round above—especially wide at the eyes, which were closed—tapering to almost nothing for a chin. Dr. Hunter told us, "Take him to my office."

M'bega, his two sons, and Sulimani picked up the little blue man between them and headed off to Dr. Hunter's very large, very beautiful house. (It has a wooden roof.) The doctor himself followed close behind them, going, "Sst! sst! careful there."

I stayed behind for a moment, walking around the rocket. The metal radiated warmth, as did the ground around it. Some of the sand had been turned to glass. The sun was fully up now, shimmering on the huge sail. It wasn't cloth, for I could see no weave,

AFRICAN BLUES

although it was like a metal fabric. But it didn't reflect quite like metal. I came back to the opening, intending to close the hatch cover, when I heard a scraping inside the rocket. I didn't know, were there more blue people in there? I was most cautious as I peered in. But it was only M'bega's littlest boy, Faki, who grinned at me from a padded chair. "See what I found, Aunt?" he said, holding up a piece of the metal-like cloth. "It was in here," he said, pointing to a little mesh bag fastened on the side of the chair.

"You come out of there," I said, and leaned in to pull him out. The rocket's—cabin, I suppose you would call it—was very cramped, and it was hot, stifling. There were many more boxes and mesh bags, many things tied to the round walls of the cabin. There were three tiny windows—no, they were television screens—on the curve of the wall before the pilot's chair. I put Faki down outside and shooed him on. Then I looked at the long cloth band I had taken from him. Too big for a headpiece and too narrow for anything else, it was smooth, thick, and quite strong. I pulled out the net bag—it had come from off the side of the chair—and closed the hatch.

Admittedly I dawdled going back to my barn. I was curious; what was this cloth for? Why should the blue man have had it nearest him? Well, something had to be nearest, I supposed. But what were these other things in the mesh bag—two pieces of very soft cloth, not metallic; a length of string; a pencil; a small vial; and a bunch of cotton waste. Strange things, but not strange enough to belong with a blue man.

Well, they were getting dusty in my hand. I put them back into the bag and went on. It was growing hotter, with the horizon shimmering all around in the distance. So flat, the savannah, with nothing but the brush and dust standing on it. But do you know, as I swung that bag while I walked, all the dust in it flew out. None of the articles, but only the dust. I looked inside and all the things were clean. It was quite odd. Do you think Europeans have such things?

I came back to my infirmary, went to see whether all was well with Llana. Ah, the poor old cow! As I approached, she was standing in her stall, shuddering in a labor pain. She strained, twitched all down the length of her hide, then relaxed. "Ah, Llana, poor girl, is it hard when you're old?" I leaned against the wooden slats for a very long time. Llana was well, just that the calf was no closer than before. The sun's rays peeped in from the cracks in the southeast corner, lighting motes in the air. It was dark and still, very quiet, but growing warm even in the shed. The hay smell was thick in the air, too, as thick as the dust out-doors.

Something about the bag's contents—the two kinds of cloth, the pencil, the cotton waste, and the string. And a small vial. It bothered me. I emptied the mesh bag out onto a manger to examine the items. The soft cloth, I found, would stick to itself, and the pencil would cut the string. It would also cut straw in half, but it would not cut my skin. I opened the little bottle, dab-bing a bit onto my fingertip. I tasted it—and it was brine! Most unusual.

The silver cloth was a sling; and its edges would hold together, making a sort of small, hollow hammock. It all bothered me. They meant something, I was sure. I felt that. Sometimes, you see, I feel as if I were all the land, that I could hear and smell every thing and every animal that walked across me, that if I could only feel just a little bit more, I should know everything and be perfect. This was the same feeling. If I could only know the why of these curious objects, I felt I should know all about the blue man.

Llana mooed very softly. I gathered the things into the bag—again all the dirt fell out—and noted the time. Forty minutes. Her waters had not yet broken, so it would be a long time yet. I thought, and made up my mind. I would go see the blue man. Maybe that would give me my hint.

Outdoors, the sky was already brass, without a cloud. The dust on the short trail to Dr. Hunter's house was stirred up just by my walking, and it settled over me, turning my arms almost as grey as the old bluejeans I was wearing. The bag I tucked under my belt. As I walked, I tied all the little braids of my hair up into a topknot, wrapping them all with my kerchief. My mother had given me the kerchief last winter, before she died. She had made me come back here to the village when I had completed school in Nairobi.

Dr. Hunter's house had been built years before, even before I was born, by a European, Herr Max. The village people had set-tled around it because he also had an artesian well drilled. There used to be a garden in back, but Dr. Hunter let it die. It is a shame; it was very beautiful.

I knocked on the wooden door and called, "Hodi?" Nobody an-swered. Again I called, "Hodi? May I come in?"

Then Dr. Hunter's voice said, "Who is it?"

"It is I, Doto," I said. "May I come in?"

There was a click as he unlatched his door. Opening it, he said, "Ka—uh, karibu, Dota. Is Jama back yet?"

"It is unlikely that he would be," I said, walking inside. "It is a very long way to Lodwar. I have come to see the blue man and ask him about his bag," which I held up. "May I see him?"

He simply looked at me, with sweat of more than heat on his brow. There, was a cry from further within the house, short, sharp, which caused Dr. Hunter to start. "Dota . . . look, the blue man is sick. He must have been injured in that landing. And I sure as Hell—that is, I may be a doctor, but that doesn't mean I necessarily know how to treat blue Martians."

"Oh. Well; I, too, am trained in medical matters. I was schooled at Corleri Veterinary Institute in the capital, and I believe I may already know what is troubling the blue man. I should like to come in." I made to enter his dispensary, but again he stopped me.

"*Dota!*" he said. "Can't I make you understand? He is an *alien*—who knows what could be wrong with him? He may have hurt organs whose normal function I couldn't know! The best thing we can do for him is try and get him comfortable until the UN or somebody can get him out of here to better care. Savvy?"

He was gripping my upper arm tightly, his face very close to mine. I do not care for this; it is not respectful. I, too, after all, am educated, perhaps not so much as Dr. Hunter; but even my knowledge of veterinary matters should count for something. And I also had the blue man's bag.

"Dr. Hunter," I said, very calm. "My name is Do*to*. You keep mispronouncing my name, which is not polite. I have come to see the blue man. I have certain things of his from the rocket which he may be needing. Hodi?"

He stared at me for quite long time. Plainly he was not happy with this situation, but when the high cry came again, he shook himself, growling, "Oh, come on in. But I'm in charge here, understand that. I don't want some back-country witch doctor fouling up interplanetary relations, y'got that?"

"Of course, Dr. Hunter. You would rather do it yourself," I said, as I went into the infirmary.

In there, on the examining table lay the blue man, awake and looking upwards. His padded suit being off, I could see he was blue all over, except for a sort of short brown pelt of hair over his scalp, apparently across his back, and running down the outside of his arms to the back of his hands. He had three fingers on each hand. He was quite thin and slight, like a young boy, with a large round head. I came a little closer and he looked at me.

How do I say it? The eyes—large and round, deep and beautiful, beautiful—like ostrich eyes, like a bowl of water reflecting sunlight. They seemed to be black, though they might have been brown. I have never seen eyes like that; I shall not forget them.

Then I looked away, down to the somewhat swollen abdomen under Dr. Hunter's modesty sheet; and everything, the bag, the belly, the sling, fell into place, as my schoolteacher used to say. "Dr. Hunter, would you want me to assist you, then?" I said to the American.

"At what?"

"The delivery. The blue man is with child."

Yes, I do say that surprised Dr. Hunter a little bit. For a long moment he gaped at the blue man, his mouth going like a fish's, until the blue man—she—groaned, gripping the sides of the table to help her bear down with the pain of labor. This brought Dr. Hunter back to himself. He snapped at me, "Move over, girl, get me—where's my stethoscope?" He fit the tips in his ears, put the cup to her belly, muttering, "All the time thought it was a second heart. *Damn*! Sell my soul for a fluoroscope. Such a thing as *too* primitive, Hunter." He flipped out the earpieces and began palpitating the abdomen. The blue man looked on, quiet again. "Oh Lord, oh Lord. Doto, you're right. How'd you know?"

I emptied the wonderful bag out onto the cabinet top. "These are the things she had nearest her—this, string, to tie the cord; this pencil is a clipper, to cut it; diapers, for herself or the child, as is also the cotton waste, for cleaning and swabbing. And this," I held up the silver cloth, "is a sling to hold the baby across her back. Or chest. It is obvious."

"Obvious, Hell," Dr. Hunter said. I tried to overlook the profanity. "How you know some alien's gonna be placental? She surely isn't mammillary, not with that practically concave chest. Genitals don't even approximate human type. Oh Lord, Lord."

"But," I said to him, "what else could it be? She *does*," I pointed it out, "have a navel."

He shook his head, his hand wiping his forehead. "Never mind. I'll accept that as a hypothesis." He looked the blue man up and down a moment, then said, "By the way she's acting, birth is imminent. So, yeah, I'll want you to assist me. Go wash up, put on these," handing me a mask, cap, and gown, "and sterilize these."

He gave me a forceps, speculum, two scalpels, and several clamps. "Wear these gloves."

He turned away as I balanced all these things in my arms. I already knew that one is supposed to do such things; Dr. Hunter, like all Europeans, is quite peremptory. Oh, I felt—but that doesn't matter. It was at that moment that I looked at the blue man again, at the deep, deep eyes... and Dr. Hunter's rudeness didn't signify. Had the blue man been a person like me, that look would have been a smile, a smile amidst all her pain. I smiled back.

So. I did as I had been told, coming back shortly with the instruments piled on Dr. Hunter's steel tray. The doctor had closed the blinds to keep out the flies and dust, and set out several clean glass dishes and test tubes. "For samples," he said. He went to wash up as well.

When he returned, he began by filling his glassware with various of the blue man's excretions. From time to time a few drops of violet-colored blood ran from her birth canal, and nothing we did seemed to stop it. The bag of waters had apparently already ruptured, although Dr. Hunter later said he didn't think there had ever been any. The pains were evident and regular, about ten minutes apart. The blue man grunted with each, holding onto my hand or the table as she bore down during the spasms. Time went on like this.

It was very close in the room, quite extremely warm. Dr. Hunter was sweating, I was sweating—even the blue man had sweat beads about her head and neck. I wiped them away and she spoke some words. They made no sense, but then what do you expect from a foreigner? Dr. Hunter listened to her belly with his stethoscope, poked and prodded, but did little else. He did not try to dilate the birth canal, which I certainly would have done by this time. He wouldn't even allow me to give the blue man some water. "We don't know if her system can tolerate real water—let alone the terrestrial organisms contaminating this stuff. God knows what airborne diseases are already infecting her. And anyway, I don't want her to drink because I sure don't need to load up her bladder right now—if she's even got a bladder." Well, that made sense, so I let the matter go.

As time went by, the sun, in its swing about the building, found a crack between the screen and the window frame. It shone in brightly, falling directly onto the blue man's face. Her eyes seemed very sensitive to our light; she squeezed them shut till I repositioned the blind. "That is the Sun," I said to her. "The Sun. And I am Doto. Do-to." She gazed at me a moment, then said—as nearly as *I* can say it—"Hckvfuhl."

"There!" I said. "That must be her name. Or possibly her country."

Dr. Hunter snorted impolitely. "Me–Man. This–Earth. Sounds more like she's clearing her throat." A moment later, the blue man spasmed again, crying out the loudest she had yet today, and he simply stood there, doing nothing.

I was annoyed. First, at this nasty drip of sweat that had run beneath my mask so I *couldn't* wipe it away; second, at Dr. Hunter. *Mostly* at Dr. Hunter. I said as evenly as I could, "Doctor, she is suffering greatly. There are drugs to relieve pain. Could you not give her a little, just to help?"

Still he did nothing, not even looking at me. Shortly, the blue man's pains ceased.

"Dr. Hunter, I am asking you to help her. Push on her belly, use the forceps, why don't you? Even Juna the midwife would have had this baby born before now. Why, I myself—"

"Oh, shove it!" he yelled at me, while a second pain arose in Hckvfuhl. He turned to me, sweating angrily, and shouted further, "You damn native bitch! What do you know—a horse doctor?! This is an alien, do you understand, an *alien*. You don't know—*I* don't know the first thing about her, her physiology, or how it functions. You and your African midwife would have had her dead by now." Yet another cry from the blue man distracted him, and he seemed to sweat even more, if possible. "There is nothing I can do but wait and watch. This may even be normal for her species. I'm not about to kill her by fooling around where I'm ignorant. Just don't you give me any flak, girl." And so he let her cry and cry and cry.

After an hour all the pains had slacked off. That is not right, it doesn't happen with people or cattle. I was alarmed that the child might be dead, but Dr. Hunter still reported hearing the fetal heartbeat. There was still that thin trickle of violet blood which would not be stopped, only slowed. Hckvfuhl moaned often from continuous pain, which was the most frightening of all. The eyes were shut tight.

Eventually it neared sunset. As the sun rimmed the unshaded window on the west side, it grew slightly cooler, quieter as both the insects and the village prepared for nightfall. It comes swiftly here. "I am hungry," I said. Dr. Hunter looked up.

"Mm, yeah, so am I. More than that, I need to take a break; and I bet you do, too. I don't think we better eat anything, we don't have time. But you go ahead. Take five minutes, then be right back."

"All right." I removed my mask and cap, peeled off my gloves. Then, as I suddenly recalled, I put my hand to my cheek, saying, "Llana! Her calf—"

"Doto." Dr. Hunter looked at me wearily. "Screw the cow. This is more important."

Well, Musa might not have agreed with him, but no matter. I took the break—oh, a most welcome relief!—pausing also for a small drink of water at the outdoor pump. It was so cool, so good going down into my belly growling of its hunger. I took a few more gulps and my stomach quieted. The sun was touching the horizon, the sky turning from yellow in the east through blue to red in the west. Tomorrow's would be much the same weather as today's.

I returned to the house and re-dressed, with fresh gloves. As I came into the dispensary, to my utter surprise I saw Dr. Hunter helping the blue man to drink from a glass beaker of water. Hckvfuhl drank it thirstily, making smacking sounds like a child, supported on the American's arm. I leaned against the doorway grinning—I confess it—like a monkey and caught Dr. Hunter's eye. He hunched embarrassedly, then shrugged to indicate the liquid. "Distilled," he said. "Shouldn't do any harm. Anyway, she was thirsty."

"Yes," I agreed, making my face *very* sober, as he carefully laid Hckvfuhl back down. He prepared to go, pulling off his gloves and unfastening his mask, saying, "I think we'll be okay if she just doesn't deliver here. It'll be safer for her in Lodwar—or better yet, Nairobi, or even the U.S. I know you meant well for the alien, but I don't want to force her baby. Do you know what I mean?"

"I think I do," I said. I couldn't help responding to the change in this Westerner. For once he seemed to worry about—how to say it, the *person,* not the "political affiliation." Till now, Dr. Hunter, in trying so hard to be "African," somehow failed to be "Brother Hunter." Then I added, "But you could have been more pleasant about it."

"Oh, excuse me," he said exaggeratedly. "Well, maybe today I haven't done things the way you would have liked, but she *is* still alive, and that's what counts, right? I think we'll just pull this one through, Doto, you and I."

I smiled. "Of course. Was there ever any doubt?"

"None at all." He patted my arm. "Now you be good and make sure the alien stays calm. I'll be going up the road to see if Jama's on the way. Hold the fort till I get back." He winked at me—not respectful, but who could mind now?—and left.

It was beginning to grow dark outside. I peered out past the window blinds at the groundsel trees silhouetted against the twilight sky: short, ugly trees, shaped like a nubby gourd on a stick. The groundsels, and all of the trees, do not grow very tall here, west of Lake Rudolf. There is not much rain.

"Snyagshe." The blue man's word turned me round. She was struggling to sit up, so I helped her. She seemed very tired, and with good reason. The sheet fell away, but it was still too warm to worry about that. Again those lovely eyes shut as she leaned against the wall, squatting on her calves. I sat down opposite her, thinking, how odd it is, that the English word "calf" means both baby cow and lower leg. I had gone from the first to the second all in one day. How utterly amazing. My own were excruciatingly tired.

After a bit I stood to light the kerosene lamp. The flame sat steady on its wick in the still air as I replaced the chimney over it. And it was just about then that the blue man cried out.

A lot of blue-tinged liquid was flooding her thighs; I could see her abdomen pulsing, rippling downward. She stood up straight on her knees, her fingers scrabbling for purchase on the wall behind her; found some, evidently. I was there in front of her in a second, pressing downward on her belly with the palm of my hand; maybe it helped. We pushed and strained together, then a little bit of grey head appeared, and more and more, stuttering outward with the pulses. Hckvfuhl was not crying any longer, but her pants were quick and loud. The baby's head was born, but there it halted.

Yet the rippling went on, and Hckvfuhl still strained against the wall. By now it was quite obvious she was placental, so perhaps the cord was restraining the baby? I felt under the child's almost nonexistent chin, barely able to fit my fingers into the tiny space; the little one was wedged tight. Indeed, it was the cord, wrapped around the neck, like a noose. I pulled it carefully, it gave slightly; pulled it downward over the child's face, it stopped short. I put my right hand under the child's head and strove to shove it back up into the womb just enough to get the umbilicus over the crown. Over its head, and then freed, the child slid out into my hands like a wet seed.

The rest was simple. The baby breathed, the cord was tied, the afterbirth came. I cleaned the child off, and Hckvfuhl as well, then carried her into Dr. Hunter's own bedroom to sleep. It was necessary; I wasn't going to allow the blue man to sleep on that mess in the infirmary. She was very light in my arms.

I brought the baby to her, with the lamp and the marvelous mesh bag; and we clothed it. It appeared to be a girl; at least, that's my guess, and it is worth that of anyone else. The baby— hummed, sort of, as we fastened the silver sling around her. It, too, had those beautiful big eyes, open already. Hckvfuhl annointed her little head with the brine from the vial. It was the most beautiful blue baby I have ever seen.

When we were done, I reached for the lamp I had set on the nightstand. Hckvfuhl lay back on the while pillow, watching me. Strange, how those eyes could catch the least ray of light, reflect the lamp like ten lamps in the night. Her hand came up, brushing the back of mine, three blue fingers against my five black ones. "Dto-dto," she said. "Khhon." A moment passed, then I left.

Well, that is what happened the day the rocket landed. Almost as soon as I emerged from the bedroom, Dr. Hunter, Brother Jama, the District Commissioner, and all the official people arrived to take Hckvfuhl off to Nairobi; and I never saw her any more. I do understand, though, that she and her daughter are well, wherever they are.

Of course, Dr. Hunter was annoyed at me for not stopping the child's birth—as if I could stop the moon and the stars, too. But he got over it when the newspapers in the capital called him a "Statue of Liberty in the savannah," keeping Hckvfuhl's "fragile spark alight." They printed my name, too.

Oh, and finally, yes, Llana came through without me well enough. Twice as well, in fact; astoundingly, she managed to produce twins. And what do you know, stingy old Musa even did pay up all that he owed.

THE MISSING ITEM
by Isaac Asimov

*Dr. Asimov's tales of the Black Widowers
usually appear in* Ellery Queen's Mystery
Magazine; *it's a pleasure to borrow the*
Black Widowers *for this issue of* IA'sf.
*The real-life model for this little
group includes among its membership*
L. Sprague de Camp *and* Martin Gardner,
*who appear elsewhere in this issue, Don
Bensen, who illustrated this episode,
your Editor, and of course Dr. Asimov
himself. The real group—alas!—has
no counterpart to the waiter, Henry,
who is wholly fictional.*

Emmanuel Rubin, resident polymath of the Black Widowers Society, was visibly chafed. His eyebrows hunched down into the upper portion of his thick-lensed spectacles and his sparse gray beard bristled.

"Not true to life," he said. "Imagine! Not true to life!"

Mario Gonzalo, who had just reached the head of the stairs and had accepted his dry martini from Henry, the unsurpassable waiter, said, "What's not true to life?"

Geoffrey Avalon looked down from his seventy-four inches and said solemnly, "It appears that Manny has suffered a rejection."

"Well, why not?" said Gonzalo, peeling off his gloves. "Editors don't have to be stupid all the time."

"It isn't the rejection," said Rubin. "I've been rejected before by better editors and in connection with better stories. It's the reason he advanced! How the hell would he know if a story were true to life or not? What's he ever done but warm an office chair? Would he—"

Roger Halsted, whose career as a math teacher in a junior high school had taught him how to interrupt shrill voices, managed to interpose. "Just what did he find not true to life, Manny?"

Rubin waved a hand passionately outward, "I don't want to talk about it."

"Good," said Thomas Trumbull, scowling from under his neatly-waved thatch of white hair. "Then the rest of us can hear each other for a while. —Roger, why don't you introduce your guest to the late Mr. Gonzalo?"

Halsted said, "I've just been waiting for the decibel-level to decrease. Mario, my friend Jonathan Thatcher. This is Mario Gon-

THE MISSING ITEM

zalo, who is an artist by profession. Jonathan is an oboist, Mario."

Gonzalo grinned and said, "Sounds like fun."

"Sometimes it almost is," said Thatcher, "on days when the reed behaves itself."

Thatcher's round face and plump cheeks would have made him a natural to play Santa Claus at any Christmas benefit, but he would have needed padding just the same, for his body had that peculiar ersatz slimness that seemed to indicate forty pounds recently lost. His eyebrows were dark and thick and one took it for granted that they were never drawn together in anger.

Henry said, "Gentlemen, dinner is ready."

James Drake stubbed out his cigarette and said, "Thanks, Henry. It's a cold day and I would welcome hot food."

"Yes, sir," said Henry with a gentle smile. "Lobster thermidor today, baked potatoes, stuffed eggplant—"

"But what's this, Henry?" demanded Rubin, scowling.

"Hot borscht, Mr. Rubin."

Rubin looked as though he were searching his soul and then he said, grudgingly, "All right."

Drake, unfolding his napkin, said, "Point of order, Roger."

"What is it?"

"I'm sitting next to Manny, and if he continues to look like that he'll curdle my soup and give me indigestion. You're host and absolute monarch; I move you direct him to tell us what he wrote that isn't true to life and get it out of his system."

"Why?" said Trumbull. "Why not let him sulk and be silent for the novelty of it?"

"I'm curious, too," said Gonzalo, "since nothing he's ever written has been true to life—"

"How would you know, since you can't read?" said Rubin, suddenly.

"It's generally known," said Gonzalo. "You hear it everywhere."

"Oh, God, I'd better tell you and end this miasma of pseudo-wit. —Look, I've written a novelette, about 15,000 words long, about a world-wide organization of locksmiths—"

"Locksmiths?" said Avalon, frowning as though he suspected he had not heard correctly.

"Locksmiths," said Rubin. "These guys are experts, they can open anything—safes, vaults, prison doors. There are no secrets from them and nothing can be hidden from them. My global organization is of the cream of the profession and no man can join the organization without some document or object of importance stolen from an industrial, political, or governmental unit.

"Naturally, they have the throat of the world in their grip. They can control the stock market, guide diplomacy, make and unmake governments, and—at the time my story opens—they are headed by a dangerous megalomaniac—"

Drake interrupted even as he winced in his effort to crack the claw of the lobster. "Who is out to rule the world, of course."

"Of course," said Rubin, "and our hero must stop him. He is himself a skilled locksmith—"

Trumbull interrupted. "In the first place, Manny, what the hell do you know about locksmithery or locksmithmanship or whatever you call it?"

"More than you think," retorted Rubin.

"I doubt that very much," said Trumbull, "and the editor is right. This is utter and complete implausibility. I know a few locksmiths and they're gentle and inoffensive mechanics with IQ's—"

Rubin said, "And I suppose when you were in the army you knew a few corporals and, on the basis of your knowledge, you'll tell me that Napoleon and Hitler were implausible."

The guest for that evening, who had listened to the exchange with a darkening expression, spoke up. "Pardon me, gentlemen, I know I'm to be grilled at the conclusion of dinner. Does that mean I cannot join the dinner conversation beforehand?"

"Heavens, no," said Halsted. "Talk all you want—if you can get a word in now and then."

"In that case, let me put myself forcefully on the side of Mr. Rubin. A conspiracy of locksmiths may sound implausible to us who sit here, but what counts is not what a few rational people think but what the great outside world does. How can your editor turn down anything at all as implausible when everything—" He caught himself, took a deep breath and said, in an altered tone, "Well, I don't mean to tell you your business. I'm not a writer. After all, I don't expect you to tell me how to play the oboe," but his smile as he said it was a weak one.

"Manny will tell you how to play the oboe," said Gonzalo, "if you give him a chance."

"Still," Thatcher said, as though he had not heard Gonzalo's comment, "I live in the world and observe it. *Anything* these days is believed. There is no such thing as 'not true to life'. Just spout any nonsense solemnly and swear it's true and there will be millions rallying round you."

Avalon nodded magisterially and said, "Quite right, Mr. Thatcher. I don't know that this is simply characteristic of our times, but the fact that we have better communications now makes it easier to reach many people quickly so that a phenomenon such as Herr Hitler of unmourned memory is possible. And to those who can believe in Mr. von Däniken's ancient astronauts and in Mr. Berlitz's Bermuda triangle, a little thing like a conspiracy of locksmiths could be swallowed with the morning porridge."

Thatcher waved his hand, "Ancient astronauts and Bermuda triangles are nothing. Suppose you were to say that you frequently visited Mars in astral projection and that Mars was, in fact, a haven for the worthy souls of this world. There would be those who would believe you."

"I imagine so," began Avalon.

"You don't have to imagine," said Thatcher. "It *is* so. I take it you haven't heard of Tri-Lucifer. That's T-R-I."

"Tri-Lucifer?" said Halsted, looking a little dumbfounded. "You mean three Lucifers. What's that?"

Thatcher looked from one face to another and the Black Widowers all remained silent.

And then Henry, who was clearing away some of the lobster shells, said, "If I may be permitted, gentlemen, I have heard of it. There was a group of them soliciting contributions at this restaurant last week."

"Like the Moonies?" said Drake, pushing his dish in Henry's direction and preparing to light up.

"There is a resemblance," said Henry, his unlined, sixtyish face a bit thoughtful, "but the Tri-Luciferians, if that is the term to use, give a more other-worldly appearance."

"That's right," said Thatcher. "They have to divorce themselves from this world so as to achieve astral projection to Mars and facilitate the transfer of their souls there after death."

"But why—" began Gonzalo.

And Trumbull suddenly roared out with a blast of anger, "Come on, Roger, make them wait for the grilling to start. Change the subject."

Gonzalo said, "I just want to know why they call them—"

Halsted sighed and said, "Let's wait a while, Mario."

Henry was making his way about the table with the brandy when Halsted tapped his water glass and said, "I think we can begin the grilling now; and Manny, since it was your remark about true-to-lifeness that roused Jonathan's interest over the main course, why don't you begin."

"Sure." Rubin looked solemnly across the table at Thatcher and said, "Mr. Thatcher, at this point it would be traditional to ask you how you justify your existence and we would then go into a discussion of the oboe as an instrument of torture for oboists. *But,* let me guess and say that at this moment you would consider your life justified if you could wipe out a few Tri-Luciferians. Am I right?"

"You are, you are," said Thatcher, energetically. "The whole thing has filled my life and my thoughts for over a month now. It is ruining—"

Gonzalo interrupted. "What I want to know is why they call themselves Tri-Luciferians. Are they devil-worshipers or what?"

Rubin began, "You're interrupting the man—"

"It's all right," said Thatcher. "I'll tell him. I'm just sorry that I know enough about that organization to be able to tell him. Apparently, Lucifer means the morning star, though I'm not sure why—"

"Lucifer," said Avalon, running his finger about the lip of his water-glass, "is from Latin words meaning 'light-bringer'. The rising of the morning star in the dawn heralds the soon-following rising of the Sun. In an era in which there were no clocks that was an important piece of information to anyone awake at the time."

"Then why is Lucifer the name of the devil?" asked Gonzalo.

Avalon said, "Because the Babylonian king was apparently referred to as the Morning Star by his flattering courtiers, and the Prophet Isaiah predicted his destruction. Can you quote the passage, Manny?"

Rubin said, "We can read it out of the Bible, if we want to. It's the 14th Chapter of Isaiah. The key sentence goes, 'How art thou fallen from heaven, O Lucifer, son of the morning!' It was just a bit of poetic hyperbole, and very effective too, but it was interpreted literally later, and that one sentence gave rise to the whole myth of a rebellion against God by hordes of angels under the leadership of Lucifer, which came to be considered Satan's name while still in heaven. Of course, the rebels were defeated and expelled from heaven by loyalist angels under the leadership of the Archangel Michael."

"Like in *Paradise Lost*?" said Gonzalo.

THE MISSING ITEM

"Exactly like in *Paradise Lost*."

Thatcher said, "The devil isn't part of it, though. To the Tri-Luciferians, Lucifer just means the morning star. There are two of them on Earth: Venus and Mercury."

Drake squinted through the curling tobacco smoke and said, "They're also evening stars, depending on which side of the Sun they happen to be. They're either east of the Sun and set shortly after Sunset, or west of the Sun and rise shortly before Sunrise."

Thatcher said, with clear evidence of hope, "Do they have to be both together; both one or both the other?"

"No," said Drake, "they move independently. They can be both evening stars, or both morning stars, or one can be an evening star and one a morning star. Or one or the other or both can be nearly in a line with the Sun and be invisible altogether, morning or evening."

"Too bad," said Thatcher, shaking his head, "that's what *they* say. —Anyway, the point is that from Mars you see *three* morning stars in the sky, or you can see them if they're in the right position: not only Mercury and Venus, but Earth as well."

"That's right," said Rubin.

"And," said Thatcher, "I suppose then it's true that they can be in any position. They can all be evening stars or all morning stars, or two can be one and one can be the other?"

"Yes," said Drake, "Or one or more can be too close to the Sun to be visible."

Thatcher sighed. "So they call Mars by their mystic name of Tri-Lucifer—the world with the three morning stars."

"I suppose," said Gonzalo, "that Jupiter would have four morning stars: Mercury, Venus, Earth, and Mars; and so on out to Pluto, which would have eight morning stars."

"The trouble is," said Halsted, "that the farther out you go, the dimmer the inner planets are. Viewed from one of the satellites of Jupiter, for instance, I doubt that Mercury would appear more than a medium-bright star; and it might be too close to the Sun for anyone ever to get a good look at it."

"What about the view from Mars? Could you see Mercury?" asked Thatcher.

"Oh yes, I'm sure of that," said Halsted, "I could work out what the brightness would be in a matter of minutes."

"Would you?" said Thatcher.

"Sure," said Halsted, "if I've remembered to bring my pocket computer. —Yes, I have it. Henry, bring me the *Columbia Ency-*

clopedia, would you?"

Rubin said, "While Roger is bending his limited mathematical mind to the problem, Mr. Thatcher, tell us what your interest is in all this. You seem to be interested in exposing them as fakers. Why? Have you been a member? Are you now disillusioned?"

"No, I've never been a member. I—" He rubbed his temple hesitantly. "It's my wife. I don't like talking about it, you understand."

Avalon said solemnly, "Please be assured, Mr. Thatcher, that whatever is said here never passes beyond the bounds of this room. That includes our valued waiter, Henry. You may speak freely."

"Well, there's nothing criminal or disgraceful in it. I just don't like to seem to be so helpless in such a silly— It's breaking up my marriage, gentlemen."

There was a discreet silence around the table, broken only by the mild sound of Halsted turning the pages of the encyclopedia.

Thatcher went on, "Roger knows my wife. He'll tell you she's a sensible woman—"

Halsted looked up briefly and nodded, "I'll vouch for that, but I didn't know you were having this—"

"Lately, Carol has not been social, you understand; and I certainly haven't talked about it. It was with great difficulty, you know, that I managed to agree to come out tonight. I dread leaving her to herself. You see, even sensible people have their weaknesses. Carol worries about death."

"So do we all," said Drake.

"So do I," said Thatcher, "But in a normal way, I hope. We all know we'll die someday and we don't particularly look forward to it, and we may worry about hell or nothingness or hope for heaven, but we don't think about it much. Carol has been fascinated, however, by the possibility of demonstrating the actual existence of life after death. It may have all started with the Bridey Murphy case when she was a teenager—I don't know if any of you remember that—"

"I do," said Rubin, "a woman under hypnosis seemed to be possessed by an Irishwoman who had died a long time before."

"Yes," said Thatcher. "She saw through that, eventually. Then she grew interested in spiritualism and gave that up. I always relied on her to understand folly when she finally stopped to think about it—and then she came up against the Tri-Luciferians. I never saw her like this. She wants to join them. She has money of her own and she wants to give it to them. I don't care about the money—well, I do, but that's not the main thing—I care about *her.* You know, she's going to join them in their retreat somewhere, become a daughter of Tri-Lucifer, or whatever they call it, and wait for translation to the Abode of the Blessed. One of these days, she'll be gone. I just won't see her anymore. She promised me it wouldn't be tonight, but I wonder."

Rubin said, "I take it you suppose that the organization is just interested in her money."

"At least the leader of it is," said Thatcher, grimly. "I'm sure of it. What else can he be after?"

"Do you know him? Have you met him?" said Rubin.

"No. He keeps himself isolated," said Thatcher, "but I hear he has recently bought a fancy mansion in Florida, and I doubt that it's for the use of the membership."

"Funny thing about that," said Drake. "It doesn't matter how lavishly a cult-leader lives, how extravagantly he throws money around. The followers, who support him and see their money clearly used for that purpose, never seem to mind."

"They identify," said Rubin. "The more he spends, the more successful they consider the cause. It's the basis of ostentatious waste in governmental display, too."

"Just the same," said Thatcher, "I don't think Carol will ever commit herself entirely. She might not be bothered by the leader's actions, but if I can prove him *wrong,* she'll drop it."

"Wrong about what?" asked Rubin.

"Wrong about Mars. This head of the group claims he has been on Mars often—in astral projection, of course. He describes Mars in detail, but can he be describing it accurately?"

"Why not?" asked Rubin. "If he reads up on what is known about Mars, he can describe it as astronomers would. The Viking photographs even show a part of the surface in detail. It's not difficult to be accurate."

"Yes, but it may be that somewhere he has made a mistake, something I can show Carol."

Halsted looked up and said, "Here, I've worked out the dozen brightest objects in the Martian sky, together with their magnitudes. I may be off a little here and there, but not by much." He passed a slip of paper around.

Mario held up the paper when it reached him. "Would you like to see it, Henry?"

"Thank you, sir," murmured Henry, and as he glanced at it

briefly, one eyebrow raised itself just slightly, just briefly.

The paper came to rest before Thatcher eventually and he gazed at it earnestly. What he saw was this:

Sun	−26.
Phobos	−9.6
Deimos	−5.1
Earth	−4.5
Jupiter	−3.1
Venus	−2.6
Sirius	−1.4
Saturn	−0.8
Canopus	−0.7
Alpha Centauri	−0.3
Arcturus	−0.1
Mercury	0.0

Thatcher said, "Phobos and Deimos are the two satellites of Mars. Do these numbers mean they're very bright?"

"The greater the negative number," said Halsted, "the brighter the object. A −2 object is two and a half times brighter than a −1 object and a −3 object is two and a half times brighter still and so on. Next to the Sun, Phobos is the brightest object in the Martian sky, and Deimos is next."

"And next to the Sun and the two satellites, Earth is the brightest object in the sky, then."

"Yes, but only at or near its maximum brightness," said Halsted. "It can be much dimmer depending on where Mars and Earth are in their respective orbits. Most of the time it's probably less bright than Jupiter, which doesn't change much in brightness as it moves in its orbit."

Thatcher shook his head and looked disappointed, "But it *can* be that bright. Too bad. There's a special prayer or psalm or something that the Tri-Luciferians have that appears in almost all their literature. I've seen it so often in the stuff Carol brings home, I can quote it exactly. It goes, 'When Earth shines high in the sky, like a glorious jewel, and when the other Lucifers have fled beyond the horizon, so that Earth shines alone in splendor, single in beauty, unmatched in brightness, it is then that the souls of those ready to receive the call must prepare to rise from Earth and cross the gulf.' And what you're saying, Roger, is that Earth *can* be the brightest object in the Martian sky."

THE MISSING ITEM

Halsted noded. "At night, if Phobos and Deimos are below the horizon, and Earth is near maximum brightness, it is certainly the brightest object in the sky. It would be three and a half times as bright as Jupiter, if that were in the sky, and six times as bright as Venus at its brightest."

"And it could be the only morning star in the sky."

"Or the only evening star. Sure. The other two, Venus and Mercury, could be on the other side of the Sun from Earth."

Thatcher kept staring at the list. "But would Mercury be visible? It's at the bottom of the list."

Halsted said, "The bottom just means that it's twelfth brightest, but there are thousands of stars that are dimmer and still visible. There would be only four stars brighter than Mercury as seen from Mars: Sirius, Canopus, Alpha Centauri, and Arcturus."

Thatcher said, "If they'd only make a mistake."

Avalon said in a grave and somewhat hesitant baritone, "Mr. Thatcher, I think perhaps you had better face the facts. It is my experience that even if you *do* find a flaw in the thesis of the Tri-Luciferians it won't help you. Those who follow cults for emotional reasons are not deterred by demonstrations of the illogic of what they are doing."

Thatcher said, "I agree with you, and I wouldn't dream of arguing with the ordinary cultist. But I know Carol. I have seen her turn away from a system of beliefs she would very much like to have followed, simply because she saw the illogic of it. If I could find something of the sort here, I'm sure she'd come back."

Gonzalo said, "Some of us here ought to think of something. After all, he's never *really* been on Mars. He's got to have made a mistake."

"Not at all," said Avalon. "He probably knows as much about Mars as we do. Therefore, even if he's made a mistake it may be because he fails to understand something we also fail to understand and we won't catch him."

Thatcher nodded his head. "I suppose you're right."

"I don't know," said Gonzalo. "How about the canals? The Tri-Luciferians are bound to talk about the canals. Everyone believed in them and then just lately we found out they weren't there; isn't that right? So if he talks about them, he's caught."

Drake said, "Not everybody believed in them, Mario. Hardly any astronomers did."

"The general public did," said Gonzalo.

Rubin said, "Not lately. It was in 1964 that Mariner 4 took the first pictures of Mars and that pretty much gave away the fact the canals didn't exist. Once Mariner 9 mapped the whole planet in 1969 there was no further argument. When did the Tri-Luciferians come into existence, Mr. Thatcher?"

"As I recall," said Thatcher, "about 1970. Maybe 1971."

"There you are," said Rubin. "Once we had Mars down cold, this guy, whoever he is who runs it, decided to start a new religion based on it. Listen, if you want to get rich quick, no questions asked, start a new religion. Between the First Amendment and the tax breaks you get, it amounts to a license to help yourself to everything in sight. —I'll bet he talks about volcanoes."

Thatcher nodded. "The Martian headquarters of the astral projections are in Olympus Mons. That means Mount Olympus and that's where the souls of the righteous gather. That's the big volcano, isn't it?"

"The biggest in the Solar system," said Rubin. "At least, that we know of. It's been known since 1969."

Thatcher said, "The Tri-Luciferians say that G. V. Schiaparelli—he's the one who named the different places on Mars—was astrally inspired to name that spot Olympus to signify it was the home of the godly. In ancient Greece, you see, Mount Olympus was—"

"Yes," said Avalon, nodding gravely, "we know."

"Isn't Schiaparelli the fellow who first reported the canals?" asked Gonzalo.

"Yes," said Halsted, "although actually when he said 'canali' he meant natural waterways."

"Even so, why didn't the same astral inspiration tell him the canals weren't there?" asked Gonzalo.

Drake nodded and said, "That's something you can point out to your wife."

"No," said Thatcher, "I guess they thought of that. They say the canals were part of the inspiration because that increased interest in Mars and that that was needed to make the astral projection process more effective."

Trumbull, who had maintained a sullen silence through the discussion, as though he were waiting his chance to shift the discussion to oboes, said suddenly, "That makes a diseased kind of sense."

Thatcher said, "Too much makes sense. That's the trouble. There are times when I want to find a mistake not so much to save Carol as to save myself. I tell you that when I listen to Carol talking there's sometimes more danger she'll argue me into being crazy than that I'll persuade her to be rational."

Trumbull waved a hand at him soothingly, "Just take it easy and let's think it out. Do they say anything about the satellites?"

"They talk about them, yes. Phobos and Deimos. Sure."

"Do they say anything about how they cross the sky?" Trumbull's smile was nearly a smirk.

"Yes," said Thatcher, "and I looked it up because I didn't believe them and I thought I had something. In their description of the Martian scene, they talk about Phobos rising in the west and setting in the east. And it turns out that's true. And they say that whenever either Phobos or Deimos cross the sky at night, they are eclipsed by Mars's shadow for part of the time. And that's true, too."

Halsted shrugged. "The satellites were discovered a century ago, in 1877, by Asaph Hall. As soon as their distance from Mars and their period of revolution was determined, which was almost at once, their behavior in Mars's sky was known."

"*I* didn't know it," said Thatcher.

"No," said Halsted, "but this fellow who started the religion apparently did his homework. It wasn't really hard."

"Hold on," said Trumbull, truculently. "Some things aren't as obvious and don't get put into the average elementary astronomy textbook. For instance, I read somewhere that Phobos can't be seen from the Martian polar regions. It's so close to Mars that the bulge of Mars's spherical surface hides the satellite, if you go far enough north or south. Do the Tri-Luciferians say anything about Phobos being invisible from certain places on Mars, Thatcher?"

"Not that I recall," said Thatcher, "but they don't say it's always visible. If they just don't mention the matter, what does that prove?"

"Besides," said Halsted, "Olympus Mons is less than 20 degrees north of the Martian equator and Phobos is certainly visible from there any time it is above the horizon and not in eclipse. And if that's the headquarters for the souls from Earth, Mars would certainly be described as viewed from that place."

"Whose side are you on?" grumbled Trumbull.

"The truth's," said Halsted. "Still, it's true that astronomy books rarely describe any sky but Earth's. That's why I had to figure out the brightness of objects in the Martian sky instead of just looking it up. The only trouble is that this cult-leader seems to be just as good at figuring."

"I've got an idea," said Avalon. "I'm not much of an astronomer, but I've seen the photographs taken by the Viking landers, and I've read the newspaper reports about them. For one thing the Martian sky in the daytime is pink, because of fine particles of the reddish dust in the air. In that case, isn't it possible that the dust obscures the night sky so that you don't see anything? Good Lord, it happens often enough in New York City."

Halsted said, "As a matter of fact, the problem in New York isn't so much the dust as the scattered light from the buildings and highways; and even in New York you can see the bright stars, if the sky isn't cloudy.

"On Mars, it would have to work both ways. If there is enough dust to make the sky invisible from the ground, then the ground would be invisible from the sky. For instance, when Mariner 9 reached Mars in 1969, Mars was having a globe-wide duststorm and none of its surface could be seen by Mariner. At that time, from the Martian surface, the sky would have had to be blanked out. Most of the time, though, we see the surface clearly from our probes, so from the Martian surface, the sky would be clearly visible.

"In fact, considering that Mars's atmosphere is much thinner than Earth's—less than a hundredth as thick—it would scatter and absorb far less light than Earth's does, and the various stars and planets would all look a little brighter than they would with Earth's atmosphere in the way. I didn't allow for that in my table."

Trumbull said, "Jeff mentioned the Viking photographs. They show rocks all over the place. Do the Tri-Luciferians mention rocks?"

"No," said Thatcher, "not that I ever noticed. But again, they don't say there aren't any. They talk about huge canyons and dry river beds and terraced ice-fields."

Rubin snorted. "All that's been known since 1969. More homework."

Avalon said, "What about life? We still don't know if there's any life on Mars. The Viking results are ambiguous. Have the Tri-Luciferians committed themselves on that?"

"Thatcher thought, then said, "I wish I could say I had read all their literature thoroughly, but I haven't. Still, Carol has forced me to read quite a bit since she said I ought not defame anything without learning about it first."

"That's true enough," said Avalon, "though life is short and there are some things that are so unlikely on the surface that one hesitates to devote much of one's time to a study of them. However, can you say anything as to the Tri-Luciferians' attitude toward Martian life from what you've read of their literature?"

Thatcher said, "They speak about Mars's barren surface, its desert aridity and emptiness. They contrast that with the excitement and fullness of the astral sphere."

"Yes," said Avalon, "and of course, the surface *is* dry and empty and barren. We know that much. What about microscopic life? That's what we're looking for."

Thatcher shook his head. "No mention of it, as far as I know."

Avalon said, "Well, then, I can't think of anything else. I'm quite certain this whole thing is nonsense. Everyone here is, and none of us need proof of it. If your wife needs proof, we may not be able to supply it."

"I understand," said Thatcher. "I thank you all, of course, and I suppose she may come to her senses after a while, but I must admit I have never seen her quite like this. I would join the cult with her just to keep her in sight; but, frankly, I'm afraid I'll end up believing it, too."

And in the silence that followed, Henry said softly, "Perhaps Mr. Thatcher, you need not go to that extreme."

Thatcher turned suddenly. "Pardon me. Did you say something, waiter?"

Halsted said, "Henry is a member of the club, Jonathan. I don't know that he's an astronomer exactly, but he's the brightest person here. Is there something we've missed, Henry?"

Henry said, "I think so, sir. You said, Mr. Halsted, that astronomy books don't generally describe any sky but Earth's, and I guess that must be why the cult-leader seems to have a missing item in his description of Mars. Without it, the whole thing is no more true to life than Mr. Rubin's conspiracy of locksmiths—if I may be forgiven, Mr. Rubin."

"Not if you don't supply a missing object. Henry?"

Henry said, "On Earth, Mercury and Venus are the morning and evening stars, and we always think of such objects as planets, therefore. Consequently, from Mars, there must be three morning and evening stars, Mercury, Venus, plus Earth in addition. That is memorialized in the very name of the cult, and from that alone I could see the whole thing fails."

Halsted said, "I'm not sure I see your point, Henry."

"But, Mr. Halsted," said Henry, "where is the Moon in all this?

It is a large object, our Moon, almost the size of Mercury and closer to Mars than Mercury is. If Mercury can be seen from Mars, surely the Moon can be, too. Yet I noticed it was not on your list of bright objects in the Martian sky."

Halsted turned red. "Yes, of course. The list of planets fooled me, too. You just list them without mentioning the Moon." He reached for the paper. "The Moon is smaller than Earth and less reflective, so that it is only 1/70 as bright as the Earth, at equal distance and phase which means—a magnitude of 0.0. It would be just as bright as Mercury, and in fact it could be seen more easily than Mercury could be because it would be higher in the sky. At sunset, Mercury as evening star would never be higher than 16 degrees above the horizon, while Earth could be as much as 44 degrees above—pretty high in the sky."

Henry said, "Mars, therefore, would have four morning stars, and the very name, Tri-Lucifer, is nonsense."

Avalon said, "But the Moon would always be close to Earth, so wouldn't Earth's light drown it out?"

"No," said Halsted. "Let's see now. —Never get a pocket computer that doesn't have keys for the trigonometric functions.— The Moon would be, at times, as much as 23 minutes of arc away from Earth, when viewed from Mars. That's three-quarters the width of the Moon as seen from Earth."

Henry said, "One more thing. Would you repeat that verse once again, Mr. Thatcher, the one about the Earth being high in the sky."

Thatcher said, "Certainly. 'When Earth shines high in the sky, like a glorious jewel, and when the other Lucifers have fled beyond the horizon, so that Earth shines alone in splendor, single in beauty, unmatched in brightness, it is then that the souls of those ready to receive the call must prepare to rise from Earth and cross the gulf.' "

Henry said, "Earth may be quite high in the sky at times, and Mercury and Venus may be on the other side of the Sun and therefore beyond the horizon—but Earth cannot be 'alone in splendor'. The moon has to be with it. Of course, there would be times when the moon is very nearly in front of Earth or behind it, as seen from Mars, so that the two dots of light merge into one that seems to make Earth brighter than ever, but the Moon is not then beyond the horizon. It seems to me, Mr. Thatcher, that the cult-leader was never on Mars, because if he had been he would not have missed a pretty big item, a world 2160 miles across. Surely you can explain this to your wife."

"Yes," said Thatcher, his face brightening into a smile, "She would have to see the whole thing is fake."

"If it is true, as you say," said Henry quietly, "that she is a rational person."

THE BLACK WIDOWERS

With arguments loud and emphatic
And logic that's sometimes erratic,
    Each member deduces
    Till Henry produces
An answer one *must* call Lunatic.

—Don R. Bensen

PERCHANCE TO DREAM
by Sally A. Sellers

> *This story, Sally Sellers's first sale, is the result of a writing workshop at the University of Michigan, headed by Lloyd Biggle, Jr. The author tells us that she wrote for as long as she can remember, but wrote only for creative writing courses while in college. Since graduation, she worked as a waitress, traveled in Europe, and worked as a medical technician in hematology. She now lives with her family, two cats, and about a hundred plants, and is a research assistant at the University of Michigan.*

From the playground came the sound of laughter.

A gusty night wind was sweeping the park, and the light at the edge of the picnic grounds swung crazily. Distorted shadows came and went, rushing past as the wind pushed the light to the end of its arc, then sliding back jerkily.

Again the laughter rang out, and this time Norb identified the creaking sound that accompanied it. Someone was using the swing. Nervously he peered around the swaying branches of the bush, but he saw no one.

He heard a click. Danny had drawn his knife. Hastily Norb fumbled for his own. The slender weapon felt awkward in his hand, even after all the hours of practice.

"It'll be easy," Danny had said. "There's always some jerk in the park after dark—they never learn." Norb shivered and gripped the knife more tightly.

Then he saw them—a young couple walking hand in hand among the trees. Danny chuckled softly, and Norb relaxed somewhat. Danny was right—this would be a cinch.

"You take the girl," Danny whispered.

Norb nodded. All they had to do was wait—the couple was headed right toward them. They were high school kids, no more than fifteen or sixteen, walking slowly with their heads together, whispering and giggling. Norb swallowed and tensed himself.

"Now!" Danny hissed.

They were upon them before the kids had time to react. Danny jerked the boy backward and threw him to the ground. Norb grabbed the back of the girl's collar and held his knife at her throat.

"Okay, just do what we say and nobody gets hurt," snarled Danny. He pointed his knife at the boy's face. "You got a wallet, kid?"

The boy stared in mute terror at the knife. The girl made small whimpering sounds in her throat, and Norb tightened his hold on her collar.

"Come on, come on! Your wallet!"

From somewhere in the shadows, a woman's voice rang out. "Leave them alone!"

Norb whirled as a dark form charged into Danny and sent him sprawling. Oh God, he thought, we've been caught! As the boy leaped to his feet and started to run, Norb made a futile swipe at him with his knife. His grip on the girl must have relaxed, because she jerked free and followed the boy into the woods.

Norb looked from the retreating kids to the two wrestling figures, his hands clenched in indecision. The dark form had Danny pinned to the ground. He was squirming desperately, but he couldn't free himself. "Get her off me!" he cried.

"Jesus!" Norb whispered helplessly. The kids had begun to scream for help. They'd rouse the whole neighborhood.

"Norb!" screamed Danny.

It was a command, and Norb hurled himself onto the woman. Twice he stabbed wildly at her back, but she only grunted and held on more tightly. He struck out again, and this time his knife sank deeply into soft flesh. Spurting blood soaked his hand and sleeve, and he snatched them away in horror.

Danny rolled free. He got to his feet, and the two of them stood looking down at the woman. The knife was buried in the side of her throat.

"Oh my God," whimpered Norb.

"You ass!" cried Danny. "Why didn't you just pull her off? You killed her!"

Norb stood paralyzed, staring down at the knife and the pulsing wound. Fear thickened in his throat, and he felt his stomach constrict. He was going to be sick.

"You better run like hell. You're in for it now."

Danny was gone. Norb wrenched his gaze from the body. On the other side of the playground, the kids were still calling for help. He saw lights up by the gate, swinging into the park drive.

Norb began to run.

The gush of blood from the wound slowed abruptly and then stopped. The chest heaved several times with great intakes of air. Then it collapsed, and a spasm shook the body. In the smooth motion of a slowly tightening circle, it curled in on itself. The heart gave three great beats, hesitated, pumped once more, and was still.

Norb caught up with Danny at the edge of the woods. They stopped, panting, and looked in the direction of the car. It had come to a stop by the tennis courts, and, as they watched, the driver cut his motor and turned off his lights.

"This way," whispered Danny. "Come on."

As they headed across the road for the gate, the car's motor suddenly started. Its lights came on, and it roared into a U-turn to race after them.

"It's the cops!" Danny yelled. "Split up!"

Norb was too frightened. Desperately he followed Danny, and the pair of them fled through the gate and turned along the street as the patrol car swung around the curve. Then Danny veered off, and Norb followed him through bushes and into a back yard. A dog began yelping somewhere. Danny scaled a fence and dropped into the adjoining back yard, and Norb followed, landing roughly and falling to his knees.

He scrambled to his feet and collided with Danny, who was laughing softly as he watched the patrol car. It had turned around and was headed back into the park.

The heart had not stopped. It was pumping—but only once every six minutes, with a great throb. At each pulse, a pinprick of light danced across the back of the eyelids. The wound attempted to close itself and tightened futilely around the intrusion of steel. A neck muscle twitched. Then another, but the knife remained. The tissue around the blade began contracting minutely, forcing it outward in imperceptible jerks.

Officer Lucas parked near the playground and started into the trees. He could not have said what he was looking for, but neighbors had reported hearing cries for help, and the way those two punks had run told him they'd been up to something. He switched on his flashlight, delineating an overturned litter basket that had spewed paper across the path. The gusting wind tore at it, prying loose one fluttering fragment at a time. Cautiously he walked forward. Gray-brown tree trunks moved in and out of the illumination as he crept on, but he could see nothing else.

He stumbled over an empty beer bottle, kicked it aside, and then stopped uncertainly, pivoting with his light. It revealed nothing but empty picnic tables and cold barbecue grills, and he was about to turn back when his beam picked out the body, curled motionless near a clump of bushes. Lucas ran forward and knelt beside the woman, shining his light on her face.

The throat wound seemed to have stopped bleeding, but if the knife had sliced the jugular vein—he leaned closer to examine the laceration. Belatedly a thought occurred to him, and he reached for the wrist. There was no pulse. He shone his light on the chest, but it was motionless.

Lucas got to his feet and inspected the area hastily. Seeing no obvious clues, he hurried back to the patrol car.

The heart throbbed again, and another pinprick of light jumped behind the woman's eyelids. The tissues in the neck tightened further as new cells developed, amassed, and forced the blade a fraction of an inch outward. The wounds in the back, shallow and clean, had already closed. The lungs expanded once with a great intake of air. The knife jerked again, tilted precariously, and finally fell to the ground under its own weight. Immediately new tissue raced to fill the open area.

The radio was squawking. Lucas waited for the exchange to end before picking up the mike. "Baker 23."

"Go ahead, Baker 23."

"I'm at Newberry Park, east end, I've got a 409 and request M.E."

"Confirmed, 23."

"Notify the detective on call."

"Clear, 23."

"Ten-four." He hung up the mike and glanced back into the woods. Probably an attempted rape, he thought. She shouldn't have fought. The lousy punks! Lucas rubbed his forehead fretfully. He should have chased them, dammit. Why hadn't he?

The heart was beating every three minutes now. The throat wound had closed, forming a large ridge under the dried blood. Cells multiplied at fantastic rates, spanning the damaged area with a minute latticework. This filled in as the new cells divided, expanded, and divided again.

Lucas reached for his clipboard and flipped on the interior lights. He glanced into the trees once before he began filling in his report. A voice crackled on the radio, calling another car. His pen scratched haltingly across the paper.

The heart was returning to its normal pace. The ridge on the neck was gone, leaving smooth skin. A jagged pattern of light jerked across the retinas. The fugue was coming to an end. The chest rose, fell, then rose again. A shadow of awareness nudged at consciousness.

The sound of the radio filled the night again, and Lucas turned uneasily, searching the road behind him for approaching headlights. There were none. He glanced at his watch and then returned to the report.

She became aware of the familiar prickling sensation in her limbs, plus a strange burning about her throat. She felt herself rising, rising—and suddenly awareness flooded her. Her body jerked, uncurled. Jeanette opened her eyes. Breathing deeply, she blinked until the dark thick line looming over her resolved itself into a tree trunk. Unconsciously her hand began to rub her neck, and she felt dry flakes come off on her fingers.

Wearily she closed her eyes again, trying to remember: Those kids. One had a knife. She was in the park. Then she heard the faint crackle of a police radio. She rolled to her knees, and dizziness swept over her. She could see a light through the trees. Good God, she thought, he's right over there!

Jeanette rubbed her eyes and looked about her. She was lightheaded, but there was no time to waste. Soon there would be other police—and doctors. She knew. Moving unsteadily, at a crouch, she slipped away into the woods.

Four patrol cars were there when the ambulance arrived. Stuart Crosby, the medical examiner, climbed out slowly and surveyed the scene. He could see half a dozen flashlights in the woods. The photographer sat in the open door of one of the cars, smoking a cigarette.

"Where's the body?" asked Crosby.

The photographer tossed his cigarette away disgustedly. "They can't find it."

"Can't find it? What do you mean?"

"It's not out there. Lucas says it was in the woods, but when Kelaney got here, it was gone."

Puzzled, Crosby turned toward the flashlights. As another gust of wind swept the park, he pulled his light coat more closely about him and started forward resignedly—a tired white-haired man who should have been home in bed.

He could hear Detective Kelaney roaring long before he could see him. "You half-ass! What'd it do, walk away?"

"No, sir!" answered Lucas hotly. "She was definitely dead. She was lying right there, I swear it—and that knife was in her throat, I recognize the handle."

"Yeah? For a throat wound, there's not much blood on it."

"Maybe," said Lucas stubbornly, "but that's where it was, all right."

Crosby halted. He had a moment of disorientation as uneasy memories stirred in the back of his mind. A serious wound, but not much blood . . . a dead body that disappeared . . .

"Obviously she wasn't dragged," said Kelaney. "Did you by chance, *Officer* Lucas, think to check the pulse? Or were you thinking at all?"

"Yes, sir! Yes, I did! I checked the pulse, and there was nothing! Zero respiration, too. Yes, sir, I did!"

"Then where *is* she?" screamed Kelaney.

Another officer approached timidly. "There's nothing out there, sir. Nothing at all."

"Well, look again," snarled Kelaney.

Crosby moved into the circle of men. The detective was running his hand through his hair in exasperation. Lucas was red-faced and defiant.

Kelaney reached for his notebook. "All right, what did she look like?"

Lucas straightened, eager with facts. "Twenty, twenty-two, Caucasian, dark hair, about five-six, hundred and twenty-five pounds. . ."

"Scars or distinguishing marks?"

"Yeah, as a matter of fact. There were three moles on her cheek—on her left cheek—all right together, right about here." He put his finger high on his cheekbone, near his eye.

Crosby felt the blood roar in his ears. He stepped forward.

"What did you say, Lucas?" he asked hoarsely.

Lucas turned to the old man. "Three moles, doctor, close together, on her cheek."

Crosby turned away, his hands in his pockets. He took a deep breath. He'd always known she'd return some day, and here was the same scene, the same bewildered faces, the same accusations. Three moles on her cheek . . . it had to be.

The wind ruffled his hair, but he no longer noticed its chill. They would find no body. Jeanette was back.

The next morning, Crosby filed a Missing Persons Report. "Send out an APB," he told the sergeant. "We've got to find her."

The sergeant looked mildly surprised. "What's she done?"

"She's a potential suicide. More than potential. I know this woman, and she's going to try to kill herself."

The sergeant reached for the form. "Okay, Doc, if you think it's that important. What's her name?"

Crosby hesitated. "She's probably using an alias. But I can give a description—an exact description."

"Okay," said the sergeant. "Shoot."

The bulletin went out at noon. Crosby spent the remainder of the day visiting motels, but no one remembered checking in a young woman with three moles on her cheek.

Jeanette saw the lights approaching in the distance: two white eyes and, above them, the yellow and red points along the roof that told her this was a truck. She leaned back against the concrete support of the bridge, hands clenched behind her, and waited.

It had been three nights since the incident in the park. Her shoulders sagged dejectedly at the thought of it. Opportunities like that were everywhere, but she knew that knives weren't going to do it. She'd tried that herself—was it in Cleveland? A painful memory flashed for a moment, of one more failure in the long series of futile attempts—heartbreaking struggles in the wrong cities. But here—

She peered around the pillar again. The eyes of the truck were closer now. Here, it could happen. Where it began, it could end. She inched closer to the edge of the support and crouched, alert to the sound of the oncoming truck.

It had rounded the curve and was thundering down the long straightaway before the bridge. Joy surged within her as she grasped its immensity and momentum. Surely this ... ! Never had she tried it with something so large, with something beyond her control. Yes, surely this would be the time!

Suddenly the white eyes were there, racing under the bridge, the diesels throbbing, roaring down at her. Her head reared in elation. Now!

She leaped an instant too late, and her body was struck by the right fender. The mammoth impact threw her a hundred feet in an arch that spanned the entrance ramp, the guideposts, and a ditch, terminating brutally in the field beyond. The left side of her skull was smashed, her arm was shattered, and four ribs were caved in. The impact of the landing broke her neck.

It was a full quarter of a mile before the white-faced driver gained sufficient control to lumber to a halt. "Sweet Jesus," he whispered. Had he imagined it? He climbed out of the rig and examined the dented fender. Then he ran back to the cab and tried futilely to contact someone by radio who could telephone the police. It was 3 AM, and all channels seemed dead. Desperately he began backing along the shoulder.

Rushes of energy danced through the tissue. Cells divided furiously, bridging gulfs. Enzymes flowed; catalysts swept through protoplasm: coupling, breaking, then coupling again. Massive reconstruction raged on. The collapsed half of the body shifted imperceptibly.

The truck stopped a hundred feet from the bridge, and the driver leaped out. He clicked on his flashlight and played it frantically over the triangle of thawing soil between the entrance ramp and the expressway. Nothing. He crossed to the ditch and began walking slowly beside it.

Bundles of collagen interlaced; in the matrix, mineral was deposited; cartilage calcified. The ribs had almost knit together and were curved loosely in their original crescent. Muscle fibers united and contracted in taut arches. The head jerked, then jerked again, as it was forced from its slackness into an increasingly firm position. Flexor spasms twitched the limbs as impulses flowed through newly formed neurons. The heart pulsed.

The driver stood helplessly on the shoulder and clicked off the flashlight. It was 3:30, and no cars were in sight. He couldn't find the body. He had finally succeeded in radioing for help, and now all he could do was wait. He stared at the ditch for a moment before moving toward the truck. There *had* been a woman, he was sure. He'd seen her for just an instant before the impact, leaping forward under the headlights. He shuddered and quickened his pace to the cab.

Under the caked blood, the skin was smooth and softly rounded. The heart was pumping her awake: Scratches of light behind the eyelids. Half of her body prickling, burning . . . A shuddering breath.

Forty-seven minutes after the impact, Jeanette opened her eyes. Slowly she raised her head. That line in the sky . . . the bridge.

She had failed again. Even here. She opened her mouth to moan, but only a rasping sound emerged.

Stuart Crosby swayed as the ambulance rounded a corner and sped down the street. He pressed his knuckles against his mouth and screamed silently at the driver: God, hurry, I know it's her.

He had slept little since the night in the park. He had monitored every call, and he knew that this one—a woman in dark clothes, jumping in front of a trucker's rig—this one had to be Jeanette.

It was her. She was trying again. Oh, God, after all these years, she was still trying. How many times, in how many cities, had she fought to die?

They were on the bridge now, and he looked down on the figures silhouetted against the red of the flares. The ambulance swung into the entrance ramp with a final whoop and pulled up behind a patrol car. Crosby had the door open and his foot on the ground before they were completely stopped, and he had to clutch at the door to keep from falling. A pain flashed across his back. He regained his balance and ran toward a deputy who was playing a flashlight along the ditch.

"Did you find her?"

The deputy turned and took an involuntary step away from the intense, stooped figure. "No, sir, doctor. Not a thing."

Crosby's voice failed him. He stood looking dejectedly down the expressway.

"To tell you the truth," said the deputy, nodding at the semi, "I think that guy had a few too many little white pills. Seeing shadows. There's nothing along here but a dead raccoon. And he's been dead since yesterday."

But Crosby was already moving across the ditch to the field beyond, where deputies swung flashlights in large arcs and a German shepherd was snuffling through the brittle stubble.

Somewhere near here, Jeanette might be lying with a broken body. It was possible, he thought. The damage could have been great, and the healing slow. Or—a chill thought clutched at him. He shook his head. No. She wouldn't have succeeded. She would still be alive, somewhere. If he could just see her, talk to her!

There was a sharp, small bark from the dog. Crosby hurried forward frantically. His foot slipped and he came down hard, scraping skin from his palm. The pain flashed again in his back. He got to his feet and ran toward the circle of deputies.

One of the men was crouched, examining the cold soil. Crosby ran up, panting, and saw that the ground was stained with blood. She'd been here. She'd been here!

He strained to see across the field and finally discerned, on the other side, a road running parallel to the expressway. But there were no cars parked on it. She was gone.

After he returned home, his body forced him to sleep, but his dreams allowed him no rest. He kept seeing a lovely young woman, with three moles on her cheek—a weeping, haunted, frantic woman who cut herself again and again and thrust the mutilated arm before his face for him to watch in amazement as the wounds closed, bonded, and healed to smoothness before his eyes. In minutes.

God, if she would only stop crying, stop pleading with him, stop begging him to find a way to make her die—to use his medical knowledge somehow, in some manner that would end it for her. She wanted to die. She hated herself, hated the body that imprisoned her.

How old was she then? How many years had that youthful body endured without change, without aging? How many decades had she lived before life exhausted her and she longed for the tranquillity of death?

He had never found out. He refused to help her die, and she broke away and fled hysterically into the night. He never saw her again. There followed a series of futile suicide attempts and night crimes with the young woman victim mysteriously missing—and then . . . nothing.

And now she was back. Jeanette!

He found himself sitting up in bed, and he wearily buried his face in his hands. He could still hear the sound of her crying. He had always heard it, in a small corner of his mind, for the last thirty years.

The street sign letters were white on green: HOMER. Jeanette stood for a long while staring at them before she turned to walk slowly along the crumbling sidewalk. A vast ache filled her chest as she beheld the familiar old houses.

The small, neat lawns had been replaced by weeds and litter. Bricks were missing out of most of the front walks. The fence was gone at the Mahews'. Jim Mahew had been so proud the day he brought home his horseless carriage, and she'd been the only one brave enough to ride in it. Her mother had been horrified.

This rambling old home with the boarded up windows was the Parkers'. The house was dead now. So was her playmate, Billy Parker—the first boy she knew to fight overseas and the first one to die. The little house across the street had been white when old Emma Walters lived there. She had baked sugar cookies for Jeanette, and Jeanette had given her a May basket once, full of violets. She must have died a long time ago. Jeanette's hand clenched. A very long time ago.

The sound of her steps on the decayed sidewalk seemed extraordinarily loud. The street was deserted. There was no movement save that of her own dark figure plodding steadily forward. Here was Cathy Carter's house. Her father had owned the buggywhip factory over in Capville. They'd been best friends. Cathy, who always got her dresses dirty, had teeth missing, cut off her own braids one day. There was that Sunday they'd gotten in trouble for climbing the elm tree—but there was no elm now, only an ugly stump squatting there to remind her of a Sunday that was gone, lost, wiped out forever. She'd heard that Cathy had married a druggist and moved out East somewhere. Jeanette found herself wondering desperately if Cathy had raised any children. Or grandchildren. Or great-grandchildren. Cathy Carter, did you make your little girls wear dresses and braids? Did you let them climb trees? Are you still alive? Or are you gone, too, like everything else that ever meant anything to me?

Her steps faltered, but her own house loomed up ahead to draw her on. It stood waiting, silently watching her approach. It, too, was dead. A new pain filled her when she saw the crumbling porch, saw that the flowerboxes were gone, saw the broken windows and the peeling wallpaper within. A rusted bicycle wheel lay in the weeds that were the front yard, along with a box of rubble and pile of boards. Tiny pieces of glass crunched sharply beneath her feet. The hedge was gone. So were the boxwood shrubs, the new variety from Boston—her mother had waited for them for so long and finally got them after the war.

She closed her eyes. Her mother had never known. Had died before she realized what she had brought into the world. Before even Jeanette had an inkling of what she was.

A monster. A freak. This body was wrong, horribly wrong. It should not be.

She had run away from this town, left it so that her friends would never know. But still it pulled at her, drawing her back every generation, pushing itself into her thoughts until she could stand it no longer. Then she would come back to stare at the old places that had been her home and the old people who had been her friends. And they didn't recognize her, never suspected, never knew why she seemed so strangely familiar.

Once she had even believed she could live here again. The memory ached within her and she quickened her pace. She could not think of him, could not allow the sound of his name in her mind. Where was he now? Had he ever understood? She had run away that time, too.

She'd had to. He was so good, so generous, but she was grotesque, a vile caprice of nature. She loathed the body.

It was evil. It must be destroyed.

Here, in the city where it was created: Where she was born, she would die.

Somehow.

The phone jangled harshly, shattering the silence of the room with such intensity that he jumped and dropped a slide on the floor. He sighed and reached for the receiver. "Crosby."

"Doctor, this is Sergeant Andersen. One of our units spotted a woman fitting the description of your APB on the High Street Bridge."

"Did they get her?" demanded Crosby.

"I dunno yet. They just radioed in. She was over the railing—looked like she was ready to jump. They're trying to get to her now. Thought you'd like to know."

"Right," said Crosby, slamming down the receiver. He reached for his coat as his mind plotted out the fastest route to High Street. Better cut down Fourth, he thought, and up Putnam. The slide crackled sharply under his heel and he looked at it in brief surprise before running out the door.

They've found her, he thought elatedly. They've got Jeanette! Thank God—I must talk with her, must convince her that she's a miracle. She has the secret of life. The whole human race will be indebted to her. Please, please, he prayed, don't let her get away.

He reached the bridge and saw the squad car up ahead. Gawkers were driving by slowly, staring out of their windows in morbid fascination. Two boys on bicycles had stopped and were peering over the railing. An officer had straddled it and was looking down.

Crosby leaped from the car and ran anxiously to the railing. His heart lifted as he saw another officer, with one arm around the lower railing and a firm grip on Jeanette's wrist. He was coaxing her to take a step up.

"Jeanette!" It was a ragged cry.

"Take it easy, Doc," said the officer straddling the railing. "She's scared."

The woman looked up. She was pale, and the beauty mark on her cheek stood out starkly. The bitter shock sent Crosby reeling backward. For a moment he felt dizzy, and he clutched the rail with trembling fingers. The gray river flowed sullenly beneath him.

It wasn't Jeanette.

"Dear God," he whispered. He finally raised his gaze to the dismal buildings that loomed across the river. Then where was she? She must have tried again. Had she succeeded?

Chief Dolenz clasped, then unclasped his hands. "You've got to slow down, Stu. You're pushing yourself far too hard."

Crosby's shoulders sagged a little more, but he did not answer.

"You're like a man possessed," continued the Chief. "It's starting to wear you down. Ease up, for God's sake. We'll find her. Why all this fuss over one loony patient? Is it that important?"

Crosby lowered his head. He still couldn't speak. The Chief looked with puzzlement at the old man, at the small bald spot that was beginning to expand, at the slump of the body, the rumpled sweater, the tremor of the hands as they pressed together. He opened his mouth but could not bring himself to say more.

§ § §

"Citizens National Bank," the switchboard operator said.

The voice on the line was low and nervous. "I'm gonna tell you this once, and only once. There's a bomb in your bank, see? It's gonna go off in ten minutes. If you don't want nobody hurt, you better get 'em outta there."

The operator felt the blood drain from her face. "Is this a joke?"

"No joke, lady. You got ten minutes. If anybody wants to know, you tell 'em People for a Free Society are starting to take action. Got that?" The line went dead.

She sat motionless for a moment, and then she got unsteadily to her feet. "Mrs. Calkins!" she called. The switchboard buzzed again, but she ignored it and ran to the manager's desk.

Mrs. Calkins looked up from a customer and frowned icily at her; but when the girl bent and whispered in her ear, the manager got calmly to her feet. "Mr. Davison," she said politely to her customer, "we seem to have a problem in the bank. I believe the safest place to be right now would be out of the building." Turning to the operator, she said coolly, "Notify the police."

Mr. Davison scrambled to his feet and began thrusting papers into his briefcase. The manager strode to the center of the lobby and clapped her hands with authority. "Could I have your attention please! I'm the manager. We are experiencing difficulties in the bank. I would like everyone to move quickly but quietly out of this building and into the street. Please move some distance away."

Faces turned toward her, but no one moved.

"Please," urged Mrs. Calkins. "There is immediate danger if you remain in the building. Your transactions may be completed later. Please leave at once."

People began to drift toward the door. The tellers looked at each other in bewilderment and began locking the money drawers. A heavyset man remained stubbornly at his window. "What about my change?" he demanded.

The operator hung up the phone and ran toward the doorway. "Hurry!" she cried. "There's a bomb!"

"A bomb!"

"She said there's a bomb!"

"Look out!"

"Get outside!"

There was a sudden rush for the door. "Please!" shouted the manager. "There is no need for panic." But her voice was lost in the uproar.

Jeanette sat limply at the bus stop, her hands folded in her lap, her eyes fixed despondently on the blur of passing automobile wheels. The day was oppressively overcast; gray clouds hung heavily over the city. When the chill wind blew her coat open, she made no move to gather it about her.

Behind her, the doors of the bank suddenly burst open, and people began to rush out frantically. The crowd bulged into the street. Brakes squealed; voices babbled excitedly. Jeanette turned and looked dully toward the bank.

There were shouts. Passing pedestrians began to run, and the frenzied flow of people from the bank continued. A woman screamed. Another tripped and nearly fell. Sirens sounded in the distance.

Above the hubbub, Jeanette caught a few clearly spoken words. "Bomb ... in the bank ..." She got slowly to her feet and began to edge her way through the crowd.

She had almost reached the door before anyone tried to stop her. A man caught at her sleeve. "You can't go in there, lady. There's a bomb!"

She pulled free, and a fresh surge of pedestrians came between them. The bank doors were closed, now. Everyone was outside and hurrying away. Jeanette pushed doubtfully at the tall glass door, pushed it open further, and slipped inside. It closed with a hiss, blocking out the growing pandemonium in the street. The lobby seemed warm and friendly, a refuge from the bitterly cold wind.

She turned and looked through the door. A policeman had appeared and the man who had tried to stop her was talking with him and pointing at the bank. Jeanette quickly moved back out of sight. She walked the length of the empty room, picked out a chair for herself, and sat down. The vast, unruffled quiet of the place matched the abiding peace she felt within her.

Outside, the first police car screamed to the curb. An ambulance followed, as the explosion ripped through the building, sending a torrent of bricks and glass and metal onto the pavement.

"Code blue, emergency room." The loudspeaker croaked for the third time as Julius Beamer rounded the corner. Ahead of him he could see a woman being wheeled into room three. An intern, keeping pace with the cart, was pushing on her breastbone at one-second intervals.

Emergency room three was crowded. A nurse stepped aside as he entered and said, "Bomb exploded at the bank." A technician

PERCHANCE TO DREAM

was hooking up the EKG, while a young doctor was forcing a tube down the woman's trachea. A resident had inserted an IV and called for digoxin.

"Okay," said Dr. Beamer to the intern thumping the chest. The intern stepped back, exhausted, and Beamer took over the external cardiac massage. The respirator hissed into life. Beamer pressed down.

There was interference. Excess oxygen was flooding the system. A brief hesitation, and then the body adjusted. Hormones flooded the bloodstream, and the cells began dividing again. The site of the damage was extensive, and vast reconstruction was necessary. The heart pulsed once.

There was a single blip on the EKG, and Beamer grunted. He pushed again. And then again, but the flat high-pitch note continued unchanged. Dr. Channing was at his elbow, waiting to take over, but Beamer ignored him. Julius Beamer did not like failure. He called for the electrodes. A brief burst of electricity flowed into the heart. There was no response. He applied them again.

The reconstruction was being hindered: there was cardiac interference. The body's energies were diverted toward the heart in an effort to keep it from beating. The delicate balance had to be maintained, or the chemicals would be swept away in the bloodstream.

A drop of sweat trickled down Julius Beamer's temple. He called for a needle and injected epinephrine directly into the heart.

Chemical stimulation: hormones activated and countered immediately.

There was no response. The only sounds in the room were the long hissssssss-click of the respirator and the eerie unchanging note of the EKG. Dr. Beamer stepped back wearily and shook his head. Then he whirled in disgust and strode out of the room. A resident reached to unplug the EKG.

The interference had stopped. Reconstruction resumed at the primary site of damage.

Rounding the corner, Dr. Beamer heard someone call his name hoarsely, and he turned to see Stuart Crosby stumbling toward him.

"Julius! That woman!"

"Stuart! Hello! What are you—?"

"That woman in the explosion. Where is she?"

"I'm afraid we lost her—couldn't get her heart going. Is she a witness?"

In emergency room three, the respirator hissed to a stop. *The heart pulsed once.* But there was no machine to record it.

In the hallway, Crosby clutched at Dr. Beamer. "No. She's my wife."

Crosby's fists covered his eyes, his knuckles pressing painfully into his forehead. Outside, there was a low rumble of thunder. He swallowed with difficulty and dug his knuckles in deeper, trying to reason. How can I? he wondered. How can I say yes? Jeanette?

The figure behind him moved slightly and the woman cleared her throat. "Dr. Crosby, I know this is a difficult decision, but we haven't much time." She laid a gentle hand on his shoulder. "We've got forty-three people in this area who desperately need a new kidney. And there are three potential recipients for a heart upstairs—one is an eight-year-old girl. Please. It's a chance for someone else. A whole new life."

Crosby twisted away from her and moved to the window. No, he thought, we haven't much time. In a few minutes, she would get up off that table herself and walk into this room—and then it would be too late. She wanted to die. She had been trying to die for years—how many? Fifty? A hundred? If they took her organs, she *would* die. Not even that marvelous body could sustain the loss of the major organs. All he had to do was say yes. But how could he? He hadn't even seen her face yet. He could touch her again, talk to her, hold her. After thirty years!

As he looked out the window, a drop of rain splashed against the pane. He thought of the lines of a poem he had memorized twenty years before.

> From too much love of living,
>   From hope and fear set free,
> We thank with brief thanksgiving
>   Whatever gods may be
> The no man lives forever,
> That dead men rise up never;
> That even the weariest river
>   Winds somewhere safe to sea.

The rain began to fall steadily, drumming against the window in a hollow rhythm. There was silence in the room, and for a brief moment, Crosby had the frightening sensation of being totally alone in the world.

A voice within him spoke the painful answer: Release her. Let her carry the burden no more. She is weary.

"Dr. Crosby . . ." The woman's voice was gentle.

"Yes!" he cried. "Do it! Take everything—anything you want. But God, please hurry!" Then he lowered his head into his hands and wept.

Grafton Medical Center was highly efficient. Within minutes, a surgeon was summoned and preparations had begun. The first organs removed were the kidneys. Then the heart. Later, the liver, pancreas, spleen, eyeballs, and thyroid gland were lifted delicately and transferred to special containers just above freezing temperature. Finally, a quantity of bone marrow was removed for use as scaffolding for future production of peripheral blood cellular components.

What had been Jeanette Crosby was wheeled down to the morgue.

The woman's voice was doubtful. "We usually don't allow relatives. You see, once the services are over . . ."

Stuart Crosby clutched his hat. "There were no services. I only want a few minutes."

The owner of the crematory, a burly, pleasant looking man, entered the outer office. "Can I do something for you, sir?"

The woman turned to him. "He wanted a little time with the casket, Mr. Gilbert. The one that came over from the hospital this morning."

"Please," Crosby pleaded. "There were no services—I didn't want any, but I just—I didn't realize there'd be no chance to say goodbye. The hospital said she was sent here, and . . . I'm a doctor. Dr. Stuart Crosby. She's my wife. Jeanette Crosby. I didn't think until today that I wanted to . . ." He trailed off and lowered his head.

The owner hesitated. "We usually don't allow this, doctor. We have no facilities here for paying the last respects."

"I know," mumbled Crosby. "I understand—but just a few minutes—please."

The manager looked at the secretary, then back to the old man. "All right, sir. Just a moment, and I'll see if I can find a room. If you'll wait here, please."

The casket was cream-colored pine. It was unadorned. The lid was already sealed, so he could not see her face. But he knew it would be at peace.

He stood dry-eyed before the casket, his hands clasped in front of him. Outside, the rain that had begun the day before was still drizzling down. He could think of nothing to say to her, and he was only aware of a hollow feeling in his chest. He thought ramblingly of his dog, and how he hadn't made his bed that morning, and about the broken windshield wiper he would have to replace on his car.

Finally he turned and walked from the room, bent over a bit because his back hurt. "Thank you," he said to the owner. Stepping outside into the rain, he very carefully raised his umbrella.

The owner watched him until the car pulled onto the main road. They he yelled, "Okay Jack!"

Two men lifted the casket and bore it outside in the rain toward the oven.

Cells divided, differentiated, and divided again. The reconstruction was almost complete. It had taken a long time, almost twenty-four hours. The body had never been challenged to capacity before. Removal of the major organs had caused much difficulty, but regeneration had begun almost at once, and the new tissues were now starting the first stirrings of renewed activity.

The casket slid onto the asbestos bricks with a small scraping noise. The door clanged shut, and there was a dull ring as the bolt was drawn.

There was a flicker of light behind the eyelids, and the new retinas registered it and transmitted it to the brain. The heart pulsed once, and then again. A shuddering breath.

Outside the oven, a hand reached for the switches and set the master timer. The main burner was turned on. Oil under pressure flared and exploded into the chamber.

There was a shadow of awareness for a long moment, and then it was gone.

After thirty minutes, the oven temperature was nine hundred degrees Fahrenheit. The thing on the table was a third of its original size. The secondary burners flamed on. In another half hour, the temperature had reached two thousand degrees, and it would stay there for another ninety minutes.

The ashes, larger than usual, had to be mashed to a chalky, brittle dust.

As Dr. Kornbluth began easing off the dressing, she smiled at the young face on the pillow before her.

"Well, well. You're looking perky today, Marie!" she said.

The little girl smiled back with surprising vigor.

"Scissors, please," said Dr. Kornbluth and held out her hand.

Dr. Roeber spoke from the other side of the bed. "Her color is certainly good."

"Yes. I just got the lab report, and so far there's no anemia."

"Has she been given the Prednisone today?"

"Twenty milligrams about an hour ago."

The last dressing was removed, and the two doctors bent over to examine the chest: the chest that was smooth and clean and faintly pink, with no scars, no lumps, no ridges.

"Something's wrong," said Dr. Kornbluth. "Is this a joke, Dr. Roeber?"

The surgeon's voice was frightened. "I don't understand it, not at all."

"Have you the right patient here?" She reached for the identification bracelet around Marie's wrist.

"Of course it's the right patient!" Dr. Roeber's voice rose. "I ought to know who I operated on, shouldn't I?"

"But it isn't possible!" cried Dr. Kornbluth.

The girl spoke up in a high voice. "Is my new heart okay?"

"It's fine, honey," said Dr. Kornbluth. Then she lowered her voice. "This is physiologically impossible! The incision has completely healed, without scar tissue. And in thirty-two hours, doctor? In thirty-two hours?"

THEY'LL DO IT EVERY TIME
by Cam Thornley

At 15, Mr. Thornley is our youngest author—a fact we discovered only after we had agreed to buy this latest entry in the horrible-pun contest. The writer also reports that he and his brother edit a school-oriented newspaper/magazine that is a lot funnier than you would think, and that he is a victim of unrequited love. This is his first sale.

The High Vavoom of Kazowie was in conference with the pilot of the scoutship which had just returned from Sol III.

"I am certain that you have much to tell us of the strange and fascinating ways of the barbaric humanoids, Captain Zot, but—"

"You wouldn't believe it, your Vavoomity! Why, they live indoors! They don't keep slaves! They even—"

"—but after skimming through your log, I have formulated a few questions which should provide the information necessary to determine whether or not the planet is ready for colonization. Now—"

"It's unbelievable, sir! They eat with pieces of metal! The men think they're better than the women! They don't—"

"—now I just want you to answer these questions as briefly and completely as possible. Do you understand?"

"They—"

"Good. First, what was the reaction of the natives upon first sighting you in the air?"

"Well, high sir, at the time I couldn't help noticing the resemblance to a glikhill that has had freem poured on it. The humanoids went into a frenzy and fired several projectiles at me, all of which fell short by several naugafrangs."

"I see. Now please describe your landing."

"Of course, high sir. When I approached the surface of the planet, I noticed that it was covered with wide black strips which appeared to be vehicular routes. As regulations strictly prohibit landing one's craft upon such routes, I looked for a better place to touch down. The only other areas that seemed to fit my craft's landing specifications were the hard-surfaced paths from the doors of the natives' houses (I will explain this later, high sir) to the vehicular routes.

"I set the ship down on one of these paths and went out to greet the humanoids. They all—"

"Wait a moment. This is extremely important. What was the reaction of the natives upon first seeing you in the flesh? Try to remember everything that happened."

"Yes, high sir. It seems that I bear a striking resemblance to one of their major religious figures. When I came out of the ship all the humanoids in the vicinity knelt and averted their eyes, and said something about the coming seconds. I think this was a reference to an event that was going to happen in the near future. At any rate, when the natives stopped talking they got up and started walking towards me with their arms stretched out in front of them. I didn't like the looks of this so I jumped into the ship and took off. The religious-figure-resemblance theory is strengthened by the fact that when I observed the landing site several weeks later through my reasonable-distance site-viewer I discovered that the natives had built a shrine there which always seemed to be full of pilgrims from many lands."

"Ah, yes. The familiar saviour-from-the-stars syndrome. It happens to every one of our astronauts on pre-colonization planets."

"What's that, high sir?"

"They worship the walk he grounds on."

WILL ACADEME KILL SCIENCE FICTION?
by Jack Williamson

Tim Kirk - WITH APOLOGIES TO REMBRANDT VAN RIJN

*A tall, easy-going, altogether friendly
man, the writer is every bit the son of
a rancher who moved his family to New
Mexico by covered wagon. But his stories
—ah!—for fifty years, Dr. Williamson
has been the leading edge of the best
in galaxy- and time- spanning science fiction.
He was a weather observer for the Army
Air Corps in the South Pacific; his
dissertation became the book,* H. G. Wells:
Critic of Progress, *and he taught SF at
the University of Eastern New Mexico
from 1964 until his retirement—from
teaching, not from writing—last year.*

99

We science-fictioneers lie stretched on a cold stone slab. The hooded academicians are slicing into us with their critical scalpels, lecturing their students on our secret inner workings and debating the function and value of this organ or that, as if we were already dead.

I don't think we are—not just yet. But a lot of us can't help wondering just how much good this scholarly dissection is going to do us. It's a new and sudden thing, all the consequences not yet clear.

Already, however, the teachers of science fiction are probably earning more out of it than the writers do. Though criticism is seldom directly paid, under the "publish or perish" laws of academic survival it's the path toward tenure and promotion. The criticism of SF has tapped rich new veins for researchers, and I can think of writers who seem to be trying harder to impress the critics than to please their readers. I'm afraid the critical tail has begun to wag the creative dog.

Personally, as writer and teacher and occasional critic, I have been in several camps. Retired from teaching now, I'm once more a full-time writer—fiction turns out to be more fun than criticism. Here, I want to try an objective survey of the benefits and hazards of this somewhat surprising academic recognition. I hope these comments will interest readers and maybe be useful to teachers.

§ § §

When I began writing, back in the 1920s, SF still had no familiar name. Hugo Gernsback was still calling it "scientifiction," a term that baffled most people—I used to tell my friends that I was writing adventure stories with a science background. With no book publishers interested—certainly no scholarly critics—it was restricted to a few such pulps as Gernsback's *Amazing Stories* and the old, all-fiction *Argosy*.

Though the SF pulps multiplied during the 1930s, we had little notice anywhere else until after World War II, when a few fans set up such small firms as Fantasy Press and Gnome Press to begin reprinting their favorite magazine serials in hard covers. Their success brought major publishers into the field, with the movies and TV soon to follow.

I think most fans catch the virus young. The early pulps carried pages of fan letters in microscopic print, most of them written by such enthusiastic kids as I was. No doubt most got over the mania, but some of us didn't.

The typical critic—like the typical writer and the typical SF teacher—is, I believe, one of those young fans who attained age and education without losing interest. Examples are such grown-up fans as Damon Knight and Tom Clareson and the late Jim Blish.

In the late 1950s a few of these fans-turned-academics, finding themselves together in the great Modern Language Association, set up a science fiction seminar. This led in time to the SFRA, the Science Fiction Research Association, which now has several hundred members.

The newsletter of the seminar has evolved into *Extrapolation,* the original scholarly fanzine. Others are listed below, among other aids for the SF teacher. In addition to these, there has been a great deal of informed comment in some of the non-academic fanzines. The first thin trickle of critical books is swelling into a flood. Taplinger, for example, is issuing a "Twenty-First Century Authors Series," the first six volumes to be about Asimov, Clarke, Heinlein, Bradbury, Dick, and LeGuin; golden ground for ambitious academics!

Though I can remember when librarians were scornfully excluding such illiterate trash as Edgar Rice Burroughs and *Astounding Stories,* a decade or two ago they suddenly began to prize it, collecting books and long runs of the brittle old pulps and the working papers of every available SF writer from Ackerman to Zelazny. Hundreds of rare old titles are being reprinted now in high-priced library editions by Gregg Press and Garland and others.

§ § §

The academic boom began with the course taught by Mark Hillegas at Colgate in 1962—Sam Moskowitz and others had conducted special lecture courses earlier. I used a news story about Mark's course to get approval for one of my own at Eastern New Mexico University, which I taught for a dozen years.

In the past decade they have multiplied wonderfully. Gathering facts in 1969 for a talk on "SF in the University," I learned of some two dozen courses. The talk led to a little publication of my own, *Teaching SF,* which was a descriptive listing intended to help convince the academic skeptics that SF had really become a legitimate subject. By 1974, when I decided to give up the project because it was getting out of bounds, I had collected descriptions of some 500 courses offered at the college level in the United States and Canada.

By that time, SF had swept on into the high schools, becoming a remarkably popular elective. A chance mention in *English Journal* brought orders for hundreds of copies of *Teaching SF*. That booklet is now out of date and out of print, but there must be several thousand high school courses, some of them in multiple sections with hundreds of students enrolled.

The courses are hard to describe because they differ so much. Most of them, I think, might be placed somewhere along a broad spectrum that ranges from futurology to fantasy. At the futurological extreme, the emphasis is on technological and sociological extrapolations in the real world; at the opposite extreme, the emphasis is on symbolic myth or "transcendence" or stylistic value or pure escape.

Most of the successful teachers are motivated, I think, by a sense that SF has a special relevance to life in our transitional times. In a world of disturbing change, it can become folklore or gospel. Hard science fiction, such as Wells's *When the Sleeper Wakes,* probes alternative futures by means of reasoned extrapolation from the known present in much the same way that good historical fiction reconstructs the probable past. Even far-out fantasy can present significant human values. Deriving its most cogent ideas from the tensions between permanence and change, SF combines the diversions of novelty with its own realistic faithfulness to the fact of change.

More than half the college courses are listed in English, but others have been offered in a score of departments ranging from astronomy and physics through the social sciences to philosophy and religion. The high school courses and a few in the lower grades are commonly taught as literature but are sometimes used to motivate reluctant readers and awaken interests generally.

Though I suppose the great majority has not yet been touched by SF, hundreds of thousands or millions of students have already been turned on—by fan friends, by juvenile novels, by *Star Trek* and *2001* and now by *Star Wars*. The alert teacher can capture their attention, simply by sharing their interest.

SF still appeals to the young, as always, because so much of it is set in the futures in which they will be living. Though the details of new inventions and alien invaders may seem fantastic, the TV kiddie shows on Saturday morning have already introduced them—SF can't be as new to anybody now as once it was for me!—and accelerating change has become almost the first fact of life.

§ § §

There is no standard syllabus for the SF course at any level. Though hundreds of teachers have been inquiring, I'm not sure we need it. One joy of the course, as things stand now, is the freedom it offers the instructor to select the writers that excite him and to communicate his own excitement.

When I began my own course, there were no special texts. I used the low-priced mass paperbacks—still low-priced then!—from such houses as Ace and Avon and Ballantine and Berkley and Bantam and DAW. They are still bargains. Issued for newsstand sale, however, they tend to drop out of print before college bookstores can stock them.

Though scholars have been trying to select a canon, the lists of books in use still vary vastly. Tabulating nearly 80 reading lists a few years ago, I found some 300 titles named, half of them only once. Even the most popular titles were used in no more than a third of the classes. That was before the special texts were numerous, and before the mass publishers began increasing their efforts to reach the schools, but the results may still be useful.

The dozen most popular titles were Asimov's *I, Robot,* Bradbury's *The Martian Chronicles,* Heinlein's *The Moon Is a Harsh Mistress* and *Stranger in a Strange Land,* Herbert's *Dune,* Huxley's *Brave New World,* Le Guin's *Left Hand of Darkness,* Miller's *Canticle for Leibowitz,* Pohl and Kornbluth's *Space Merchants,* Silverberg's *Science Fiction Hall of Fame,* Vol. I, and Wells's *Time Machine* and *War of the Worlds.*

Ingenious teachers have brought life to their classes with all sorts of challenging projects, such as designing new worlds and creatures to fit them. Good audiovisual aids are now available, some described below. Such classic SF films as *Metropolis* can be rented for nominal fees. SF writers can be invited to visit the classroom—a few command high lecture fees, but many are pleased to meet new readers anywhere. (There is a writers bureau as part of the Science Fiction Writers of America; the address is listed at the end of this article.)

§   §   §

Though no course is typical, I suppose my own is a reasonable random sample. Offered at the junior level in college, it generally drew more people than I really wanted for the mixed lecture-and-discussion approach. A few were veteran fans, a few more wanted to write, most were simply curious about science fiction or looking for three upper-division hours in English.

Working toward a general appreciation of SF, we considered definitions and origins; history and types; writing techniques and markets; the uses of SF for entertainment, prediction, and social comment; standards and literary values.

(Science fiction, as I like to define it, is fiction based on the imagined exploration of scientific possibility. The distinction from fantasy—or from other sorts of fantasy—lies in the word *possibility*. In a different way than SF, fantasy asks for Coleridge's famous poetic faith resulting from a willing suspension of disbelief in the impossible.

(This sense of possibility is of course only a small part of the effect of any individual story. Once embarked on the narrative flow, the reader is caught and carried on by the old appeals of mood and style and theme, drawn by the drama of characters in conflict. But still, I think, he wants the assumption that just maybe, somewhere, somehow, it really could happen. Any crude violation of accepted science can break the spell.)

The history of SF can begin nearly anywhere, even with the prehistoric Greeks. If we look at it as a response to technological change, however, it is only in the last couple of centuries that this has been apparent. Brian Aldiss makes a good case for Mary Shelley's *Frankenstein,* published in 1818, as the starting point.

Poe wrote SF not much later, in the same Gothic tradition. He influenced Jules Verne, whose lively tales of new inventions and far adventure earned world acclaim. H. G. Wells, however, was the real founding father of modern SF. A student under T. H. Huxley, he had learned evolution and become our first futurologist, gaining an understanding of our nature and our niche in an uncaring cosmos that Poe and Verne had lacked.

Scholars and anthologists have classified SF in all sorts of ways. Asimov, for example, once called it primitive (1818–1926), adventure (1926–1938), gadget (1938–1945), and social science fiction (1945 to the present)—the only sort worth critical attention. This scheme does fit the American SF magazines, but I can't quite agree that Wells was primitive.

A more meaningful distinction, I believe, certainly one more rewarding in the classroom, is the division between the utopians and the dystopians, between the optimists and pessimists about man's place in the universe and his chances of using reason and science to build a better future.

This issue is probably older than the art of lighting fire, but it is now more urgent every day, as the whole world must somehow balance all the increasing expectations of growing populations against the limits of our resources and the dangers of environmental damage.

Swift foresaw this war, and the Luddites were early skirmishers. Sir Charles Snow described it 20 years ago, in his defense of the culture of science against the traditional literary academics. New battles are raging now over every pipeline, every strip mine, every nuclear reactor. The conflict is clearly coming toward some kind of climax, the outcome not yet sure. We're all involved. The issue has been a central theme of SF, at least since Wells, and students are likely to be delighted with fiction that expresses their own concerns.

Class readings on the dystopian side can begin with the last two books of *Gulliver*—Swift is satirizing the pioneer scientists in the Royal Society. I think Wells, especially in *The Island of Dr. Moreau* and *The First Men in the Moon,* is writing more voyages for Gulliver. Zamyatin's *We* echoes Wells; Aldous Huxley and George Orwell echo both. This dystopian line comes on down through my own *Humanoids,* through Fred Pohl and the New Wave, to Harlan Ellison and others enough.

The utopians are seldom quite so effective—I think the dystopians have an accidental advantage in the tragic drama inherent in their doomsdays. But there is faith in man's reason and hope for his future in the *Odyssey,* in Plato's *Republic*, in Lord Bacon, in Heinlein's juvenile explorers of the universe and Asimov's positronic robots and Clarke's visions of human evolution from caveman to spaceman.

A writer myself, I probably gave more classroom attention to technique than most teachers would. We discussed problems of plot and character and theme and style and viewpoint, sometimes using a little paperback of my own, *People Machines.* Students did two assignments each semester, either critical or creative.

Most of them wrote stories—or sometimes turned in a poem, a chapter of a novel, an original panting, a cartoon strip, a recorded SF drama, a futuristic costume—any of which I cheerfully accepted. Few of the stories reached the professional level, but they were nearly always interesting, the writing often remarkably better than that in the ordinary term paper.

The whole class shared in reading and evaluation, and we read outstanding items aloud. Now and then, when students volunteered to be editors, we produced a class magazine; and a good many of our productions reached the school's literary magazine—which I was sponsoring—to win awards there.

For students who were interested, we discussed the worlds of fandom and writing as a career, passing around a variety of fanzines, prozines, original anthologies, criticism, and the new SF picture books. A few students have reported sales, and at least one has an accepted novel in progress—student writers are sometimes highly gifted, but—fortunately for us professionals—they are very seldom obsessed enough with success to make the sort of sustained effort that it took for even such able people as Bradbury and Ellison to break into the game.

Considering the uses of science fiction, I think it must first of all offer entertainment, before the futurology or the social comment can matter. For most readers, entertainment means escape. Though a few young writers are scornful of that, creating good escape fiction is a high and admirable art. Even when the writer aims at something more, entertainment is basic. The bored reader is lost.

Here, I suspect, the critics are becoming a threat. Praising obscure symbolism, far-out experiments in style, and adherence to party dogma, they are too often able to persuade a talented writer to neglect essential story values. (In my own uninvited opinion, Chip Delany has sometimes been among the victims.)

In a limited but significant way, SF is predictive—predicting nearly everything, we're sometimes right! The limits are narrow. As Wells discovered with *When the Sleeper Wakes,* futurology and fiction mix rather poorly. The writer in search of originality and story drama often does well to select the less likely future.

Yet, as everybody knows, we did foresee space flight and atomic bombs and organ transplants. That's a key item in our popular image and a chief reason for the growing popularity of science fiction. In our age of runaway technological change, future shock is real and common. I think SF can be our best defense, allowing us to learn to ride tomorrow's waves before they break over us.

Much SF is social comment—in a sense, perhaps it all is, being produced by present-day writers for present-day readers, its imagined futures all drawn from present-day concerns. Mainstream critics tend to see no other use. Kingsley Amis, for example, considered SF as social satire and not much else in *New Maps of Hell*.

On literary value, we must appeal to Ted Sturgeon's Law: Nine-tenths of anything is crap. The other tenth of SF is, I think, comparable in lasting worth and interest to the best tenth of any body of work being done today. Witness the widening international recognition of such writers as Phil Dick and Ursula Le Guin and Stanislaw Lem.

Yet, despite all we claim for it, SF is still widely suspect, still fatally stained from its pulp past. In the publishing industry, it's merely another category, like mystery or western or Gothic. If the SF label on a recognizable package can assure moderate sales, it seems also to prevent large sales. Winning best-seller status, such writers as Vonnegut deny the label.

A few people have decided that SF should stand for something else—speculative fiction or speculative fantasy or speculative fabulation. I think they're mistaken. I'm afraid the climb up the giddy spires of Literary Art has taken them too far from any solid base in scientific believability and human interest.

To a limited extent, as others have suggested, SF may be merging into the mainstream. Certainly, as it grows in popularity, more and more mainstream writers are attracted to it. Often, however, they show little understanding of either the methods of science or the tested conventions of SF. Or perhaps my old prejudices are showing.

In any case, there's room for everybody. The SF audience has many appetites. Burroughs' tales of Barsoom are still in wide demand, along with Vonnegut's satire and Phil Dick's probing of apparent realities and Chip Delany's *Dhalgren*.

§ § §

Getting back at last to our initial question: *Will academe kill SF?* I don't think so. The effects of our late welcome into the ivory tower will probably be mixed, but SF is a sturdy young giant with a history of survival. The New Wave is a case in point. Greeted with cries of alarm, it has receded to leave the whole field richer in technique and awareness.

I do suspect that the critics are luring a few promising writers into the formless indulgence and the willful obscurity that has destroyed the popularity of modern poetry. I must admit, too, that many of the new teachers are not at home with SF—their desperate appeals for help are proof of that.

Ben Bova and Jim Gunn have debated the teaching of SF, in *Analog* editorials. Both are respected experts, Ben as editor and writer, Jim as writer, critic, and teacher of an outstanding SF course at the University of Kansas. Ben, still smarting under the way the TV industry mauled and cheapened Harlan Ellison's fine original concept for *Starlost,* was afraid that poorly qualified teachers would do the same sort of thing in the classroom, turning students off. Jim, speaking from his college experience, is convinced that good SF, in spite of untrained teachers, will turn them on.

I think Jim is right. In our TV world, many students don't arrive as serious readers. Leading them to appreciate Shakespeare or Joyce or Dostoevsky is always difficult, often impossible. I have found it far easier to involve them in SF, perhaps because its futures have come to seem more real and challenging than the past.

§ § §

In the high schools alone, hundreds of thousands of kids are being exposed each year to classic SF. Some few teachers, I suppose, limit them to the dated works of Hawthorne and Poe, or take them on searches for symbols and themes the writers never intended, or bog them down in dry research assignments, but many another teacher is as creative and enthusiastic as our arthritic educational establishment allows. Many a bright student, no matter where he first meets SF, will recognize it as an exciting and essential new language, invented to make better sense of our fast-evolving world.

For the teacher at any level who understands and cares about SF, the course is a rare opportunity. There are aids waiting, some outlined below. Though paths enough have been explored, there is freedom left to select your own direction, toward a broad humanism or toward nearly any special field. Most of the students will be above average; a few will be fans, already full of the writers they admire. For all, there is enjoyment and intellectual liberation in science fiction. Far from killing it, academe promises to enrich it with new readers, new writers, and new dimensions of interest.

RESOURCES FOR THE SF TEACHER

Periodicals:

Besides the small handful of such professional magazines as *IA'sfm,* there are at any time several hundred fanzines, dozens worth reading. Labors of love, they appear unannounced and vanish untraced. They have printed some of the best SF criticism, and some of the worst, all of it hard to locate now. Here are a few important and stable titles:

Locus. Edited by Charles N. Brown, Box 3938, San Francisco, CA 94119. (12 issues, $9.00) The indispensable SF news magazine.

Extrapolation. Edited by Thomas D. Clareson, Box 3186, The College of Wooster, Wooster OH 44691. "The Journal of the MLA Seminar on Science Fiction, also serving the Science Fiction Research Association." (2 issues yearly, $4.00) The oldest of the academic fanzines.

Science Fiction Studies. Edited by R. D. Mullen and Darko Suvin, Department of English, Indiana State University, Terre Haute, IN 47809. (3 issues, $6.00) Seriously academic and often useful, but sometimes too pedantic and doctrinaire for my taste.

Foundation. Edited by Peter Nicholls, North East London Polytechnic, Longbridge Road, Essex, RM8 2AS, England. Brighter and more relaxed than most academic journals.

Delap's F&SF Review. Edited by Richard Delap, 1226 North Laurel Ave., W. Hollywood CA 90046. (12 issues, $13.50; libraries, $18.00) Full and knowledgeable reviews of SF in all forms, essential for librarians, recommended for the teacher and the serious reader.

Algol. Edited by Andrew Porter, PO Box 4175, New York NY 10017. Non-academic, but handsome, informed, and readable.

Science Fiction Review. Edited by Richard E. Geis, PO Box 11408, Portland OR 97211. Highly personal comment by an intelligent and articulate critic.

Audiovisual Aids:

James Gunn has produced a series of filmed lectures on SF by writers and editors in the field, available for rental or purchase from the Audio-Visual Center, the University of Kansas, Lawrence KS 66045. Especially recommended are those by Asimov and Pohl, and the one by Ackerman on SF films.

Science Fiction: Jules Verne to Ray Bradbury is a slide-cassette program (3 cassettes and 240 slides) issued by the Center for the Humanities, Inc., 2 Holland Ave., White Plains NY 10603. ($169.50) A basic introduction, which I like.

For visiting science fiction lecturers, write to the Science Fiction Writers Speakers Bureau, care of Mildred Downey Broxon, 2207 Fairview Avenue East, Seattle, WA 98102. Send a stamped, self-addressed envelope for a descriptive brochure.

Handbooks for Teachers

Calkins, Elizabeth, and Barry McGhan. *Teaching Tomorrow: A Handbook of Science Fiction for Teachers*. Pflaum/Standard, 1972. Brief paperback for high school teachers.

Friend, Beverly: *Science Fiction: The Classroom in Orbit*. Educational Impact, 1974. Short paperback for both high school and college teachers.

Williamson, Jack, ed. *Science Fiction: Education for Tomorrow*. Mirage Press, PO Box 7687, Baltimore MD 21207. (Delayed, due in early 1978.) A comprehensive teaching guide in three sections, "The Topic," "The Teachers," "The Tools." Articles by Asimov, Bova, Gunn, Le Guin, Pohl, and 20-odd others. Introduction by Carl Sagan.

Criticism and History:

Aldiss, Brian. *Billion Year Spree*. Doubleday, 1973. An outstanding critical history to about 1950, rather superficial on period since.

———. *Science Fiction Art*. Bounty Books (Crown Publishers), 1975. A stunning picture book with intelligent text.

Barron, Neil. *Anatomy of Wonder: Science Fiction*. Bowker, 1976. Recent, scholarly, and comprehensive. Lengthy annotated bibliography, essential for librarians and collectors.

Bretnor, Reginald, ed. *The Craft of Science Fiction*. Harper & Row, 1975. The best text on writing SF.

———. *Science Fiction, Today and Tomorrow*. Harper & Row, 1974. (Also in Penguin paperback) A broad and useful survey by some 15 writers.

Clareson, Thomas D. *Science Fiction Criticism: An Annotated Checklist*. Kent State U. Press. 1972. Useful listing, 800 items.

Gunn, James E. *Alternate Worlds*. Prentice Hall, 1975. (Also in paperback) A fine critical history with hundreds of photographs.

Hillegas, Mark Robert. *The Future as Nightmare: H. G. Wells and the Anti-Utopians*. Oxford, 1967. An outstanding study of Wells and his pessimistic followers.

Johnson, William, ed. *Focus on the Science Fiction Film*. Prentice-Hall, 1972. Recommended.

Williamson, Jack. *H. G. Wells: Critic of Progress*. Mirage, 1973. On the futurology and the great early SF of Wells.

Wollheim, Donald A. *The Universe Makers*. Harper and Row, 1971. Personal comment by an influential editor and publisher.

Classroom Texts:

Scarce at first, special SF texts are now too numerous to list in full. Since they are expensive, many instructors will prefer to use the lower-priced books from the mass publishers, which have become easier for schools to obtain. Here are typical titles:

Allen David. *Science Fiction: An Introduction.* Cliff Notes, 1973. Includes useful essays on a dozen important sf novels.

Allen, Richard Stanley, ed. *Science Fiction: The Future.* Harcourt, 1971. An excellent anthology; futurological emphasis.

Bova, Ben, ed. *Science Fiction Hall of Fame,* Vols. IIA & IIB. Doubleday, 1973. (Also in Avon paperback—a bargain!) Classic SF novelettes to 1965.

Gunn, James E., ed. *The Road to Science Fiction: From Gilgamesh to Wells.* Mentor, 1977. A fine new historical anthology. Recommended.

Katz, Harvey A., Patricia Warrick, and Martin Harry Greenberg, eds. *Introductory Psychology through Science Fiction.* Rand McNally, 1974. Typical of numerous collections by these and other editors, using SF to introduce nearly everything.

Sargent, Pamela, ed. *Women of Wonder: Science Fiction Stories by Women about Women.* Vintage, 1975. An excellent collection; outstanding introductory essay.

Scholes, Robert, and Eric S. Rabkin. *Science Fiction: History, Science, Vision.* Oxford, 1977. (Paper, $2.95) A thorough and excellent recent text. Recommended.

Silverberg, Robert, ed. *The Mirror of Infinity: A Critics' Anthology of Science Fiction.* Harper & Row, 1970. (Also in paperback) Well-chosen stories, each with a foreword by a different critic, making the book a useful historical survey of SF from Wells to the seventies.

_____. *Science Fiction Hall of Fame,* Vol. I. Doubleday, 1971. (Also in Avon paperback—another bargain!) Classic short stories to 1965, selected by members of the SFWA.

Spinrad, Norman. *Modern Science Fiction.* Doubleday (Anchor paperback), 1974. Good historical anthology with essays defending the New Wave.

Wells, H. G. *The Time Machine / The War of the Worlds; A Critical Edition,* ed. Frank D. McConnell. Oxford, 1977. (Paper, $4.00) Wells's two most popular SF novels, with well-chosen critical essays.

Wilson, Robin Scott. *Those Who Can: A Science Fiction Reader.* Mentor, 1973. Twelve writers accompany their reprinted short stories with essays on plot, character, setting, theme, point of view, and style.

HEAL THE SICK, RAISE THE DEAD
by Jesse Peel

*Mr. Peel tells us that he is 29, married,
with two children. During his yearning-to-
be-a-writer-someday-when-I-have-time period,
he has been a lifeguard, a swimming teacher,
an aluminum-salesman-&-fork-lift-operator,
a private investigator, a kung-fu instructor,
and a male nurse. Currently, he's working
at a family medical clinic as a Physician's
Assistant—sort of half-nurse, half-doctor,
half-technician, and general flunky. The
writer lives with his family in the bayous
of Louisiana; this story is his first sale.*

After I finished attaching the last of the electrodes to the body,
I looked at the girl, making it into a question with my raised
eyebrows. She nodded, her thin-and-young face very pale. I turned
back to my instruments—all the connections seemed to be

correct—so I punched the power switch. The body gave a small, convulsive twitch; there was the smell of burned hair, then . . . nothing.

"Sometimes it takes a while," I said. Anything important usually does. I thought about my own decision. Soon, I'd likely be lying on a table like the one I now stood next to.

She nodded again, and I wanted to tell her, that in this case, it might take longer than a while—it might well take forever.

Despite the cryo-table and the holding-embalm, six days was a long time, a hell of a long time. I didn't know of any case ever brought back over a week or eight days, and anything over five days was usually good enough to make the medical journals.

The girl stood by the body, her slight frame tense and trembling. Her fingers were knitted together, the knuckles white and bloodless. Small beads of sweat stood out on her upper lip and neck, despite the hard chill of the crematorium. Her eyes never left the inert form of the dead boy.

I mostly watched my instruments, lost in my own thoughts. It was cold, and I always got cramps from standing too long when it was cold. I moved about, shifting from one leg to the other, to keep the circulation going. The smell of burnt hair was rivaled by that of stale death; there were over a thousand bodies lying on tables around us.

There was nothing yet to see on the scopes. The EEG was flat, the ECG straight-lined. Total Systems Output was nil, and enzymes were dormant. The polyvital injection/infusion was running well, despite the collapsed state of the blood vessels, but six days was still six days.

I glanced at the lifeless body, and tried to see myself there. I couldn't picture it, being dead. I wondered again how much that had to do with the whole business.

§ § §

I'd figured her for a grafter this morning when she first came in. But the spiderweb skintight she wore was revealing enough to show that she had no obvious scars from prior surgery. No matter how good a medic is, there is always something—a discoloration here, a stretchmark there. She was clean, like a baby.

She had high, small breasts and a thin, leggy body. Her feet were covered with clear spray-on slippers. There was an odor of some musky perfume about her that was pleasant enough, and I figured that she was maybe fifteen.

No graft marks, so today might be her first time. The latest was to have the little finger of the right hand replaced with a live coral snake. Deadly, but who cared? It was novel—this month. Last big fad had everyone wearing raccoon tails for crotch cover. Next month, who could tell?

"What can I do for you?" I asked, giving her my best professional medic smile. I wondered if I had any snakes left in the cryo-tank—business had been good this month.

"I want a Reconstruct," she blurted, her voice a high quaver.

Reconstruct? Damn! So much for my *augenblick* diagnosis of neophyte grafter! I tried to hide my surprise with a question. "How old are you?"

She hesitated for a second. "Thirteen—almost fourteen!"

Missed again. I'd thought fifteen generous, but thirteen? That was much too young to be asking for a Reconstruct. Legally, anyway. Not that too many people paid a hell of a lot of attention to the laws these days.

"Who's this package you want defrosted? Parent?"

She shook her head, and looked down at the floor.

"Sibling?"

She brought her eyes up to meet mine. "Pronger," she said softly.

Well. She didn't look thirteen, and I supposed that if they were big enough, they were old enough. I looked at her small-and-slim body, and sighed. They were maturing earlier all the time, those that were left. When I was young, they'd have put you under the jail and left you there for sleeping with a girl that age. Except that a mob would probably have dragged you out and hanged you from the nearest tree in short order.

I sighed again. When I was young. That was so long ago, it seemed like a million years.

Maybe I was getting senile, living in the past, I thought. Sure, senile at fifty-four.

That was young, fifty-four. If you wanted to bother, you could figure on three times that age before you died, given the state of modern medicine. If you wanted to bother. Hardly anybody did, I mean, what for? I was one of the oldest people I knew—maybe one of the oldest, period.

I pulled myself back to the girl. "When did he terminate?"

"Last Friday."

Today was Thursday. That irritated me! Damn people who held off until the last minute! What did they expect, miracles? "Waited kind of long, didn't you?"

"I was . . . afraid." It was a whimper, a plea.

Go on, I scolded myself, make the little girl cry.

"How old was he?"

"Fourteen."

Another child. "How'd he die? Accident?"

She took a deep breath, and said it with a rush. "Self 'struct!"

God Damn! Tired of life at that tender age! Suddenly I felt very old and tired and alone. I looked quickly down at my desk, visualizing the plastic bottle of capsules there. I was nearly four times his age, I had that kind of right—but God, a fourteen-year-old boy?

§ § §

On my scopes, I was finally getting some activity. A small spiking on the EEG, not much, but something, at least.

I increased the power input slightly. Easy does it, I told myself, don't fry him. I was curious to hear his version, provided I could land him, and it would be good work. Good work was something to be proud of, something else people rarely bothered with any more.

He had been a handsome kid when he was alive. Some medic had done a rotten job on a pair of matched leopard-fur shoulder caplets. They were the only transplants he'd been wearing when he'd died. A few scars were scattered over his body, remnants of past surgeries, but not all that many. Pretty conservative, for a teener.

I looked around the crematorium, noticing how nearly full it was. Looked like they'd have to run the ovens in a day or two, to clear the tables for the next batch. I could taste the bitter dregs of the holding-embalm left in the air by the air'ditioners, and I felt the cold worse because of the clammy dead, I fancied. I spotted only two guards roaming about, but I knew that there were others. There were certain . . . people in our society who had all sorts of uses for fresh bodies.

Another blip on my scopes—some ventricular fib on the ECG. The heart was tough, even after death. I began to think that I might get this boy moving after all. The timer said twenty minutes had passed, and that wasn't good, but there was still a chance out to half an hour.

But five more minutes passed without any change. Then seven. Eight. Crap, the organs must be too far gone. Sorry, kid, I thought, as I reached for the power switch.

Just then, the body turned its head. The girl squealed and I turned up the strength on the booster-relay. I had gross muscle!

Three more minutes passed and then the fibrillation converted. Damned if I didn't get a spotty, but definite sinus rhythm! A block, sure, but it was pumping! If autonomics were still workable, that meant some fine control was possible. Maybe even speech.

The EEG had steeled down to only a mild epileptogenic focus, so I fed the neural circuits more juice. Oxy-lack damage was difficult to overcome, but the polyvital could soothe a great deal of brain damage and rot—temporarily.

Now or never, I thought. I kicked in the bellows pump, and the lungs started to inflate. If they held. . . .

"Uuunnhhh." A windy moan, the voice of the dead.

"Roj? Oh, Roj! I'm here!"

His eyes opened. They were cloudy, of course, and blind. Optic nerves were always the first to go—very few Reconstructs were sighted, even those only a day or two gone. But the eighth cranial, the auditory, hung on for some reason. It was always the last to leave, so it was likely that he'd be able to hear.

". .Te. .Tefi?" Ah, some vocal cords. It was that eerie drone of speech I had heard so many times before. Mostly wind, rushing through a voice-box that had lost much of its elasticity. There was little tongue or lip involved.

"Oh, Roj!" She cried, reaching out to touch him.

"Don't!" I yelled, my voice an echo in the vast room. "You'll short him out!" She jerked her hand back, and I relaxed a little. Likely short yourself out too, I thought. Besides, you wouldn't like the feel of his flesh. It would be like a just-thawed steak.

". .efi?. . .wh. .why...didn' . .youuu..uuhhh...you.....uuhhh. . ."

The girl started to cry. "I'm sorry," she whispered with a sob. I watched as a tear fell onto the cryo-table. It spattered, and froze into a thousand smaller tears.

"After you, I mean, I was scared, after you were. . . ."

" 's okay. .swee'..efi. . .uuhhh...'s..like they ssaid. . . ."

The dead boy struggled, fighting against the bellows pump which restricted his speech. He fought for air which had no other use to him now except to run his decaying vocal cords.

"..onderful..here.. .like   they   ssaid...'eaceful.   'alm...sso.nice." Another pause, waiting for the air. "...friendss...here...all of the...but..youuu... ."

She started to sob, her body shaking. The knobs of my instruments felt suddenly hard and lifeless in my hands. Even after all this time, I could still feel the sadness. Even after all the people I'd brought back.

A self'struct pact. Only she couldn't go through with it at the end. So she had brought him back. For what? To say she was sorry? Could that matter to him? Or to find out if it were really true, what they said about the Other Side? To hear it from one she knew and could trust, to know that Life After Death existed, after all.

But did she know? The boy's story was familiar. It was like, but unlike many others I had heard. It was good to hear it, since I had almost decided. It helped to push my fears into the distance. It helped.

But looking at the girl's face, I wasn't happy. She was getting the same message, more, it was her dead lover saying it. No, I thought, not you. Me, certainly, but not you, not at your age. Don't listen. Wait—thirty, or forty years, a hundred years, then decide. But not now!

I jerked my eyes down, to see the digitals dropping. He was fading. It had taken every bit of my skill, along with a great deal of luck to pull him in, and now I was losing him. But I tried, for her sake—and my own. I punched in full power. The smell of burning hair grew stronger. The body shook, but it was no good. He was gone, this time, forever.

Once, we healed the sick. Now, we raised the dead. I was as bad as all the rest, I did it too. That ability, that power of god-like strength, that curse was going to be the death of mankind. I looked at the girl, and I knew.

"I'm sorry," I said, not just meaning the loss of the boy.

"Don't be," she said, smiling through the tears. "It's all right now."

But I knew that it wasn't all right. Not now, not ever. She had made up her mind, but it wasn't all right. It was wrong, and it was as much my fault as any man's.

I repacked my instruments. Even after thirty years as a medic, I still hated to lose a patient, regardless that he was already dead. All I wanted to do now was get out, into the city-stale but alive air.

Inside my ancient and much-repaired hovercraft, we sat quietly for a minute, letting the autoglide fly us back to my office. I knew what she was thinking, but it was wrong.

Why?, Shouted a voice inside my head. Weren't you thinking the same thing?

That's different, I argued with myself. I am older. I—

Hah!, said the voice.

"So you are going to do it," I said. It was not a question.

She nodded, smiling and unafraid now.

"You can't! You're only a child!" I exploded.

"Roj is waiting for me!"

"There are a thousand boys—"

"No! They are not Roj!"

"But to kill yourself—"

"So what? Here is only here! There is perfect! It's like everybody said, you heard him!"

Yes, I'd heard him. Him, and all the others. Still, I had to try.

"You don't know what life has to offer!"

"I do so! I'm not a baby! I've been places, done things! Why go through it all over again? Why does it even matter? Roj is *there*, waiting for me!"

"But—"

"You heard him!" She threw herself back deeply into the hover-craft's worn seat, her arms crossed to shut me out.

How could I argue with it? How could I fight a voice from the lips of her own dead lover? Who would not be taken in, convinced totally by the words of a father, mother, or a sister—or a wife?

I stared through the pitted plastic window at the city beneath us. Mostly deserted now, a far cry from the days before the Reconstruct process. Maybe if Mali had lived, had made it until the process had been perfected.... No. It was long past, and I'd never hear it from my own wife.

I turned back to the girl. "Listen," I said, feeling desperate. For some reason, it was important that she know, that she understand. I caught her shoulders, feeling her smooth skin and firm muscle under my hands.

"When the Reconstruct concept was first created, there were a lot of theories. One of the most important was thrown out, because nobody wanted to believe it. That theory says that what the dead say is not real!"

She shook her head and struggled, but I wouldn't let her go.

"It says that the human brain refuses to accept its own death, so it makes up a story, to convince itself that it will not die! That what the dead say when you bring them back is only that story, played back a final time, like a recording! That's why the stories are different, because they are subjective, not because there are really different realities on the Other Side!"

She stared at me, not wanting to hear it.

"Don't you understand? It could all be a lie! You could be killing yourself for nothing!" There. I'd said it. But who was I really trying to convince?

"You heard, you heard!" She screamed, starting to cry. "Roj said, he said, he said—"

I let her go, and slumped back into my seat. Yes. Roj had said.

§ § §

The girl was gone, and I sat alone at my desk, staring at the drawer. Had I convinced her? Planted a seed of the smallest doubt? I didn't know. Probably not, but maybe. Somebody had to convince them, the young ones. What if the theory was wrong?

What even, if the theory was valid? Suppose there was Life After Death—what then? Why would there be any point in staying alive. Or what point in being born in the first place? It was a question that had been debated by the best minds we had, and no answer had been found.

At least, not in this life. There was one way for anyone who wished to find out. I took the bottle of capsules from the drawer, and shook them about inside their plastic prison. I was older than most, surely I had the right to do as I wished. I had heard all the stories: It was Heaven, Valhalla, Nirvana, Paradise. Nobody ever said it was Hell—at worst, it was much better than here.

But if I did it, who would be left to try and keep the young ones going? And what if it were a lie? What if the whole thing was a massive con game, a trick of the human mind on itself; who would be around to try and keep the human race going?

I was supposed to be a healer, a life-giver, a medic. It was my job, wasn't it? But I was tired, and how much could one man be expected to do?

I poured the blue-and-green capsules out onto the desk, touching the slick-and-light one-way tickets to where? Heaven, or oblivion? I stirred them around with my finger, hearing the tiny sound they made on my plastic desk. I was almost sure, until I had met the girl today, and brought back her dead lover.

Was this the way the world was to end, not with a bang or a whimper, but with an expectant smile?

Could all those people be wrong?

There was only one way I could be sure, only one way.

Carefully, I put the capsules back into the bottle, and snapped the lid shut. Not today, I thought.

Not today.

HOME TEAM ADVANTAGE
by Jack C. Haldeman II

The author reports that he is now 34; he lives with his wife, Vol, their two daughters, two cats, and an alligator in a weathered cedar cabin full of tree frogs. Mr. Haldeman further reports hard times in the swamp these days: the alligators have been seen selling apples and pencils along the canal.

Slugger walked down the deserted hallway, his footsteps making a hollow ringing sound under the empty stadium. Turning a corner, he headed for the dugout. He was early. He was always early. Sportscasters said he'd probably be early for his own funeral.

He was.

Slugger sat on the wooden bench. It was too quiet. He picked up a practice bat and tapped it against the concrete floor. Normally he and Lefty would be razzing Pedro. Coach Weinraub would be pacing up and down, cursing the players, the umpire. There would be a lot of noise, gum popping, tobacco spitting, and good-natured practical jokes. The Kid would be sitting at the far end of the bench, worrying about his batting average and keeping his place in the starting lineup. The Kid always did that, even though he had a .359 average. The Kid was a worrier, but he wouldn't worry anymore. Not after yesterday. Not after the Arcturians won the series and ended the season. Not after they won the right to eat all the humans.

Tough luck about being eaten, but Slugger couldn't let himself feel too bad about that; he had led the league in homers and the team had finished the regular season 15 games out in front. Except for the series with the Arcturians, it had been a good year. Slugger hefted the practice bat over his shoulder and climbed the dugout steps, as he had done so many times before, up to the field. This time there were no cheers.

The early morning wind blew yesterday's hot dog wrappers and beer cups across the infield. It was cool; dew covered the artificial grass, fog drifted in the bleachers. Slugger strode firmly up to the plate, took his stance, and swung hard at an imaginary ball.

In his mind there was a solid crack, a roar from the crowd and the phantom ball sailed over the center field fence. He dropped the bat and started to run the bases. By the time he rounded third, he had slowed to a walk. The empty stadium closed in on him, and when he reached home plate he sat down in the batter's box to wait for the Arcturians.

He wasn't alone very long. A television crew drove up in a large van and started setting up their cameras. Some carpenters quickly erected a temporary stage on the pitcher's mound. The ground crew half-heartedly picked up the hot dog wrappers and paper cups. Slugger started back to the dugout but he didn't make it. He ran into the Hawk.

Julius Hawkline was a character, an institution of sorts in the sports world. In his early days as a manager, the Hawk had been crankier and more controversial than the legendary Stengel. In his present role as television announcer and retired S.O.B., the Hawk was more irritating and opinionated than the legendary Cosell. True to his name, the Hawk was descending on Slugger for an interview.

"Hey Slugger!"

"Gotta go."

"Just take a minute." A man was running around with a camera, getting it all on tape. "You owe it to the fans."

The fans. That got to Slugger. It always did.

"Okay, Hawk. Just a minute. Gotta get back to the locker room. The guys'll be there soon."

"How's it feel to have blown the game, the series—to be responsible for the Arcturians earning the right to eat all the humans?"

"We played good," said Slugger, backing away. "They just played better. That's all."

"That's *all*? They're going to *eat* us and you blew it four to three. Not to mention Lefty—"

"Don't blame Lefty. He couldn't help it. Got a trick ankle, that's all."

"*All*? They're going to gobble us up—you know, knives, forks, pepper, Worcestershire sauce, all that stuff; every man, woman, and child. Imagine all those poor children out there covered with catsup. All because of a trick ankle and a couple of bonehead plays. Sure we can blame Lefty. The whole world will blame Lefty, blame you, blame the entire team. You let us down. It's all over, buddy, and your team couldn't win the big one. What do you have to say to that?"

"We played good. They played better."

The Hawk turned from Slugger and faced the camera. "And now you have it, ladies and gentlemen, the latest word from down here on the field while we wait the arrival of the Arcturians for their post-game picnic. Slugger says we played good, but let me tell you that this time 'good' just wasn't good enough. We had to be *great* and we just couldn't get it up for the final game. The world will little note nor long remember that Slugger went ten for seventeen in the series, or that we lost the big one by only one run. What they *will* remember is Lefty falling down rounding first, *tripping* over his own shoelaces, causing us to lose the whole ball of wax."

Slugger walked over to the Hawk, teeth clenched. He reached out and crumpled the microphone with one hand.

"Lefty's my friend. We played good." He turned and walked back to the dugout.

The Hawk was delighted. They'd gotten it all on tape.

When Slugger got back to the dressing room, most of the team was there, suiting up. Everything was pretty quiet, there was none of the horseplay that usually preceded a game. Slugger went to his locker and started to dress. Someone had tied his shoelaces together. He grinned. It was a tough knot.

Usually coach Weinraub would analyze the previous day's game—giving pointers, advice, encouragement and cussing a few of the players out. Today he just sat on the bench, eyes downcast. Slugger had to keep reminding himself that there wouldn't be any more games; not today, not tomorrow. Never again. It just didn't seem possible. He slipped his glove on, the worn leather fitting his hand perfectly. It felt good to be in uniform, even if it was just for a picnic.

The noise of the crowd filtered through to the dressing room; the stadium was filling up. The Arcturians would be here soon. Reporters were crowding at the door, slipping inside. Flashbulbs were popping.

Lefty snuck in the back way and slipped over to his locker. It was next to Slugger's. They had been friends a long time, played in the minors together.

"Mornin' Lefty," said Slugger. "How's the wife and kids?"

"Fine," mumbled Lefty, pulling off the false mustache he'd worn to get through the crowd.

"Ankle still bothering you?"

"Naw. It's fine now."

"Can't keep a good man down," said Slugger, patting Lefty on the back.

A microphone appeared between them, followed by the all too familiar face of the Hawk.

"Hey Lefty, how about a few words for the viewing public? How does it feel to be the meathead that blew the whole thing?"

"Aw, come on, Hawk, gimme a break."

"It was a team effort all the way," said Slugger, reaching for the microphone.

"These things cost money," said the Hawk, stepping back. The coach blew his whistle.

"Come on team, this is it. Everybody topside." The dressing room emptied quickly. Nobody wanted to be around the Hawk. Even being the main course at the picnic was better than that.

On the field the Arcturians had already been introduced and they stood at attention along the third base line. One by one the humans' names were called, and they took their places along the first base line. The crowd cheered Slugger and booed Lefty. Slugger felt bad about that. The stage on the pitcher's mound had a picnic table on it and the Arcturian managers and coaches were sitting around it, wearing bibs.

After they played both planets' anthems, George Alex, the league president, went to the podium set up on the stage.

"Ladies and gentlemen, I won't keep you in suspense much longer. The name of the first human to be eaten will be announced shortly. But first I would like to thank you, the fans, for casting so many ballots to choose the person we will honor today. As with the All-Star game, the more votes that are cast make for a more representative selection. All over the country—the world, for that matter—fans like you, just plain people, have been writing names on the backs of hot dog wrappers and stuffing them in the special boxes placed in all major league stadiums. I'm proud to say that over ten million votes were cast and we have a winner. The envelope, please."

A man in a tuxedo, flanked by two armed guards, presented the envelope.

"The results are clear. The first human to be eaten will be ... the Hawk! Let's hear it for *Julius W. Hawkline!*"

The stadium rocked with cheers. The Hawk was obviously the crowd's favorite. He was, however, reluctant to come forward and had to be dragged to the stage. The other reporters stuck microphones in his face, asking him how it felt to be the chosen one.

For the first time in his life the Hawk was at a loss for words.

The coach of the Arcturians held the Hawk with four of his six arms and ceremoniously bit off his nose. Everyone cheered and the Arcturian chewed. And chewed. The crowd went wild. He chewed some more. Finally, he spat the Hawk's nose out and went into a huddle with the other coaches.

Undigestible, was the conclusion, unchewable; humans were definitely inedible. Something else would have to be arranged.

Slugger smiled to himself, thinking ahead to next season. You had to hand it to the Hawk; he was one tough old bird.

A SOLUTION TO THE DEFECTIVE DOYLES
(from page 45)

The algorithm uses the binary system. Take 1 doyle from the first can, 2 from the second, 4 from the third, 8 from the fourth, 16 from the fifth, and 32 from the sixth. These numbers, 1, 2, 4, 8, . . . , are powers of 2, and every integer is the sum of a unique set of such powers, provided no two are alike.

Place the 63 doyles on the scale and write down the excess weight in milligrams as a binary number. The position of each 1 in the number, counting from the *right*, identifies a defective can. Example: the excess weight, is 22 milligrams. In binary, 22 = 10110. Therefore the second, third, and fifth cans hold defective doyles.

Several months later, after a third shipment, the following message came. "Due to computer error, each can contains only two dozen doyles. Any can may be full of defective doyles, each one milligram overweight. Destroy defective doyles."

"The binary system won't work now," said Watts. "It requires 32 doyles from one can, but no can has that many."

Shurl said nothing. He retired to his room where he gave himself an injection of Fermataine, a drug that increases one's ability to do number theory in book margins, and scraped for a while on his musical saw. When he returned he said:

"I've done it again, Watts. One weighing suffices. A most singular solution."

See page 213 for the answer.

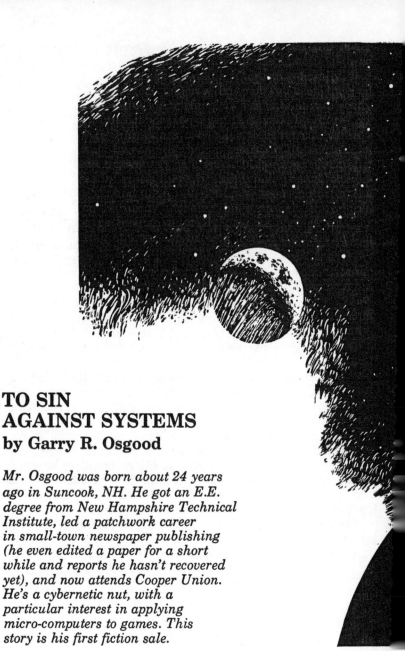

TO SIN
AGAINST SYSTEMS
by Garry R. Osgood

*Mr. Osgood was born about 24 years
ago in Suncook, NH. He got an E.E.
degree from New Hampshire Technical
Institute, led a patchwork career
in small-town newspaper publishing
(he even edited a paper for a short
while and reports he hasn't recovered
yet), and now attends Cooper Union.
He's a cybernetic nut, with a
particular interest in applying
micro-computers to games. This
story is his first fiction sale.*

With a defiant squeak, the chalk finished its last block diagram for the year while I concluded to the blackboard, "So the classical tube amplifier can be represented by the block μ times the load resistor, R_L, divided by R_L plus plate resistance r_p. This transfer function represents the ideal gain of the system and relates the time varying function at the block's input port to the output function."

I turned to the young faces of the class and pitched the chalk stub in the wastepaper basket. The classroom was hot. My shirt was sticking to my back, and I had beads of perspiration growing on my forehead. There was one last hurdle between these kids and the summer vacation.

"The final for this course will be held in the lecture hall L-212, I guess." I peered at the assignment sheet posted on the bulletin board, to keep up the appearance that I was myopic. "On Friday, first period—nice and early in the morning." Nobody laughed. I sat down on the desk and mulled over the various bits of wisdom that a professor should pass on to his departing students. There were damn few items that weren't already stale. I rubbed my chin, peered out the window, and decided on a few classics.

"Everybody should bring a pencil, I guess. A school that can't afford individual terminals probably can't afford pencils—or a sharpener, so bring a spare." That was classic enough, so I left them with some personal philosophy: "I think if you go into this thing with the idea of memorizing a lot of equations, you'll run into a great deal of trouble. Remember the underlying concepts, the reasons why the equations are written the way they are. We are dealing with integrated and inter-related systems here, and not discrete pieces. Nowhere in the exam are you given equations. You are given a system. Take the overview approach and look at the system as a whole, and the proper relations will suggest themselves if you don't bury yourself in minute and unimportant aspects."

Well, that's what all engineering profs say anyway, so I guess I didn't add anything new to student lore.

"See you next year—some of you. Get lost." And away they went. Some were intent and some were asleep; I wondered if teachers were ever any use. Chances were I wouldn't be seeing them again next year, anyway. I was feeling the weather in my joints, and I didn't like getting up in the morning anymore. Both were signs that soon I would have to hole up somewhere and go through a metamorphosis. I didn't think that I could leave it for

TO SIN AGAINST SYSTEMS

another year; and after it was done I would have to be someone else—two lifetimes of Professor Gilbert Fenton were more than I could take. It had been fun for a while, teaching these kids; but the subject matter was getting stale of late. I had taught it too many times. I'd be doing myself and these kids a favor if I became somebody else.

I walked out of the old ivy-covered brick building into the heat of a midwestern day in May. I found myself wandering down a shady, sleepy walk of American academe. It was one of those late spring days that whisper, like the wind through the trees, "Summer is here." The students who had doubts about their futures were hitting the books and typewriters for their final papers and whatnots. Those who were in no doubt—the 'smart' and the otherwise—were infesting the beer halls and hangouts of the college town.

It had been my pleasure to have for the last few days a companion, of sorts, though I knew neither who he was nor where he came from. I hadn't even spoken with him. He was a slender youth, dressed in the standard uniform of T-shirt and jeans. He didn't amount to anything save for those eyes of his. He had first caught my attention, then my curiosity. As I turned the corner of the lane on that sleepy summer day, my companion of sorts saw me; upon seeing me, he propelled himself down the street like the boy who had made the acquaintance of the preacher's daughter and the sheriff; the latter being an unplanned circumstance. Seeing him struck me as a very curious thing, for apparently I had gone through most of the year without noticing him; and when I finally did I couldn't avoid him. This sometimes happens with me: to be aware of people is to see them; but I don't think I would have noticed this particular youth in the first place if it had not been for those eyes. He reminded me of a friend; Sheridan had eyes like that youth: steel grey eyes that penetrated and calculated, windows to a sharp intellect. Sheridan was a living embodiment of von Neumann's ideal game player: perfectly intelligent and perfectly ruthless. In all my years he has been the only one to really guess who I am.

Damn him.

While I have laid low in life, Sheridan always grabbed the limelight, always wanted still more; though age was slowing him down at last. He and I first met in a rooming house on Fulton Street in New York City, in the year 1912. He was a lad of twenty and I . . . well I was passing through, in need of folding money or a man who was handy with a printing press. Sheridan had both. But he was also a most perceptive lad, and he picked up something that had kept him on my trail ever since. I considered the memory. It has been ninety years since I made that acquaintance. Sheridan was now very old, and very rich—and very persistent. I decided that I might just put old Gilbert Fenton to rest that night; Sheridan's grey eyes might run in the family. After I metamorphose I generally make myself quite different and turn up quite far from where I start, and Sheridan usually loses me for a spell. If I pulled the dodge one more time, I probably wouldn't have to worry again. I set off with decision in my step, lighthearted, in a way; I was about to begin again.

Perhaps I shouldn't be harsh on Sheridan, though. For all that I abhor his fascination with wealth and power, I haven't come one iota closer to the Universal Why than he has: which is to say, not at all. I have been looking for some time, too. I recalled, as I walked down the lane, That Woman—metamorphosing always makes me nostalgic—she had had an insight that impressed me deeply. She was old—mentally old—for an ephemeral. I had thought that with two of us on the job, the Universal Why wouldn't be too hard to find, so on her eightieth birthday I gave her the insight I have been able to exercise on myself as a gift to celebrate our fifty-five-year-old friendship. Afterwards, she was very quiet; and some time later she found the Universal Why at the bottom of a mine shaft. I was very thoughtful about the matter of self-annihilation after that, and I swore that I would understand a human being *thoroughly* before I tried the stunt again. I started the new policy with myself, and I'm still working with the first candidate.

You can understand how thoughtful a man becomes when considering such terribly human matters. That day I should have been careful. I am not immortal: I am a well-tuned mechanism, granted, but I can break. I should have paid attention to the crunch of gravel on the road as the car coasted along in neutral, the engine off. The car came alongside me (lost as I was in fond reverie), and a door opened.

"Hey, Bill! Wanna ride?"

Well, it wasn't my name but I looked up anyway. The youth with steel grey eyes was adding sounds of plausibility to what amounted to a kidnapping—though I was far too old to be a kid. I felt a little twinge of pain and a mild feeling of regret. A quick investigation of my chemical systems told me that the sedative was fast-acting and already rooted in too many places for me to whip up an effective counter-agent.

Shucks. Can't win 'em all.

They were gentle with me. I suspect they all had hospital experience; Sheridan knew how to pick his staff. I was sure I was going to see him again. I can't call him friend, but it's people like him who make the world go round the way it does: sadly.

§ § §

The ride up to the Polar Orbital Station, administrative offices of The Sheridan Group Industries, was uneventful. I'd have been drugged to the gills if I had any.

It was a peaceful awakening, considering the abruptness of my abduction. I found myself in a nice, soft bed in a room of pastel colors. In the background there was the rustle of pink noise, which at one moment suggested the wind through tree branches, at another, the dance of water through rocks. I had the warm feeling that follows a good long sleep, but I was not at all sure how this next meeting with Sheridan would go. I looked for a clock but couldn't find one. I sat back on my pillows with the vague disquiet that comes when I'm completely disoriented in time. I don't think the temporal displacement would have been all that bad, if I hadn't found that I had company.

A male steward. A large male steward. Rather larger than four of me in fact.

I gave him what I imagined was a glower but it didn't seem to scare him.

"Hey, Shorty. How about telling your Boss that I'm awake?" I said.

He looked over his shoulder at me, uncrossed his arms from behind his back, turned, bowed curtly. From anyone else, the gesture would have looked ridiculous, but he gave it an air of poetry; and besides, he was bigger than I, so I didn't laugh. Through his smile he said,

"Mr. Sheridan will be with you presently. In the meantime, if there is anything that I can do—"

"Leave," I suggested.

"That would not be possible, I'm afraid." A smile, a bow. I rapped out a few drum rolls with my fingers and thought a few thoughts.

"Hmm. Can you dance? Do magic tricks? How about some clothes? Sure as taxes your Boss man is going to chew the fat with me eventually." Why else would he go to all this trouble?

"Certainly." He snapped his fingers, and another version of him, somewhat smaller perhaps, appeared. This didn't help, I thought. It wasn't that I wanted privacy so I could escape—where could I escape to, on Sheridan's own orbital satellite? I didn't think they'd lend me a shuttle; assuming I could find a shuttle, assuming I could run a shuttle, or assuming that I could go through the bang, bang, shoot-'em-up heroics that would be required to get one. I haven't lived since A.D. 900 by giving people excuses to shoot at me. I wanted privacy because I was prudish, and if I asked for anything else, I'd probably get a brass band to watch me dress.

"How 'bout some privacy? You expect me to dress to an audience?" They both complied. In unison they turned their backs. The choreography was superb.

I knew Sheridan was well off, but I began to wonder if even that could adequately describe a man who owned his own space station. When I first met him he was just another two-bit waterfront chiseler with an accommodating smile and a printing press that spit out sawbucks and fins. On the side he could do magic with a piece of paper. He could match stock certificates to inks and to presses. He could take a document from any institution and turn out a very reasonable facsimile lickety-split.

At the time, the various patrons I served in the booking industry were tossing those significant glances my way that told me that it was time to move on, and like Tammany Hall, I did. I picked Sheridan because I needed the various bits of paper naming an individual to be crisp and well done. Sheridan was just a kid, but he was beginning to get the reputation of being a phenomenally skilled kid. True to form, he was thorough with his patrons and kept an eye on me even after I thought I had finished doing business with him. My thirteenth metamorphosis had had a cheering section.

The togs fit perfectly. One of the goons brought me a mirror, and I saw that I liked the cut and style of the clothes. Warm color, simple, with no baroque frills. Sheridan remembered my tastes and had gained some skill on the soft pedal. It was very different from the techniques that he had used on me before; the last time we met, Sheridan caressed me with an india rubber hose.

He has had a long time to learn, I reflected. Sheridan must be at least a hundred and ten, and still a captain of industry. He should have become an honorary member of the Board of the

Sheridan Group Industries forty years ago, but he didn't retire. He still had enough energy to secure his position in the business and chase me all over India, when he got wind of me there. I looked around the compartment. It was well appointed. I could have been on the Terran surface. Sheridan was a scoundrel who would sell his mother down the river; but he was a capable, intelligent, and gifted scoundrel. One of the goons cleared the ceiling and I amused myself by watching the activity on the Station's Hub.

In a short while I heard the door mechanism. The two goons got up to go as the compartment door slid quietly into the bulkhead.

It was Sheridan.

Oh, he was old, and very thin, but I couldn't make the word 'frail' hang on him. His was the distinguished kind of old that one associates with the occupants of stone castles, who cultivate very fine wines. His back was straight. He was neat as a pin, and though his cheeks were sunken he still had the hawk nose and the penetrating, steel grey eyes. I had the urge to stand up in his presence, to forget about the abduction and the rubber hose: he had an atmosphere of command just like that. I almost got up—but I didn't.

"Good afternoon—Gilbert, is it?" he asked, and held out a hand that I didn't take. He had a nice, rich voice, with just a slight trace of a piping waver. Ordinarily, I would like a man with a voice like that.

I scratched my head, still sprawled out on the bed, looked up at the Hub, and said it was as good a name as any. "Is it afternoon? Heck, Pappy, I should be hungry now. Got anything to eat in this oversized bicycle wheel?"

" 'Afternoon' by Greenwich Mean. I suspect it would be early in the morning in Midwestern America. You either will, or already have notified the college that you have been taken ill."

"Thanks, Pappy, I guess. You always were thorough." The last time we had met he had been a near youngster, and I'd been apparently in my late seventies. I wasn't a youngster at the moment, but the apparent age-spread between us was the same, only the sign had been changed.

"Chester," he addressed one of the goons by the door, "attend to dinner for Mr. Fenton and myself. Have it served in the Observatory. After that, you and the staff shall retire from my living quarters until 0800 tomorrow."

"Very good, Mr. Sheridan." Chester and the other goon left in a butlerish sort of way.

Sheridan turned his attention back to me, saying, "To the Observatory, sir? The view of the Earth is magnificent—Olympian, even."

"As beheld by an Olympian god, perhaps?" I asked.

Sheridan smiled, ignored my sally and asked: "Have you ever seen the Earth from this vantage point?"

"Naw," I replied. "This is a first. First time in orbit, too. Can't say that it's much different from any Terran flophouse—purtier, maybe."

Sheridan allowed a calculated degree of surprise. "The first time? I thought that you had the time to try everything." Sheridan arched his eyebrows just so.

"What? Impossible. Sir, I have just begun!" I replied.

". . . And at an age when most men have long retired from their affairs," Sheridan added. Then he cocked his eyebrow and fixed me with a steely sidelong glance. "Except that it's 'all men' in your case, Gilbert?"

"Speak for yourself, Chief," I retorted. "You aren't doing too badly either. Banging around in orbit. Hell, you got your start out of the backside of a horse-drawn wagon. Are you telling me that you've finally figured it out for yourself and you don't need my services?"

"Business after lunch, Fenton. We old fellows shouldn't rush about. Let us say I have changed my mind on certain fundamental points in our century-old cat-and-mouse game."

"You've decided to be the mouse?" I asked with staged surprise.

"Maybe, Fenton, I have been the mouse all along. Quiet, now." We had been riding in a slidevator that ran along the rim of the Station. It had reached its last stop, and the doors slid open. Sheridan guided me to another set of double doors. With his finger poised over the opening plate, he turned to me and whispered: "Hold on; this view will take your breath away. I've had people faint here."

The doors opened into an oval room with dark walls and unobtrusive lights scattered about the ceiling. Save for small islands and threadlike catwalks, the floor opened out into parsecs of inky black space, scattershot with points of light. The Milky Way was drifting with stately dignity beneath our feet.

"Walk out onto it. The floor is quite an engineering feat itself."

And I saw Earthrise at the Polar Orbital Station.

Moving with a graceful pace, Northern Europe hove into view, dressed in the satin white lace of a fair-weather system. To my left, protracted, was the North American continent, glowing under a late morning sun. White and sapphire, russet and green, Terra spun slowly against a velvet backdrop; and behind her, the Milky Way drifted in the vastness of the expanding Universe. I was awestruck, thunderstruck, and struck by a million items so vanishingly small, yet so brilliantly resolved: the sun's highlight on the Atlantic, individual textures of clouds, the incredibly involved texture of the land. If ever I had a feel for the comprehension of the Universal Whole, it was in that Observatory.

I wasn't going to fall . . . but I wasn't going to let go of Sheridan, either.

"Sher—Sheridan?"

"Sir."

"I'm impressed. Where can I sit down?"

Sheridan helped me along the walk, over the Mid-Atlantic, and sat me down at a table somewhere above the Ural Mountains. For some time I had forgotten to breathe. I checked my pulse, spent some minutes doing something about all the adrenalin my glands had so thoughtlessly dumped into my bloodstream, and soothed senses that *swore* I was going to fall out of the place. There were a number of body-keeping chores that I had to attend to right there.

"Do you have a fear of heights?" Sheridan asked pleasantly.

"Only—recently, Sheridan. I didn't think they could make a transparent shield of such dimensions."

"Anything can be done with money, Gilbert. The costs of developing the Observatory were indeed high, but you should see the effect it has on the stockholders. Between you and me and the Board, the principal stockholders require little additional conditioning after they've been in this room. They respond to this place as they would to a religious experience; indeed, for some it's the only religious experience they ever have."

Conditioned stockholders. A typical Sheridan scheme. But, I had to admit to myself, I hadn't been moved like this since I was sixteen and inside my first cathedral. Life was more carefree then; I didn't have to trouble myself with the schemings of old men—or escaping from their space stations to protect the secret of longevity. For all its faults, the world didn't deserve an immortal Sheridan.

I think Sheridan felt embarrassed in the silence that followed his remark. I peered at him in the green and blue earthlight, and he fumbled with his fingers and then burst out: "Oh, the conditioning isn't that severe! We have no use for a bunch of Pavlov dogs! The conditioning is very subtle, and actually falls into that never-never land between conditioning, convincing, and educating. They aren't even aware of it. The only form it takes is the inclination to invest in one kind of a scheme, every now and then, rather than another; and to keep re-electing the present Board of Directors and myself. That's hardly dictating their every movement! And we're only dealing with one-thousandth of one percent of the world's population."

"The ones with money," I said, levelly.

"Well, that is hardly an abuse of power," he said, forcing conviction into his voice.

"Did I sound like I was objecting?" I asked.

"Oh . . ." Sheridan seemed surprised. Poor fella; he was warming up to a justification speech that he found out he didn't need. He didn't know what to do with his mouth—and I felt good. At least for that instant he wasn't in the driver's seat.

"I rather thought you would," he said, a little lamely. "You always were a liberal moralist, Gilbert. You objected to the printing of bogus money even as you were accepting your degree from—'Matheus University'? I think that was the place I gave you." I got a thin smile as soft sounds from the ramp announced Chester's arrival with the chow.

Chester was unimpressed by the spectacle beneath his feet. The green-blue light from the floor lit him up like an apparition from the Ektachrome of a bad horror movie.

I replied to Sheridan's comment, "Times change; so do the opinions of cantankerous old men."

Sheridan nodded thoughtfully. He began to cut carefully into the steak. Since my background lacked grace and form, I attacked my portion in the spirit of an Apache raid on an intruding wagon train.

In time I asked through the music of utensils on porcelain, "So, Pappy; how's the printing business?"

Sheridan stopped the elegant business of eating. He looked at me and tried to gauge any hidden meaning in my question.

"I sold it to someone who could appreciate it. I purchased a bakery and sold it as a bread company. I bought into Rockwell International and recommenced the manufacture of the Shuttle when the energy depletion scare finally blew away. It was difficult, but men aren't all that difficult to control, if they are ambitious. You figure out what they want, and then you make them think you've delivered it to them—all for a price, mind you."

"Hmm," I said. He had suggested something to me . . . but what was it? A plan, a whole brazen plan flashed in front of me and—I lost it. My glimmer didn't reach the gleam stage.

Sheridan, asked, between bites, "And how are you proceeding, sir?"

As if he didn't know. "I've been trying my hand as an engineering prof in a diploma mill," I replied. "I have no illusions about the sanctity of the learning process. There are people who learn—and people who look for the instructions on things."

"Education, a personal process, what?"

"Yep." I launched my last piece of steak on its next phase of existence and said around the bite, "Maybe the process is easier in defined atmospheres, with research material and someone to help you who knows the ropes; but it's still a personal process. Maybe the word 'teacher' is meaningless. Maybe 'learning assistant' is better."

Chester was gone. We were alone now.

"I am going to make a proposition, Gilbert."

"Anything like the last one? As I recall, you presented it with a great deal of persistent vigor."

Sheridan laughed a polite laugh, which revealed a row of perfect teeth. The floor was opaquing in response to a local sunrise. "And I would have continued to do so if you hadn't found a door I didn't know existed."

That wasn't how I had gotten out; but if that was what he wanted to think, then I wasn't going to disillusion him.

Sheridan continued: "But you must admit that I have developed a great deal of sophistication since those days. Here we are in an orbital station, amid the offices and laboratories of the Sheridan Group Industries. A thousand office workers and technicians and their families reside here. No one knows you are here but you and I."

"What about Chester?"

"Chester? He thinks you're someone who has to be persuaded to do a little business. He has no idea that you are a millennium old or what you are here for. He rather hopes to help out in a little accident that will occur in your local area if you can't be persuaded. But he shall be disappointed this time, fortunately."

"You mean you'd let me go if I didn't tell you how I do what I do?" I asked.

"I haven't planned what I'd do with you if you refused me," replied Sheridan, easily. I couldn't imagine a situation where Sheridan hadn't laid a plan for each detail. Sheridan was meticulous.

"You see," he said after a pause to consider his last piece of steak, "I am rather confident that we have come to an agreement, shall we say." Sheridan carefully arranged his silverware on his plate. "I considered that I might have to demonstrate to the authorities that you were never here, of course. Let us say that it comes to unpleasantness. Several people might swear that you were uncommonly careless in the traffic lanes near Des Moines, Iowa, say. But I don't intend to harm you. We are life-long companions, of sorts, equal gentlemen, you and I; and I have a proposition." He neatly swiped at his mouth with his napkin.

"Sheridan," I said warily, "I do not use the term 'gentleman' for someone who uses rubber hose diplomacy."

Sheridan winced and with a waving hand cleared the air of my ungentlemanly observation. "Oh, please don't say that. I've grown up, Fenton. At a hundred and ten I can see myself in perspective. I've come to realise that I am dependent on you for just a little flow of information. I can't beat you to death, you'd die with the secret and a smirk on your lips, I know. I'd be as badly off as I was before I brought you up here, worse because you'd be dead; and there isn't another man on the face of the Earth that knows what you know."

"Maybe. Folks like us are mighty particular with our identities."

"You mean there are *others* . . .?" Sheridan's expression told me I'd better can that line, or my life wouldn't be worth one of Sheridan's funny-money sawbucks.

"How the hell do I know? You've been looking around, have you found any?"

Sheridan looked bitter. "No, but I have you. A bird in hand. No, Gil, I was wrong to try to beat it out of you, though I wouldn't admit it at the time. I was extraordinarily lucky that I didn't kill you; for I was strong as an ox, and I had all the passion of youth. But then you were out that extra door, Gil, and I swore that someday I would be in a position to buy you, if I had to. In a way, you are responsible for Sheridan Group Industries; you are its prime mover. I merely gathered the resources to track you down."

"And now you've got all that dough and I'm not the least

interested in it," I said tiredly. "I generally outlive the local currency standards. What is wealth then? If that's the basis of your proposition, to trade your future for your empire... You've bored me, Sheridan."

Sheridan pushed his empty plate back and rose from his chair. He began to pace the floor, now fully occluded and pearly white from the attenuated sunlight.

"No, Gil. I could offer you lifelong wealth as a part of the commission, which for you would be quite a pile, but that is not my intention. Gil, my proposition is that I won't pay you a red cent. I'll pay Humanity."

I smiled. Deathbed morality catches up with the richest man in the world. "Do tell, I say."

"Gil, I know you want a better Humanity. Beneath your cynicism you want every person to live better and far longer. Maybe you want them to live indefinitely. Am I right?"

I shrugged, suppressing a thrill of wonder. "Has he changed?" I asked myself, then a mental chuckle re-aligned the errant neurons.

"That what all right-thinking people on the globe want—for the record. Have you got something concrete to back up those pleasant words?" I smiled and watched him pace to my side of the table.

"I have been amassing wealth, Gil; but more important, I have been amassing *control.*

"Fact:" announced Sheridan. "Since the depression that preceded World War II, and in a larger sense since the Industrial Revolution, the gross economic trend has been the concentration of wealth into the hands of a smaller and smaller circle of people and institutions. At first it was direct personal wealth. Personal wealth purchases goods and services—and money is purchasable, like beer and pickles. Hence we have people who sell money, for profit; they rent out a commodity that won't wear out and is guaranteed by the governments of the world. Since the members of the service class are wealthy to start with, they become wealthier—"

"Positive feedback," I said.

"Eh?"

"Positive feedback. Like a feedback circuit where the linkage is multiplicative with a positive sign at the circuit's summation point. The output shows an exponential change in magnitude to the limits of the supply, or it steals wind from other supplies."

Sheridan seemed to like the engineering. He beamed, "An essentially similar viewpoint, Gil. I didn't think you had it in you.

"Anyway, there is a tendency for wealth to concentrate. To control the concentrations of wealth is to have that wealth, and the power it represents, in your hands. My strategy for the last sixty years has been to allow other people's wealth to accumulate, so I can then take control of it. I have not been troubled by the politics of the masses.

"Now, what to do with that power? One can purchase or develop technological means to control people who control wealth. Right hemisphere implants—a crude method—chemotherapy via food doping, non-volitional conditioning..." He paused. "Anyway, we've developed many techniques here at the Station. Fact. Sheridan Group Industries can now control the purchasing and investment habits of twenty-five percent of the pivotal individuals and institutions."

I shrugged. Sheridan was getting excited in the pearly sunlight. "So? You've dedicated a century of living to get control, but you're dying just the same. Tell me, Sheridan, what's the point? I'd really like to know—I've got a hunch that civilization is a circus we've all put on to keep our minds off the main question: 'What happens after I shoot through..?' "

"That doesn't have to be the point. I represent a potential that has never existed before. I represent the apex of economic control. I can devastate the world economy by changing the value of paper tokens, simply by launching a series of booms, which trigger the busts. I can make the system oscillate wildly; I can destroy the links between the economic communities: people will go back to direct barter. Or, I can make the system work better because I can control enough of the system to reroute it—to improve it. That's a much harder trick; for it takes knowledge, experience, control—and *time*. There have been people like me before, but they gained the first three elements at the expense of the fourth, and whatever potential they had was cut off by the vanishingly small time they had left to use it in.

"Gil, you represent that fourth element, and I represent the other three. All four elements in one man, Gil; it would be tremendous." Sheridan waited, hesitant, expecting a reaction.

"Who gets the four elements?"

"I do, Gil. You give me the fourth element."

"And what's in it for me?"

"Nothing, Gil. There's nothing in it for you. I can't buy you a

140   TO SIN AGAINST SYSTEMS

whore or bribe you with money, and at one time that annoyed me. But I've learned that I can rely on your higher principles. Trust me and give me longevity, and I'll use the time, control, knowledge and experience to pass that longevity on to humanity. I have the tools to do it.

"I'm not Pappy the Printer anymore. Diligence and unorthodox financial techniques have brought me to the brink of economic domination of the world. As I've watched this globe wheel beneath my feet, Gil, I've gained an understanding of what could be done. It'll take several years to re-tune the global economy to tolerate longevity, of course. I know what needs to be done. But I'll be dead before I can do it. I have the vision; give me the *time*."

The opalescent half-light sharpened to needle points as the floor cleared to reveal again the timeless Milky Way. Sheridan waited. He had spoken his piece.

Three seconds brought me almost—but not quite—to the conclusion that Sheridan was full of that elegant stuff that fills a soul while the body is on Death Row and that he would revert to his old foolishness if he got a pardon. Let us say that I was ninety percent sure of this. But as I am damned to see every side to a circular question, I was ten percent in doubt now and would be

more than ten percent doubtful later and—*damn!*—I would most assuredly have to kill Sheridan if I didn't join him. What an awesome decision. My killing Sheridan, my being his executioner, could result only from an act of judgment. I have fundamental reservations about executing a man I haven't properly judged; to do so is to send him to that state that I have not yet had the courage to face myself.

Troubled, I tabled the thought. I said into the utter silence of that room, "Thank you."

"Eh?" was Sheridan's response.

"You are the first man who has tried to appeal to me with neither a sexy kitten nor a pile of gold. Instead, you've appealed to my morals. I thank you for the compliment."

Sheridan nodded tiredly. "I need what you have but there is nothing in the world that I can give you in trade. So I'll tell you of my purpose and I ask you to judge if it's a worthy one. I am completely dependent upon your believing me. I ask you to trust me, Gil, to judge me; to let me work, or to condemn me and watch me die." Still holding at ten percent, I thought.

But to have civilization on a leash! What a heady thought. And Sheridan had what it took. Almost. "What if I . . . don't decide immediately?"

"Wait," he answered. "I won't let you go, until you have decided; I think you owe me that."

"And if I . . . never decide?" I asked.

Sheridan played with his fork, smiled a bitter smile, and looked directly at me.

"Why," he said, "that would be the same as judging against me, wouldn't it?" He paused. "I've been dodging it for some time. We've used some pretty powerful techniques to keep me alive. I've made it to a hundred and ten; but the repair rate is getting out of hand. The doctor thinks I can live six more months." And Sheridan looked at me with twinkling, intelligent, predatory eyes.

"I think you had better prepare your guest room, Pappy."

"I'm not Pappy anymore. His attitude is dead."

"So he says."

"You'll see," said Sheridan, unruffled. "I can wait—for a little while. In the meantime, we'll need to keep you occupied. You'll be my personal assistant."

Sheridan and I walked through his personal section of the Station—two of the twenty-four major compartments circling the rim. The interior was decorated in subtle whites and greys, with

142   TO SIN AGAINST SYSTEMS

curved floors, plants, sculpture, and paintings scattered about. One compartment was a guest area, which contained along with a get-together room, visiting quarters and servants' area, the Observatory. The other compartment was Sheridan's *sanctum sanctorum*. Sheridan led me past its locked door and into a wide room tastefully done in the same white and grey décor. In one corner of the main room, a terminal to the Station's library silently presented a menu of games and reading material. Sheridan watched me while I browsed through some of the 1-person games, happy as a clam. Then he switched the terminal to the novice mode and showed me the query generator, commenting that this was one of the only two unsealed terminals in the Station, the other being in his room. "Look at anything you want," he said. "My life's work is on line." He then retired for the evening while I amused myself with the terminal.

I quickly discovered that the station library, and the station itself, were manifestations of Sheridan's interests. The station was his 'activity module', I suppose the best word is that; his library showed a preponderance of sociology, psychology, and biology, with an impressive number of unpublished papers. Sheridan had been gunning for the Fountain of Youth for some time, it seemed. A lot of his inquiries concerned genetic engineering—a practice banned on the surface—and he had on his staff Dr. William Vonner, who had gone into hiding when the scientific community announced its self-imposed moratorium on the design and manufacture of new species. It was good to know how the Doctor was biding his time.

A few touches of the paging stud informed me that Sheridan, while prospecting for the Fountain of Youth, had come up with a swarm of useful techniques. He had put brain implants and gene doping on a practical basis, if I interpreted this three-year-old report correctly, and had developed a system of protein fabrication that fit learning into little pills. He had been using it to teach languages to his staff and 'investment techniques' to clients who subscribed to his service. I whistled in appreciation: not only did Sheridan control his investors, they were paying for the privilege! He would have been a hell of a horse trader, back when.

After two hours at the data bank I sat back, amazed. Sheridan's inquiries into the science of direct and indirect control of the human subject were the most exhaustive I had ever seen. He had hit the problem on both the macro and micro levels. He was developing a mathematics of n-dimensional topological spaces, and investigating how a functional projection of degree (n–1) onto a given topological space could serve as a model for various macro-phenomena—how a crowd will sell, or buy, or revolt. On the micro level he was developing subtle methods of direct individual control like his 'subscription service.'

The man had no competition in the science of manipulation. With all of these control mechanisms at his command, he could have become dictator of the Earth in the most subtle way, and no one would have been particularly aware of it—

I jerked up.

Maybe he was now. Maybe he just needed me to assure his subsequent terms in office.

Or maybe he was still consolidating his position and treading water until he was sure he could direct all phases of the program personally, without having to be inconvenienced halfway through by dropping dead.

Or maybe deathbed morality had changed his reach, redirected his vision, and he was waiting for me to give him the go-ahead, the time to do the world right—the world he had so sorely cheated. The groundwork was there for something magnificent, shenanigans or otherwise.

I turned off the terminal, stretched out on the resilient floor, and threw a pillow over my head.

I had, I thought, a powerful investigative tool that would clear out a lot of the guesswork—the longevity therapy itself. I discovered shortly after my first metamorphosis that I could gain access to other people's minds if they 'let me in'. The process is a little more complicated than that, but that is the best I can do with the language. Once I was let in I had a wide communication spectrum with a subject, and I could see—Hell, it isn't 'see' but that's the best word going—I could see his neural network and his chemical systems as well as he could; better, because I knew where to 'look' and he didn't. Telepathy and this clear inner eye and control of one's inner processes seem to go hand in hand and indeed, might even be the same phenomenon. I could learn a lot about what really went on in Sheridan's mind during the initial rapport, and I could pull out if I saw anything I didn't like. If he were being totally deceptive he might even balk at a telepathic link-up, and my decision would be easy—though getting out of the station might be pretty hard. I rather liked that alternative. I took off the pillow and smiled to myself. There just might be a way out.

I slept on the problem until a female voice by my head said, "Mr. Sheridan asked me to remind you that it is 0600, and that you are to meet with him at 0700 in the Administration Compound, segment zero one hundred, room thirteen."

"Fair 'nuff," I muttered. I wandered into the bathroom, and cycled the refresher cube until I was reasonably awake. Breakfast was a problem, and fresh clothing; and I pondered the point in my birthday suit until I remembered the terminal. I negotiated a large breakfast and a small wardrobe; in two minutes a chime rang out and I had what I'd asked for, although the surrogate coffee needed some development work.

I headed to work on my first job with the great Mr. Sheridan.

I found segment zero one hundred between zero two hundred and two four hundred. A 'can you tell me where Mr. Sheridan's office is?' got me the rest of the way.

"Good morning!" greeted Sheridan.

"It'll be a while before I have an opinion on it," I replied. He smiled. "I've got a job for you. Come with me, I'm starting on my rounds." We went through a priest's hole and into some unlisted corridor.

"The thing, is I'm getting forgetful in my old age," he said. "Every day I walk around to all of the departments and see the heads, trade a few words with the help. There are over a thousand people employed here, Fenton; and I know all of their names and faces—and all about their wives, husbands, lovers, families, and kids too. I used to remember all the things they told me, important or not. People work better for me when they think I care about them."

I nodded.

"But as I said, I'm getting forgetful, so I'd like you to tag along and keep track of things for me."

"Besides, you would always have your eye on me," I said.

"There's that too, isn't there," agreed Sheridan. "Of course, if you find the job offensive, I can always find another one for you. Engineering is a forte of yours. I have some systems work—"

"No, no. Don't go to a lot of trouble," I said. "I just might want to keep an eye on you too."

"Ha! Fenton, if life were any different, we just might have been friends—we still could be. But I must ask you to be quiet, and careful as to what you say, for on the other side of these doors are the public corridors."

The large doors slid easily in their slots to reveal a businesslike corridor. To the left, at various intervals, were the slidevator stations; to the right were the working spaces appropriate for the pinnacle of the Sheridan Group Industries.

We went into a bio lab.

Some people, working at individual terminals, looked up. Sheridan got a chorus of 'Good Morning, Mr. Sheridan' and a few 'Hi Sher's.

"Morning, crew. Is Bill around?"

"In the office, Chief."

"Thanks, Frank. Group, I'd like you to meet Gil, my new memory man. If it's important, tell him. Gil is going to be the fellow who tells me what to do from now on."

Sheridan plowed to a hubward compartment, with me in tow.

The compartment was well laid out. There were happy plants all over the place, gentle curves, and light colors. We found the occupant contemplating the Hub with a ghost of a smile on his lips.

"Good Morning, Dr. Vonner," said Sheridan. I arched my eyebrows.

"Hi, Sher. I've got a biggie," announced Bill as he swung his feet to the floor. There was enthusiasm in his eyes, a sheaf of papers in his hand. He was young, sandy haired and pudgy, late of the genetic engineering effort on the surface.

"Look at this, Sher: a definitive carrier loop that can modulate codon transfer during the pre-meiotic stage ..."

And off he went, bubbling, enthusiastic, optimistic: a delighted child who had just learned a new magic trick. I could have been happy for him if I weren't so busy taking notes.

After about fifteen minutes, Vonner wound down and Sheridan was nodding thoughtfully. He handed back the sheaf to Vonner and said, "If you think you can control a mutation like that without radiation, Bill, then be my guest. Just don't let a hairy monster out into the lab."

"Hairy monster?" Vonner looked indignant. "I happen to be careful with my facilities—not like those jackasses on the surface, who probably wash their equipment in the nearest stream. Anything that I make will be so weak that it will self-destruct if I look at it cross-eyed."

Sheridan's bantering tone vanished. "I know you're careful, Bill. I'm basically conservative, that's all."

Vonner cooled off and his enthusiasm resurfaced. "You'll see the most wonderful things from this! History will be made in these labs!"

"I'd say you've made history in these labs already, Bill. When we release some of your experiments to a—more understanding world, your name will rank with Salk and Pasteur."

Sheridan wheeled out of the office, leaving Vonner in a happy, creative flush. Before we got any distance, I had notes on two birthdays and an anniversary, along with two get-well cards.

When we got to the slidevator, Sheridan was in a thoughtful mood. He said, in part to himself, "You know, Vonner's lucky that he's up here. If his own safeguards fail, and worse comes to worse, there is always the ultimate safeguard."

"Such as?" I asked. Sheridan looked up at me.

"Oh! Well, Space itself. Genetic labs are ideally suited to orbit because that big old vacuum out there will get anything the radiation misses. If something—unpleasant—does happen up here, then I have deadman instructions controlling a nuclear device located in the Hub. Couldn't have that kind of safeguard anywhere on the surface."

"How about traffic to and from the Station between the time a bug gets loose and when the first symptoms show up?" I asked.

Sheridan looked surprised. "I *am* getting senile! Note somewhere on that pad that I should issue a general three-week quarantine on personnel leaving the Station. Call it General Instruction Q3. The Station Provost Officer is going to inundate me with grievances by tomorrow night, dollars to donuts."

Sheridan fell to inspecting his tightly cropped fingernails. I had a doomsday thought.

"Sheridan, suppose there is a plague in the near future, after you and I resolve our . . . differences," I asked, "would you blow yourself up with the Station?"

Sheridan fixed me with his eyes, his steely glinting eyes.

"I have you thinking about it, haven't I?"

"Maybe."

"You're thinking about it. Progress, I can't complain." Sheridan sat back and a relieved expression crossed his face.

"Would you blow yourself up if the Incurable X disease slipped out of Vonner's test tube?" I pushed the matter. It was important.

The slidevator had stopped at the next station. Sheridan kept his bony fingers on the HOLD and DOOR CLOSE buttons, and said in a soft voice, tight with tension: "I have told you not to talk about this matter in public places. I suspect you made your way through the Black Plague in a manner that the contemporary alchemists would have found amazing, not to mention the present ones. It turns on what you teach me, Gil. Now *can it!*" The door opened and a perfectly composed Sheridan slipped out with a thoughtful memory man padding along behind.

There were sixteen anniversaries, two-score birthdays, ten get-well cards and thirty pages of notes from Sheridan to others via my aching fingers. My feet were killing me. Sheridan was just starting his day. I saw data processing and genetic experiments, high vacuum industrial experiments, and crystal-growing experiments, and I had notes to get data sheets on a dozen more.

"We do a lot of research here," remarked Sheridan as we headed back to his office. "This is the only private industrial facility in orbit, and we have clients who need testing done in the high vacuum and zero-g—plus all of the housework from the industries in the Group."

When we got into his office I gave him the note pad. Sheridan looked at my tight notes, diagrams, circles, arrows, and three-colored inserts and made a tsk, tsk, sound.

"Good heavens, Fenton, do you think the way that you write notes?"

I marveled, as I wriggled in my seat, how a fellow barely a century old could make me, with my ten centuries' seniority, feel like a junior office boy.

"This is the most amazing aggregation of mixed-up markings. . . . Here." Sheridan opened a drawer, exactly the one he wanted; reached in; and picked out a sealed metal cylinder. He snapped it open and rolled a large green pill onto his felt desk-top.

"Take it. It's a special shorthand that I can read and you can take, real-time, without looking at the notepad."

I looked dubiously at the pill, tapped my teeth with my pencil, and thought of that investment subscription service of his.

"Come on, I wouldn't poison you now, would I?" laughed Sheridan.

I was thinking of Vonner's enthusiasm—genuine human reaction or derived from a German language pill? Everyone that Sheridan dealt with was respectful, loyal, and even loving in a businesslike way. Was it love and respect on a human to human basis, or were they chemically treated dogs and yes-men?

I didn't know. It was all as enigmatic as Sheridan himself. But I knew my body chemistry and I had my inner 'eyes' and 'hands'. I made a bet with myself that I could nullify any chemical in that pill should it get out of hand. Swallowing it, I noted a slight suggestion of the taste/feel of dry peach rind, before the skin breaks. It was an interesting gamble, the kind that adds gusto to one's life. Besides, I was interested in how that pill would work on me.

"It'll be a while," remarked Sheridan. "Some of the secretaries say that when it starts to hit, it's best to draw some audio from the Station's library and practice. Others say to sleep on it. Do what comes naturally, and I'll see you tomorrow."

"Sure," I said, and I went to my quarters with my inner eyes watching.

§ § §

It was a pleasant inner show, that pill. It didn't touch my value areas one bit. Any fragment of protein that banged on the doors in that neighborhood got a gruff 'We don't want any'. The protein looked at its instructions, said, 'Excuse me!' and moved on. When it got to the area that decided whether a sound should be shunted to a higher level or acted on right there, the proteins slipped in and established a correspondence between a sequence of motor instructions and phonal groups. The causality between 'loud noise: jump and cuss' which worked within a certain small loop suddenly had company in the form of such correspondences as 'freedom: motor instructions 4FEA'. There was a blocking neuron that controlled the loop, making it a function of will, so I wouldn't continually be urged to write everything I heard. When I *did* will the routine in, I would automatically write the shorthand analog of each word, knee-jerk fashion.

I suppose I could have done something similar myself, if I knew how; but there is a lot that I don't know about me. I do know the various control nexi and can manipulate a variety of neural, electrical, and chemical circuits. Since I see the body as a whole, I can appreciate the wide variety of 'domino chains' throughout the body: almost every circuit is linked to its neighbors, and an intentional adjustment will often trigger side effects in a (seemingly) unrelated function. Thus when I treat hardening of the arteries, I affect bone-cell manufacture. Though I know the nexi and how they can be excited, I still have to respect the overall body and its inter-related systems. In order for me to do that neural adjustment myself, I would be obliged to trace out all of the domino chains. Why Sheridan's little green pill failed to trigger any side effects is a mystery that goes to show how little I understand me, in spite of the intimate relationship that I enjoy with myself.

Which brought me to the problem of Sheridan, the next order of business after the Pill. My idea of what was on the man's mind and how it might be probed during the intimate link-up of the Therapy had taken a severe blow when I saw how Sheridan was received by his employees.

They liked him.

No one liked Sheridan when he was on Fulton Street. People did business with him because he was efficient, not because he was pleasant. Had he changed over the years?

Possibly Sheridan had changed. On the other hand, if it were deathbed morality, then I might miss it: unconscious self-deception, I cannot detect. I had missed That Woman's suicide tendency, and I was a hell of a lot more intimately bound to her than to Sheridan; and had rambled through her head for hours on end. And I now had the feeling that once I got inside of Sheridan, I would find answers that would beget more questions until it was *all* questions again.

In between arguing with myself, I watched the scenery that evening. The ceiling was cleared, and it treated me to alternate views of Space, then Earth, and then a period of occlusion while the sun was in view.

Good old Terra, I thought. Even she is a spaceship, with naturally evolving controls, hierarchies of systems, diverse phenomena working hand in hand: all of it fitting together so *right*. And the human creature is an outgrowth of that fit. Oh, he had a learning period, I thought, when he messed with chemicals that didn't dovetail with naturally existing systems; and when his material use was straight line, and not a loop that fed itself; but when the economics of recycling made themselves felt in the latter half of the depletion age, humankind learned the first aspect of systems; a lesson that John Donne put into the words: 'No man is an island'.

Indeed, no *thing,* man or otherwise, is an island: everything is adjacent in one way or another in the intricate universal topology, related, in a web of relationships, where everything can be connected implicitly or explicitly to every or any other thing in the web. Changes in one portion of the web mean changes in all other portions of the web and once this fundamental rule of systems was learned by Humankind, he was forever more careful with his garbage, especially when it became profitable to do so.

The ceiling occluded and I was cut off, for a time, from the outside.

I am a frail creature, dogged with uncertainty, lacking in personal self-worth at times; but I see that things fit together—click—joyfully like fine machinery, and that understanding is the basis of my morals; for I respect and wish to preserve that fit. It is the reason I believed that longevity was safe with me at the time, for I wouldn't spread it—willy-nilly—throughout Mankind until I had carefully traced out all of the domino chains—

I stopped, thunderstruck. Sheridan had shoved the job of judgment on me as if I were the sole judge, as if the buck could stop with me, and that is not the way things work at all, at all! I admired—marveled at—the man's postures, choice of words, styles of talking, and the way he maneuvered me into the role of an arbitrator, giving me the obligations of a judge—omniscient but detached—when I was intimately woven into the problem. Sheridan knew that, when he forced himself on me and displayed himself as a person loved and respected, I wouldn't have the courage to watch him die. He knew I was particularly sensitive to death. He gambled that I would keep him alive even if I didn't give him the full therapy. He gambled that I would remain in the judge's role long enough for the responsibilities of that august position to cloud my vision; until I would say to myself: 'Why am I keeping this guy on tenterhooks?' and give in. I jumped off the bunk, resolved. Sheridan played a skillful game, a damned skillful game, and he had come perilously close to winning.

But he didn't. And I knew exactly what to do.

I fixed myself an elegant meal with some help from the terminal. Just as I sat down, the compartment bell set up an enormous clatter. Annoyed, I put down my chopsticks, rose, and touched the door plate. My visitor was evidently in a hurry.

"Mr. Fenton, you are to come with me immediately. I—"

I stepped on the brakes gently. "Easy, son. I can't think offhand why I should neglect dinner on your say-so, can you?"

"Mr. Fenton, please, I understand you give security personnel a difficult time as a matter of course, but this is serious. Can you run?"

So we ran. We ran to the slidevator, which then skipped every stop until we reached the sickbay compound. Shortly I was in an emergency care room, and my guess was verified. A young doctor with a stormy look in his eyes confronted me.

"Mr. Fenton? I'm Mr. Sheridan's physician. Mr. Sheridan has had a severe coronary, which at his age—anyway, he wants you

here." I peeked past the doctor.

Sheridan wore a mask and had things wired to his chest. His eyes were closed and he was breathing with quick shallow breaths. He looked awful, very old-looking now, frail, the dynamic personality gone. There was a small pick-up on his pillow. His eyes opened a crack, he turned slightly toward us and whispered, "Jim."

"Mr. Sheridan." The doctor turned, businesslike.

"Get lost—clear room of—everyone—but Fenton."

"Mr. Sheridan, I have the responsibility. . . ."

"Jim." The doctor stopped abruptly. I looked at Sheridan. Despite the attack that had beaten his body, despite the tinny speaker and phone amplifier, the voice still carried command.

"Jim—I am a dying—man. Washed up. You—wouldn't deny—a dying man—his last—wish?"

The doctor turned red. Sheridan could still do it, turn a person against himself with a carefully composed sentence. Sheridan was a marvel.

The doctor and nurses and technicians retired behind the door. They were not to return until I allowed them.

Sheridan was peering at me again with that intense predatory look. I looked down at him, waiting.

"Your . . . decision, Fenton."

I checked my thoughts. It would be a calculated gamble; chances were there would be unfortunate aspects no matter what the outcome.

"Welcome to the Longevity Club. We're a small and select group."

"What . . . What . . . " Sheridan seemed almost surprised. Did he have last minute doubts about his game? I tabled the thought.

"All you have to do is relax and give me eye contact. Don't think of anything and when you feel me, *don't resist!*"

I found a chair to sit down on, cradled my head in my hands, and took a stab. I was in. Information flow was very wide and the exchange rate was fast.

"SHERIDAN!"

"Yes . . . "

"Don't will anything. Go to sleep."

"The pain . . . " I altered the firing threshold of a bundle of synapses.

"What did you do?"

"Later, sleep now. This is not the metamorphosis, this is just to patch you together."

It wasn't the worst session I'd had with death. My fourteenth metamorphosis, the short one, somehow found me in France during the year 1916. I called the shot that World War One wouldn't happen and got drafted in the French infantry. A moment of carelessness found me stitched up the side with a machine-gun burst. I had to keep myself alive *and* metamorphose at the same time. At least Sheridan wasn't halfway sawed through and lying in a trench.

Patchwork kept me busy for about an hour. Sheridan was in relatively healthy shape, so I took the liberty of hyper-regenerating the arterial walls. I worked on the local timing too, so I was sure the heart wouldn't stop on us. With the somatic problems mostly settled and the consequences of a few dozen toppled domino chains cleared up, I woke Sheridan.

"Sheridan."

"Yes."

"How do you feel?"

"Good! Is it over?"

"We haven't even begun. I just rewired you so you can make it

TO SIN AGAINST SYSTEMS 153

through the short haul, which is going to be a rough one. I am going to go through a metamorphosis step by step and you are to take notes. The first thing I'll show you is direct-memory access so you won't forget anything that I show you."

"I could use that trick in a thousand and one ways."

"Now a lot of these processes are traumatic and set up noise in the nervous system. It's painful. I also won't touch the exterior much. That's finishing and I'll leave it to you as practice; besides, it's best not to upset the doctor too much."

"Understandable."

"You ready?"

"Yes."

"This is going to hurt as much as your rubber hose."

I gave Sheridan very practical instruction. If you ever buy a piece of complicated machinery a field representative will come with it. That field representative will give you point-by-point instructions: this knob does this; that lever controls that. He isn't teaching you an overall philosophy, he's telling you how that button sorter can be specifically operated to sort buttons. It's the exact opposite of how I teach control systems and the exact opposite of how I taught That Woman because the two teaching methods stem from entirely different points of view.

Sheridan didn't seem to object.

"It's done."

"That was very comprehensive, Fenton; and this link-up is a very effective method of getting ideas across."

"True, but it's an 'and' link: both of us have to agree to it and either of us can cut at any time." I finished with my voice. "So it's subject to my vagaries."

Sheridan shook his head. The cyanosis was gone, but his exterior, to the quick glance, was about as old as when I first came on board.

Sheridan looked at the clock. "It's been two hours. Gil, let the doctor in; he'll be having kittens."

I opened the door and the doctor was about standing on it with a battalion of security men, it seemed.

"Good Heavens! I was about to break in, Fenton. What...?"

"Are you sure there is anything wrong with Mr. Sheridan? He and I had a good long chat and he doesn't seem the least bit ill," I said innocently. The doctor shoved past me and bee-lined to the telemetry equipment.

"What happened?" he kept on saying through his teeth.

"Security, you're dismissed," Sheridan commanded. "Fenton, if I pull through," with amusement in his eyes, "I'll be in direct contact with you."

Near as I could tell, that ten percent chance was shrinking, and Sheridan would soon be up to his old tricks. I had made my move, however, and only time would tell if I had made the right one.

§ § §

Three days.

I had expected things to happen, but Sheridan was working on a grand scale. The afternoon of the metamorphosis, he had the doctors take him to his personal quarters, where he got out of bed and dismissed them. He relieved his physician and gave him a research post he was after. He then announced that Sheridan Industries would be marketing another First.

Three days. I knew my plan would work, but it might take a week. Meanwhile, Sheridan was going to town.

Sheridan had invited me to the Observatory for a private breakfast. Sheridan had dismissed his personal staff and made his domain 'taboo', while I was forbidden to go into the rest of the Station. I watched the Earth spin silently below my feet. "You've put up with a lot of silliness," I said to her. She bore the comment in silence. I wondered, for the umpteenth time, if my timing was off. A perfectly good scheme shot to Hell by poor timing still loses the war. If my timing was off, could I still patch up the pieces?

Sheridan came strutting down the catwalk. Oh God, I thought for the seventh time that day, Doc Savage and Conan rolled into one.

Sheridan was a magnificent specimen. His skin was bronzed, with muscles rippling smoothly beneath. His hair was blond again and close-cropped. The only real constants, his eyes, were still the same—steel grey and penetrating. He tried a mental hook-up, but I had the 'bug-off' shield up. So he shrugged and sat down to a breakfast that was large enough to feed the Golden Horde. Well, he was half of it, anyway. I nursed a cup of coffee—my seventh cup.

"You're bigger than yesterday," I said. "Have you got the inner man represented yet?"

"Yes, I do, and I feel at peace with myself and my exterior, thanks to you." He shot me an engaging, genuine smile. I suspect, knowing his mentality, that Sheridan considered me his only equal; his staff were people with whom words and charm sufficed.

"Don't thank me, you are what you are because ... well, that's the way you want to be," I said.

"But you taught me how to live and how to do this," said Sheridan, gently flexing his body beautiful. "You pulled me from the grave with your teachings."

"I taught you nothing. You taught yourself. I just told you a few things that you used according to a certain philosophy."

"You're modest, Fenton. That's your only shortcoming: you have no assertive qualities. You neither assert yourself nor impose your ideas on your surroundings. No wonder you've been in the background for a millennium."

"Where would you foreground people be if it wasn't for us background people giving you something to stand out from?"

"True, true—it takes all kinds to make a world. I am going to take advantage of this boon."

"You're going to charge a membership fee to the longevity club."

"More than that, Gil. I am going to make the Sheridan Group the most powerful organization that has ever existed." Sheridan stalked around the room, lecturing me. I finally got around to breakfast, hoping that my timing wasn't off, ready to hear the worst, if it was.

"Nationwide, then worldwide hook-up, right on Day One." Sheridan paced around the room with Terra wheeling beneath his feet. He turned to me.

"Why can't today be Day One?"

"Too soon," I replied around a dripping jam sandwich. "Take it from the authority on longevity. You need a little more practice."

"Hard to believe."

"Besides," I replied, "if you announce today you'll hit the North American continent on Friday. If you wait two days you'll hit 'em on a Monday. There ain't *nothin'* to look forward to on a Monday but another lousy week. The announcement of immortality will break up an otherwise dull day."

"That would be better," Sheridan acquiesced. Turning to an unpowered holographic rig, he said, "People of the nation, I am the director of the Sheridan Group Industries and I have an Important Announcement to make." He smiled and turned back to me. "Sheridan Industries are now offering options on Immortality. You and I will give the first lessons and hire the ones we've processed until we have a good line going. Then you'll be my chief engineer and I'll go back to the management of the Group. The price: no money, just the adoption of The Sheridan Plan; a plan of recommended, rational behavior based on chemotherapy and classroom teaching. It's going to be a wonderful world, Gil."

"Do tell." I chased a bit of egg around. "What about population control?"

"That's in the plan—some special instructions for women," beamed Sheridan. "Having kids will be a privilege."

"I see, always the girl who carries the burden," I observed to Terra, turning slowly in space.

"Well, there's physical evidence if we catch her. I'm thinking in terms of logistics."

"Or stagnation?" I asked. "How about genetic remixing? How will the gene pool get stirred around?"

"I think Vonner and his boys can handle that; as for senility— well, you know the answer to that one."

"I don't mean senility. What will happen to the culture if the same points of view get banged around century after century?"

"Nor do I see any objection there, Gil; there's no point of view like the right point of view; and that's what The Sheridan Plan is for." He smiled, his hands on his hips. "Next objection! You see I've thought out this entire business of world direction. I am the first scientific ruler this planet has ever had, thanks to you."

Remembered as Sheridan's 'Dr. Frankenstein'? I was horrified.

"We've been over this teaching business," I said. "So what are the logistics of handling everybody and his uncle?"

Sheridan became serious, calculating. "We have to be rather exclusive in our clientele in the first phase. Between you and me, Sheridan is still consolidating its position. We will have to do business with potential investors and world rulers at first, and make the club exclusive, and use the *promise* of longevity to control the masses. As we go along, tying in more rulers and investors, we can consolidate our position and give permission to those populations who are most in tune with the Sheridan Group." The word 'Industries' had disappeared.

"As near as I can tell," I said musingly, watching the world turn, "we'll have, a century from now, a population with the right point of view, chemically cultivated by the Sheridan Group, which is an instrument of your philosophy." I looked at Sheridan and he nodded. I continued, "People will be born at an insignificant rate, to replace those who were careless with machinery or political points of view. Those born could easily be dealt with early in life, separately, for together they might brew up some silly ideas. Once cultivated, they pose no threat. Most everybody will sit around for millennia on end, nodding to each other, thinking the right kind of thoughts, a worldwide Roman Empire without the boon of the Huns to stir up the show." I again looked at Sheridan. He nodded.

And continued nodding.

Nodding, with a blank stare.

Nodding, with a growing look of horror on his face.

Nodding, he grabbed at what he thought was the table and seized air.

Nodding, he shook and stumbled, as neural networks crumbled and revolted.

Nodding, he fell, soaked with sweat, trembling lips trying to form words, with chemical circuits awry, neural circuits oscillating or disengaging, his entire body politic in revolt.

I scratched the back of my head, much relieved. There were a few blows against my bug-off screen, but they weakened, and vanished.

"G-G-G-G-G-G-G—Gil!"

"Nothing I can do about it, chum; you are what you are and that is the bed of roses. Don't complain."

"What's happening? *God,* it hurts!"

"Easy question. You're dying."

"Impossible—I can't reach anything—falling apart. . . . *Help me!* Help the world—"

"I'm helping the world in the most humane way I can; and I guess that means your elimination. Sorry, Sheridan, but I abide by the circumstances of your passing." I folded my hands on the table and watched the heaving, sweating, crawling man.

"You judged me . . . *worthy!*" he growled out. He tried to fix his grey eyes on me but the head kept oscillating about the proper line of sight, giving Sheridan the appearance of nodding yes, no, yes, no.

"Before you pass on, Sheridan, I would like you to know that I almost fell for your judgment game: but I didn't. I never judged you. I did, however, give you an examination, knowing that I could live with the results of the examination—whether you passed or failed."

"Y-y-y-you gave me—*ability!*"

"I didn't know if you truly appreciated the obligations of one who instigates change. Many changes introduced to the culture have had vast side effects, such as the petroleum dirt of our late, great automobile; we lived through that era, you and I. And I, in search of that Universal Why, have come to respect the interrelatedness of things. I wondered if you had. I knew Terra was a network of dependencies. I also knew you had big plans for it. So after I got out from under that judgment syndrome you offered me, I gave you a microcosm to play with: yourself."

"Long—" Sheridan had stopped trembling now. He drooled.

"No, it wasn't longevity. I showed you a number of system controls that *could* have been used to promote your longevity wish. They could also make you big and handsome overnight. Used with the understanding that the body is an interrelated complex, where introduced changes in themselves trigger related changes, they could make you do a thousand different things. Used without the understanding of the relatedness of things, they kill you. You made yourself big and handsome, pushed your skeleton around, forced growth there, retarded activity here as if your body were one great plaything. Now you die, because you weren't sensitive to the chemical, neural, and electrical systems you bowled over. You kicked over too many domino chains." I looked at him. "And you were on the verge of doing it with Terra. Sheridan, if you can't run yourself right, how the hell do you expect to keep a *planet* straight?"

"You . . . tested me?"

"And you flunked."

Sheridan understood. Before Sheridan shot through, he understood, and died without fear.

And I sat for a long time at the breakfast table, wondering if, philosophies aside, Sheridan was a better man than I for facing fearlessly that which frightens me so. I could have changed him, tweaked a neuron or so while he was asleep to make him a less ambitious man.

But he had called me a man of principles: I didn't approve of his sawbucks, and I didn't approve of his conditioning either. Sheridan died Sheridan.

And at the breakfast table I mourned him for what he could have been.

I finished my sixteenth metamorphosis and attended to Sheridan's rounds. I sent the security force chasing around for a Gilbert Fenton, laid the plans for some very careful dismantling; cancelled an announcement that I had made the previous week, when I was ill and given to curious things. All in all, it was a productive Monday; and I finished out the day, alone, amused at the circumstances that induced me to metamorphose into a very old man.

SURE THING
by Isaac Asimov

*In response to Mr. Clarke's
challenge in the matter of SF puns,
our Good Doctor here offers a
short-short, this one written especially
for this contest. The Editor, however,
hastens to assure all of you that
these will not be a* **permanent**
feature of this magazine.

As is well-known, in this 30th Century of ours, space travel is
fearfully dull and time-consuming. In search of diversion many
crew-menbers defy the quarantine restrictions and pick up pets
from the various habitable worlds they explore.

Jim Sloane had a Rockette, which he called Teddy. It just sat
there looking like a rock, but sometimes it lifted a lower edge and
sucked in powdered sugar. That was all it ate. No one ever saw it
move, but every once in a while it wasn't quite where people
thought it was. There was a theory it moved when no one was
looking.

Bob Laverty had a Heli-worm he called Dolly. It was green and
carried on photosynthesis. Sometimes it moved to get into better
light and when it did so it coiled its worm-like body and inched
along very slowly like a turning helix.

One day, Jim Sloane challenged Bob Laverty to a race. "My
Teddy," he said, "can beat your Dolly."

"Your Teddy," scoffed Laverty, "doesn't move."

"Bet!" said Sloane.

The whole crew got into the act. Even the Captain risked half a
credit. Everyone bet on Dolly. At least it moved.

Jim Sloane covered it all. He had been saving his salary
through three trips and he put every millicredit of it on Teddy.

The race started at one end of the Grand Salon. At the other
end, a heap of sugar had been placed for Teddy and a spotlight for
Dolly. Dolly formed a coil at once and began to spiral its way very
slowly toward the light. The watching crew cheered it on.

Teddy just sat there without budging.

"Sugar, Teddy. Sugar," said Sloane, pointing. Teddy did not
move. It looked more like a rock than ever, but Sloane did not
seem concerned.

160

Finally, when Dolly had spiralled half-way across the salon, Jim Sloane said casually to the Rockette, "If you don't get out there, Teddy, I'm going to get a hammer and chip you into pebbles."

That was when people first discovered that Rockettes could read minds. That was also when people first discovered that Rockettes could teleport.

Sloane had no sooner made his threat when Teddy just disappeared from its place and re-appeared on top of the sugar.

Sloane won, of course, and he counted his winnings slowly and luxuriously.

Laverty said, bitterly, "You *knew* the damn thing could teleport."

"No, I didn't," said Sloane, "but I knew he would win. It was a sure thing."

"How come?"

"It's an old saying everyone knows. Sloane's Teddy wins the race."

Wolf Tracks

They've found wolf tracks
Down at the Aeronautics-
And-Space Museum.
Not once, three times.
And they're talking crazy.

First time, they let it go.
Just pranksters, they said,
And told the security cops,
You guys keep a sharp eye out.
Second time, they brought in
A German Shepherd.
He told them, That's wolf,
No doubt about it.

Now, they're talking crazy:
Burglars, plots & counter-plots;
Terrorists, hijackers, spies;
One guy says its lycanthropes.
They've bugged the place, and
Lay traps at night—those big,
Steel traps with all the teeth.
They've even hung some wolfbane.
And one CIA-type's got
A .45 with silver bullets.

Me, I think it's wolves, too.
Not sheep's-clothing wolves,
And not Russo-Sino wolves;
Not werewolves. *Real* wolves.
I think they come to see
The Apollo exhibits, just
Like everybody else does.

Lupine geologists, maybe,
Come to read the moon rocks.
Who could do it better?

Or some wolf-composer,
Seeking inspiration
For a new moon hymn.
Because, who loves the moon
More than a wolf does?

Could be there are wolves
On the moon, and these
Earth-wolves are looking
For some sign of Otherness
That's somehow a Sameness
—Just as we are looking.

Scientiest would say that's bunk.
There's no air on the moon,
Ergo: there are no wolves.
(On the other hand, I've seen
Those moonscapes on TV, and
That's wolf country, alright.)

Down at the A&S Museum,
Nobody says "wolf tracks."
They all call it "spoor,"
Even the security guards.
They've got the jargon pat.
Despite the head-scratching,
They're experts, all, down there.

But, last night, the wolves
Started howling, everywhere,
Howling the whole world over.

The TV commentators say
That wolf packs have been seen
Moving on the highways.

People are getting afraid.
But I've heard the howls,
And they're full of sorrow.

Maybe all the wolves want
Is some word about the moon.
After all, wolves have been
Moon watchers a long time.

Some people say that it's
Something much more sinister,
Nothing to do with the moon.

Meanwhile at the A&S,
They haven't figured out
Anything. But it's okay.
They've got the janitors
Talking about "canis lupus."
I suppose that's progress.

They're keeping sharp eyes out.
Probably, so are the wolves.
You keep a sharp eye, too.

—Donald Gaither

165

THE ASTRONOMICAL HAZARDS OF THE TOBACCO HABIT
by Dean McLaughlin

*Resublimated thiotimoline, we must explain, is a highly improbable compound with the even more improbable property of dissolving shortly **before** being placed in water. Dr. Asimov's papers on the subject are here augmented by an interesting letter brought to our attention by Dean McLaughlin, the son of a noted astronomer.*

Dr. Isaac Asimov
Director; Thiotimoline Research Foundation
Trantor MA 31416

Dear Dr. Asimov:
   You may recall that, some years ago, astronomers at a certain French observatory noticed the sudden, temporary appearance of potassium lines in the spectra of three otherwise quite ordinary stars. They interpreted these lines as evidence of powerful eruptions of ionized material on the surfaces of these stars—flares—which contained an unusual concentration of the element potassium.
   But they weren't sure.
   To begin with, each star had shown the lines only once. Each star was different from the others except for that one similarity, and none was a type that could be expected to display such behavior. And though the observatory set up a watch on these stars, none repeated the performance.
   Those considerations didn't entirely rule out flares as an explanation. Flares can be brief and, for a given star, they can be rare. But unique events—especially three within a short time span—must be considered with caution.
   Instead of publishing a report, therefore, the

166

French astronomers quietly inquired of other observatories around the world: had they, too, noticed anything unusual about those stars? Or similar stars?

No such luck.

But a group of California astronomers did come up with what seemed the answer. Having obtained a foundation grant—mostly for chalk and coffee, plus a few books of matches—they inquired whether perhaps the French astronomers might be victims of the tobacco habit. Most of them were. Well then, said the Californians, might it be possible that the Frenchmen had succumbed to the weed during business hours? Might they, perhaps, have struck matches while the crucial spectra were exposed, contaminating them?

Unchristian comments were heard from a cerain French mountain top. The case seemed closed.

While I do not doubt the California group's work has identified previously unrecognized relationships surrounding the events, I am less certain their analysis correctly identified the true causal sequence. Rather, I suspect they remarked upon the one—perhaps too obvious—possibility, neglecting to consider others equally consistent with the available data.

Specifically, I believe it reasonable to suggest that, by striking a match on the telescope (or perhaps the krinkle finish of the spectrograph housing) while in the act of photographing a star's spectrum, the star might be caused to emit a potassium flare. This hypothesis, if correct, would have a very interesting consequence: bearing in mind that the stars in question were all several hundred light years distant, meaning that the light recorded on the spectrum plates departed those stars several hundred years in the past, it follows that the act of striking the match "now" caused the star to emit its flare an equal number of hundred years previous.

I believe this interpretation of the data calls for thorough study. It is of interest not only for its own sake (basic research always pays off!), and for the light (sic) it might shed on the nature of time (and is it possible that in this process, the telescope is functioning as a psionic device? Is it necessary for the spectrograph to contain a photographic plate?). There is also this very sobering question: if our astronomers, here, can cause such an event on distant stars, might it not be equally possible that astronomers in other solar systems—assuming they exist—could cause our own sun to similarly misbehave? (Bearing in mind, of course, they will not strike their matches until several centuries from now.) Therefore, I enclose my formal research grant application to your Foundation.

I am confident you will view it with interest, inasmuch as your favorable response arrived in yesterday's mail. Most of the requested funds, you will note, will go for chalk, matchbooks, and coffee. Or possibly beer.

Sincerely yours,

Willem O. Kamm

AIR RAID
by Herb Boehm

Raised in Texas, Herb Boehm now lives among the tall trees of Oregon—a state that has recently been building up a very respectable population of SF writers. Mr. Boehm tells us he has no occupation but writing; and says that if things keep going as well as they have, he may never have to do another lick of work. He's very much a supporter of the women's movement, trying to people his stories with a majority of females.

I was jerked awake by the silent alarm vibrating my skull. It won't shut down until you sit up, so I did. All around me in the darkened bunkroom the Snatch Team members were sleeping singly and in pairs. I yawned, scratched my ribs, and patted Gene's hairy flank. He turned over. So much for a romantic send-off.

Rubbing sleep from my eyes, I reached to the floor for my leg, strapped it on and plugged it in. Then I was running down the rows of bunks toward Ops.

The situation board glowed in the gloom. Sun-Belt Airlines Flight 128, Miami to New York, September 15, 1979. We'd been looking for that one for three years. I should have been happy, but who can afford it when you wake up?

Liza Boston muttered past me on the way to Prep. I muttered back, and followed. The lights came on around the mirrors, and I groped my way to one of them. Behind us, three more people staggered in. I sat down, plugged in, and at last I could lean back and close my eyes.

They didn't stay closed for long. Rush! I sat up straight as the sludge I use for blood was replaced with supercharged go-juice. I looked around me and got a series of idiot grins. There was Liza, and Pinky and Dave. Against the far wall Cristabel was already turning slowly in front of the airbrush, getting a caucasian paint job. It looked like a good team.

I opened the drawer and started preliminary work on my face. It's a bigger job every time. Transfusion or no, I looked like death. The right ear was completely gone now. I could no longer close

169

my lips; the gums were permanently bared. A week earlier, a finger had fallen off in my sleep. And what's it to you, bugger?

While I worked, one of the screens around the mirror glowed. A smiling young woman, blonde, high brow, round face. Close enough. The crawl line read *Mary Katrina Sondergard, born Trenton, New Jersey, age in 1979: 25*. Baby, this is your lucky day.

The computer melted the skin away from her face to show me the bone structure, rotated it, gave me cross-sections. I studied the similarities with my own skull, noted the differences. Not bad, and better than some I'd been given.

I assembled a set of dentures that included the slight gap in the upper incisors. Putty filled out my cheeks. Contact lenses fell from the dispenser and I popped them in. Nose plugs widened my nostrils. No need for ears; they'd by covered by the wig. I pulled a blank plastiflesh mask over my face and had to pause while it melted in. It took only a minute to mold it to perfection. I smiled at myself. How nice to have lips.

The delivery slot clunked and dropped a blonde wig and a pink outfit into my lap. The wig was hot from the styler. I put it on, then my pantyhose.

"Mandy? Did you get the profile on Sondergard?" I didn't look up; I recognized the voice.

"Roger."

"We've located her near the airport. We can slip you in before take-off, so you'll be the joker."

I groaned, and looked up at the face on the screen. Elfreda Baltimore-Louisville, Director of Operational Teams: lifeless face and tiny slits for eyes. What can you do when all the muscles are dead?

"Okay." You take what you get.

She switched off, and I spent the next two minutes trying to get dressed while keeping my eyes on the screens. I memorized names and faces of crew members plus the few facts known about them. Then I hurried out and caught up with the others. Elapsed time from first alarm: twelve minutes and seven seconds. We'd better get moving.

"Goddam Sun-Belt," Cristabel groused, hitching at her bra.

"At least they got rid of the high heels," Dave pointed out. A year earlier we would have been teetering down the aisles on three-inch platforms. We all wore short pink shifts with blue and white stripes diagonally across the front, and carried matching shoulder bags. I fussed trying to get the ridiculous pillbox cap pinned on.

We jogged into the dark Operations Control Room and lined up at the gate. Things were out of our hands now. Until the gate was ready, we could only wait.

I was first, a few feet away from the portal. I turned away from it; it gives me vertigo. I focused instead on the gnomes sitting at their consoles, bathed in yellow lights fro their screens. None of them looked back at me. They don't like us much. Our fat legs and butts and breasts are a reproach to them, a reminder that Snatchers eat five times their ration to stay presentable for the masquerade. Meantime we continue to rot. One day I'll be sitting at a console. One day I'll be *built in* to a console, with all my guts on the outside and nothing left of my body but stink. The hell with them.

I buried my gun under a clutter of tissues and lipsticks in my purse. Elfreda was looking at me.

"Where is she?" I asked.

"Motel room. She was alone from 10 P.M. to noon on flight day."

Departure time was 1:15. She cut it close and would be in a hurry. Good.

"Can you catch her in the bathroom? Best of all, in the tub?"

"We're working on it." She sketched a smile with a fingertip drawn over lifeless lips. She knew how I like to operate, but she was telling me I'd take what I got. It never hurts to ask. People are at their most defenseless stretched out and up to their necks in water.

"Go!" Elfreda shouted. I stepped through, and things started to go wrong.

I was faced the wrong way, stepping *out* of the bathroom door and facing the bedroom. I turned and spotted Mary Katrina Sondergard through the haze of the gate. There was no way I could reach her without stepping back through. I couldn't even shoot without hitting someone on the other side.

Sondergard was at the mirror, the worst possible place. Few people recognize themselves quickly, but she'd been looking right at herself. She saw me and her eyes widened. I stepped to the side, out of her sight.

"What the hell is . . . hey? Who the hell. . . . " I noted the voice, which can be the trickiest thing to get right.

I figured she'd be more curious than afraid. My guess was right. She came out of the bathroom, passing through the gate as if it wasn't there, which it wasn't, since it only has one side. She had a towel wrapped around her.

"Jesus Christ! What are you doing in my—!" Words fail you at a time like that. She knew she ought to say something, but what? *Excuse me, haven't I seen you in the mirror?*

I put on my best stew smile and held out my hand.

"Pardon the intrusion. I can explain everything. You see, I'm—" I hit her on the side of the head and she staggered and went down hard. Her towel fell to the floor. "—working my way through college." She started to get up so I caught her under the chin with my artifical knee. She stayed down.

"Standard fuggin' *oil!*" I hissed, rubbing my injured knuckles. But there was no time. I knelt beside her, checked her pulse. She'd be okay, but I think I loosened some front teeth. I paused a moment. Lord, to look like that with no make-up, no prosthetics! She nearly broke my heart.

I grabbed her under the knees and wrestled her to the gate. She was a sack of limp noodles. Somebody reached through, grabbed her feet, and pulled. *So long, love! How would you like to go on a long voyage?*

I sat on her rented bed to get my breath. There were car keys and cigarettes in her purse, genuine tobacco, worth its weight in blood. I lit six of them, figuring I had five minutes of my very own. The room filled with sweet smoke. They don't make 'em like that anymore.

The Hertz sedan was in the motel parking lot. I got in and headed for the airport. I breathed deeply of the air, rich in hydrocarbons. I could see for hundreds of yards into the distance. The perspective nearly made me dizzy, but I live for those moments. There's no way to explain what it's like in the pre-meck world. The sun was a fierce yellow ball through the haze.

The other stews were boarding. Some of them knew Sondergard so I didn't say much, pleading a hangover. That went over well, with a lot of knowing laughs and sly remarks. Evidently it wasn't out of character. We boarded the 707 and got ready for the goats to arrive.

It looked good. The four commandos on the other side were identical twins for the women I was working with. There was nothing to do but be a stewardess until departure time. I hoped there would be no more glitches. Inverting a gate for a joker run into a motel room was one thing, but in a 707 at twenty thousand feet . . .

172   AIR RAID

The plane was nearly full when the woman that Pinky would impersonate sealed the forward door. We taxied to the end of the runway, then we were airborne. I started taking orders for drinks in first.

The goats were the usual lot, for 1979. Fat and sassy, all of them, and as unaware of living in a paradise as a fish is of the sea. *What would you think, ladies and gents, of a trip to the future? No? I can't say I'm surprised. What if I told you this plane is going to—*

My alarm beeped as we reached cruising altitude. I consulted the indicator under my Lady Bulova and glanced at one of the restroom doors. I felt a vibration pass through the plane. *Damn it, not so soon.*

The gate was in there. I came out quickly, and motioned for Diana Gleason—Dave's pigeon—to come to the front.

"Take a look at this," I said, with a disgusted look. She started to enter the restroom, stopped when she saw the green glow. I planted a boot on her fanny and shoved. Perfect. Dave would have a chance to hear her voice before popping in. Though she'd be doing little but screaming when she got a look around . . .

Dave came through the gate, adjusting his silly little hat. Diana must have struggled.

"Be disgusted," I whispered.

"What a mess," he said as he came out of the restroom. It was a fair imitation of Diana's tone, though he'd missed the accent. It wouldn't matter much longer.

"What is it?" It was one of the stews from tourist. We stepped aside so she could get a look, and Dave shoved her through. Pinky popped out very quickly.

"We're minus on minutes," Pinky said. "We lost five on the other side."

"Five?" Dave-Diana squeaked. I felt the same way. We had a hundred and three passengers to process.

"Yeah. They lost contact after you pushed my pigeon through. It took that long to re-align."

You get used to that. Time runs at different rates on each side of the gate, though it's always sequential, past to future. Once we'd started the snatch with me entering Sondergard's room, there was no way to go back any earlier on either side. Here, in 1979, we had a rigid ninety-four minutes to get everything done. On the other side, the gate could never be maintained longer than three hours.

"When you left, how long was it since the alarm went in?"

"Twenty-eight minutes."

It didn't sound good. It would take at least two hours just customizing the wimps. Assuming there was no more slippage on 79-time, we might just make it. But there's *always* slippage. I shuddered, thinking about riding it in.

"No time for any more games, then," I said. "Pink, you go back to tourist and call both of the other girls. Tell 'em to come one at a time, and tell 'em we've got a problem. You know the bit."

"Biting back the tears. Got you." She hurried aft. In no time the first one showed up. Her friendly Sun-Belt Airlines smile was stamped on her face, but her stomach would be churning. *Oh God, this is it!*

I took her by the elbow and pulled her behind the curtains in front. She was breathing hard.

"Welcome to the twilight zone," I said, and put the gun to her head. She slumped, and I caught her. Pinky and Dave helped me shove her through the gate.

"Fug! The rotting thing's flickering."

Pinky was right. A very ominous sign. But the green glow stabilized as we watched, with who-knows-how-much slippage on the other side. Cristabel ducked through.

"We're plus thirty-three," she said. Thers was no sense talking about what we were all thinking; things were going badly.

"Back to tourist," I said. "Be brave, smile at everyone, but make it just a little bit too good, got it?"

"Check," Cristabel said.

We processed the other quickly, with no incident. Then there was no time to talk about anything. In eighty-nine minutes Flight 128 was going to be spread all over a mountain whether we were finished or not.

Dave went into the cockpit to keep the flight crew out of our hair. Me and Pinky were supposed to take care of first class, then back up Cristabel and Liza in tourist. We used the standard "coffee, tea, or milk" gambit, relying on our speed and their inertia.

I leaned over the first two seats on the left.

"Are you enjoying your flight?" Pop, pop. Two squeezes on the trigger, close to the heads and out of sight of the rest of the goats.

"Hi folks. I'm Mandy. Fly me." Pop, pop.

Half-way to the galley, a few people were watching us curiously. But people don't make a fuss until they have a lot more to go on. One goat in the back row stood up, and I let him have it.

By now there were only eight left awake. I abandoned the smile and squeezed off four quick shots. Pinky took care of the rest. We hurried through the curtains, just in time.

There was an uproar building in the back of tourist, with about sixty percent of the goats already processed. Cristabel glanced at me, and I nodded.

"Okay, folks," she bawled. "I want you to be quiet. Calm down and listen up. *You*, fathead, *pipe down* before I cram my foot up your ass sideways."

The shock of hearing her talk like that was enough to buy us a little time, anyway. We had formed a skirmish line across the width of the plane, guns out, steadied on seat backs, aimed at the milling, befuddled group of thirty goats.

The guns are enough to awe all but the most foolhardy. In essence, a standard-issue stunner is just a plastic rod with two grids about six inches apart. There's not enough metal in it to set off a hijack alarm. And to people from the Stone Age to about 2190 it doesn't look any more like a weapon than a ball-point pen. So Equipment Section jazzes them up in a plastic shell to real Buck Rogers blasters, with a dozen knobs and lights that flash and a barrel like the snout of a hog. Hardly anyone ever walks into one.

"We are in great danger, and time is short. You must all do exactly as I tell you, and you will be safe."

You can't give them time to think, you have to rely on your status as the Voice of Authority. The situation is just *not* going to make sense to them, no matter how you explain it.

"Just a minute, I think you owe us—"

An airborne lawyer. I made a snap decision, thumbed the fireworks switch on my gun, and shot him.

The gun made a sound like a flying saucer with hemorrhoids, spit sparks and little jets of flame, and extended a green laser finger to his forehead. He dropped. All pure kark, of course. But impressive.

And it's damn risky, too. I had to choose between a panic if the fathead got them to thinking, and a possible panic from the flash of the gun. But when a 20th gets to talking about his "rights" and what he is "owed," things can get out of hand. It's infectious.

It worked. There was a lot of shouting, people ducking behind seats, but no rush. We could have handled it, but we needed some of them conscious if we were ever going to finish the Snatch.

"Get up. Get *up*, you *slugs!*" Cristabel yelled. "He's stunned, nothing worse. But I'll *kill* the next one who gets out of line. Now *get to your feet* and do what I tell you. *Children first! Hurry,* as fast as you can, to the front of the plane. Do what the stewardess tells you. Come on, kids, *move!"*

I ran back into first class just ahead of the kids, turned at the open restroom door, and got on my knees.

They were petrified. There were five of them—crying, some of them, which always chokes me up—looking left and right at dead people in the first class seats, stumbling, near panic.

"Come on, kids," I called to them, giving my special smile. "Your parents will be along in just a minute. Everything's going to be all right, I promise you. Come on."

I got three of them through. The fourth balked. She was determined not to go through that door. She spread her legs and arms and I couldn't push her through. I will *not* hit a child, never. She raked her nails over my face. My wig came off, and she gaped at my bare head. I shoved her through.

Number five was sitting in the aisle, bawling. He was maybe seven. I ran back and picked him up, hugged and kissed him, and tossed him through. God, I was beat, but I was needed in tourist.

"You, you, you, and you. Okay, you too. Help him, will you? Pinky had a practiced eye for the ones that wouldn't be any use to anyone, even themselves. We herded them toward the front of the plane, then deployed ourselves along the left side where we could cover up the workers. It didn't take long to prod them into action. We had them dragging the limp bodies forward as fast as they could go. Me and Cristabel were in tourist, with others up front.

Adrenalin was being catabolized in my body now; the rush of action left me and I started to feel very tired. There's an unavoidable feeling of sympathy for the poor dumb goats that starts to get me about this stage of the game. Sure, they were better off, sure they were going to die if we didn't get them off the plane. But when they saw the other side they were going to have a hard time believing it.

The first ones were returning for a second load, stunned at what they'd just seen: dozens of people being put into a cubicle that was crowded when it was empty. One college student looked like he'd been hit in the stomach. He stopped by me and his eyes pleaded.

"Look, I want to *help* you people, just . . . what's going *on?* Is this some new kind of rescue? I mean, are we going to crash—"

I switched my gun to prod and brushed it across his cheek. He gasped, and fell back.

AIR RAID

"Shut your fuggin' mouth and get moving, or I'll kill you." It would be hours before his jaw was in shape to ask any more stupid questions.

We cleared tourist and moved up. A couple of the work gang were pretty damn pooped by then. Muscles like horses, all of them, but they can hardly run up a flight of stairs. We let some of them go through, including a couple that were at least fifty years old. *Je*-zuz. Fifty! We got down to a core of four men and two dropped. But we processed everyone in twenty-five minutes.

The portapak came through as we were stripping off our clothes. Cristabel knocked on the door to the cockpit and Dave came out, already naked. A bad sign.

"I had to cork 'em," he said. "Bleeding Captain just *had* to make his Grand March through the plane. I tried *everything*."

Sometimes you have to do it. The plane was on autopilot, as it normally would be at this time. But if any of us did anything detrimental to the craft, changed the fixed course of events in any way, that would be it. All that work for nothing, and Flight 128 inaccessible to us for all Time. I don't know sludge about time theory, but I know the practical angles. We can do things in the past only at times and in places where it won't make any difference. We have to cover our tracks. There's flexibility; once a Snatcher left her gun behind and it went in with the plane. Nobody found it, or if they did, they didn't have the smoggiest idea of what it was, so we were okay.

Flight 128 was mechanical failure. That's the best kind; it means we don't have to keep the pilot unaware of the situation in the cabin right down to ground level. We can cork him and fly the plane, since there's nothing he could have done to save the flight anyway. A pilot-error smash is almost impossible to Snatch. We mostly work mid-airs, bombs, and structural failures. If there's even one survivor, we can't touch it. It would not fit the fabric of space-time, which is immutable (though it can stretch a little), and we'd all just fade away and appear back in the ready-room.

My head was hurting. I wanted that portapak very badly.

"Who has the most hours on a 707?" Pinky did, so I sent her to the cabin, along with Dave, who could do the pilot's voice for air traffic control. You have to have a believable record in the flight recorder, too. They trailed two long tubes from the portapak, and the rest of us hooked in up close. We stood there, each of us smoking a fistful of cigarettes, wanting to finish them but hoping there wouldn't be enough time. The gate had vanished as soon as we tossed our clothes and the flight crew through.

But we didn't worry long. There's other nice things about Snatching, but nothing to compare with the rush of plugging into a portapak. The wake-up transfusion is nothing but fresh blood, rich in oxygen and sugars. What we were getting now was an insane brew of concentrated adrenalin, super-saturated hemoglobin, methedrine, white lightning, TNT, and Kickapoo joyjuice. It was like a firecracker in your heart; a boot in the box that rattled your sox.

"I'm growing hair on my chest," Cristabel said, solemnly. Everyone giggled.

"Would someone hand me my eyeballs?"

"The blue ones, or the red ones?"

"I think my ass just fell off."

We'd heard them all before, but we howled anyway. We were strong, *strong*, and for one golden moment we had no worries. Everything was hilarious. I could have torn sheet metal with my eyelashes.

But you get hyper on that mix. When the gate didn't show, and didn't show, and *didn't sweetjeez show* we all started milling. This bird wasn't going to fly all that much longer.

Then it did show, and we turned on. The first of the wimps came through, dressed in the clothes taken from a passenger it had been picked to resemble.

"Two thirty-five elapsed upside time," Cristabel announced.

"Je-zuz."

It is a deadening routine. You grab the harness around the wimp's shoulders and drag it along the aisle, after consulting the seat number painted on its forehead. The paint would last three minutes. You seat it, strap it in, break open the harness and carry it back to toss through the gate as you grab the next one. You have to take it for granted they've done the work right on the other side; fillings in the teeth, fingerprints, the right match in height and weight and hair color. Most of those things don't matter much, especially on Flight 128 which was a crash-and-burn. There would be bits and pieces, and burned to a crisp at that. But you can't take chances. Those rescue workers are pretty thorough on the parts they *do* find; the dental work and fingerprints especially are important.

I hate wimps. I really hate 'em. Every time I grab the harness of one of them, if it's a child, I wonder if it's Alice. *Are you my kid, you vegetable, you slug, you slimy worm?* I joined the Snatchers right after the brain bugs ate the life out of my baby's head. I couldn't stand to think she was the last generation, that the last humans there would ever be would live with nothing in their heads, medically dead by standards that prevailed even in 1979, with computers working their muscles to keep them in tone. You grow up, reach puberty still fertile—one in a thousand—rush to get pregnant in your first heat. Then you find out your mom or pop passed on a chronic disease bound right into the genes, and none of your kids will be immune. I *knew* about the para-leprosy; I grew up with my toes rotting away. But this was too much. What do you do?

Only one in ten of the wimps had a customized face. It takes time and a lot of skill to build a new face that will stand up to a doctor's autopsy. The rest came pre-mutilated. We've got millions of them; it's not hard to find a good match in the body. Most of them would stay breathing, too dumb to stop, until impact.

The plane jerked, hard. I glanced at my watch. Five minutes to impact. We should have time. I was on my last wimp. I could hear Dave frantically calling the ground. A bomb came through the gate, and I tossed it into the cockpit. Pinky turned on the pressure sensor on the bomb and came running out, followed by Dave. Liza was already through. I grabbed the limp dolls in stewardess costume and tossed them to the floor. The engine fell off and a piece of it came through. I grabbed the cabin. We started to depressurize. The bomb blew away part of the cockpit (the ground crash crew would read it—we hoped—that part of the engine came through and killed the crew: no more words from the pilot on the flight recorder) and we turned, slowly, left and down. I was lifted toward the hole in the side of the plane, but managed to hold onto a seat. Cristabel wasn't so lucky. She was blown backwards.

We started to rise slightly, losing speed. Suddenly it was uphill from where Cristabel was lying in the aisle. Blood oozed from her temple. I glanced back; everyone was gone, and three pink-suited wimps were piled on the floor. The plane began to stall, to nose down, and my feet left the floor.

"Come on, Bel!" I screamed. That gate was only three feet away from me, but I began pulling myself along to where she floated. The plane bumped, and she hit the floor. Incredibly, it seemed to wake her up. She started to swim toward me, and I grabbed her hand as the floor came up to slam us again. We crawled as the plane went through its final death agony, and we came to the door. The gate was gone.

There wasn't anything to say. We were going in. It's hard enough to keep the gate in place on a plane that's moving in a straight line. When a bird gets to corkscrewing and coming apart, the math is fearsome. So I've been told.

I embraced Cristabel and held her bloodied head. She was groggy, but managed to smile and shrug. You take what you get. I hurried into the restroom and got both of us down on the floor. Back to the forward bulkhead, Cristabel between my legs, back to front. Just like in training. We pressed our feet against the other wall. I hugged her tightly and cried on her shoulder.

And it was there. A green glow to my left. I threw myself toward it, dragging Cristabel, keeping low as two wimps were thrown head-first through the gate above our heads. Hands grabbed and pulled us through. I clawed my way a good five yards along the floor. You can leave a leg on the other side and I didn't have one to spare.

I sat up as they were carrying Cristabel to Medical. I patted her arm as she went by on the stretcher, but she was passed out. I wouldn't have minded passing out myself.

For a while, you can't believe it all really happened. Sometimes it turns out it *didn't* happen. You come back and find out all the goats in the holding pen have softly and suddenly vanished away because the continuum won't tolerate the changes and paradoxes you've put into it. The people you've worked so hard to rescue are spread like tomato surprise all over some goddam hillside in Carolina and all you've got left is a bunch of ruined wimps and an exhausted Snatch Team. But not this time. I could see the goats milling around in the holding pen, naked and more bewildered than ever. And just starting to be *really* afraid.

Elfreda touched me as I passed her. She nodded, which meant well-done in her limited repertoire of gestures. I shrugged, wondering if I cared, but the surplus adrenalin was still in my veins and I found myself grinning at her. I nodded back.

Gene was standing by the holding pen. I went to him, hugged him. I felt the juices start to flow. *Damn it, let's squander a little ration and have us a good time.*

Someone was beating on the sterile glass wall of the pen. She shouted, mouthing angry words at us. *Why? What have you done to us?* It was Mary Sondergard. She implored her bald, one-legged twin to make her understand. She thought she had problems. God, was she pretty. I hated her guts.

Gene pulled me away from the wall. My hands hurt, and I'd

broken off all my fake nails without scratching the glass. She was sitting on the floor now, sobbing. I heard the voice of the briefing officer on the outside speaker.

"... Centauri 3 is hospitable, with an Earth-like climate. By that, I mean *your* Earth, not what it has become. You'll see more of that later. The trip will take five years, shiptime. Upon landfall, you will be entitled to one horse, a plow, three axes, two hundred kilos of seed grain ... "

I leaned against Gene's shoulder. At their lowest ebb, this very moment, they were so much better than us. I had maybe ten years, half of that as a basketcase. They are our best, our very brightest hope. Everything is up to them.

"... that no one will be forced to go. We wish to point out again, not for the last time, that you would all be dead without out intervention. There are things you should know, however. You cannot breathe our air. If you remain on Earth, you can never leave this building. We are not like you. We are the result of a genetic winnowing, a mutation process. We are the survivors. but our enemies have evolved along with us. They are winning. You, however, are immune to the diseases that afflict us ... "

I winced, and turned away.

"... the other hand, if you emigrate you will be given a chance at a new life. It won't be easy, but as Americans you should be proud of your pioneer heritage. Your ancestors survived, and so will you. It can be a rewarding experience, and I urge you ... "

Sure. Gene and I looked at each other and laughed. *Listen to this, folks. Five percent of you will suffer nervous breakdowns in the next few days, and never leave. About the same number will commit suicide, here and on the way. When you get there, sixty to seventy percent will die in the first three years. You will die in childbirth, be eaten by animals, bury two out of three of your babies, starve slowly when the rains don't come. If you live, it will be to break your back behind a plow, sun-up to dusk. New Earth is Heaven, folks!*

God, how I wish I could go with them.

BOARDER INCIDENT
by Ted Reynolds

*Here is another story from Lloyd Biggle's
writing class at the University of
Michigan. The author, Mr. Reynolds, is
well over 30; he's been a copy boy,
egg candler, interpreter, yachtsman,
teacher, accountant, and planetarium
operator—among other jobs. He's
traveled leisurely through some six
continents, and asked us especially to
mention eleven archipelagoes, but
neglected to tell us which ones.*

He strolled out of the alley, trying not to look like an alien who
had just buried his spaceship under the forsythia bushes. The
house he sought stood at the corner, high-peaked and gaunt. The
sign in the lower window proclaimed: MRS. DOGEN, FINE ROOMS FOR
RENT.

On the front steps, he paused to tuck in a stray tastestalk that
had somehow slipped from under his rubberoid head covering. It
was his careful attention to details like these that had made him
such a valuable first contact man for Galactic Empire, Inc.

He rang the bell.

The last landlady he had encountered had been sesquipedal and
oviparous, but the type was universal. With a shudder he began a
sputtering explanation. Mrs. Dogen seemed wilfully bent on not
comprehending him.

"Just a moment," she said finally. "Your name is Astroven?"

"In effect. And I request only that—"

"Why do you want to live in *my* attic? I have nice rooms available on both the first and second floors."

"I don't precisely intend to live in it," Mr. Astroven explained in
his rubbery voice, "just set up a hyperdimensional interstellar
space-warp booster station in it. I shall *live* in the stairwell cupboard."

Mrs. Dogen rotated her head. "Out of the question," she announced.

Mr. Astroven took a synthekit from his pocket and synthesized
a small diamond. Mrs. Dogen watched the performance suspiciously until Mr. Astroven placed the gleaming end product in her

183

hand. "As a stipend, perhaps one of these per week," he suggested. "Its intrinsic value would equal some two hundreds of your dollars."

Mrs. Dogen's expression altered. "Perhaps," she announced, "some kind of explanation is in order."

§ § §

They sat in the cool living room and Mr. Astroven explained ... and explained ... and explained, and with deepening misgivings, for Mrs. Dogen obviously was gleaning not a tithe of it.

"So you see," Mr. Astroven said, bringing his explanation to a conclusion for the third time, "if we can't set up on Earth, we'll have to set up at least four booster stations and go several parsecs out of the direct route to the Persean spiral arm. We prefer worlds with no natives; and if there must be natives, we'd much prefer civilized ones; but in dry regions like this we have to make do with what is available."

"I see," Mrs. Dogen said, though she was still looking at the diamond. "Then what you're saying is that my attic is one of the three places on Earth where your gadgets will work."

"Yes, ma'am. One of the other two is a nexus at the bottom of the Marianas trench, under six miles of water. Its use poses certain inherent difficulties. The other place—" He shuddered. "The other place is in a bar in Belfast."

Mrs. Dogen nodded. "Under the circumstances, I think ... perhaps ... *ten* of these per week ..."

Mr. Astroven expelled a hissing breath and agreed.

"But there is one thing. I notice that you are concealing your actual features under a headmask. I trust you are not keeping anything important from me?"

"We merely try to be discreet on first contact," Mr. Astroven said. "However, if it is a condition for renting ..." He pulled off the mask and showed his real face. It was garish, variegated, surreal, and mostly green.

Mrs. Dogen was visibly relieved. "Perhaps it was foolish of me," she said. "I was afraid you might be black."

She paused to chase the cat from Mr. Astroven's lap for the tenth time. "Very well," she went on. "Kitty likes you, and I trust her judgment. You may—ah—bring your—er—friends through the attic as long as none of you create any disturbance, and your weekly rent will be—did we say—fifteen of these?"

Mr. Astroven expelled another hissing breath and while Mrs.

Dogen looked on greedily he operated his synthekit fourteen more times. "We use it more often to synthesize coal," he remarked.

He finished, and Mrs. Dogen counted fifteen and thanked him, and he returned her thanks. "And now," he said, "I must leave you temporarily."

"Please don't let Kitty out," Mrs. Dogen said. "She hasn't been fixed."

Mr. Astroven regarded her perplexedly. "Oh, I'm not going out-*side*. It will be unnecessary to use your doors from now on."

He climbed to the attic, where he set up a tiny pendulum disc, touched it, and . . . *went*.

§ § §

For the first few days, there were no difficulties. Mr. Astroven's visitors, whoever or whatever they were, kept to the attic and behaved quietly. Still, there *was* the old friend he brought downstairs to introduce to Mrs. Dogen. It was a tritubiculated monosculate tissue culture from Mirfak, and it somewhat resembled a purple sea-cucumber. When it got a good look at Mrs. Dogen, it screamed in terror.

§ § §

"Mrs. Dogen," Mr. Astroven said petulantly, "could you kindly explain to your domestic symbiote that the Phlegoorian Ambassador is not a rat? She appears painfully intent on ingesting him."

§ § §

"You know this is a non-drinking house, Mr. Astroven. Perhaps you have a reasonable explanation for that strong stench of alcohol?"

"Why, yes, ma'am, I believe I do. The carbon rings at the basis of Danubian metabolism are made up in the following interesting arrangement—"

"That does not sound like a reasonable explanation," Mrs. Dogen said frostily. "If you're suggesting that some of your visitors smell like alcohol, then I insist that they use perfume."

"But my dear ma'am—what you are smelling *is* perfume!"

§ § §

Mr. Astroven clumped down the stairs in awed excitement. "Ma'am—Mrs. Dogen!" he called.

She regarded him irritably.

"The Imperial Cortege will be passing through your attic next week," he blurted, panting his excitement. "The Galactic Empress

Herself has expressed the wish for your presentation to Her."

Mrs. Dogen frowned. "Does *she* use perfume?"

"My dear ma'am! As a royal personage, naturally only the very finest—"

"You will kindly give her my regrets," Mrs. Dogen said firmly. "As a loyal American, I don't believe in royalty."

§ § §

"Mr. Astroven, I don't care if there *is* a war out there somewhere! Feet tramping noisily through my attic from one to seven AM is something I cannot tolerate. I'm giving you notice."

Mr. Astroven sighed. "Perhaps if I were to increase the stipend—it is rather important to us—an additional ten diamonds a week?" He got out his synthekit.

"Twenty," Mrs. Dogen said, holding out her hand.

§ § §

Mr. Astroven said apologetically, "The Loobite is forced to remain here until the proper cycle in its binary destination. Do you think you could turn the thermostat up forty degrees for a few days?"

"*Really*, Mr. Astroven!"

"It must have warmth to survive, you see."

"Out of the question," Mrs. Dogen said firmly.

"Perhaps for an additional five diamonds a week?"

"For ten diamonds," Mrs. Dogen said, "I'll rent the oven to you."

§ § §

"I regret to inform you," Mr. Astroven announced, "that my synthekit is broken. And therefore this week's stipend . . ."

"I'm giving you notice," Mrs. Dogen announced coldly. "Effective at once."

Mr. Astroven sighed. "Actually, that was my intention. Giving notice, I mean. My superiors feel that a weekly stipend of two hundred diamonds is excessive. The wear and tear on synthekits has become intolerable. Therefore we have decided to transfer operations to the other route, the one with the four additional booster stations."

"Under the circumstances," Mr. Dogen said, "I'll waive the required period of notice. Peace and quiet, and an absence of peculiar odors, are to be prized in one's home above diamonds."

"Indeed, yes," Mr. Astroven murmured; he knew it would take her years to dispose of the hoard she had accumulated. "Indeed, yes. Kindly express my farewell regards to Kitty."

He touched the pendulum disc and vanished. The disc remained. There was no way it could transport itself, or it would have gone, too.

§ § §

The same evening, Kitty went to the attic in search of her friend, Mr. Astroven. She batted the pendulum disc. She *went*.

§ § §

Mrs. Dogen sent several furiously worded notes out into the galaxy by space warp . . . "send me back my cat or else!" The cat did not return.

§ § §

Mrs. Dogen began dumping daily loads of trash into the galaxy by space warp. They sped to various stations within the Sagittarian or Perseid spiral arms and were duly noticed. Shortly afterward, the cat reappeared.

§ § §

Mrs. Dogen's joy in the reunion with her pet was sharply tempered by the realization that Kitty was in the family way. When the kittens arrived, her first impulse was to drown them. They were a constant reminder of the sights and sounds and odors of Mr. Astroven's tenancy, all of which she preferred to forget.

But they *were* cute, and now that they're old enough to talk . . .

A DELICATE SHADE OF KIPNEY
by Nancy Kress

/G.Barr

*Ms. Kress is 29; she holds a Master's
degree in education. She used to teach
the fourth grade; her current occupation
is a juggling act, involving a typewriter
and two small sons. She reports that the
one time that she met Dr. Asimov—at a
pot-luck dinner when he was lecturing at
a local college—he was more impressed
in the brownies she had prepared than
in her interest in writing science fiction.*

Sullen gray clouds lay heavily on the low sky, and below them gray fog shrouded the land. It had just finished drizzling, or was about to drizzle, or perhaps even was drizzling with fine clammy droplets that were indistinguishable from the ever-present mist. In the East the lowering clouds were paling almost imperceptibly, and the stunted kiril trees that dotted the plain hastily turned their gray-green leaves toward the thin light before any of it should be wasted.

A boy sat on the hill that poked abruptly from one side of the plain, just before it broke into irregular rocky ravines. His already muscular arms were clasped around knees that, child-like, were scraped from falls. Under his coarse, dull-colored tunic, his bare buttocks pressed against the damp, straggly grass. He sat unmoving, absorbed, staring raptly toward the drab eastern sky.

"Wade?"

The boy turned without getting up, and peered through the shifting fog. It was difficult to see clearly more than a few yards.

"Wade! Are you there?"

"Oh, it's you, Thekla. I'm over here."

"Who else did you think it would be?" Spectrally his sister materialized from the fog, her gray tunic blending with it at the edges, her younger child astride one hip. The baby stared at Wade with round solemn eyes.

"I thought I'd find you here. How was it today?"

Wade shook his head, inarticulate. "Really beautiful. Much brighter than the sunset ever is. Thekla, look at this color." He held out a leaf. The underside was a delicate gray, lightly shined with silver.

"Mmmm, what a pretty shade of tlem."

"It's the exact color I need for the painting. If only I could figure out a way to mix it!" He gazed hopefully at Thekla, only four years his senior but always so much more deft at the endless foraging and fashioning of supplies. "Got any ideas?"

"No, but I'll think about it. Wade, you'd better come down to breakfast now. Mother sent me to get you. She's almost ready to serve."

The cords in Wade's neck grew taut. "I thought it was earlier than that."

"It is. I mean, we're having breakfast earlier this morning because Brian woke us up when he was news-spreading. Jenny had her baby last night, it's a girl, and they're both all right!" Thekla smiled, and he saw that it was still the dazzling, comradely smile which had made the toddler Wade follow her everywhere, stumbling gaily after her through the wet mist, and which lately had become so rare. But now it somehow—*jarred* with her too-thin face, and with the awkward way she stood, one shoulder hoisted a little higher than the other. Something had gone wrong with one hip when the last baby had been born; they hadn't told Wade just what. Painfully he looked away, watching instead the perfect, disembodied fog.

"I'm glad. I was thinking about Jenny." He added, after a pause, "Maybe that will put *him* in a good mood, too. Forty-nine now."

They both looked down from the hill, down to the plain, where the small stone cabins huddled around the lifeless hulk of the ship. The fog shifted, and for a moment they could see her clearly, the long, grotesquely mangled wreckage barnacled with rust, and, at a sharp angle to the rest, the rear observation section, miraculously snapped free and preserved whole by the inexorable vectors of chance. Then the fog closed once more.

The pause lengthened, broken only by the soft cry of a small creature shrouded somewhere in the formless gray mist: "Keeday! Kee-day!"

"Well, come on then," Wade said heavily. "I guess we have to go down."

§ § §

The inside of the small cabin fairly vibrated with color.

Every wall was covered with pictures, glossy prints carefully torn from an art book and cemented to the walls in close rows, as though to blot out as much of the native stone as possible. Masterpieces from several centuries elbowed each other crazily, with no regard to chronology, all seemingly chosen only for their glowing colors and pure, hard lines. Picasso, Van Eyck, Miro, Vermeer, Grunewald, Reznicki.

In the center of the wall opposite the fireplace was a group of landscapes done on split kirilwood boards. The drawing showed obvious skill, but the colors were garish, larger than life, put on with a lavish desperate hand by an almost-artist who had forgotten that nature could be subtle. The Grand Canyon at sunset screamed orange and red and acid yellow; a kelly green forest grew lushly under a turquoise sky; Victoria Falls threw up a lurid, brassy rainbow.

The others were already seated at the long table. Wade slid into his place, glanced once at Mondrian's *Broadway Boogie-Woogie* on the wall opposite him, and shuddered. He dropped his eyes quickly to his plate, thinking of his own paintings prudently stored in the sleeping loft, dwelling on their soft, almost imperceptible shadings; the last one carried the blending right to the edge of what the eye could discern, he was pretty sure. Now if he could only mix that shade of tlem, the one you only saw when the light had just—

"Wade, Jenny had her baby last night," his mother said in her soft voice. "A little girl, thank God."

"Thekla told me," Wade said. He looked at his mother's worn face with affection. "They're both all right. That's wonderful."

"Forty-nine, by God!" his grandfather cackled. "Forty-nine, and two more pregnant right this minute—Cathy, and Tom's youngest girl, what's-her-name—Suja. We'll make it yet!"

"Yes, sir," Wade agreed. His grandfather was elated, as he always was when another addition arrived to the colony, and maybe this morning he would let Wade alone, let him escape the usual . . . Quickly he began eating.

Thekla finished strapping her baby into a tall wooden chair, and began putting food on her five-year-old's plate. The little girl was rhythmically kicking her heels against the legs of the rough wooden bench, and the old man frowned.

"Stop that, Malki, right now! A Strickland is reverent when grace is said, remember that!"

Damn. No escape after all.

The grandfather swept his gaze around the table to make sure the four of them all folded their hands and bowed their heads. Thekla's baby stared at him soberly.

"Earth, let us see you once again, green and blooming, if it is possible. If not—" there was always an agonized pause here, and Wade wondered what awful scenes of desolation howled in his grandfather's mind, "—if not, then let us see your offspring, New Earth, and carry to her a loyal band of colonists to help prepare for the Return. If even that is not possible—" again than anguished quaver, "—then be sure that we will rebuild Earth here, preserving, above all, the great cultural traditions entrusted to us so long ago, and someday carrying them ourselves to the stars!"

Wade caught Thekla's eye out of the corner of his own; she smiled faintly and shook her head. Malki piped, "What's a star, Great-Grandfather?"

The rheumy old eyes glared at her fiercely. "You asked that yesterday, Malki, and I told you then. It's a big ball of fire in the sky that makes light and heat."

The child looked at the stone fireplace, where a fire was kept constantly against the pervasive damp of the fog. She opened her mouth, her eyes full of doubt, glanced at her great-grandfather's glowering face, and said instead, "I caught a non-frog."

"Did you now?" the grandfather asked, amusement replacing annoyance with the fitfulness of the old, and the adults around the table relaxed. "And what did you do with him?"

"Oh, I let him go. He was pretty, though. He was tlem."

"What?" asked the grandfather, puzzled.

"What did the non-frog say, Malki?" Thekla asked hastily.

"He went like this: kee-day, kee-day, kee-day!" The high, childish voice piped such a close imitation that even the grandfather, smiled.

"After breakfast, I'll show you a picture of a real frog, Child, in the Book. It was painted long ago, by a man called Nussivera." He glanced lovingly at the wall, where five well-worn books were enthroned. *History of Western Art*; Petyk's *A Thousand Years of Painting,* now cannibalized to provide the pictures on the walls; *Complete Shakespeare*; the Bible; and a dubious novel popular fifty-three years before, *Love Until the Sky Falls*. The five books that had been shelved on the rear observation deck when the Emergency Landing deteriorated into the Crash.

On a little carved bracket, set well enough below the shelf to make even the remote chance of fire impossible, a candle burned day and night.

"What's a real frog, Grandfather?"

"It's a small green amphibian. It looks a little like a non-frog, but it goes 'ribbit-ribbit'."

The little girl's eyes grew round. "*Nothing* goes like that!"

Wade smiled. "Nothing that lives here, Malki. But, remember, Keedaithen isn't the only—" he stopped abruptly, groaning inwardly, knowing it was already too late.

His grandfather rose to his feet, trembling violently. "This is not 'Keedaithen!'" he shouted. This is 'Exile', and don't you forget it, young man! Exile! *Exile!* Not a home you give a name to! A 'home', this dingy, mildewed ... mildewed...." he broke off, his face flushed hectically, his eyes straining out of their sockets. Wade's mother hurried over to him.

"Sit down, Father, right here; it's all right. You shouldn't get that excited, you know it's bad for you, the boy didn't mean anything. . . ." Her eyes signalled for Wade to leave. He was half-way to the door when his grandfather's voice, wheezing and jagged, stopped him.

"Just a minute, boy. You think I don't know that you kept on with that stuff you call painting. The hell I don't—" wheeze, wheeze, "—carry on cultural heritage . . . must preserve—" wheeze, "—no composition or values or even geometric grouping. . . ."

"Now, Father, just sit quietly for a few minutes and you'll be all right. Thekla, bring a dipper of water. There, that's better, just sit still."

". . . perverting sacred trust. . . ." he began coughing hard.

Wade made his escape.

§ § §

All morning he hoed non-potatoes, savagely driving his hoe deeper than necessary into the spongy wet earth. In the afternoon he cut kirilwood, choosing trees set far enough into the ravines to require much heaving and pulling. By evening Wade's back muscles ached all the way to the base of his skull, but he felt that he had control enough of himself to return to the cabin. Still, he was aware that somewhere, deep inside, his resentment was only precariously banked.

The sunset damped it down a little more. He watched the fading light raptly, leaning on his ax, his eyes glued to the soggy clouds glimpsed through the mist as they shaded from gray to tlem to slate and all the way to a delicate kipney. The fog carried the mingled smells of rainplant, decaying wet leaves, and the pungent richness of cut kirilwood.

It won't all get into even this last painting, he thought with a curious mixture of gratitude and despair. No artist could get it all—not even me, damn it. The shaded softness, the grayness, the—the *rightness* of the way it looks just before dark. God, the world is so damn beautiful.

He shifted a little, gingerly flexing his cramped muscles, keeping his eyes turned upwards to the foggy sky, and the gray lichens beneath his boots crunched softly. He bent over and carefully scraped them off the rocks. What if he powdered them, maybe adding a little thinned river clay—would they mix into that silvery shade of tlem?

He began to whistle a wordless, excited little tune, unaware that he did so, as he intently rubbed the gray lichens into the back of his hand and squinted at the resulting shades. He didn't see the figure gliding through the fog until his mother materialized next to him.

"Wade? Are you all right?"

All his life, that had been her greeting—a tentative request for reassurance, made as though she questioned her own right to ask it. Incongruously, Wade thought of the three headstones in the little cemetery with "Beloved Child of Janice" on them, as well as that other one bearing the name of the man assigned to sire two of them and Wade himself.

"Yes, Mother, I'm all right." He half-held out his lichen-colored hand, then drew it back. Better show Thekla instead.

They were silent, smelling the wet air, watching the way the gray mist softened the tools leaning against the stone cabin. Simple tools, simply made; the improvisations of a pioneer society starting over.

"He's very old, Wade. You don't always remember that," his mother said abruptly. Wade said nothing, his lips pressed tightly. Somewhere among the rocks a non-frog shrilled: kee-day, kee-day.

"Eighty-three, by that reckoning system he insists on using." Her voice was softer now, pleading, amost apologetic. "Eighty-three, and the last one left. We can't know what it was like for them, Wade. Leaving behind them a world on the edge of war, taking all those books and art treasures with them to the only place of safety left, and then, after sleeping all those years—" he caught the little stumble in her voice, the psychological balk at hurdling the illogical concept, "—to miss it by so little."

"Oh, Mother, it's not so little," Wade said impatiently. "It's a whole planet away! A whole different world!"

His mother sighed. "I know it seems that way to us. But after they traveled all that way—nine 'light years'—" again that little stumble, "—being just one planet away *seems* like a little. I guess."

She stared at the darkening clouds, behind which were—somewhere—that just-missed Earth-like world, with its flourishing commemorative colony, New Earth. Behind them, too, was the sun, which the grandfather insisted they refer to as "Beta Hydri," and all the other unimaginable "stars." Wade fidgeted impatiently. If he mixed the powdered lichens with a little pale kipney—

"You know, when I was a little girl," his mother went on, "and all of the Five Survivors were alive, I would hear them have the same conversation over and over. I used to wonder why it was so interesting to them. Mother would wail about all the books and paintings that were destroyed in the Crash. Uncle Peter would shake his head and say how much they would have meant to New Earth. Then Father would brace his shoulders—I know you don't remember him strong and healthy, Wade, but I do—and say in a deep, artificial voice, 'If you were marooned on a desert island and could only take one book . . .' The others would laugh, but not happily, and Father would add, 'But we've got five of them. Well, four decent ones, anyway. A whole culture!' and then Aunt Alia would simper and say that it wouldn't have meant so much without a real artist and art historian like Professor James Strickland to help pass on that culture, and that even though New Earth had suffered his loss, it was Exile's gain."

Wade shifted his weight from one foot to the other. It was growing very dark. His mother reached up her hands and rested them on his shoulders.

"He's not well, Wade. He never leaves the fire anymore, and he can't bear to even look outside—and even close to the fire he coughs from the damp. And these scenes just upset him so. Yes, I know, you kept your temper this morning, but what about yesterday, or the day before? It can't be much longer. Please, Wade."

"Please what?" he asked through suddenly stiff lips.

"Please don't paint those gray-mist pictures anymore. Paint the way he needs you to."

"I can't!"

"Then don't paint at all. Please. I can say they need everyone for some harvest emergency or other; he can't keep track of the work any more."

Not to paint. Not to feel the smoothness of the whittled brush handle between your fingers, and the power flow down your arm, and the ultimate, wholly enormous satisfaction of the subtle shades drifting over the kirilwood board seemingly without even touching it and the. . . .

"Please, Wade. It means so much to him, this passing on of a heritage. It's all that's kept him going, that's carried him—and all of us with him, don't you ever forget that—this far."

Her face was completely obscured. He put out a finger and touched the worn cheeks, the skin still soft from the eternal damp but hollowed out, stretched tautly in the contours of a face that had looked steadily at backbreaking work and compulsory childbearing and the thin edge of survival every day of her life, with no space for the luxury of painting that was her son's inheritance from her labor.

"What about you, Mother?" he asked desperately, his voice cracking from its new deep tones upward into a childish wobble. "It's always *him*, everything's always *him*. What about you? Don't you have an opinion about it? What cultural heritage do *you* want me to have?"

She took her hands from his shoulders, and through the sodden darkness her voice was weary with all those weeks and months and years of unbroken work. "I don't know, Wade. I don't have one to give you."

§   §   §

He didn't paint. He harvested non-potatoes, and hunted the small, quick glarthen, and cut kirilwood, and didn't paint. He took his turn on the hand loom and helped roof the Ciegler cabin for the winter, and went on a foraging trip to haul rock salt, and didn't paint. In the mild autumn evenings he sat with the others by the fireplace and listened to his grandfather read alien, outlandish plays from Shakespeare or discuss the turn-of-the century Delineists. While his grandfather talked, Wade made himself keep his eyes focused on the trembling, liver-spotted hands that would never hold a paintbrush again.

Once, almost formally, the old man showed him a seventeeth-century Tohaku in the Book. It was a pine forest, seen through early-morning mist. "See," he quavered, "there's a fog, but the emphasis is still on the trees, the composition and values are preserved. Now if you would use your talent to do something like that, boy, instead of those formless, colorless blobs, it would be part of a great tradition!"

For a moment Wade saw everything red, an ugly livid red that made his body recoil even while his mind winced away from the knowledge that, coming from his grandfather, this was a peace offering. Peace, when it might be years—oh, God, surely not *years*—before he would paint again, and the old man kept on shoving those hard ugly drawings at him and he was probably going to live till a hundred and what kind of a person would *wish* for another human's death? What did that make him?

The grandfather was shrinking back on his bench, clutching the book and staring at Wade's face. Wade shook his head convulsively, saw his mother fearfully watching him from across the room, and managed to say in a voice that was almost steady, "I wasn't *trying* to paint the way a landscape looks in fog."

There was a long, painful pause. Finally the grandfather dropped his eyes; he hardly spoke to Wade the rest of the winter.

As winter wore on, the usual stretching of provisions began. Wade lost ten pounds and his mother watched him anxiously. In the longer evenings, desperate to put some object into fingers that seemed to constantly curve into the hold for a brush, he tried to help Thekla teach Malki to read. Malki had always come to him, hanging around underfoot and fiddling with his tools, but now she climbed into her mother's lap when Wade fixed her with his flat, tense gaze that seemed to see nothing.

§ § §

The spring came early. The fog lost its winter clamminess and chill, and smelled of new gray-green life and wet dirt. Wade, restless, took to long twilight walks, meandering aimlessly through the dank fog, refusing even Thekla's company. As he walked, he held his right hand firmly imprisoned in his left.

He returned one night well after dark. His mother watched him as he came in, looking as though she were going to urge him again to eat something, but he avoided her eye and climbed up to the sleeping loft. She sighed and went back to helping his grandfather touch up the colors in his Terran landscapes.

"More red in that, Janice," the old man was saying fretfully. "Can't you see it's too drab? The damn fog fades everything. It should be scarlet, or even crimson, damn it."

The loft seemed cramped and suffocating. Wade lay on his pallet and stared at the peak of the kirilwood ceiling, where a nonspider was spinning an intricate gray web. He tossed to his side and examined the weave of the heavy, dull blanket. He lay on his stomach and tried to bring sleep by sheer effort of will. At last he rolled off the pallet and slowly, his calloused fingers trembling a little, opened the little cupboard he himself had built under the low eaves.

They were gone.

A few chips of dried paint shimmered on the rough shelves. His brushes were all there, and the little dippers of the powders he had made, and one thin kirilwood board, painstakingly sanded but still as yet empty. But the paintings, all of them, were, unbelievably, gone.

"Mother! Thekla! *Malki!*" Wade clattered down the ladder, sprang at the child bent over her lesson slate. "Malki! You were in my things again! What did you do with them, where are they, oh my God—"

Malki squealed and ran for her mother. Wade caught her by the shoulders and started shaking her violently, like a rag doll. Thekla hit at his arms, screaming, and finally her words pierced the red mist in his brain.

"She didn't take them, Wade! She didn't take them! Leave her alone, you're hurting her! Wade! She didn't take them!"

He dropped Malki, who climbed, sobbing, into Thekla's arms. Wade straightened slowly, and slowly, leadenly, his eyes swung to his grandfather.

"No," he whispered, "you couldn't have."

The old man shrank back on his bench. "You weren't painting anything: you have talent only you just don't *use* it, boy; you have an obligation to the colony...," he began to sputter, his words slurring together as the quavering, cracked voice rose higher. "You *can* do it, but this damn stinking hell cast a spell on you, and they were holding you back, those other ones, don't you see I *had* to burn them! I had no choice!"

Wade took a step forward, woodenly, feeling his fists clenching themselves at his sides.

"... and who the hell d'you think you are, anyway?" his grandfather shouted, pulling himself up with his stick. "All of us ... obligation ... to cult'al heritage ... memory of Earth...."

"Memory of Earth!" Wade shouted. "My God, I hate the damned place! Earth! What good have your memories of Earth ever done but strangle us! This isn't Earth, it's Keedaithen, and you're just too rotten stubborn to admit it! But I won't go down with you, you hear me, old man? You destroyed my p-paintings." he bent over in a ragged, shuddering sob, then sprang, his face demented, to the fireplace. The grandfather tried to scurry behind the table, but Wade rushed past him. He grabbed the books from their homemade altar and hurled them, one by one, into the fire.

"This is what I think of Earth! My God, my God, all my work—" The Shakespeare hit the center of the flames and sent red sparks leaping. The Bible joined it a second later and the two of them, old and brittle, blazed passionately. *A Thousand Years of Painting* landed a little to one side and began to char, its edges graying ghoulishly.

The grandfather started forward with a strangled cry, his face dull purple, his eyes bulging fron their sockets. Wade began to claw at the walls, ripping the prints into tatters, hurling the paper fragments into the fire. The kirilwood landscapes, more solid, hit the back of the stone fireplace with a dull 'thunk'.

"And this damned memory, and this one, and this one! 'Cultural heritage!' 'Memories of Earth!' Damn the stinking place, it's probably nothing but a pile of rubble by now—"

The old man fell to his knees. Spittle covered his chin and his face was ashen, but he made no sound. He seemed to fall very slowly, his body twisting from the waist, like a feather from a kel bird and floating through the shifting fog, cutting secret little paths that soundlessly closed behind it. When he hit the stone floor there was scarcely a noise at all.

§ § §

The mist hung in dark gray curtains into the oblong hole, filling it, asserting first rights over the kirilwood box that would soon take its place. Wade stood a little apart from the rest, numb with guilt and unexpected grief, isolated less by any action of the others than by his own frozen immobility. A baby whimpered in its mother's arms, was impatiently hushed, and quieted.

Thomas, now the eldest colonist, stepped forward and began the service. He recited it haltingly, hesitating often, and when Wade realized why the man had to rely on his uncertain memory, he moaned softly, an inarticularte keening, unaware that he did so. Thekla put out her hand and gently touched his arm.

"As for man, his days are as grass ... and ... as a flower of the field, so he ... flourisheth."

His mother, dry-eyed, watched Wade anxiously. It began to drizzle.

"For the wind passeth over it, and it is gone, and ... and ... the place thereof shall know it no more."

The light rain fell on Wade's face, fragrant with the smell of new grass and wet slate. The frozen immobility cracked a little, began to break up.

Eighty-three years. 'He's not well, Wade. It can't be long.' And time passing, relentless as the squalling clouds, in the unimaginable light-years among those stars he only half-believed in, anyway. 'As a flower of the field.'

But there were no field flowers here, he thought haltingly. None of those garish, over-colored daisies or zinnias or roses in the Impressionist paintings that now existed nowhere in the world. And the wind never passed *over* anything; it got tangled in the mist and the clouds and made beautiful shifting shapes of its own.

Wade unclenched his fists and surreptitiously flexed his hands; the right one began to curve gently. There must be someone, he thought, either among these 48 or yet to come, who could see words as purely as he could see colors. Someone who could write a new funeral service—as well as sonnets, plays, celebrations, all of it—to fit here, and now, on Keedaithen.

THROUGH TIME AND SPACE WITH FERDINAND FEGHOOT—TWICE!

by Grendel Briarton

Here is another entry in the IA'sf *competition to determine, finally, if anyone can write worse puns than Dr. Asimov. Mr. Briarton is another member of the Oregon SF colony, having moved there from the San Francisco Bay area at the same time as his close associate, Reginald Bretnor, who is the editor of the unsurpassed symposium on writing SF:* The Craft of Science Fiction.

ON POACHING

"I'm so glad you've returned, Mr. Feghoot," said Queen Victoria, as they sipped Highland whiskey in her sitting room at Balmoral Castle. "We do have a *most* difficult problem."

"Och, aye," declared John Brown, her devoted Scottish gamekeeper and friend. "It's that domned poacher, ye ken."

"You mean you still haven't caught him?" asked Feghoot.

"Sir, the problem is we *have* caught him—that is, we ken weel who he is, and there's naught to be done about it. He's Sir Andrew MacHaggis, Lord Chief Justice of Scotland, and there's scarce a day when he doesn't shoot a good dozen of our cock pheasants. Then he hides the birrds in a hole in the wall, and comes here bold as brass to pay his reespects. He desairves to be shot, but ye canna shoot a Lord Chief Justice of Scotland."

"No," sighed the Queen. "Nor can we drag him to court like a common criminal. We must think of public opinion. Yet punished he must be. Oh, Mr. Feghoot, what shall we do?"

Feghoot thought for a moment. Then, "Your Majesty," he announced, "I have a solution of which I'm sure Prince Albert would have approved. You can charge Sir Andrew quite properly with male pheasants in orifice."

ON PRAYING

Had it not been for Ferdinand Feghoot's quick thinking, Sir Richard Burton would never have become famous as the first Unbeliever to reach Mecca, and his translation of the Arabian Nights never would have been published. Feghoot (who had made the trip many times over the centuries) kindly went with him, posing as a humble used-camel dealer.

As the caravan started out, the fierce desert sheik who was convoying it stared at Burton suspiciously. "Who is this man, Honest Akbar?" he demanded. "He doesn't look like a Moslem to me."

"He's a Pathan from faraway Hind," Feghoot told him. "That is why his appearance and accent are strange."

The sheik glared for a moment and galloped away, and poor Burton sighed in relief. Then, at the mid-day halt, when they were all called to prayer, he made his mistake. He threw down his prayer rug, and prostrated himself—not to the East, like everyone else, *but to the West.*

Instantly the sheik and his men were upon him, their scimitars drawn, shrieking, "Slay him! Slay the uncircumcised infidel!"

"Stop!" shouted Ferdinand Feghoot in the nick of time. "O Sons of the Prophet, he didn't do it on purpose! He's just Occident prone!"

THE SMALL STONES OF TU FU
by Brian W. Aldiss

*The author has been writing and
selling SF at an enviable rate since his
first sale, which appeared in 1954.
British by birth and current residence,
Mr. Aldiss describes himself as in the
travel belt: after Poland, Czechoslovakia,
and Ireland in 1976, he
visited the U.S.S.R. as a guest of the
Soviet Writers' Union, and is now preparing
for trips to Scandinavia and Italy. He
still hopes to get to China one day,
the setting of this unclassifiable tale.*

On the 20th day of the Fifth Month of Year V of Ta-li (which would be May in A.D. 770, according to the Old Christian calendar), I was taking a voyage down the Yangtse River with the aged poet Tu Fu.

Tu Fu was withered even then. Yet his words, and the spaces between his words, will never wither. As a person, Tu Fu was the most civilised and amusing man I ever met, which explains my long stay in that epoch. Ever since then, I have wondered whether the art of being amusing, with its implied detachment from self, is not one of the most undervalued requisites of human civilization. In many epochs, being amusing is equated with triviality. The human race rarely understood what was important; but Tu Fu understood.

Although the sage was ill, and little more than a bag of bones, he desired to visit White King again before he died.

"Though I fear that the mere apparition of my skinny self at a place named White King," he said, "may be sufficient for that apparition, the White Knight, to make his last move on me."

It is true that white is the Chinese colour of mourning, but I wondered if a pun could prod the spirits into action; were they so sensitive to words?

"What can a spirit digest but words?" Tu Fu replied. "I don't entertain the idea that spirits can eat or drink—though one hears of them whining at keyholes. They are forced to lead a tediously spiritual life." He chuckled.

This was even pronounced with spirit, for poor Tu Fu had recently been forced to give up drinking. When I mentioned that sort of spirit, he said "Yes, I linger on life's balcony, ill and alone, and must not drink for fear I fall off."

Here again, I sensed that his remark was detached and not self-pitying, as some might construe it; his compassion was with all who aged and who faced death before they were ready— although, as Tu Fu himself remarked, "If we were not forced to go until we were ready, the world would be mountain-deep with the ill-prepared." I could but laugh at his turn of phrase.

When the Yangtse boat drew in to the jetty at White King, I helped the old man ashore. This was what we had come to see: the great white stones which progressed out of the swirling river and climbed its shores, the last of the contingent standing grandly in the soil of a tilled field.

I marvelled at the energy Tu Fu displayed. Most of the other passengers flocked round a refreshment-vendor who set up his pitch upon the shingle, or else climbed a belvedere to view the landscape at ease. The aged poet insisted on walking among the monoliths.

"When I first visited this district as a young scholar, many years ago," said Tu Fu, as we stood looking up at the great bulk towering over us, "I was naturally curious as to the origin of these stones. I sought out the clerk in the district office and enquired of him. He said, 'The god called the Great Archer shot the stones out of the sky. That is one explanation. They were set there by a great king to commemorate the fact that the waters of the Yangtse flow East. That is another explanation. They were purely accidental. That is a third explanation.' So I asked him which of these explanations he personally subscribed to, and he replied, 'Why, young fellow, I wisely subscribe to all three, and shall continue to do so until more plausible explanations are offered.' Can you imagine a situation in which caution and credulity, *coupled with extreme scepticism,* were more nicely combined?" We both laughed.

"I'm sure your clerk went far."

"No doubt. He had moved to the adjacent room even before I left his office. For a long while, I used to wonder about his statement that a great king had commemorated the fact that the Yangtse waters flowed East; I could only banish the idiocy from my mind by writing a poem about it."

I laughed. Remembrance dawned. I quoted it to him.

> "I need no knot in my robe
> To remember the Lady Li's kisses;
> Small kings commemorate rivers
> And are themselves forgotten."

"There is real pleasure in poetry," responded Tu Fu, "when spoken so beautifully and remembered so appositely. But you had to be prompted."

"I was prompt to deliver, sir."

We walked about the monoliths, watching the waters swirl and curdle and fawn round the base of a giant stone as they made their way through the gorges of the Yangtse down to the ocean. Tu Fu said that he believed the monoliths to be a memorial set there by Chu-Ko Liang, demonstrating a famous tactical disposition by which he had won many battles during the wars of the Three Kingdoms.

"Are your reflections profound at moments like this?" Tu Fu asked, after a pause, and I reflected how rare it was to find a man, whether young or old, who was genuinely interested in the thoughts of others.

"What with the solidity of the stone and the ceaseless mobility of the water, I feel they should be profound. Instead, my mind is obstinately blank."

"Come, come," he said chidingly, "the river is moving too fast for you to expect any reflection. Now if it were still water. . ."

"It is still water even when it is moving fast, sir."

"There I must give you best, or give you up. But, pray, look at the gravels here and tell me what you observe. I am interested to know if we see the same things."

Something in his manner told me that more was expected of me than jokes. I looked along the shore, where stones of all kinds were distributed, from sand and grits to stones the size of a man's head, according to the disposition of current and tide.

"I confess I see nothing striking. The scene is a familiar one, although I have never been here before. You might come upon a little beach like this on any tidal river, or along the coasts by the Yellow Sea."

Looking at him in puzzlement, I saw he was staring out across the flood, although he had confessed he saw little in the distance nowadays. Because I sensed the knowledge stirring in him, my role of innocent had to be played more determindly than ever.

"Many thousands of people come to this spot every year," he said. "They come to marvel at Chu-Ko Liang's giant stones, which are popularly known as 'The Eight Formations', by the way. Of course, what is big is indeed marvellous, and the act of marvelling is very satisfying to the emotions, provided one is not called upon to do it every day of the year. But I marvel now, as I did when I first found myself on this spot, at a different thing. I marvel at the stones on the shore."

A light breeze was blowing, and for a moment I held in my nostrils the whiff of something appetising, a crab-and-ginger soup perhaps, warming at the food-vendor's fire further down the beach, where our boat was moored. Greed awoke a faint impatience in me, so that I thought, before humans are old, they should pamper their poor dear bodies, for the substance wastes away before the spirit, and was vexed to imagine that I had guessed what Tu Fu was going to say before he spoke. I was sorry to think that he might confess to being impressed by mere numbers. But his next remark surprised me.

"We marvel at the giant stones because they are unaccountable. We should rather marvel at the little ones because they are accountable. Let us walk upon them." I fell in with him and we paced over them: first a troublesome bank of grit, which grew larger on the seaward side of the bank. Then a patch of almost bare sand. Then, abruptly, shoals of pebbles, the individual members of which grew larger until we were confronted with a pile of lumpy stones which Tu Fu did not attempt to negotiate. We went round it, to find ourselves on more sand, followed by well-rounded stones all the size of a man's clenched fist. And they in turn gave way to more grit. Our discomfort in walking—which Tu Fu overcame in part by resting an arm on my arm—was increased by the fact that these divisions of stones were made not only laterally along the beach but vertically up the beach, the demarcations in the latter division being frequently marked by lines of seaweed or of minute white shells of dead crustaceans.

"Enough, if not more than enough," said Tu Fu. "Now do you see what is unusual about the beach?"

"I confess I find it a tiresomely *usual* beach," I replied, masking my thoughts.

"You observe how all the stones are heaped according to their size."

"That too is usual, sir. You will ask me to marvel next that students in classrooms appear to be graded according to size."

"Ha!" He stood and peered up at me, grinning and stroking his long white beard. "But we agree that students are graded according to the wishes of the teacher. Now, according to whose wishes are all these millions upon millions of pebbles graded?"

"Wishes don't enter into it. The action of the water is sufficient, the action of the water, working ceaselessly and randomly. The playing, one may say, of the inorganic organ."

Tu Fu coughed and wiped the spittle from his thin lips.

"Although you claim to be born in the remote future, which I confess seems to me unnatural, you are familiar with the workings of this natural world. So, like most people, you see nothing marvellous in the stones hereabouts. Supposing you were born—" he paused and looked about him and upwards, as far as the infirmity of his years would allow— "supposing you were born upon the moon, which some sages claim is a dead world, bereft of life, women, and wine... If you then flew to this world and, in girdling it, observed everywhere stones, arranged in sizes as these are

208   THE SMALL STONES OF TU FU

here. Wherever you travelled, by the coasts of any sea, you saw that the stones of the world had been arranged in sizes. What then would you think?"

I hesitated—Tu Fu was too near for comfort.

"I believe my thoughts would turn to crab-and-ginger soup, sir."

"No, they would not, not if you came from the moon, which is singularly devoid of crab-and-ginger soup, if reports speak true. You would be forced to the conclusion, the inevitable conclusion, that the stones of this world were being graded, like your scholars, by a superior intelligence." He turned the collar of his padded coat up against the breeze, which was freshening. "You would come to believe that that Intelligence was obsessive, that its mind was terrible indeed, filled only with the idea—not of language, which is human—but of number, which is inhuman. You would understand of that Intelligence that it was under an interdict to wander the world measuring and weighing every one of a myriad myriad single stones, sorting them all into heaps according to dimension. Meaningless heaps, heaps without even particular decorative merit. The farther you travelled, the more heaps you saw—the myriad heaps, each containing myriads of stones—the more alarmed you would become. And what would you conclude in the end?"

Laughing with some anger, I said, "That it was better to stay at home."

"Possibly. You would also conclude that it was *no use* staying at home. Because the Intelligence that haunted the earth was interested only in stones; that you would perceive. From which it would follow that the Intelligence would be hostile to anything else and, in particular, would be hostile to anything which disturbed its handiwork."

"Such as human kind?"

"Precisely." He pointed up the strand, where our fellow-voyagers were sitting on the shingle, or kicking it about, while their children were pushing stones into piles or flinging them into the Yangtse. "The Intelligence—diligent, obsessive, methodical to a degree—would come in no time to be especially weary of human kind, who were busy turning what is ordered into what is random."

Thinking that he was beginning to become alarmed by his own fancy, I said, "It is a good subject for a poem, perhaps, but nothing more. Let us return to the boat. I see the sailors are going aboard."

We walked along the beach, taking care not to disturb the stones. Tu Fu coughed as he walked.

"So you believe that what I say about the Intelligence that haunts the earth is nothing more than a fit subject for a poem?" he said. He stooped slowly to pick up a stone, fitting his other hand in the small of his back in order to regain an upright posture. We both stood and looked at it as it lay in Tu Fu's withered palm. No man had a name for its precise shape, or even for the fugitive tints of cream and white and black which marked it out as different from all its neighbours. Tu Fu stared down at it and improvised an epigram.

> "The stone in my hand hides
> A secret natural history:
> Climates and times unknown,
> A river unseen."

I held my hand out. "You don't know it, but you have released that stone from the bondage of space and time. May I keep it?"

As he passed it over, and we stepped towards the refreshment-vendor, Tu Fu said, more lightly, "We take foul medicines to improve our health; so we must enterain foul thoughts on occasion, to strengthen wisdom. Can you nourish no belief in my Intelligence—you, who claim to be born in some remote future—which loves stones but hates human kind? Do I claim too much to ask you to suppose for a moment that I might be correct in my supposition. . ." Evidently his thought wandered slightly, for he then said, after a pause, "Is it within the power of one man to divine the secret nature of the world, or is even the whisper of that wish a supreme egotism, punishable by a visitation from the White Knight?"

"Permit me to get you a bowl of soup, sir."

The vendor provided us with two mats to lay over the shingle. We unrolled them and sat to drink our crab-and-ginger soup. As he supped, with the drooling noises of an old man, the sage gazed far away down the restless river, where lantern sails moved distantly towards the sea, yellow on the yellow skyline. His previously cheerful, even playful, mood had slipped from him; I could perceive that, at his advanced age, even the yellow distance might be a reminder to him—perhaps as much reassuring as painful—that he soon must himself journey to a great distance. I recited his epigram to myself. "Climates and times unknown, A river unseen."

Children played round us. Their parents, moving slowly up the gangplank on to the vessel, called to them. "Did you like the giant stones, venerable master?" one of the boys asked Tu Fu, cheekily.

"I like them better than the battles they commemorate," replied Tu Fu. He stretched out a papery hand, and patted the boy's shoulder before the latter ran after his father. I had remarked before the way in which the aged long to touch the young.

We also climbed the gangplank. It was a manifest effort for Tu Fu.

Dark clouds were moving from the interior, dappling the landscape with moving shadow. I took Tu Fu below, to rest in a little cabin we had hired for the journey. He sat on the bare bench, in stoical fashion, breathing flutteringly, while I thought of the battle to which he referred, which I had paused to witness some centuries earlier.

Just above our heads, the bare feet of the crew pattered on the deck. There was a prolonged creaking as the gangplank was hoisted, followed by the rattle of the sail unfolding. The wind caught the boat, every plank of which responded to that exhalation, and we started to glide forward with the Yangtse's great stone-shaping course towards the sea. A harmony of motion caused the whole ship to come alive, every separate part of it rubbing against every other, as in the internal workings of a human when it runs.

I turned to Tu Fu. His eyes went blank, his jaw fell open. One hand moved to clutch his beard and then fell away. He toppled forward—I managed to catch him before he struck the floor. In my arms, he seemed to weigh nothing. A muttered word broke from him, then a heavy shuddering sigh.

The White Knight had come, Tu Fu's spirit was gone. I laid him upon the bench, looking down at his revered form with compassion. Then I climbed upon deck.

There the crowd of travellers was standing at the starboard side, watching the tawny coast roll by, and crying out with some excitement. But they fell silent, facing me attentively when I called to them.

"Friends, " I shouted. "The great and beloved poet Tu Fu is dead."

A first sprinkle of rain fell from the west, and the sun became hidden by cloud.

Swimming strongly on my way back to what the sage called the remote future, my form began to flow and change according to time pressure. Sometimes my essence was like steam, sometimes like a mountain. Always I clung to the stone I had taken from Tu Fu's hand.

Back. Finally I was back. Back was an enormous expanse yet but a corner. All human kind had long departed. All life had disappeared. Only the great organ of the inorganic still played. There I could sit on my world-embracing beach, eternally arranging and grading pebble after pebble. From fine grit to great boulders, they could all be sorted as I desired. In that occupation, I fulfilled the pleasures of infinity, for it was inexhaustible.

But the small stone of Tu Fu I kept apart. Of all beings ever to exist upon the bounteous face of this world, Tu Fu had been nearest to me—I say 'had been', but he forever *is*, and I return to visit him when I will. For it was he who came nearest to understanding my existence by pure divination.

Even his comprehension failed. He needed to take his perceptions a stage further and see how those same natural forces which create stones also create human beings. The Intelligence that haunts the earth is not hostile to human beings. Far from it—I regard them with the same affection as I do the smallest pebble.

Why, take this little pebble at my side! I never saw a pebble like that before. The tint of this facet, here—isn't that unique?

I have a special bank on which to store it, somewhere over the other side of the world. Only the little stone of Tu Fu shall not be stored away; small kings commemorate rivers, and this stone shall commemorate the immortal river of Tu Fu's thought.

A SECOND SOLUTION TO THE DEFECTIVE DOYLES
(from page 125)

From the six cans remove 11, 17, 20, 22, 23, and 24 doyles. Every subset of these six numbers has a different sum. This makes it easy to identify all defective cans in one weighing. For instance, suppose the scale registers an overweight of 53 milligrams. The only way to obtain 53, as a sum of distinct numbers in the set of six, is $11 + 20 + 22$. This shows that cans one, three, and four hold the overweight doyles.

POLLY PLUS
by Randall Garrett

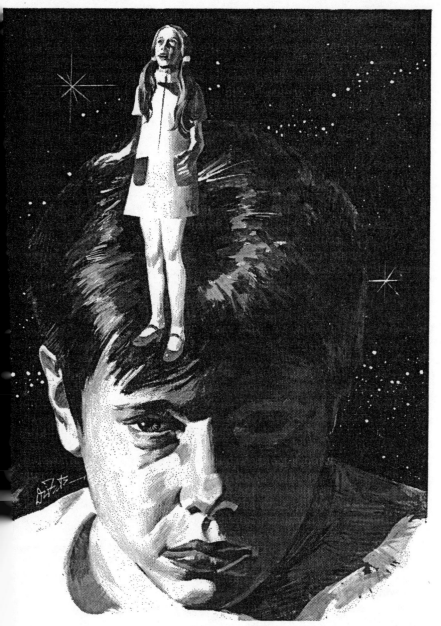

Mr. Garrett tells us that he is neither as young as Isaac Asimov nor as old as Harlan Ellison, but somewhere between the two. He wrote his first science fiction story when he was 14, and it was published in the old Astounding Science-Fiction *in 1944, after John W. Campbell had sat on it for years. By that time, the author was in the United States Marine Corps.*

By courtesy of the GI Bill, the author majored in chemistry, with minors in physics and math, at Texas Tech. After working in several industrial laboratories, he decided he'd get farther by writing. If dress suits for dinosaurs were a dime a dozen, he warns us, a BS in chemistry would buy a bow tie for a bumblebee. Like the Good Doctor, he would rather write about science than do it.

It wasn't the first clue I had, but it was the incident of the parrot that first got me to really thinking about Willy.

Everyone always asks me about Dawn Kelley as soon as they find out that I am the Janet Sadler mentioned in her best-selling autobiography. I can understand that; as her grade-school teacher, I am presumed to be an extraordinary woman myself because I helped to mold the childhood of a *truly* extraordinary woman.

Dawn Kelley has won three Oscars for the only three pictures she has appeared in, and for two others she directed. She had earned doctorates in medicine, law, and physics; and has made widely-acclaimed contributions to all three fields. Her television program has been in the top ten of the ratings for the past seven years. Everyone who knows her loves her, and she still looks a beautiful twenty-five, although she is only fifteen years younger than I, and I am over seventy.

Yes, Dawn Kelley is a remarkable woman, but everyone has read and heard about her for years. Instead of re-hashing old material, I would like to tell you about an even more remarkable person of whom you have never heard.

As I said, it was the parrot that really got me to thinking, but there were clues before that.

I was in my mid-twenties at the time; I'd only had my teaching certificate three years, and I was still naïve enough to think that four years of college and a year of graduate work had taught me all I needed to know about teaching. I was shy, I know, and I covered that tendency with an over-precise pedantry and an avoidance of emotional involvement with my students. I conceived of myself as a lofty being who knew everything—at least, everything that a child needed to know—and whose job it was to pour as much of that knowledge into childish minds as those receptacles would hold. I was, I fear, a rather stuffy prig.

It was Willy who gave me my first real comeuppance, but the fault was my own, not his. I had always disliked nicknames and diminutives—I still do, but I'm a great deal more tolerant now. When, on Willy's first day in my fifth-grade class, I asked each child to stand and tell me his or her name, Willy stood and said: "Willy Taylor."

"William Taylor," I said, by way of correction. Like a damn fool, I hadn't looked over the prepared roster yet. I had already corrected "Susie" to "Susan" and "Bobby" to "Robert" without repercussions, and expected none now.

"No, ma'am," he said with precision. "Willy. Doubleyou, eye, ell, ell, wye. Willy."

" 'Willy'," I replied with equal precision, "is a diminutive for 'William'."

"Yes, ma'am, sometimes," he said agreeably, "but not this time. Willy's my real name. It's German. You've heard of Willy Brandt and Willy Ley."

I had, of course. I was caught, and I knew it. I should have had sense enough to drop it right there, but my mouth was moving before I could stop it. "Are you German?"

Now what difference would that make? I had a David who was not Hebrew, a Marguerite who was not French, and a Paula who was not Italian; I hadn't carped at those. Because of my shyness, I was suddenly on the defensive.

"No, ma'am." Still polite. "But my name is."

By then, I had control. "I see. Thank you, Willy. You may sit down."

He did, and that was the end of it. But I remember it.

I sensed from the beginning that Willy was an intelligent child. His intelligence quotient, according to the tests, was 136; bright, but hardly brilliant. The transfer record from his previous school showed a nice B+ average. But almost from the very first I had the feeling that he was holding himself back, that he was trying to hide his real abilities. That sort of behavior is not as rare as you might think; the merely bright children show it in school and get themselves thoroughly hated by their duller classmates, while the truly brilliant child is wise enough not to be that offensive.

But Willy did the same thing in sports, which was overdoing it. At softball, touch football, volleyball, and the various track sports that nine- and ten-year-olds can play, he never ranked higher than second best, and never lower than fourth. He was trying to keep his B+ average.

Now that, I thought, *is ridiculous.* A boy might want to keep his mind under cover—no one likes being called "teacher's pet" or "bigdome"—but why do so at sports, where excellence is approved of, lauded, and looked up to by faculty and students alike?

I remember the basketball especially. You see, I lived right across the alley from the Taylors, and I could see the back yard of their house from my second-floor apartment window. His father had set up a basketball hoop on the garage wall, and the boy often went out there after school to practice.

No. Not really to practice. To have fun.

Do you remember how much fun it was to skip stones across a pond? Or to throw snowballs against the side of a house, just to watch them splash? You never missed the pond or the house, did you?

Willy had fun throwing at the hoop, always on the move. Underhand, overhand, one-handed, two-handed, or over his head, facing away from the hoop, it didn't matter. He never missed. Never.

Except when schoolmates came by to play, or when he was playing at school. Then he became merely very good. But not exceptional.

We have a term for that sort of thing in the teaching profession: underachievement. I resolved to speak to his father about it.

I never got around to it, of course. Mr. Taylor never came to PTA meetings, and, somehow, I never found any excuse for asking him to see me. It's hard to do that when a boy is, actually and really, doing very well in school. If he'd ever got in a fight—

I often daydreamed that Orville Goldman, a tease and semi-bully, would go too far with Willy some day, but he never did.

If Willy would only get caught smoking a cigarette or drinking a beer or—

But no.

Damn it, if he would at least tease Paula, or react to the way she teased him. She discovered a series of rhymes which tickled her not-too-bright little mind, a chant that went "Silly Willy, full of chili, has a face like a water-lily!" He responded by helping her with her math lessons, and the chant was dead within three days. And Paula's arithmetic improved.

And then came the parrot incident.

We had a "nature study" program (call it "biology," and some clot-headed parent will think you're teaching sex) at Kilgore School. A part of that program consisted of teaching the children how to feed and care for small animals. Ann Simons, who was in charge of the program, was an absolute genius at it.

One thing that it is important for a human being to learn is that other people hurt. One of the best ways, in my opinion, is to teach them that *all* animals feel pain. Small children are solipsists at heart; they don't know that those people out there are pretty much like this person in here. Particularly, children are unaware that an adult can be hurt. An adult seems too big, too powerful, to suffer. It takes a child time to learn that an adult can be hurt, both physically and emotionally, by a child.

Ann's theory—and I think it a good one—is to show this with animals.

"A little rabbit may not be able to talk, and he can't learn the things you can learn; but he can feel pain just the way you do, so you must be very careful. It's easy to hurt him because he's so much smaller and you're so much stronger. And even though he's small, he can hurt you, too, if you hurt him or tease him. If you're ever unlucky enough to have a rabbit sink his teeth in you, you'll know what I mean. I hope that never happens, because if it does it means you were hurting or teasing the rabbit."

She had many kinds of birds and small beasts: rabbits, white rats, snakes, chickens, ducks, and the like. Plus a few exotics: a kinkajou, an ocelot, a boa constrictor, and a parrot.

Named Jeremiah.

Jeremiah was Ann's personal property and a personal friend, and she'd had him for years. She had originally named him Onan "because he spilled his seed upon the ground," but she changed his name when she brought the bird to school because some parent might catch on to the joke. (I later found that Ann had borrowed the gag from Dorothy Parker.)

One of the phrases the bird had learned was "Woe is me," so Ann renamed him Jeremiah.

Part of Ann's program was to allow certain very carefully selected children to "borrow" an animal and take it home for a weekend. (Some were not borrowable; the kinkajou, for instance. You wouldn't believe what a kinkajou can do to your home!) It was something like borrowing a book from the library; the child was supposed to learn from it, and had damn well better bring it back in good condition. Mostly, they did.

But, there again, one had to watch out for the parents.

A white rat, bred for thousands of generations in the laboratory, is about as harmless as an animal can get. But there were mamas and papas who were horrified at the very *word* "rat"—to say nothing of having one in their home. Believe me, Ann Simons had to be a top-flight diplomat. She felt obliged to teach the parents as well as their children.

Willy Taylor was very good with animals. Ann said that his father must have taught him how to handle them from the very beginning.

"How about his mother?" I asked.

"Didn't you know?" Ann looked a little sad. "Mrs. Taylor—well, the way Willy puts it is that she 'went to a better world' right after he was born."

At any rate, it was because of his way with animals that Ann made the decision she did.

Willy, you see, was particularly fond of Jeremiah, and the bird seemed fond of him. A big green parrot can be dangerous; that beak could take off the end of a child's finger if the bird put power in it. Jeremiah had no record of that sort of behavior, but Ann was reluctant to loan him out. She had never really put him on the "non-circulating" list, like the kinkajou or the ocelot, but she usually convinced a child that another animal would be more suitable. Somehow, she wasn't able to resist Willy; and one fine spring Friday afternoon, Willy, with his father's permission, took Jeremiah home for the weekend.

Saturday afternoon, I was sitting at home, near the living room window, reading a book on child psychology. (I forget the title and the name of the author, but I remember being convinced that the psychologist hadn't been anywhere near a living child for forty years.) I had opened the window to enjoy the cool westerly breeze and the fragrances it carried with it: the sweet scent of the blooming lemon bushes beneath my window; the tangy smell of cut grass; the mouth-watering aroma of Mrs. Jackson's homemade bread.

Once, as I glanced out, I noticed Willy in his back yard playing with Jeremiah. Their voices came clearly.

"Hello, Jeremiah, hello."

"Hello. Hello. Yawwwk! Hello."

The bird's wings had been clipped, and he had a leather collar around one leg, attached to a long leash, so it was perfectly safe to let him wander around on the fenced-in lawn of the back yard.

"Jeremiah! Yawwk! Silly bird! Silly bird! Yaawwk!"

Wishing I could go out and play on such an afternoon, I went back to my book. The parrot-boy talk went on, but I ignored it.

A chapter or so later, though, Willy's voice penetrated my block.

"Dad! How come Jeremiah can talk, but can't *really* talk?"

I looked out the window and listened carefully. The father's answer to a question like that would tell me a great deal about the man.

I couldn't see him; he was inside the house. But his low tenor voice carried well through the open window.

"You mean he can't carry on a conversation?"

"Yeah, that's right," Willy agreed.

"Well, Jeremiah's brain is something like a tape recorder that's attached to a simple computer. A tape recorder can talk, but it can't think. Jeremiah can't think, either, not like you and I can, but his little computer can make certain responses to certain input signals and come out with recorded sounds."

"Oh, I see. Yeah, that makes sense. Thanks, Dad."

"Any time."

"Yaawwk! What time is it? Eight bells and all's well!"

Remarkable! I found myself liking Mr. Taylor very much.

But I went back to my book.

It must have been well over an hour later that I heard the screaming.

I want to say here that I am fond of cats. I have always lived with at least one, and the sad part is that I have outlived so many of them. The one I had then—Tamantha, I believe it was—was curled up on my lap at the time. In general, cats are nice people.

But there are exceptions.

The big orange tom was one of them. Nobody knew who he belonged to; he'd hang around the neighborhood for a few days, then disappear for a while. He was feral, and he was mean. He only had three things on his mind, and the other two were food and fighting.

When I heard the screaming, I think I knew it was Orange Tom before I looked up.

I almost screamed, myself. All I saw was a flurry of fur and feathers.

What happened took place in far less time than it takes to tell it. The cat had evidently come over the fence and decided that Jeremiah was good for at least two of the things on his mind.

The screaming was from both of them. Jeremiah was fighting back, beak and claw. But he was no match for that big tom. Then Willy came slamming out of the back door, adding his scream to the others, and running straight toward the combat.

He handled it beautifully. If he had tried to kick the two apart, or, worse, pull them apart with his hands, there might have been far worse damage done. He didn't; instead, he came down solidly on Orange Tom's tail with his right foot. It is difficult to step on a cat's tail if he's wary, but Orange Tom was preoccupied.

Not for long. He let go of the bird and turned. As he was turning, Willy let up on the tail, drew back, and kicked.

It was lovely. He didn't kick the way you'd kick a football, with the toe. Even under pressure like that, he did not want to hurt the cat. His instep caught Orange Tom right under the belly, lifting him in a high arc that took him clear over the fence. He landed neatly, as cats do, and vanished in an orange streak.

But Jeremiah was an unmoving mop of green feathers.

By that time, Mr. Taylor had come out, less than a second after the boy. Willy knelt down by Jeremiah, not touching him.

"Dad! He's dead! That damn cat killed Jeremiah!"

I had never heard Willy swear before. Under the circumstances, I didn't blame him.

I didn't hear what Mr. Taylor said. His voice was too soft, too gentle to be intelligible at that distance.

During those several seconds, I had stood frozen at the wondow, not even realizing that I had unceremoniously dumped Tamantha off my lap when I stood up. She had leaped to the window sill and was looking out to see what all the fuss was about.

Then I realized something. I had an excuse to go over to the Taylor house! The fight wasn't exactly the one I had envisioned, but it was certainly school business, and I had been a witness.

I changed clothes quickly; shorts and halter are not for a teacher who is visiting a parent.

By the time I had gone down the block, around the end at Dillon Street, and back up to the Taylor House, ten minutes or so had passed. I went up the walk to the porch and pushed the door-bell button.

The man who opened the door was tall, like his son, and had one of the strongest faces I have ever seen. He was not really handsome, but there was character there. Strength, compassion, and a touch of deep-seated sadness which even his smile did not erase.

"Yes?"

"I—I'm Janet Sadler. One of Willy's teachers." I suddenly felt very awkward and foolish. "I—uh—I live just across from your back yard. I saw—what happened."

"I see." His smile faded a little, but did not vanish. "Will you come in, Miss Sadler?"

By that time, Willy was at the door. He had a grin on his face of sheer happiness. I was momentarily shocked.

"He's all right, Miz Sadler! Jeremiah's all right! Dad fixed him!" He looked up at his father. "Dad, will you teach me how to fix things like that?"

"Certainly, Willy," Mr. Taylor said. He was still looking at me. "Jeremiah wasn't really hurt at all, Miss Sadler. He's fine. Mostly shock, I think. Not a scratch on him."

"My God!" I said. "*Really*? It looked to me as though he'd been torn to bits."

"Come see," he said. "He's lost a few feathers and, for a while, his dignity, but he's in perfect health."

He led me into a pleasant living room. Jeremiah was preening himself on the crossbar of the wooden T-stand that was his perch. He looked great. I just stared.

"Say something, Jeremiah," Mr. Taylor said.

"Jeremiah! Yawwwk! Silly bird! Silly bird!"

I got over my shock. "Well, he certainly seems all right. I'm very glad. Mrs. Simons would have had a fit if something had happened to Jeremiah. Are you sure we shouldn't take him to a veterinarian?"

"We can if you want, but I don't think he'll find a thing wrong with the bird."

"I really think we should," I said.

And we did. There wasn't a thing the doctor could find wrong with Jeremiah.

As we were driving back, I realized that Willy had said nothing for a long time. I thought I knew why.

He was in the back seat with the parrot; I was in the front with his father. "Willy," I said without looking at him, "I don't think we need to say anything to Mrs. Simons about this. Jeremiah wasn't hurt, and it wasn't your fault. But if we tell Mrs. Simons, it will make her worry and she'll be unhappy. Of course, if she asks either of us, we'll have to tell the truth, but I don't see why she should, do you?"

"No, ma'am. Thank you."

"That's very good of you, Miss Sadler," his father said. "I wouldn't like the boy to lose his borrowing privileges. And next time, there'll be no leaving an animal in the back yard unguarded, will there, son?"

"No, *sir!* I promise. Next time I need a drink of water, I'll bring whatever it is in with me."

"That's fine." He gave me a quick glance and then looked back out the windshield. "He'll keep his word."

"I know," I said.

It wasn't until he drove me up to the front door of my apartment building that I realized I hadn't said a word about Willy's underachievement. It was far too late then.

Twelve days later, on a Thursday, Ann Simons came into my classroom after the children had been dismissed for the day. She looked worried.

"Janet, are you particularly busy right now?"

"No," I told her, "I was just getting ready to go home."

"Have you got a few minutes? Jeremiah's behaving—well, *peculiarly.*"

I know that one's heart does not literally leap into one's throat at a time like that, but it certainly feels like it.

I got up from my desk. "All the time in the world. What do you mean 'peculiarly'? Is he sick?"

"Nnnno—not sick. Come along, I'd rather show you."

She led me into the nature study section, and I followed, worried. If there was something wrong with the bird, I'd have to tell her what had happened nearly two weeks before—and that would be embarrassing.

Jeremiah was sitting on his perch, looking jauntily around. He speared us with a bright eye.

"Yawk! Good morning, Miz Simons!"

Ann said, "What time is it?"

"What time is it? Five of twelve. Yaawwwk! Lunchtime in five minutes. Be patient."

"Where does the kinkajou come from?"

"Where does the kinkajou come from? Does anybody know? Yawwk. I think it comes from South America, Miz Simons."

I wish I had a hologram of my face at that moment. Or, rather, a flat photo; there were no pocket holo cameras in those days.

Ann went over to the cage where Flower, the denatured skunk, was watching with evident interest. "Name this animal, Jeremiah."

Jeremiah eyed it carefully, looked around the room, then looked back at Flower. *"Skunk. Mephitis mephitis. A carnivorous mammal which lives mostly on other small mammals, birds' eggs, and insects. Yawk."*

I think I was actually frightened. My mouth felt dry.

Ann said, "Janet, you know the question everybody asks a parrot. Ask him."

It took me a moment to find my voice. I looked at the bird and said: "Polly wanna cracker?"

He looked at me speculatively. Momentarily the nictitating lid filmed his eye. Then, distinctively: *"Graham, fire, or Georgia?"*

I looked at Ann. Now I *knew* that I was frightened. "Ann, can that damned bird *think?*"

"Think?" said Jeremiah. *"Think, children, think! Yaawwwk!"*

"Let's go to the teacher's lounge," Ann said quietly. "There's still some coffee in the urn."

Neither of us said another word until we were seated in a couple of soft chairs with mugs of hot, black coffee in our hands. Then I said, "Well? *Does* he think?"

She frowned a little. "Well, yes. All animals do, to a limited degree. They have to reason, to make decisions. The chimpanzee experiment at the University of California at Santa Barbara showed that chimps can carry on a conversation—a real, if limited, conversation—even if they can't talk. They use plastic symbols instead of words, but they can communicate.

"And that's the difference, Janet. Jeremiah can't communicate with us."

"It certainly sounded like it to me," I said flatly.

She shook her head. "I don't think so. A bird just doesn't have the brain for that sort of thing. A bird's brain isn't connected up that way. Oh, they can communicate with each other. The best examples are in the crow family—ravens, jays, jackdaws, magpies—that bunch. The parrots are halfwits in comparison."

"That little chit-chat we were just having with Jeremiah didn't sound halfwitted to me," I said.

"*Sound* like it," Ann said. "That's the clue, you see. A parrot's brain can be compared to—"

"To a tape recorder connected to a computer," I said.

She tried to keep from looking surprised, and almost succeeded. "Yes, that's—that's very appropriate. Look; suppose you're an actor who wants to memorize a part in a play. You could read all the other parts into a tape recorder, leaving properly timed blanks for the part you were trying to memorize. Then you practice, and memorize your part. By the time you get through, it'll *sound* like you were having a conversation with your recorder.

"Now carry it one step further and connect in a computer that can recognize any of the lines you deliver, pick out the appropriate response from the tape, and play it back. Make up a sufficiently long list of statements and responses, and it will sound like a conversation, possibly a very sophisticated one."

"And that's all Jeremiah's doing?"

"I think so." She grinned oddly. "God, I *hope* so." She took a sip of her coffee. "So far, that's what it seems to be. Every one of the answers he gave was something he had heard in class—word for word."

"Even that part about the crackers?" I asked.

She chuckled. "No, I tried to teach him that one a year or so ago, but it didn't seem to take. He apparently dug it up out of his memory." She grew more serious.

"What makes that sort of thing sound so much like a conversation is that most conversations you hear *are* just that sort of thing. Somebody throws you a line, and you give them a stock answer without having to think.

" 'Good morning, Ann.'

" 'Good morning, Janet.'

" 'How are you this morning?'

" 'Just fine. How are you?'

" 'Just fine. Lovely weather, isn't it?'

" 'Absolutely marvelous.'

"Hell, Janet, you can program a computer for a lot more sophisticated dialogue than that. There's a program now that will do Rogerian psychotherapy, using just that sort of system. It's so spooky that it scares people. Of course, you have to communicate by typewriter, but it still seems as though the machine knows what it's talking about. The thing it can't do is ignore or comment on nonsense, the way a real psychotherapist would. If you type in, "My head aches,' it will type back, "Why do you think your head

226   POLLY PLUS

aches?' But if you type in, 'My frammis pilks,' it will say, 'Why do you think your frammis pilks?' instead of saying, 'Your *what* does *what?*' the way a real person would do."

"Do you think Jeremiah could do that?" I asked.

She shook her head. "I don't think his internal circuits are set up for it. But I'm going to test that out. I'm going to take that bird home again, and I'm going to set up a testing program before I let him hear another word.

"I don't think he is any more a reasoning being than he was before. He isn't some strange super-parrot; he's got no more abilities than any other parrot. But he can certainly use them a damn sight more efficiently." She grinned at me suddenly. "I'm going to get the best tape recorder and the best movie camera, all the best equipment I can afford. If I don't get a doctorate out of this, I'll *eat* that bird."

I didn't tell her anything about what had happened to Jeremiah twelve days before, and I'm glad I didn't. She would have thought shock had something to do with it, and only God knows how many parrots would have had nervous breakdowns before she decided that line was a dead end.

Ann went to work on her project as though there were nothing in the world but her and that parrot. She didn't actually neglect the children, but they didn't get the extra attention she had given them before. She worked twice as hard, and I've never seen a tireder, happier woman.

It was late in May when the final incident occurred.

Little Paula ran across the street during recess to get a rolling ball. She ran between two parked cars, and the oncoming driver didn't see her until too late. It was almost a textbook case of that kind of accident. If the driver had been exceeding the twenty-five mile speed limit, Paula would have been killed instantly.

I didn't see it, thank Heaven; I was inside, grading papers. I heard the ambulance, but I didn't pay much attention; it was a block away, on the other side of the school grounds. The first I heard about it was when Willy came bursting into the room. There were tears in his eyes.

"Miz Sadler! Miz Sadler! Polly's hurt!"

"Paula," I corrected him automatically. "Calm down. What happened?"

He didn't calm down. "She got hit by a car! Her head's all smashed in and some of her bones are broken and she's bleeding and they won't let me fix her! They wouldn't let me anywhere near her! I can do it, 'cause my dad showed me how, but they wouldn't let me near her! Now they're taking her to the hospital and I asked could I come and see her and they said no I couldn't because I'm too little!" He stopped for breath.

"That's right," I said, "they don't let children into the emergency ward." I was more shaken than I let on, but I thought that by remaining calm myself, I could calm the boy down.

It was a mistake.

"You don't care either! You don't understand! Those doctors can't help you! Polly's gonna *die* if I don't fix her! you *hear* me? She's gonna die!"

"Willy! Calm down!"

"Please Miz Sadler! *Please* take me to the hospital! If I'm with a grownup, they'll let me in!"

I shook my head. "No, they won't, Willy. They wouldn't even let me in. Even her parents couldn't see her until she's out of Emergency."

"Then the next time they see her, it'll be to identify her body." His voice and his manner had changed startlingly. He was suddenly very coldly angry. "She'll go from Emergency to the morgue. I'm glad my education on this snijjort planet is nearly done." (That's as close as I can come to spelling the word he used.) "We're going to see Mother pretty soon."

I just gawped.

"Wait!" He felt in his pocket and came out with a small wad of dollar bills. "Yeah. I can make it." And he was gone.

I just sat there, not thinking. I didn't want to think. It's taken me nearly half a century to really think about it.

I think he took a taxi. I'm sure he got into the Emergency Room somehow, although nobody saw him. I'm sure because a miracle happened. Paula was back in school three days later.

A nurse who was a friend of mine said that the doctors reported that there was nothing wrong with Paula but shock, and they only kept her in the hospital for observation. But it was the doctors who were shocked. One minute, Paula was a smashed and dying thing. Then—something—happened.

The next minute, she was perfectly well.

They couldn't explain it, so they pretended, even to each other, that it hadn't happened. I can't explain it, either, but I think I know a great deal more about what happened than they did.

Mr. Taylor took Willy out of school the next day. The boy was having nervous trouble, emotional shock brought on by seeing the accident, he said.

They moved out the day before Polly came back to school.

I never saw them again.

Ann Simons finally got her doctorate, but it was for another study. Jeremiah was unique, you see, and the experiment, as well documented as it was, was not reproducible. He was a better parrot, the best parrot he could be.

After all, when you fix something that's broken, you fix it so that it will operate at optimum, don't you?

I don't know why Paula Kelley changed her name to Dawn, but there are times when I wish it had been I, rather than she, who had been hit by the car. And there are other times when I wonder if Willy loved *me* enough to break his cover.

THE SEVERAL MURDERS OF ROGER ACKROYD
by Barry Malzberg

The Good Doctor wrote to me recently, saying, "At the November writers' party we both attended, I spoke to Barry Malzberg and urged him to send us a story. He said he can't undertake to write stories with humor and clean language and so on. I said, 'I know that, Barry, but if you should happen to write such a story by accident, *why not send it in?' So he sent one to me, saying that he knew he should send it to you, but I was the one who asked. So I read it, and I liked it.—Would you therefore look this one over?" Well I did, I liked it too, so—*

Dear Mr. Ackroyd:

    Your application for the position of mysterist has been carefully reviewed in these offices.

    While there are many impressive aspects to your credentials and while we fully recognize your qualifications for the position of mysterist, I regret to inform you that the very large number of highly qualified applications for the few openings which do exist means that we must disappoint many fine candidates such as yourself.

    Rest assured that this decision is not intended as a commentary upon your abilities but only upon the very severe competition encountered during the current application period.

    Truly do we wish you success in all future endeavors.

Regretfully,
A. HASTINGS/for the Bank

Dear Mr. Hastings:

    I have received your outrageous letter rejecting

me for the position of mysterist. I demand more than a form reply!

If you have truly reviewed my application you know that I have dedicated my life to achieving this position and am <u>completely</u> qualified. I know the major and minor variations of the locked room murder, I know the eighteen disguising substances for strychnine to say nothing of the management of concealed relationships and the question of Inherited Familial Madness. I know of the Misdirected Clue and the peculiar properties of the forsythia root; not unknown to me are the engineering basis and exhilarating qualities of antique vehicles known as "cars". In short I know everything that a mysterist must know in order to qualify for the Bank.

Under these circumstances, I refuse to accept your bland and evasive reply. I have a right to know: why are you turning me down? Once I am admitted to the Bank I am <u>positive</u> that I can find a huge audience which wants something more than the careless and unmotivated trash that your current "mysterists", and I dignify them by use of that name, are propounding. This, then, is to your benefit as well as mine.

Why have I been rejected?
Will you reconsider?

Hopefully,
ROGER ACKROYD

Dear Mr. Ackroyd:

Because we received several thousand applications, many of them highly qualified, for a mere twenty-five vacancies for mysterists in the Interplanetary Program Entertainment Division for the period commencing in Fourthmonth 2312, it was necessary for us to use a form reply. This letter, however, is personally dictated.

I am truly sorry that you are taking rejection so unpleasantly. No insult was intended nor were aspersions cast upon your scholarly command of the mysterist form, which does indeed appear excellent.

Your application was carefully reviewed. In many ways you have talent and promise is shown. But because of extraordinarily heavy competition for the limited number of banks, applications even more qualified than your own were rejected. As you know, the majority of the Interplanetary Program Entertainment Division channels are devoted to westernists, sexualists, gothickings, and science-fictionists with only a relatively few number of mysterists to accommodate the small audience still sympathetic to that form. At present all twenty-five vacancies have been filled by superb mysterists, and we anticipate few openings in the foreseeable future.

I can, of course, appreciate your dismay. A career to which you have dedicated yourself seems now closed. I remind you, however, that a man of your obvious intelligence and scholarship might do well in some of the other branches offering current vacancies. For instance and for example we have at this time an opening for a science-fictionist specializing in Venerian counterplot and Saturnian struggle.

If you could familiarize yourself with extant materials on the subject and would like to make formal application we would be pleased to forward proper forms. Just refer to this letter.

Sincerely,
A. HASTINGS/for the Bank

Dear Mr. Hastings:

I don't <u>want</u> to be a science-fictionist specializing in Venerian counterplot. We have <u>enough</u> science-fictionists, westernists, sexualists, and gothickings. They are all dead forms. The audience will wise up to that sooner or later and all go away and where will your Interplanetary Program Entertainment Division be then?

What they are seeking is fine new mysterists with new approaches. Such as myself.

I did not prepare myself for years in order to become a hack churning out visuals of the slime jungles. I am a dreamer, one who looks beyond the technological barriers of our civilization and understands the human pain and complication within, complication and pain which can only be understood by the mysterist who knows of the unspeakable human heart.

The Interplanetary Program Entertainment Division was, in fact, originally conceived for people such as myself, the great mysterists who would bring a large audience ever closer to the barriers of human experience. Hundreds of years ago mysterists were responsible for all of your success. (I have read some history.) Only much later did the science-fictionists and the rest move in to make a wonderful entertainment device a dull nuisance predicated upon easy shocks drained of intellection. The audience was corrupted by these people. But now a wind is rising. It is time for the mysterists to return to their original and honored place.

You would insult me by offering me Venerian combat science-fictionist! I tell you, you people have no sense of the dream. You have no heart. I have devoted my life to mastery of the craft: I am a good mysterist on the verge of becoming great.

I demand a supervisor.

Bitterly,
ROGER ACKROYD

Dear Mr. Ackroyd:

I am a Supervisor. All applications must be reviewed by a Supervisor before final disposition. Complaints such as yours reach even higher; I am writing you on advice. I am highly trained and skilled and I know the centuries-long history of the International Division much better than you ever will.

In fact, I find your communication quite offensive.

I fear that we have already reached the logical terminus of our correspondence. There is nothing more to be done. Your application for mysterist -- a position for which there is small audience and little demand -- was carefully reviewed in the light of its relation to many other applications. Although your credentials were praiseworthy they were surpassed by candidates more qualified. You were, therefore, rejected. Mysterist is a small but useful category and we respect its form and your dedication, but the audience today is quite limited. We are not mindless bureaucrats here, but on the other hand we accept the fact that the Division must give the audience what it wants rather than what we think it should want, and gothica and science-fictionists are what most people like today. We are here to make people happy, to give them what they want. We leave uplift to our very competent Interplanetary Education Division and they leave entertainment to us.

There is a tiny demand for mysterists.

If you do not wish to be a science-fictionist specializing in Venerian counterplot or to apply for other fine positions available as westernist, it must be your decision. We recognize your abilities and problems but you must recognize ours. You can give up and go to work.

A. HASTINGS/for the Bank

Dear Mr. Hastings:

I choose to ignore your offensive communication and give you one last benefit of the doubt. This is your last chance. May I be a mysterist? Do send me the proper authorization.

Reasonably,
ROGER ACKROYD

Dear Roger Ackroyd:

Mr. A. Hastings, Supervisor for the Eastern Application Division, Interplanetary Programming and Entertainment Division, has asked me to respond to your communication.

There are no vacancies for mysterist.

M. MALLOWAN/Over-Supervisor

Dear Hastings and Mallowan:

I gave you every chance.

You were warned.

As I did not see fit to tell you until now (having as well an excellent command of the deus-ex) I have a close friend who is already a mysterist although not as good as myself and who, for certain obscure personal reasons, owes me several favors.

234   THE SEVERAL MURDERS...

He has given me tapes; I have completed them. I have turned them over to him.

He has done with them the requisite.

I am already on the banks!

My mysteries are already available on the banks and I think that you will find what the reaction is very soon. Then you will realize your folly. Then you will realize that Interplanetary Programming, which I sought initially in the most humble manner and which could have had me in their employ on the easiest terms is now at my mercy. Completely at my mercy!

You are bent, as the science-fictionists say, completely to my will!

It did not have to be this way, you know. You could have judged my application fairly and we could have worked together well. Now you shall pay a Much Higher Price.

Wait and see.

Triumphantly,
ROGER ACKROYD

DIVISION: SEND ENDING ABC MURDERS. TAPE MYSTERIOUSLY MISSING. SEND AT ONCE. DEMAND THIS.

▣ Interplanetary STOP How did they get off that island QUERY Where is final material QUERY I insist upon an answer at once STOP ∆∆ +

DIVISION - THIRD REPRESENTATIVE DIVISION EASTERN DISTRICT DEMANDS KNOWLEDGE WHY POIROT DIED - REPEAT - WHY DID HE DIE QUESTION MARK NO FURTHER EXCUSES EXCLAMATION POINT COMMITTEE LICENSES PREPARED FULL ASSEMBLE TOMORROW FOR INVESTIGATION UNLESS MATERIALS SUPPLIED EXCLAMATION POINT

DIVISION: WHO KILLED THE INSPECTOR? ENDING MISSING. REPLY AT ONCE. MCGINNITY FOR THE PRESIDENT.

DIVISION - FIFTY-SEVEN MILLION NOW DEMAND ....

ON THE MARTIAN PROBLEM
by Randall Garrett

I am not at liberty to reveal whence I obtained the Xerox copy of this letter, nor why it was specifically sent to me rather than, say, Mr. Philip José Farmer, who would be far more qualified than I for the honor of putting it before the public. My duty, however, was clear, and with the kind co-operation of Dr. Isaac Asimov and Mr. George Scithers, it is herewith submitted for your perusal. The letter itself is written in a bold, highly legible, masculine hand. The heading shows that it was written in Richmond, Virginia, and it is addressed to a numbered postal box in Nairobi. The bracketed notes after certain of the writer's expressions were added by myself.

My dear Ed,

Since your secret retirement to Africa, we have had much less communication than I would like; but, alas, my duties at home have kept me busy these many years. It is, however, a comfort to know that, thanks to the Duke's special serum, you will, barring accident or assassination, be around as long as I.

I am sorry not to have answered your last letter sooner, but, truth to tell, it caused me a great deal of consternation. I fear I had not been keeping up with the affairs of Earth as much as I perhaps should have, and I had no idea that the Mariner and Viking spacecraft had sent back such peculiar data.

One sentence in your last letter made me very proud: "I would rather believe that every man connected with NASA and JPL is a liar and a hoaxer than to believe you would ever tell me a deliberate lie." But, as you say, those photographs are most convincing.

Naturally, I took the photoreproductions you sent to a group of the wisest savants of Helium, and bade them do their best to solve the problem. They strove mightily, knowing my honor was at stake. Long they pondered over the data, and, with a science that is older and more advanced than that of Earth, they came up with an answer.

The tome they produced is far longer and far heavier than any book you have ever published, and is filled with page after page of abstruse mathematics, all using Martian symbolism. I could not translate it for you if I wished.

In fact, I had to get old Menz Klausa to explain it to me. He is not only learned in Martian mathematics, but has the knack of making things understandable to one who is not as learned as he. I shall endeavor to make the whole thing as clear to you as he made it to me.

First, you must consider in greater detail the method I use in going to Mars. There are limitations in time, for one thing. Mars must be almost directly overhead, and it must be about midnight. To use modern parlance, my "window" is small.

At such times, Mars is about 1.31×10^6 *karads* [4.88×10^7 miles] from Earth.

I call your attention to my description of what happens when I gaze up at the planet of the War God. I must focus my attention upon it strongly. Then I must bring to the fore an emotion which I can best describe as *yearning*. A moment's spark of cold and dark, and I find myself on Mars.

There is no doubt in my mind that I actually travel *through* that awful stretch of interplanetary void. It is *not* instantaneous; it definitely requires a finite time.

And yet, for all that I travel through nearly fifty million miles of hard vacuum naked, or nearly so, I suffer no effects of explosive decompression, no lack of breath, no popping of the eardrums, no nosebleed, no "hangover" eyeballs.

Obviously, then, I am exposed to those extreme conditions *for so short a time that my body does not have the time to react to them!*

Consider, also, that the distance is such that light requires some 296 *tals* [262 seconds] to make the trip. Had I been in the void that long, I would surely have been dead on arrival. Quite obviously, then, when I make such trips, *I am traveling faster than light!*

There is, unfortunately, no way of telling *how* much faster, for I have no way of timing it, but Menz Klausa is of the opinion that it is many multiples of that velocity.

Now we must consider what is known to Earth science as the "time dilation factor." I must translate from Martian symbols, but I believe it may be expressed as:

$$T_v = T_0[1 - (v^2/c^2)]^{1/2}$$

where T_v is time lapse at velocity v, T_0 is the time lapse at rest, v is the velocity of the moving body, and c is the velocity of light.

The Martians, however, multiply this by another factor:

$$[(c-v)/(c^2-2cv+v^2)^{1/2}]^{1/2}$$

Thus, the entire equation becomes:

$$T_v = T_0[1-(v^2/c^2)]^{1/2} \cdot [(c-v)/(c^2-2cv+v^2)^{1/2}]^{1/2}$$

As you can clearly see, as long as the velocity of the moving body remains below the velocity of light (443,778 *haads* per *tal*), the first factor is a positive number, and the second factor has a value of +1. This, I believe, is why it has never been discovered by Earth scientists; multiplying a number by +1 has no effect whatever, and is not noticeable.

When v is exactly equal to c, both factors become zero; in other words, the moving body experiences zero time. Its clock stops, so to speak.

However, when v exceeds c, the equation assumes the form:

$$T_v = T_0(xi)\,(i)$$

where i is the square root of minus one, and x is a function of v.

If the second, or Martian, factor is neglected, it is obvious that the experienced time of the moving body would become imaginary, which is unimaginable in our universe.

However:

$$(xi)\,(i) = xi^2 = -x$$

In other words, if the body is moving at greater than the velocity of light, the elapsed time becomes negative. *The body is moving backwards in time!*

According to the most learned savants in Helium, this is exactly what happened to me. Indeed, so great was my velocity that I traveled an estimated 50,000 years into the past!

Thus, the Mars that I am used to has, in Earth terms, been dead for fifty millennia.

This explanation seemed perfectly sound when Menz Klausa first elucidated it, but suddenly a thought occurred to me.

Why did I always go forward *in time when I returned to Earth?*

For surely that must be so, else I could not be here today. If that formula I quoted were complete, when I returned the first time, I should have found myself a hundred thousand years in the past, in about the year 98,000 B.C. Considering the number of trips I have made, I should, by now, be somewhere back in the Miocene.

However, that, too, is explained by our Martian theorists. Another factor comes into play at ultralight velocities, that of gravitation field strength. At light velocity, this factor accounts for the gravitational red-shift of light when it is attempting to escape from a strong gravitational field, and the violet-shift when the light is falling toward the gravity source.

At velocities greater than that of light, the factor becomes +1 when the direction of travel is from a greater gravitation field force to a lesser one, and –1 when the direction is from a lesser to a greater. Thus, when I return to Earth, the negative time factor becomes positive, and I go into the "future" of Mars, which is your "present."

I trust that is all very clear.

Unfortunately, there is no way I can translate the gravity factor into Earth's mathematical symbolism. I can handle simple algebra, but tensor calculus is a bit much. I am a fighting man, not a scientist.

By the way, it becomes obvious from this that the Gridley Wave is an ultralight and trans-time communicator.

Another puzzle that the photos brought out was that they show no trace of the canals of Mars. And yet, Giovanni Schiaparelli saw them. Percival Lowell not only saw them, but drew fairly accurate maps of them. I can testify to that, myself. And yet they do not show on the photographs taken from a thousand miles away. Why?

The answer is simple. As you know, certain markings that are quite unnoticeable from the ground are easily seen from the air. An aerial photograph can show the San Andreas Fault in California quite clearly, even in places where it is invisible from the ground. The same is true of ancient meteor craters which have long since weathered smooth, but have nonetheless left their mark on the Earth's surface. From an orbiting satellite, more markings become visible when there is a break in the cloud cover.

Many modern paintings must be viewed from a distance to understand the effect the artist wished to give. Viewed under a powerful magnifying glass, a newspaper photo becomes nothing but a cluster of meaningless dots. One is too close to get the proper perspective.

Thus it is with the canals of Mars, long since eroded away, from your viewpoint in time. In order to see those ancient markings properly, you have to stand back forty or fifty million miles.

But what is going to happen to the Mars I love? Or, from Earth's view point, what *did* happen to it?

According to Menz Klausa, that is explained by one significant feature on the photos you sent.

Remember, even "today" (from the Martian viewpoint), Mars is a dying planet. Our seas have long since vanished; our atmosphere is kept breathable only by our highly complex atmosphere plant. Martians have long since learned to face death stoically, even the death of the planet. We can face the catastrophe that will eventually overtake us.

From Earth's viewpoint in time, it happened some forty thousand years ago. A great mountain of rock from the Asteroid Belt—or perhaps from beyond the Solar System itself—came crashing into Mars at some 24 *haads* per *tal* [10 miles per second]. So great was its momentum that it smashed through the planetary crust to the magma beneath.

The resulting explosion wrought unimaginable havoc upon the planet—superheated winds of great velocity raced around the globe; great quakes shook the very bedrock; more of the atmosphere was literally blown into space, irretrievably lost.

But it left no impact crater like those of the Moon. The magma, hot and fluid, rushed up to form the mightiest volcano in the Solar System: Olympus Mons.

And the damned thing landed directly on our atmosphere plant!

However, we won't have to worry about that for another ten thousand years yet. Perhaps I won't live that long.

Give my best regards to Greystoke. Your Aunt Dejah sends her love.

All my best,

Uncle Jack

A CHOICE OF WEAPONS
by Michael Tennenbaum

*The author tells us that he is a writer
and film teacher in New York City, a
resident of Brooklyn, and an avid
collector of all things trivial. He
also expresses concern that his
introduction might exceed the
length of this—ah—thing,
which certainly appears to be
the horridest pun yet.*

The lecture began seriously enough.

"Of course, the system was not always crime-free. Near the end of the 22nd Century, roving gangs of criminals made interspace travel quite dangerous. Historians are still fascinated with the ritualistic aspects of these gang wars.

"I am reminded of the story of the maimed Taurog who, while awaiting shipment of replacement limbs, was visited by the Clemmian who had wounded him (as was the custom). The Clemmians, you will recall, were fierce traditionalists, bound by the morals and methods of their ancestors. Their weaponry was, in fact, so archaic that it was a wonder to all that they were as successful as they had been.

"It was this point that bothered the Taurog most of all. After some minutes of idle small talk, all pretense of pride was dropped and the question that had hung in the air like a lead cloud was finally asked.

" 'What,' queried the Taurog, 'was that laser you sawed me with last night?'

"The Clemmian just smiled. 'That was no laser,' he replied. 'That was my knife.' "

LOW GRADE ORE
by Kevin O'Donnell, Jr.

The author was born 26 years ago in
Cleveland, Ohio, where he grew up.
He spent two years in Korea, one in
Hong Kong, and one in Taipei. Like many
writers, he's worked at a wide range of
jobs: groundskeeping, teaching English,
managing a dining hall, and various
positions in a hospital. He now lives in New
Haven with his wife, Lillian, where he
is working on a novel along with his
short stories—of which he's sold 19.

Nobody knew the teleport's name. Unless she'd come alone, her parents had also disappeared. Repeated appeals through the scratchy loudspeaker system had drawn no one willing to claim knowledge of her, much less a relationship. Perhaps they were peasants, fearful of reprisals if her identity were known.

By 14:49, the Director of the Calcutta Evaluation Center was answering the rapid-fire questions of fifty unruly newsmen. He spoke in English, probably to avoid accusations of regional favoritism. "Yes," he was saying, "we should be able to find it from her computer card, as we did on the three previous occasions, but—" He spread his dusky hands in dismay.

A cameraman from a local station lined his equipment up to frame the Director's pudgy figure with the ever-shifting colors of the Pukcip hologram.

"To the best of our admittedly limited knowledge, the child did present her card; the question now is, where has it gone? You must understand that immediately after she teleported to Pukci, at 13:46, there arose more commotion than the staff could cope with, yet—" as the photographer readied his video-tape camera, the Director, a political appointee, dried his forehead, "—I assure you, gentlemen, that as soon as conditions permit we shall cross-check all cards on file quite thoroughly, and—"

A little girl's desperate shriek froze everyone. The audience's attention shifted from the Director; he swayed visibly, as though brushed by a gust of wind. The camera whirred while its handler murmured clipped phrases of excitement into its microphone.

Between the straining reporters and the hologram stood the six-year-old whom the Pukcip screening had swallowed. Her hair was gone, shaved to the scalp; her dark skin was streaked and smeared with blood. She was naked except for wires that flapped from her wrists, her ankles, and her knobbly bald head.

They began to mutter. Was this what the Pukcip did to the children who precipitated out? Slowly, their hostility focused on the intermediary—

The child's second scream was ghastly in its inhumanity. It was the throat-tearing cry of a mortally wounded animal. Staggering towards them, she raised her tiny hands as though to beg their help.

A few in the front shook off their numbness, opened their arms, stepped—

Two Pukcip warriors materialized; the almost-saviors lurched back as if from a gout of flame. Each warrior held a gun in its

246   LOW GRADE ORE

posterior hands; each trained one stalked eye on the startled newsmen. Their anterior hands reached for the girl. She dodged. They teleported to either side of her. One seized her arms; the other, her legs. The one whose kaleidoscopic carapace was more ornate dipped its eyestalks at the crowd that had begun to press forward. An instant later, all three—warriors and child, aliens and human—had vanished as though they'd never been.

The heavy silence of shock hung over the room for an awful minute, then burst into a monsoon rain of anger. The Director was its center. Bodies shoved; voices shouted. His mouth worked frantically, but futilely, against the frustration that mounted like a storm's static charge.

"Gentlemen, gentlemen, please, this is no—" His fat hands waved in vain. He was the lightning rod; their hatred, a rising surf, needed a rock on which to break. A fist beat against his face, and then another. He gave one strangled cry before his final, fatal inundation.

Even as the white-helmeted police were cracking enough black-haired skulls to disperse the mob, a bruised witness described the cameraman. Through channels hypersensitive to bad publicity flashed the order to suppress the tape.

The station manager surrendered it, though he protested that the government should not obscure the truth, not when a thousand hugely distorted rumors were flickering like cobra tongues through the Calcutta slums.

His superiors, apparently confident that tempers ignited by gossip needed hard fact to sustain their heat, ignored him.

They were wrong.

Calcutta burned.

A step ahead of the flames worked a score of foreign agents, laboring to discover just why the uneasy peace had been shattered. One "cultural attaché" after another spoke to the survivors of the press conference; one government after another decided that it had to view the tape.

New Delhi, resisting their demands, insisted that it was a purely internal affair. In private and off the record, its distracted officials promised to distribute the tape once the civil disorders had ended.

Russian and American strategic analysts were skeptical. Oft-declared "states of emergency" had overprotected the Indian government from reality; it could not, they maintained, outlast an actual emergency.

Red phones buzzed; edgy leaders conferred. For once agreement came swiftly: they would force New Delhi, in the few remaining hours of its life, to relinquish the tape before it was buried under the wreckage of the regime.

The Indians were obdurate, at least until the fighters, scrambling off the carrier decks, made like a cloud of locusts for the subcontinent. The camel's back snapped; the tape was broadcast to the satellite network.

Televisions lit up policy rooms around the world; sweat dampened the shirts of the watchers. What if a teleport returned to Shanghai, or Los Angeles, or Rome? A tense, resentful public would lash out . . . possibly with the deep-gut fervor of Calcutta. Scrub as they might, the giant air machines couldn't filter out the stench of that fear.

Because if Calcutta was the rock, Wichita was the hard place.

On the afternoon of 23 June 1979, five hours after the then-President of the US surrendered to end the Two Minute War, the Pukcip had staged a demonstration on the Kansas plains. Their small expeditionary force had slammed into Wichita with more fury than any tornado had ever unleashed; their grim sweep missed but four of the town's three hundred thousand residents. The rest lay rotting in the corn-growers' sun.

When it was over, their Commander had pre-empted the nation's communication networks. As cameras inched over the dark stains on the carapace he'd refused to cleanse, he said through his interpreter: "You see now our seriousness. Do as you are told, and all will be well. Oppose us even lightly, and a larger city will suffer the same fate."

Like a dynamite blast in a coal mine, Wichita crumbled America's solidity. While the last twitches of the President's feet were reflected in the gleaming tiles of a White House bathroom, politician after politician hurried to add his frightened constituency to the swelling list of those that would follow orders. By midnight the country had committed itself to cooperation.

Two years had passed since the headlines, the half-masted flags, the muffled drumbeats on Pennsylvania Avenue. The impact had yet to fade. The annual tribute of four or five widely separated children was clearly the lesser evil. They went so quickly, so completely . . . they left no bones to be washed by the summer rains . . . one could almost pretend that they, and the Pukcip, had never existed.

The alien presence on Earth was nearly invisible: a small embassy at the United Nations, regular equipment deliveries to the many Evaluation Centers, and an occasional spot-check of children reported to have been tested. Scientists were prohibited from examining them; even diplomats met them only at lengthy intervals.

They were strangers, and clever conquerors. Importing no overlords, advisors, or enforcers, they presented no targets. Like Mafiosi handing their victim a shovel, they made Terrans do the work. Any rebellion would have to attack the governments that traded a few children's futures for many citizens' lives.

Any successful rebel would have to raze the Centers, would have to cut off the steady trickle of teleports to Pukci.

Any such interruption would invite Pukcip retaliation on a scale that would dwarf Wichita and utterly discredit the rebels.

The options seemed stark to most leaders: they could protect escaping teleports, and be punished; or they could do nothing, be overthrown, and then watch their populaces be savaged.

In the gray light of dawn, with the sun only a band of pink promise on the horizon, the President reached his decision. America would continue to cooperate with the Pukcip—up to a point. However, any returning children would find armed troops eager to defend them.

The men at the Cabinet meeting saw him hammer his fist on the long table, felt his agony of soul as though it were theirs, and shared his determination when he vowed: "No kid of ours goes to Pukci twice! Send in the Army."

§ § §

Colonel Mark Hazard Olsen, spine straight as a pine from his native Vermont, meditated in the passenger seat of the Jeep. The wind, the smooth humming roar of the motor, the dawn-dappled rows of abandoned buildings, were all locked out of his thoughts. His entire being sought serenity.

Yet the housefly flitting of Pukcip warriors refused to respect the pattern and the peace of his mantra. He forced himself to persevere, but after a few minutes more opened his eyes. Maybe later, once the bright plating of his hunger had been corroded by hours of forced alertness, he could try again.

At the moment, all he wanted to do was kill a few Pukcip.

Olsen had been a major during the Two Minute War. When the Pukcip squad had wink-blinked onto his post, he'd been dictating a new page for the MP training manual. Scattered shots had drawn him to the window.

His uncomprehending blue eyes had seen the bright shells of the Pukcip, had seen the running, falling, sprawling blurs of khaki. More shots: a pitifully few steady growls punctuated by flurries of single cracks that seemed always to end in astonished screams of pain.

Hanging out the open window, he'd watched his men race for the armory, where all the weapons except the guards' were kept under lock and key. The first to emerge had taken cover, were waiting for the enemy to come carelessly into range. There! The machine gun roared, its tracers leaping out to the—but the foe was already gone, had already shielded itself inside a squad of stunned GI's.

"NO GRENADES!" he'd shouted. "NO GRENADES!" The din was too great for his order to be audible, but his men didn't need it. They wouldn't hurl indiscriminating death into their own ranks, not even to kill the commingling aliens.

The phone had rung; an enraged General had had to scream, "Surrender, you damn fool!" four times before its import had sunk in. A word to his secretary, a frantic realignment of intercom switches, and his hollow voice, pregnant with feedback squeal, had echoed through the firefights.

Afterwards the clean-up, as integral a part of modern warfare as hot turkey on Thanksgiving, or cold beer on the Fourth. Three hundred GI's lay dead and dying; another five hundred were wounded. In the pools of blood, under the half-wrecked armory, were found four bullet-riddled shells. The Pukcip, as contemptuous of their own dead as of the human living, had left them behind.

Olsen, after wondering what to do with them, had decided to ship them to a nearby university. He'd taken the alien weapons—the post had specialists who could say if they deserved detailed study—and then ordered a dozen sullen GI's to load the death-dulled shells onto a van.

Before the van had cleared the gate, the news of Wichita had crackled through every radio on the post. The GI's, without communication or negotiation, responded to the same instincts. They'd parked the van on the parade ground.

Gasoline burns hot and quick; Pukcip horn merely chars. The billows of black smoke had drawn the survivors, who'd contributed wood, and more gas, and phosphorus grenades. A wasp-bitter helicopter had offered a load of napalm. And through it all the men had stood, helpless rage under the dirty sweat of their

250

empty-eyed faces. Among them was Mark Hazard Olsen, who'd waited till the last crisp curl of carapace had folded upon itself to give the order for bulldozed burial.

By then he'd been informed that his was one of the three US posts assaulted by the invaders. There had been no tactical or strategic reason for the attack—the motive had been psychological. Deliberately flaunting their ability to rain chaos on any defensive installation, the Pukcip had hoped to demoralize the military.

Their ploy had failed. Olsen had already started to work out tactics for the next engagement, tactics—the convoy jolted to a stop amid the potholes of a long-neglected parking lot; he dismounted and surveyed the old, two-story school building—which would be invaluable if the Pukcip came to Hartford.

§ § §

Ten minutes later, Walter F. Dortkowski, Director of the Hartford Evaluation Center, groaned aloud. The blacktop lawn of the commandeered school was littered with Jeeps, deuce-and-a-half's, and milling squads of soldiers. Cursing, he rammed his battered Volvo into his reserved space. Things weren't red-taped enough, they had to saddle him with the Army, too.

As he switched off the ignition, he brightened. Maybe the Governor, finally keeping her promise, had convinced the Army to take over. Maybe he could throw away his plasticized ID badge, break his clipboard over his knee, and go home a free man. God knew he'd tried to resign often enough before.

In July of 1979, when the Governor had named him Director, he'd accepted the appointment for two reasons, and on one condition. The condition had been that he'd step down within six months.

The reasons had been almost classically simple: first, a very important job had to be done with a minimum of time, money, and effort. Dortkowski, who had earned his MBA at Columbia before finding the fascination of educational administration, had realized—had been sweet-talked into realizing—that he could establish a better Center than any one else under consideration. The stakes had been too high for his hatred of the Pukcip to interfere. He'd felt—he'd been urged to feel—a responsibility to the public.

Then, once he'd truly understood—had been made to understand—how he could guarantee the safety of three and a half million people, the Governor had pulled out the plum: after six months of designing, implementing, and refining the evaluation system, he'd be named State Commissioner of Education. It would have been a wonderful 45th birthday present.

But difficulties arose. January, 1980: the administration could find no qualified successor, could he hold on for a few months more? Yes, he could. April, 1980: The Commissionership received too much exposure to be held by someone who symbolized Pukcip oppression; they'd find him another slot, but in the meantime . . . and the meantime became all the time, and the bars of inertia, animosity, and indispensability had grown around him like bamboo.

At last, I'm quitting! he'd declared, to the deputies and assistants and administrators who'd hemmed him in. He'd continued to say it; in the end, even to the Governor herself.

Warm sympathy had flowed across her face. Sadly, she'd told him she was sorry, she couldn't let him quit. She needed him too badly. And if he did just walk away from it, as he'd threatened to do, she personally had it in her power to make sure that he. Never. Worked. Anywhere. At anything. Again. And in her face had glittered the eyes of a krait.

So he'd stayed, depsite the vociferous hatred of people he'd never met, despite the pleas of his ostracized family. He'd stayed because he had no choice, because the Directorship—carrion-strewn plateau that it was—was his only pathway to the peak, and if he ever climbed down from it, they'd never let him near the mountain again.

Now, for the first time in months, a smile disturbed his sunken cheeks. Adjusting his tie, checking his frizzy gray hair in the rear-view mirror, he stepped into the early sun. Already the day felt hot. A shirtsleeve day. His small, neatly shod feet were light as he walked expectantly to the door. If he could transfer power quickly, he might have time for his fishing rod.

He might even get away before the first child arrived.

§   §   §

Someone was shaking Jonathan's shoulder. It was his daddy, telling him to get up. He pushed his heavy eyelids open, but it was still dark. That meant it was going to rain a lot, 'less it was real early. Gradually, he remembered. Today he'd be 'valuated.

"You 'wake, boy?" gruffed his daddy.

"Yowp." It was true, too. He sat up, feeling alive and excited all over. "How soon we leaving, Daddy?"

"Soon's your mama fix us some breakfast. Get dressed, now."

"Okay, I be quick." He slid out from under the much-mended sheet, and started grabbing for the clothes his mama had laid out on his dresser. "I be real quick, Daddy. Don't wanna be late for my 'valuation." As he pulled on his underwear, he puzzled over his daddy's wordless turn and hasty exit.

§ § §

Dortkowski stared into Olsen's face. Long and lean, dark from years of weather, lined by innumerable hard decisions, it was utterly impassive. Only two things hinted at the Colonel's feelings: the grinding of his teeth on the burnt-out stub of a cigar, and the ambiguous softness in his clear blue eyes.

"Sorry as hell to give you the wrong impression, Mr. Dortkowski," Olsen was saying. "We're here for one reason, and one reason only: to protect any kid who happens to come back from Pukci. We'll give you any assistance we can, but . . . we're not going to run your operation."

"It's my fault, Colonel." The words were very hard to get out. To be trapped in reality's field after free-falling through fantasy like a wide-eyed child . . . a glider pilot must feel the same, when he's lost the thermals and the ground is rushing up at him. "Thanks for, uh, letting me down easy."

He turned away. Hands behind his back, shoulders slumped, he entered the I-shaped school building. The place would consume him yet. Already it had cost him his friends, his reputation as a concerned administrator . . . what next? His wife? His life? Olsen had said his Calcutta counterpart had been torn to pieces by an enraged mob. That might be better. One white-hot moment of pure, unmasked hatred—despite the agonies of dying—might be preferable to years of uncomfortable silences, of embarrassed breakings-off.

Hand kneading his belly, where the ulcer had awakened with its usual rumbling torment, he trudged down the stem of the I. As he did every morning, he paused by the door that led to the memory-wiping machinery. That had earned him more abuse than anything else.

The test could be invalidated if the children knew what to expect, so the Pukcip had designed equipment to keep the already-screened from describing it to the untested. There had yet to be a single adverse reaction to the erasing—if nothing else, the Pukcip were unparalleled in neuroelectronics—but every mother despised him for exposing her child's mind to a callous alien machine.

The dials glittered in the slanting sunlight. If only the scales

were larger; if only the gauges measured months instead of minutes ... to go in, to strip his brain of its experience, to tear from it the skills that made him indispensable to the political establishment ... they'd have to let him resign, then. They'd have no use for a seventeen-year-old mind in a forty-six-year-old body ...

He unlocked the door to his office. The small cubicle smelled of arguments and dust, of hysteria and decay. He forced a swollen window up six inches, as high as it would go. Rubbing the neck muscle that had protested the exertion, he dropped into the chair behind his desk.

On the blotter lay a computer printout naming the 250 children who would pass through the building that day. The coldly efficient type face hit him like a slap in the face. Lowering his head to his crossed arms, he wished he could be as pragmatic about it as the Colonel was.

§ § §

Olsen was stationing his men just outside the projection room. His blue eyes, as if belying Dortkowski's assessment, held real anger whenever they glanced through the next doorway.

"They were too slow in Calcutta," he was telling his lieutenant. "They gawked like raw recruits while the Puks took the kid back. I won't put up with that kind of horseshit. The odds are against its happening here—that was Calcutta's third or fourth teleport, and this Center hasn't even had one yet—but if it does, so help me God, you'll either save the child or face a firing squad." He removed his cigar and spat out a shred of tobacco for emphasis. "Do I make myself clear?"

LOW GRADE ORE

"Perfectly, sir." The lieutenant was relaxed but watchful: he knew Olsen prized performance above all else. "Are there any limitations on what weapons we may use, sir?"

Olsen studied the dingy anteroom before replying. A touch of claustrophobia flicked him from a distance, warned him of the oppressiveness it could bring to bear.

The ceiling sagged in the middle; any significant explosion would bring it down on everyone's head. "No grenades." Even a firefight would weaken it, perhaps disastrously. "Sidearms and M-16's only." He'd have to risk it, no matter what memories it teased into life.

In 'Nam once, during his first tour on the Delta, he'd led a company of men into a subterranean VC arms cache. An observer silent in a treetop had pressed the button of a small radio transmitter; the plastique had gone up and the tunnel roof had come down. The memory of muffled screams, of tattered fingernails clawing at soggy earth, still haunted Olsen.

But now it had competition: the tape he'd seen over closed-circuit TV that morning would stalk his dreams for months to come.

"There's one advantage to this kind of confined space," he said to his lieutenant. "They won't be able to ride their carousel."

Films of the Two Minute War had revealed distinct patterns—predictable patterns—in the Pukcip style of skirmishing. Each warrior moved through a standard series of positions, a series as immutable as an 18th Century waltz. To defeat them on the battlefield, a foe had merely to determine each warrior's starting point, and fire there a fraction of a second before the Pukcip was due to materialize.

That called for a special soldier: one who could make sense of the shifting, surging intermingling of gaudy shells and faded khaki; one who could synchronize his trigger squeezes with the rhythm of their maneuvers; one who could stand fast even when a Pukcip blinked into the space next to him.

Olsen had asked for permission to select and train an elite detachment of such soldiers. Civilian eyebrows had lifted—there was no future, they thought, in preparing to fight an enemy that could depopulate a continent if it chose—but the political pressure to develop contingency plans had meshed with the Pentagon's desire for revenge. He had received his colonelcy.

"Two last things," Olsen said, staring at the cracked plaster of the anteroom walls. "First, make sure you rotate your men, keep 'em fresh. Those idiots in Calcutta were probably asleep on their feet."

"Consider it done, sir."

"Second, if a kid shows up, aim above his head and hose the room. That should catch the Puks by surprise, and leave 'em no place to jump except back home. All right?"

"Yes, sir."

"Carry on." The far doorway called him. Scowling, he crossed to it, and scanned the holographic projection of the—reception room? laboratory? zoo?—on Pukci. All shimmers of swirling blues and purples, it stood in haughty contrast to the peeling green paint of the Center. Olsen glared at the metallic glints in the odd-shaped tiles of its floor, as if he could dissolve the deception through sheer force of will. The vivid image remained unaltered. The Pukcip equipment was too good.

Spurred by an impulse as inexplicable as fate, he stepped forward. The lieutenant's surprised gasp plucked at his shoulder, but he didn't respond. He had no time. Gravity grasped him, ripped him through the planes of colored light. An instant later, he was bouncing softly on the nylon mesh strung beneath the doorway.

Damn effective, he thought. *If I hadn't known—if I'd been a trusting six year old—I'd have expected it to be solid. Shit, even knowing, I was startled.*

A child's world is tinged with the mysterious and the irrational. To him, fantasy is merely fact in which he can not participate. What looks like a room must be a room, if he can enter it.

Two hundred fifty children ran, skipped, hopped, or walked into the Pukcip projection every day. Passage over the threshhold triggered the test which, for one uncaring nanosecond, pitted the law of gravity against the child's belief that he was in a room whose floor could support his weight. If reality won, the testee tumbled; if faith overrode it to write its own version of natural law, the child either levitated in blissful ignorance . . . or teleported directly to the original room, somewhere on Pukci.

Roughly eleven of every million testees had faith enough to warp reality.

§   §   §

Jonathan was in the front seat, between his mama and his daddy. He'd wanted to ride in the back—both his parents were pretty big, and there wasn't much room. They'd told him that just that once they wanted to be together. It was sort of nice to be able to lean against his mama's softness, but there wasn't any air. If

256   LOW GRADE ORE

he were sitting where he always sat, the wind would be buffeting his face, and he'd have to half-close his eyes, which made the whole world look different.

"Is it long time, Daddy?" he asked.

"Most an hour, boy." He took his eyes off the road and gazed down at his only son. "Don't be in such a hurry, y'hear? We gonna get there, we just gonna have to sit and wait till they ready for us anyhow."

Jonathan nodded solemnly. He'd been wanting to ask his daddy why he was driving so much slower than usual.

§ § §

The stone floor was worn; Olsen's combat boots set up a hollow ringing. The old school building had, at that hour of the morning, the semi-deserted air of a shut-down refinery. It was hard to believe how crowded the empty corridors would become; harder still to think how many people had passed through them in either of the building's two lifetimes, ironic that each involved some sort of screening.

The silence was almost good. Dortkowski's crew would shatter it within the next half hour, but the first children weren't due till nine o'clock, more than an hour away. That would be time enough to look things over, to smooth out the jangle of his thoughts. It bothered him that he would have to stand idle while the Pukcip equipment assayed the value of two hundred fifty children.

He left-faced into the main wing. Rickety metal folding chairs lined the walls; he repositioned one that had wandered out a few feet. A stencil on the seat's underside declared it to be the property of a local funeral home. Disgusted, he kicked it. The impact chipped paint off the crumbly cinderblocks; quarter-sized flakes of green skittered down to the baseboard.

Damn the Pukcip for their ability to teleport. And damn the civilians for being so easily cowed! The Army could have taken them, once it had recovered from the initial shock. Their weapons weren't very good, no matter what the hysterical media claimed, and the carouselling warriors took longer to aim than a GI did. If their tiny expeditionary force hadn't held most of the government hostage . . .

The fact that every other officer in the world had succumbed to the same ruse didn't lessen the shame. If anything, it heightened it. A professional respects his opposite numbers, often to the point of judging himself by his perception of how well he could do against them. When not a single human officer proves himself capable of beating off a handful of stalked-eyed child thieves ...

Only revenge could remove the stigma. But the Pukcip were immune—Earth neither knew where Pukci was, nor had the star drive to get troops there. In a year or two, though ...

The US and the USSR were co-developing a faster-than-light drive. If it were possible, if it weren't a mirage hanging stubbornly above the horizon, they'd launch a grim fleet and ransack space for Pukci. Fueled by a bitterness that wouldn't fade with the generations, they'd find it, and avenge Wichita, Lyons, Serpukhov, all the other demonstration cities ... the Pukcip warriors could dance quadrilles on the asteroids, but their planet wouldn't be able to dodge the swollen tips of the nuclear missiles.

One fear dogged Olsen, as it did everyone who hungered for satisfaction; if an FTL drive could be invented, why were the Pukcip allowing work on it to continue?

If it couldn't be invented, why had the joint communique announcing the project provoked the invasion?

It was obvious, in the crystallized brilliance of hindsight, that the Pukcip had spied on Earth for years. They'd done nothing to reveal themselves until the release of the joint communique, but within twelve hours of that first, hope-stirring news flash, the four-armed teleports had stormed the world.

Olsen had his own theory: that the Pukcip theoreticians had decided FTL *travel* was impossible, but that research into it would somehow uncover natural teleports. So the Pukcip warriors, as edgily suspicious as military men anywhere, had opted to remove Earth's teleports before they could spearhead an invasion of Pukci.

That fit neatly with the intelligence analysis that only the enemy's soldiers could teleport. If, in their culture, the power had purely military applications, their experts would naturally have decided that Earth would also exploit it for war.

They were afraid, Olsen thought. *They knew that once we started roaming the stars, we'd find them ... shit, and I thought* we *were xenophobic. Or maybe they know how xenophobic we are, and figured they'd eliminate our space capability before we'd discovered we had it ... or maybe their motive is completely different—like they wanted to maximize the return on their investment, and so they held off while our population grew, until it seemed that we were ready to find, and use, the raw materials they needed ...* he gave up the effort at triple-think with a tired shake of his head. The *why* of the situation didn't really matter, not to him. The specialists could worry about it.

His job was to be ready to fight them.

His hope was that he'd get the chance.

§ § §

Dortkowski lifted his clipboard, recorded the Center's need for more Pukcip ink, and looked the room over one more time. Everything seemed to be ready for the children. The question was, would he be ready for the parents?

He'd explained it ten thousand times himself; he'd had every newspaper in the state run articles on it; he'd even scraped together the funds for a brochure distributed at the door. But still they screamed their outrage when they saw the tricolored tattoo on their children's wrists.

What could he say that he hadn't said before? Clearly the best thing was simply to start up the mental tape recorder, let the tired neutral words fall as they had so often before, and then wear the stoic face while spittle spattered his cheeks.

The Pukcip wanted their slag heaps labeled. What else could he say? To tell a mother that her child likes something she doesn't is to incite the hurricane; to tell a father that the process is painless is to ignore the very real hurt he feels at his child's disfigurement.

The bureaucrat had but one defense: *I'm sorry, it's not my idea, I didn't make that rule, if it were up to me I wouldn't, I can't make an exception, I'm sorry, but I'm just following orders.* His ulcer pinched, as if to extend the range of his soul pain. It was a lousy defense and he knew it. The fact that every word was true made him no happier.

What the parents couldn't understand was what he didn't dare forget: any deviation from the Pukcip procedures might be discovered in one of the irregular Pukcip spotchecks. Such a discovery could condemn an entire city.

The headache was starting up again; his ink-stained fingers massaged the bulging vein in his temple. It was going to be one of those days ... but maybe he'd get lucky. Maybe a parent would get infuriated enough to put him into the hospital.

Immediately he sighed. That was wishful thinking. There was always an aide, a cop, *somebody* to step in officiously and protect him from the lesser suffering. Why would no one do it for the greater?

His hands groped for the center drawer of his desk; warped wood screeched as he pulled it out. It overflowed with the debris of bureaucracy: forms, stamp pads, pencils ... brushing them to one side, he uncovered the small green bottle. He shook it. The lethal white pills rattled like castanets.

They were his ticket out. If the Center uncovered a teleport—no, *when* it did, because eventually it had to—he'd screw off the top, tilt back the bottle, and empty dusty release down his throat ... because it would have been his fault. Without his administrative expertise, it never would have happened ... and he could see no other means of atonement.

Then he laughed, sourly, and the acid bit at the back of his throat. Atonement? He knew himself better. It was escape, the modern man's escape: swallow the pills and dodge the pain. Let chemistry exorcise reality. Let death deny his responsibility for losing a child to the Pukcip pipeline.

§ § §

They were driving straight at the sun, and if it didn't rise up off the end of the road before they got there, they were going to have a whole lot of trouble getting to his 'valuation.

Jonathan squirmed around so the bright streaks wouldn't be flying into his eyes. Catching his mama looking down at him, he asked the question that had been floating around in his head for the last couple days. "Mama, why they wanna 'valuate me for anyway?"

"They doing it to all the little children, honey."

"But how come they want *me*, Mama?"

"Cause the government say you gotta."

"Oh." He considered that for a moment, then shrugged. If his daddy listened to the government, whoever that was, he guessed he'd better, too. Sure didn't sound like his mama liked that guy, though. Her voice had done the same thing to "government" that it always did to "landlord."

§ § §

Olsen strode through a classroom to a window above the parking lot. The April day was going to be hot; a tang of soft asphalt was beginning to permeate the air. Below, the unseasonally cruel sun tormented a cluster of anxious parents. They probably hadn't slept all night. Unable to stand the suspense, they'd come early, to get it over and quickly. Poor bastards. Their faces were as gray as Dortkowski's hair.

The odds were against any of them losing a kid—from the initial statistics, only one in a million could teleport—in fact, they were ten times more likely to go home with a levitator. Still, the possi-

260   LOW GRADE ORE

bility that their child might wind up a nugget in a Pukcip pocket was enough to make most of them despair.

Leaning on the dusty windowsill, he clenched his teeth. He had a boy of his own—Ralph, four years old, now. In less than two years' time he'd be shuffling through the corridors of a Center much like this, one more big-eyed kid in a line that stretched all the way back to the world's maternity wards. As a father, he knew that the most nerve-wracking aspect was that if your kid should go to Pukci, you'd never know what they did to him.

Not that Calcutta wasn't giving him some very nasty ideas.

He couldn't decide whether he should tell Grace about the video-tape. If one of the networks was leaked a copy, of course, he wouldn't have to, but if its icy horror kept it off the air . . . *could* he tell her?

No. From a comment or two dropped into her conversations, he knew she was expecting him to find and pull the string that would exempt Ralph. He'd explained, more than once, that there was no such string—that even the President's grandson had endured the evaluation—but she behaved as though she'd never heard him.

It was either acute tunnel vision—she saw what she wanted to see, and no more—or she had a very touching faith in him.

Straightening, brushing the dust off his hands, Olsen gazed into the sky. He wouldn't tell her. There was always the random factor to consider—why make her fret for two years if there was even the slightest chance that the armies of Earth could hurl themselves against the Pukcip warriors?

If it didn't happen, she'd wax hysterical while Ralph was being tested, but once he came through alive she'd calm down.

If it did happen . . . either the Centers would be leveled by jubilant wrecking crews, or there'd be no citizens to fill their halls.

§ § §

"We here," his daddy grunted. "Looks like they just opening the doors."

"Jonathan, child—" suddenly his mama turned sideways, and her soft round eyes practically swallowed up his own "—you gonna be all right, honey, y'hear?"

"Yowp." His head bobbed up and down, till he twisted to see his daddy, who cleared his throat with embarrassing loudness. "You all right, Daddy?"

"Just fine, boy." He pushed his door open, but before he threw his long legs into the parking lot, he gave Jonathan his hand. "Do what they tell you, boy, and everything's gonna be okay."

Jonathan didn't say anything. He was too busy wondering what they were so nervous about.

§ § §

Olsen stood by the door to the anteroom, eyes restless, muscles panther-loose. Facing him was Dortkowski, thin frame draped in a soft white lab coat. Behind him was the Specialist 5th Class who ran the communications gear. It was a mild reassurance to know that if anything happened, the entire chain of command would hear of it within seconds. It was less reassuring to recall that the Calcutta guards had had exactly seven seconds in which to react.

He glanced at Dortkowski, whose bony hand was massaging his stomach. Evidently the tension was gnawing at the Director. It was understandable: the children came so slowly; the parents hovered so watchfully. From the other's impatient checking of his watch, Olsen guessed that they'd fallen behind schedule. Any further delays would probably drive Dortkowski into a nervous fit.

The short, shabby corridor seemed to quiver with an air of expectancy. Everyone was uptight, jerking about at the slightest noise, as if convinced that It was going to happen. Eventually, of course, It would. The only question was when.

Dortkowski's statistics were no help. They said one in a million, but refused to say which of those million it would be. He'd have to imitate the bureaucrat: test them all, hold his breath on each, and—if he was there long enough—swig the Maalox after every five or six. Olsen knew, with a pawn's despair, that even when they lost one, he wouldn't be able to relax. Though there would be only two in two million, they could come consecutively.

He wondered what was in Dortkowski's other pocket, the one he patted every few minutes. It wasn't ulcer medicine. The outlined bottle was too small.

Fighting back the temptation to pace, he leaned against the wall. He had to be near enough to hear the voice patterns echo through the anteroom.

First the flare of fright as the child fell, then a gasp, then bewilderment rushing to the brink of tears. If the costumed clown by the safety net caught the kid's attention quickly, the thin, confused voice would switch to giggles in mid-sob. If not, they had to hold everything until the child was safely inside, out of earshot of the text testee.

A little black boy was walking towards him. All dressed up,

LOW GRADE ORE

with his shoes shined and his hair in a neat Afro, he looked scared. He was probably getting too much attention. All the adults were eyeing him, and their expressions would be hard for a kid to read. But his jaw was set, and he put one foot in front of the other with praiseworthy determination.

Dortkowski smiled down at the boy, which seemed to help a little, and one of the black soldiers winked. His voice was still tiny, though, when he said his name was Jonathan. Yes, sir; he'd go into the next room and wait.

Olsen watched his small back pass through the rainbow doorway. As he braced himself for the cry of betrayal, his back tingled. The boy was too quiet. The air smelled . . . odd, and its pressure seemed to have dropped.

Barely noticing the green bottle in Dortkowski's hand, he looked. Jonathan was standing on glistening tiles, apparently inspecting the spacious room. Doors opened in the shiny walls; Olsen saw Pukcip heads come around the edges. The boy sat down and started to sob.

Dortkowski gave a sound, almost a whimper, of relief, and sagged against him, murmuring, "It's a levita—"

But Olsen shouted, "Hell with that, it's a space warp! Get in there, you bastards, *get in there and take that place!!!*"

Within seconds, his and other booted feet were skidding across Pukcip stone; back in Hartford, his Spec 5 was demanding reinforcements for the bridgehead; and Olsen, automatic in hand, was cradling the terrified boy.

§ § §

Jonathan was frantic to know what he'd done wrong. After all, they'd *told* him to go into the room, even though they must have known how far away it was. It was very confusing. If they knew he couldn't go there, why did they get so excited when he brought there here?

§ § §

With almost clinical dispassion, Dortkowski watched his skinny fingers tighten the cap on the bottle. He'd come *that* close. He almost hadn't had the courage to look. If Olsen's uncompromising eyes hadn't swept over him . . .

They should have guessed. When the test provoked two different paranormal reactions, one less common than the other, they should have guessed that it might provoke a third, even more rare. This boy, neither levitator nor teleport, was something else entirely: a talent capable of wedding Earth to Pukcip via another dimension, and of keeping them joined, perhaps indefinitely. Continued testing might eventually have uncovered a fourth kind of power . . . but he didn't have time for that, not now.

Though the halls were a blur, he knew he should clear them for the Army. He walked up to the crowd of parents and children, spread his arms, said, "That's all, folks, it's all over, go on home, there won't be any more evaluations."

And the tears on his cheeks made his smile more profound.

§ § §

The war was short, and perhaps more savage than it should have been, but no one knew how long Jonathan could hold open the doorway. Besides, the once humbled generals wanted an unconditional surrender, and quick. And more than a few of the infantrymen had had friends or relatives in Wichita.

The Pukcip contributed heavily to their own defeat. Most of their tiny army was elsewhere, and had to be recalled. By the time it was ready to skirmish, a thousand GI's had spread throughout the neighborhood. The entire 82nd Airborne was in position before the aliens had deduced the existence, and the location, of the doorway. Their assault on it ran headlong into Olsen's special forces, and was repulsed with heavy casualties.

Furious, humiliated, and totally unaccustomed to defensive warfare, the Pukcip wasted the little strength they had. They launched a dozen vindictive raids on Terran cities, and lost soldiers in each. Then, before their terrorism could take effect, their panic-stricken government called them home. Ordered to destroy the invaders, they tried—but pent-up hatred and sheer numbers more than cancelled their carouselling multiplicity. With the arrival of the 101st Airborne, the battles tapered into sniper attacks, and those into silence.

If they'd reacted less emotionally—if they'd had any experiences with invasions—if they'd studied Russian or Chinese military history . . . but they hadn't, so the war was short. And perhaps more savage than it should have been.

The Army took two sets of documents from Pukcip archives before closing the doorway on chaos.

The first included blueprints for a functioning starship.

The second included invoices for FTL drive units sold to the shipyards on Rigel VI. Each unit was identified by its city of origin. Four had come from Calcutta.

DANCE BAND ON THE *TITANIC*
by Jack Chalker

*Mr. Chalker, doing business as Mirage Press, publishes books about fantasy and science fiction. He teaches in the Baltimore public schools, is becoming known as a SF novelist—*Midnight at the Well of Souls, *from del Rey Books, is one he's particularly happy with—and chases ferryboats as a hobby.*

The young woman was committing suicide again on the lower afterdeck. They'd told me I'd get used to it, but after four times I could still only pretend to ignore it, pretend that I didn't hear the body go over, hear the splash, and the scream as she was sucked into the screws. It was all too brief, and becoming all too familiar.

When the scream was cut short, as it always was, I continued walking forward, toward the bow. I would be needed there to guide the spotlight with which the captain would have to spot the buoys to get us all safely into Southport harbor.

It was a clear night; once at the bow I could see the stars in all their glory, too numerous to count or spot familiar constellations. It's a sight that's known and loved by all those who follow the sea, and it had a special meaning for us, who manned the *Orcas*, for the stars were immutable, the one unchanging part of our universe.

I checked the lines, the winch, and ties in the chained-off portion of the bow, then notified the captain by walkie-talkie that all was ready. He gave me "Very well," and told me that we'd be on the mark in five minutes. This gave me a few moments to relax, adjust my vision to the darkness, and look around.

The bow is an eerie place at night, for all its beauty; there is an unreality about a large ferryboat in the dark. Between where I stood on station and the bridge superstructure towering above me there was a broad area always crowded with people in warm weather. That bridge—dominating the aft field of vision, a ghostly, unlit white-gray monolith, reflecting the moonlight with an almost unreal cast and glow. A silent, spinning radar mast on top, and the funnel, end-on, in back of the bridge, with its wing supports and mast giving it some futuristic cast, only made the scene more alien, more awesome.

I glanced around at the people on deck. Not as many as usual, but then it was very late, and there was a chill in the air. I saw a few familiar faces, and there was some lateral shift in focus on a number of them, indicating that I was seeing at least three levels of reality that night.

Now, that last is kind of hard to explain. I'm not sure whether I understand it, either, but I well remember when I applied for this job, and the explanations I got then.

Working deck on a ferryboat is a funny place for a former English teacher, anyway. But, while I'd been, I think, a good teacher, I was in constant fights with the administration over their lax discipline, stuff-shirt attitudes toward teaching and teachers, and the like. The educational system isn't made for mavericks; it's designed to make everyone conform to bureaucratic ideals which the teacher is supposed to exemplify. One argument too many, I guess, and there I was, an unemployed teacher in a time when there were too many teachers. So, I drifted—no family, no responsibilities. I'd always loved ferryboats—raised on them, loved them with the same passion some folks like trains and trolley cars and such—and when I found an unskilled job opening on the old Delaware ferry, I took it. The fact that I was an ex-teacher actually helped; ferry companies like to hire people who relate well to the general public. After all, deck duty is hectic when the ferry's docking or docked, but for the rest of the time you just sort of stand there, and every tourist and traveller in the world wants to talk. If you aren't willing to talk back and enjoy it, forget ferry runs.

And I met Joanna. I'm not sure if we were ever in love, but we got along. No, on second thought, I shouldn't kid myself—I *did* love her, although I'm pretty sure I was just convenient from her point of view. For a while things went smoothly—I had a job I liked, and we shared rent. She had a little daughter she doted on, and we hit it off, too.

And in a space of three weeks my neat little complacent world ended. First she threw that damned party while I was working, and a cigarette or something was left, and the apartment burned. They saved her—but not her little girl. I tried to comfort her, tried to console her, but I guess I was too full of my own life and self-importance, I didn't see the signs. The woman hanged herself, again while I worked the boat.

A week after that the damned bridge-tunnel put the ferry out of business, too.

I was alone, friendless, jobless, and feeling guilty as hell. I seriously thought about ending it all myself about then, maybe going down to the old ferryboat and blowing it and me to hell in one symbolic act of togetherness. But, then, just when I'd sunk to the depths, I got this nice, official-looking envelope in the mail from something called the Bluewater Corporation, Southport, Maine. Just a funny logo, some blue water with an odd, misty-looking shape of a ship in it.

"Dear Mr. Dalton," it read. "We have just learned of the closing of the Delaware service, and we are in need of some experienced ferry people. After reviewing your qualifications, we believe that you will fit nicely into our company, which, we guarantee, will not be put out of business by bridge or tunnel. If this prospect interests you, please come to Southport terminal at your earliest convenience for a final interview. Looking forward to seeing you soon, I remain, sincerely yours, Herbert V. Penobscot, Personnel Manager, Bluewater Corp."

I just stood there staring at the thing for I don't know how long. A ferry job! That alone should have excited me, yet I wondered about it, particularly that line about "reviewing my qualifications" and "final interview". Funny terms. I could see why they'd look for experienced people, and all ferry folk knew when a line was closed and might look for their own replacements there, but—why me? I hadn't applied to them, hadn't ever heard of them or their line—or, for that matter, of Southport, Maine either. Obviously they preselected their people—very odd for this particular business.

I scrounged up an old atlas and tried to find it. The letterhead said **"Southport—St. Michael—The Island"**, but I could find nothing about any such place in the atlas or an almanac. If the letterhead hadn't been so damned convincing, I'd have sworn somebody was putting me on. As it was, I had nothing else to do, and it beat drinking myself to a slow death, so I hitchhiked up.

It wasn't easy finding Southport, I'll tell you. Even people in nearby towns had never heard of it. The whole town was about a dozen houses, a seedy ten-unit motel, a hot dog stand, and a very small ferry terminal with a standard but surprisingly large ferry ramp and parking area.

I couldn't believe the place warranted a ferry when I saw it; you had to go about sixty miles into the middle of nowhere on a road the highway department had deliberately engineered to miss some of the world's prettiest scenery and had last paved sometime before World War II just to get there.

There was a light on in the terminal, so I went in. A gray-haired man, about fifty, was in the ticket office, and I went over and introduced myself. He looked me over carefully, and I knew I didn't present a very good appearance.

"Sit down, Mr. Dalton," he offered in a tone that was friendly but businesslike. "I've been expecting you. This really won't take long, but this final interview includes a couple of strange questions. If you don't want to answer any of them, feel free, but I must ask them nonetheless. Will you go along with me?"

I nodded, and he fired away. It was the damndest job interview I'd ever had. He barely touched on my knowledge of ferries except to ask if it mattered that the *Orcas* was a single-bridge, twin-screw affair, not a double-ender like I'd been used to. It still loaded on one end and unloaded on the other, though, through a raised bow, and a ferry was a ferry to me and I told him so.

Most of the questions were on my personal life, my attitudes. Like this one: "Have you ever contemplated or attempted suicide?"

I jumped. "What's *that* have to do with anything?" I snapped. After all this I was beginning to see why the job was still open.

"Just answer the question," he responded, almost embarrassed. "I told you I had to ask them all."

Well, I couldn't figure out what this was all about, but I finally decided, what the hell, I had nothing to lose and it was a beautiful spot.

"Yes," I told him. "Thought about it, anyway." And I told him why. He just nodded thoughtfully, jotted a little something on a preprinted form, and continued. His next question was worse.

"Do you now believe in ghosts, devils, and demonic forces?" he asked in the same tone that he would ask whether I did windows.

I couldn't suppress a chuckle. "You mean the ship's haunted?"

He didn't smile back. "Just answer the question, please."

"No," I responded. "I'm not very religious."

Now there was a wisp of a smile there. "And suppose, with your hard-nosed rationalism, you ran into one? Or a whole bunch of them?" He leaned forward, smile gone. "Even an entire shipload of them?"

It was impossible to take this seriously. "What kind of ghosts?" I asked him. "Chain rattlers? White sheets? Foul forms spouting hateful gibberish?"

He shook his head negatively. "No, ordinary people, for the most part. Dressed a little odd, perhaps; talking a little odd perhaps, but not really very odd at all. Nice folks, typical passengers."

Cars were coming in now, and I glanced out the window at them. Ordinary-looking cars, ordinary-looking people—campers, a couple of tractor-trailer rigs, like that. Lining up. A U.S. customs man came from the direction of the motel and started talking to some of them.

"They don't look like ghosts to me," I told my interviewer.

He sighed. "Look, Mr. Dalton. I know you're an educated man. I have to go out and start selling fares now. She'll be in in about forty minutes, and we've only got a twenty-minute layover. When she's in, and loads, go aboard. Look her over. You'll have free rein of the ship. Take the complete round trip, all stops. It's about four hours over, twenty minutes in, and a little slower back. Don't get off the ship, though. Keep an open mind. If you're the one for the *Orcas,* and I think you are, we'll finish our talk when you get back." He got up, took out a cash drawer and receipt load, and went to the door, then turned back to me. "I hope you are the one," he said wearily. "I've interviewed over three hundred people and I'm getting sick of it."

We shook hands on that cryptic remark, and I wandered around while he manned his little booth and processed the cars, campers, and trucks. A young woman came over from one of the houses and handled the few people who didn't have cars, although how they ever got to Southport I was at a loss to know.

The amount of business was nothing short of incredible. St. Michaels was in Nova Scotia, it seemed, and there were the big runs by CN from a couple of places and the Swedish one out of Portland to compete for any business. The fares were reasonable but not merely cheap enough to drive this far out of your way for, and to get to Southport you *had* to drive out of the way.

I found a general marine atlas of the Fundy region in his office and looked at it. Southport made it, but just barely. No designation of it as a ferry terminal, though, and no funny line showing a route.

For the life of me I couldn't find a St. Michael, Nova Scotia—nor a St. Clement's Island, either—the mid-stop that the schedule said it made.

And then there was the blast of a great air horn, and I rushed out for my first look at the *Orcas*—and I was stunned.

272   DANCE BAND ON THE TITANIC

That ship, I remember thinking, *has no right to be here. Not here, not on this run.*

It was *huge*—all gleaming white, looking brand-new, more like a cruise ship than a ferryboat. I counted three upper decks, and, as I watched, a loud clanging bell sounded electrically on her and her enormous bow lifted, revealing a grooved raising ramp, something like the bow of an old LST. It docked with little trouble, and the ramp came down slowly, mating with the ferry dock, revealing space for well over a hundred cars and trucks, with small side ramps for a second level available if needed.

It was close to sundown on a weekday, but they loaded over fifty vehicles, including a dozen campers and eight big trucks. Where had they all come from, I wondered. And why?

I walked on with the passengers, still in something of a daze, and went up top. The lounges were spacious and comfortable, the seats padded and reclining. There was a large cafeteria, a newsstand, and a very nice bar at the stern of passenger deck 2. The next deck had another lounge section, and a couple of dozen staterooms up front, while the top level had crew's quarters and a solarium.

It was fancy; and, after it backed out, lowered its bow, and started pouring it on after clearing the harbor lights, the fastest damned thing I could remember, too. Except for the slight swaying and the rhythmic thrumming of the twin diesels you hardly knew you were moving. It was obviously using enormous stabilizers.

The sun was setting, and I walked through the ship, just looking and relaxing. As darkness fell and the shoreline receded into nothingness, I started noticing some very odd things, as I'd been warned.

First of all, there seemed to be a whole lot more people on board than I'd remembered loading, and there certainly hadn't been any number staying on from the last run. They all looked real and solid enough, and very ordinary, but there was something decidedly weird about them, too.

Many seemed to be totally unaware of each other's existence, for one thing. Some seemed to shimmer occasionally, others were a little blurred or indistinct to my eyes no matter how I rubbed them.

And, once in a while, they'd walk through each other.

Yes, I'm serious. One big fellow in a flowered aloha shirt and brown pants carrying a tray of soft drinks from the cafeteria to his wife and three kids in the lounge didn't seem to notice this woman dressed in a white tee shirt and jeans walking right into him, nor did she seem aware of him, either.

And they met, and I braced for the collision and spilled drinks—and it didn't happen. They walked right *through* each other, just as if they didn't exist, and continued obliviously on. Not one drop of soda was spilled, not one spot of mustard was splotched.

There were other things, too. Most of the people were dressed normally for summer, but occasionally I'd see people in fairly heavy coats and jackets. Some of the fashions were different, too—some people were overdressed in old-fashioned styles, others wildly underdressed, a couple of the women frankly wearing nothing but the bottoms of string bikinis and a see-through short cape of some kind.

I know I couldn't take my eyes off them for a while, until I got the message that they knew they were being stared at and didn't particularly like it. But they were generally ignored by the others.

There were strange accents, too. Not just the expected Maine twang and Canadian accents, or even just the French Canadian accents—those were normal. But there were some really odd ones, ones where I picked out only a few words, which sounded like English, French, Spanish, and Nordic languages all intermixed and often with weird results.

And men with pigtails and long, braided hair, and women with shaved heads or occasionally beards.

It was weird.

Frankly, it scared me a little, and I found the purser and introduced myself.

The officer, a good-looking young man named Gifford Hanley, a Canadian by his speech, seemed delighted that I'd seen all this, and not the least bit disturbed.

"Well, well, well!" he almost beamed. "Maybe we've found our new man at last, eh? Not bloody soon enough, either! We've been working short-handed for too long and it's getting to the others."

He took me up to the bridge—one of the most modern I'd ever seen—and introduced me to the captain and helmsman. They all asked me what I thought of the *Orcas* and how I liked the sea, and none of them would answer my questions on the unusual passengers.

Well, there *was* a St. Clement's Island. A big one, too, from the

274   DANCE BAND ON THE TITANIC

looks of it, and a fair amount of traffic getting off and wanting on. Some of the vehicles that got on were odd, too; many of the cars looked unfamiliar in design, the trucks very odd, and there were even several horse-drawn wagons!

The island had that same quality as some of the passengers, too. It seemed never to be quite in focus just beyond the ferry terminal, and lights seemed to shift, so that where I thought there were houses or a motel suddenly they were somewhere else, of a different intensity. I was willing to swear that that motel had two stories; later it seemed over on the left, and four stories high, then farther back, still later, and single-storied.

Even the lighthouse as we sped out of the harbor changed; one time it looked very tall with a house at its base; then, suddenly, it was short and tubby, then an automated light that seemed to be out in the water, with no sign of an island.

This continued for most of the trip. St. Michael looked like a carbon copy of Southport, the passengers and vehicles as bizarre, and there seemed to be a lot of customs men in different uniforms dashing about, totally ignoring some vehicles while clearing others.

The trip back was equally strange. The newsstand contained some books and magazines that were odd to say the least, and papers with strange names and stranger headlines.

This time there were even Indians aboard, speaking odd tongues. Some looked straight out of *The Last of the Mohicans,* complete with wild haircut, others dressed from little to heavy, despite the fact that it was July and very warm and humid.

And, just before we were to make the red and green channel markers and turn into Southport, I saw the girl die for the first time.

She was dressed in red t-shirt, yellow shorts, and sandals; she had long brown hair, was rather short and overweight, and wore oversized granny glasses.

I wasn't paying much attention, really, just watching her looking over the side at the wake, when, before I could even cry out, she suddenly climbed up on the rail and plunged in, very near the stern.

I screamed, and heard her body hit the water and then heard her howl of terror as she dropped close enough in that the prop wash caught her, tucked her under, and cut her to pieces.

Several people on the afterdeck looked at me quizzically, but only one or two seemed to realize that a girl had just died.

There was little I could do, but I ran back to the purser, breathless.

He just nodded sadly.

"Take it easy, man," he said gently. "She's dead, and there's no use going back for the body. Believe me, we *know*. It won't be there."

I was shocked, badly upset. "How do you know that?" I snapped.

"Because we did it every time the last four times she jumped, and we never found her body then, either," he replied sadly.

I had my mouth open, ready to retort, to say *something;* but he got up, put on his officer's hat and coat, said, "Excuse me, I have to tend to the unloading," and walked out.

As soon as I got off the ship it was like some sort of dreamy fog had lifted from me. Everything looked suddenly bright and clear, and the people and vehicles looked normal. I made my way to the ferry terminal.

When they'd loaded and the ship was gone again, I waited for Mr. McNeil, the ticket agent, to return to his office. It looked much the same, really, but a few things seemed different. I couldn't quite put my finger on it, but there *was* something odd— like the paneling had been rosewood before, and was now walnut. Small things, but nagging ones.

McNeil, the ticket-agent, came back after seeing the ship clear. It ran almost constantly, according to the schedule.

I glanced out the window as he approached, and noticed uniformed customs men checking out the debarked vehicles. They seemed to have a different uniform than I'd remembered.

McNeil came in, and I got another shock. He had a beard.

No, it was the same man, all right. No question about it. But the man I'd talked to less than nine hours earlier had been clean-shaven.

I turned to where the navigation atlas lay, just where I'd put it, still open to the Southport page.

It showed a ferry line from Southport to a rather substantial St. Clements Island now. But nothing to Nova Scotia.

I turned to the bearded McNeil, who was watching me with some mild amusement in his eyes.

"What the *hell* is going on here?" I demanded.

He went over and sat down in his swivel chair. "Want the job?" he asked. "It's yours if you do."

I couldn't believe his attitude. "I want an explanation, damn it!" I fumed.

He chuckled. "I told you I'd give you one if you wanted. Now, you'll have to bear with me, since I'm only repeating what the Company tells me, and I'm not sure I have it all clear myself."

I sat down in the other chair. "Go ahead," I told him.

He sighed. "Well, let's start off by saying that there's been a Bluewater Corporation ferry on this run since the mid-1800s—steam passenger and freight service at first, of course. The *Orcas* is the eleventh ship in the service, put on a year and a half ago."

He reached over, grabbed a cigarette, lit it, and continued.

"Well, anyway, it was a normal operation until about 1910 or so. That's when they started noticing that their counts were off, that there seemed to be more passengers than the manifests called for, different freight, and all that. As it continued, the crews started noticing more and more of the kind of stuff you saw, and things got crazy for them, too. Southport was a big fishing and lobstering town then—nobody does that any more, the whole economy's the ferry.

"Well, anyway, one time this crewman goes crazy, says the woman in his house isn't his wife. A few days later another comes home to find he has four kids—and he was only married a week before. And so on."

I felt my skin start to crawl slightly.

"So, they send some big shots up. The men are absolutely nuts, but *they* believe in what they claim. Soon everybody who works the ship is spooked, and this can't be dismissed. The experts go for a cruise and can't find anything odd, but now two of the crewmen claim that it *is* their wife, or their kid, or somesuch. Got to be a pain, though, getting crewmen. We finally had to center on loners—people without family, friends, or close personal ties. It kept getting worse each trip. Had a hell of a time keeping men for a while, and that's why it's so hard to recruit new ones."

"You mean the trip drives you crazy?" I asked unbelievingly.

He chuckled. "Oh, no. *You're* sane. It's the rest of 'em. That's the problem. And it gets worse and worse each season. But the trip's *extremely* profitable. So we try and match the crew to the ship, and hope they'll accept it. If they do, it's one of the best damned ferry jobs there is."

"But what causes it?" I managed. "I mean—I saw people dressed outlandishly. I saw other people walk *through* each other! I even saw a girl commit suicide, and nobody seemed to notice!"

McNeil's face turned grim. "So that's happened again. Too bad. Maybe one day there'll be some chance to save her."

"Look," I said, exasperated. "There must be some explanation for all this. There *has* to be!"

The ticket agent shrugged and stubbed out the cigarette.

"Well, some of the company experts studied it. They say nobody can tell for sure, but the best explanation is that there are a lot of different worlds—different Earths, you might say—all existing one on top of the other, but you can't see any one except the one you're in. Don't ask me how that's possible or how they came up with it, it just *is,* that's all. Well, they say that in some worlds folks don't exist at all, and in others they are different places or doing different things—like getting married to somebody else or somesuch. In some, Canada's still British, in some she's a republic, in others she's a fragmented batch of countries, and in one or two she's part of the U.S. Each one of these places has a different history."

"And this one boat serves them all?" I responded, not accepting a word of that crazy theory. "How is that possible?"

McNeil shrugged again. "Who knows? Hell, I don't even understand why the little light goes on in here when I flip the switch. Do most people? I just sell tickets and lower the ramp. I'll tell you the company's version, that's all. They say that there's a crack—maybe one of many, maybe the only one. The ship's route just happens to parallel that crack, and this allows you to go between the worlds. Not one ship, of course—twenty, thirty ships or more, one for each world. But, as long as they keep the same schedule, they overlap—and can cross into one or more of the others. If you're on the ship in all those worlds, then you cross, too. Anyone coexisting with the ship in multiple worlds can see and hear not only the one he's in but the ones nearest him, too. People perception's a little harder the farther removed the world you're in is from theirs."

"And you believe this?" I asked him, still disbelieving.

"Who knows? Got to believe *something* or you go nuts," he replied pragmatically. "Look, did you get to St. Michaels this trip?"

I nodded. "Yeah. Looked like this place, pretty much."

He pointed to the navigation atlas. "Try and find it. You won't. Take a drive up through New Brunswick and around to the other side. It doesn't exist. In this world, the *Orcas* goes from here to St. Clement's Island and back again. I understand from some of the crew that sometimes Southport doesn't exist, sometimes the Island doesn't, and so forth. And there are so many countries involved I don't count."

I shook my head, refusing to accept all this. And yet, it made a crazy kind of sense. These people didn't see each other because they were in different worlds. The girl committed suicide five times because she did it five times in five different worlds—or was it five different girls? It also explained the outlandish dress, the strange mixture of vehicles, people, accents.

"But how come the crew sees people from many worlds and the passengers don't?" I asked him.

McNeil sighed. "That's the other problem. We have to find people who would be up here, working on the *Orcas*, in every world we service. More people's lives parallel than you'd think. The passengers—well, they generally don't exist on a particular run except once. The very few who do still don't take the trip in every world of service. I guess once or twice it's happened that we've had a passenger cross over, but if so we never heard of it."

"And how come I'm here in so many worlds?" I asked him.

McNeil smiled. "You were recruited, of course. The Corporation has a tremendous, intensive recruiting effort involving ferry lines and crewmembers. When they spot one, like you, in just the right circumstance in all worlds, they recruit you—all of you. An even worse job than you'd think, since every season one or two new Bluewater Corporations put identical ferries on this run, or shift routes slightly and overlap. Then we have to make sure the present crew can serve them, too, by recruiting your twin on those worlds."

Suddenly I reached over, grabbed his beard, and yanked.

"*Ouch!* Dammit!" he cried, and pulled my hand away.

"I—I'm sorry, I—" I stammered.

He shook his head, then smiled. "That's all right, son. You're about the seventh person to do that to me in the last five years. I guess there's a lot of varieties of *me*, too."

I thought about all that traffic. "Do others know of this?" I asked him. "I mean, is there some sort of hidden commerce between the worlds on this ferry?"

He grinned. "I'm not supposed to answer that," he said carefully. "But, what the hell. Yes, I think—no, I *know* there is. After all, the shift of people and ships is constant. You move one notch each trip if all of you take the voyage. Sometimes up, sometimes down. If that's true, and if they can recruit a crew that fits the requirements, why not truck drivers? A hell of a lot of truck traffic through here year 'round, you know. No reduced winter service. And some of the rigs are really kinda strange-looking." He sighed.

"I only know this—in a couple of hours I'll start selling fares again, and I'll sell a half-dozen or so to St. Michael—and *there is no St. Michael*. It isn't even listed on my schedules or maps. I doubt if the Corporation's actually the trader, more the middle-man in the deal. But they sure as hell don't make their millions off fares alone."

It was odd the way I was accepting it. Somehow, it seemed to make sense, crazy as it was.

"What's to keep me from using this knowledge somehow?" I asked him. "Maybe bring a team of experts up?"

"Feel free," McNeil answered. "Unless they overlap they'll get a nice, normal ferry ride. And if you can make a profit, go ahead, as long as it doesn't interfere with Bluewater's cash flow. The *Orcas* cost the company over twenty four million *reals* and they want it back."

"Twenty four million *what?*" I shot back.

"Reals," he replied, taking a bill from his wallet. I looked at it.

I looked at it. It was printed in red, and had a picture of some-one very ugly labeled "Prince Juan XVI" and an official seal from the "Bank of New Lisboa". I handed it back.

"What country are we in?" I asked uneasily.

"Portugal," he replied casually. "Portuguese America, actually, although only nominally. So many of us Yankees have come in you don't even have to speak Portuguese any more. They even print the local bills in Anglish now."

Yes, that's what he said. Anglish.

"It's the best ferryboat job in the world, though," McNeil con-tinued. "For someone without ties, that is. You'll meet more dif-ferent kinds of people from more cultures than you'll ever im-agine. Three runs on, three off—in as many as twenty-four differ-ent variations of these towns, all unique. And a month off in winter to see a little of a different world each time. Never mind whether you buy the explanation—you've seen the results, you know what I say is true. Want the job?"

"I'll give it a try," I told him, fascinated. I wasn't sure if I *did* buy the explanation, but I certainly had something strange and fascinating here.

"O.K., here's twenty *reals* advance," McNeil said, handing me a purple twenty from the cashbox. "Get some dinner if you didn't eat on the ship, get a good night at the motel, then be ready to go on at four tomorrow afternoon."

I got up to leave.

"Oh, and Mr. Dalton," he added, and I turned to face him.

"Yes?"

"If, while on shore, you fall for a pretty lass, decide to settle down, then do it—*but don't go back on that ship again!* Quit. If you don't she's going to be greeted by a stranger, and you might never find her again."

"I'll remember," I told him.

§ § §

The job was everything McNeil promised and more. The scenery was spectacular, the people an ever-changing, fascinating group. Even the crew changed slightly—a little shorter sometimes, a little fatter or thinner, beards and moustaches came and went with astonishing rapidity, and accents varied enormously. It didn't matter; you soon adjusted to it as a matter of course, and all shipboard experiences were in common, anyway.

It was like a tight family after a while, really. And there were women in the crew, too, ranging from their twenties to the early fifties, not only in food and bar service but as deckhands and the like as well. Occasionally it was a little unsettling, since, in two or three cases out of the crew of 66, they were men in one world, women in another. You got used to even that. It was probably more unsettling for them; they were distinct people, and *they* didn't change sex. The personalities and personal histories tended to parallel, regardless, though, with only a few minor differences.

And the passengers! Some were really amazing. Even seasons were different to some of them, which explained the clothing variations. Certainly what constituted fasion and moral behavior was wildly different, as different as what they ate and the places they came from.

And yet, oddly, people were people. They laughed, and cried, and ate and drank and told jokes—some rather strange, I'll admit—and snapped pictures and all the other things people did. They came from places where the Vikings settled Nova Scotia (called Vinland, naturally), where Nova Scotia was French, or Spanish, or Portuguese, or very, very English. Even one in which Nova Scotia had been settled by Lord Baltimore and called Avalon.

Maine was as wild or wilder. There were two Indian nations running it, the U.S., Canada, Britain, France, and lots of variations some of which I never got straight. There was also a temporal difference sometimes—some people were rather futuristic, with gadgets I couldn't even understand. One truck I loaded was powered by some sort of solar power and carried a cargo of food service robots. Some others were behind—still mainly horses, or old-time cars and trucks. I am not certain even now if they were running at different speeds from us or whether some inventions had been made in some places and not in others.

And, McNeil was right. Every new summer season added at least one more. The boat was occasionally so crowded to our crew eyes that we had trouble making our way from one end to the other. Watching staterooms unload was also wild—it looked occasionally like the circus clown act, where 50 clowns get out of a Volkswagen.

And there *was* some sort of trade between the worlds. It was quickly clear that Bluewater Corporation was behind most of it, and that this was what made the line so profitable.

And, just once, there was a horrible, searing pain that hit the entire crew, and a modern world we didn't make any more after that, and a particular variation of the crew we never saw again. And the last newspapers from that world had told of a coming war.

There was also a small crew turnover, of course. Some went on vacation and never returned, some returned but would not re-board the ship. The company was understanding, and it usually meant a little extra work for a few weeks at most until someone new came on.

§ § §

The stars were fading a little now, and I shined the spot over to the red marker for the Captain. He acknowledged seeing it, and made his turn in, the lights of Southport coming into view and masking the stars a bit.

I went through the motions mechanically, raising the bow when the captain hit the mark, letting go the bow lines, checking the clearances, and the like. I was thinking about the girl.

We knew that people's lives in the main did parallel from world to world. Seven times now she'd come aboard, seven times she'd looked at the white wake, and seven times she'd jumped to her death.

Maybe it was the temporal dislocation, maybe she just reached the same point at different stages, but she was always there and she always jumped.

I'd been working the *Orcas* three years, had some strange experiences, and generally pleasurable ones. For the first time I had a job I liked, a family of sorts in the crew, and an ever-changing assortment of people and places for a three-point ferry run. In that time we'd lost one world, and gained by our figures three others. That was 26 variants.

Did that girl exist in all 26? I wondered. Would we be subjected to that sadness 19 more times? Or more, as we picked up new worlds?

Oh, I'd tried to find her before she jumped in the past, yes. But she hadn't been consistent, except for the place she chose. We did three runs a day, two crews, so it was six a day more or less. She did it at different seasons, in different years, dressed differently.

You couldn't cover them all.

Not even all the realities of the crew of all worlds, although I knew that we were essentially the same people on all of them and that I—the other mes—were also looking.

I don't even know why I was so fixated, except that I'd been to that point once myself, and I'd discovered that you *could* go on, living with the emotional scars, and find a life.

I didn't even know what I'd say and do if I *did* see her early. I only knew that, if I did, she damned well wasn't going to go over the stern that trip.

In the meantime, my search for her when I could paid other dividends. I prevented a couple of children from going over through childish play, as well as a drunk, and spotted several health problems as I surveyed the people. One turned out to be a woman in advanced labor, and the first mate and I delivered our first child—our first, but the *Orcas'* nineteenth. We helped a lot of people, really, with a lot of different things.

They were all just spectres, of course; they got on the boat often without us seeing them, and they disembarked for all time the same way. There were some regulars, but they were few. And, for them, we were a ghost crew, there to help and to serve.

But, then, isn't that the way you think of anybody in a service occupation? Firemen are firemen, not individuals; so are waiters, cops, street sweepers, and all the rest.

We sailed from Point A to Point C stopping at B, and it was our whole life.

And then, one day in July of last year, I spotted her.

She was just coming on board at St. Clement's—that's why I hadn't noticed her before. We backed into St. Clement's, and I was on the bow lines. But we were short, having just lost a deckhand to a nice-looking fellow in the English Colony of Annapolis Royal, and it was my turn to do some double duty. So, there I was, routing traffic on the ship when I saw this little rounded station wagon go by and saw *her* in it.

I still almost missed her; I hadn't expected her to be with another person, another woman, and we were loading the Vinland existence, so in July they were more accurately in a state of undress than anything else, but I spotted her all the same. Jackie Carliner, one of the barmaids and a pretty good artist, had sketched her from the one time she'd seen the girl and we'd made copies for everybody.

Even so, I had my loading duties to finish first—there was no one else. But, as soon as we were underway and I'd raised the stern ramp, I made my way topside and to the lower stern deck. I took my walkie-talkie off the belt clip and called the captain.

"Sir, this is Dalton," I called. "I've seen our suicide girl."

"So what else is new?" grumbled the captain. "You know policy on that by now."

"But, sir!" I protested. "I mean still alive. Still on board. It's barely sundown, and we're a good half hour from the point yet."

He saw what I meant. "Very well," he said crisply. "But you know we're short-handed. I'll put Caldwell on the bow station this time, but you better get some results or I'll give you so much detail you won't have time to meddle in other people's affairs!"

I sighed. Running a ship like this one hardened most people. I wondered if the captain, with nineteen years on the run, even understood why I cared enough to try and stop this girl I didn't know from going in.

Did *I* know, for that matter?

As I looked around at the people going by I thought about it. I'd thought about it a great deal before.

Why *did* I care about these faceless people? People from so many different worlds and cultures that they might as well have been from another planet. People who cared not at all for me, who saw me as an object, a cipher, a service, like those robots I mentioned. They didn't care about me. If *I* were perched on that rail and a crowd was around most of them would probably yell "Jump!"

Most of the crew, too, cared only about each other, to a degree, and about the *Orcas,* our rock of sanity. I thought of that world, gone in some atomic fire. What was the measure of an anonymous human being's worth?

I thought of Joanna and Harmony. With pity, yes, but I realized that Joanna, at least, had been a vampire. She'd needed me, needed a rock to steady herself, to unburden herself to, to brag to. Someone steady and understanding, someone whose manner and character suggested that solidity. She'd never really even considered that I might have my own problems, that her promiscuity and lifestyle might be hurting me. Not that she was trying to hurt me—she just never *considered* me.

Like those people going by now. If they stub their toe, or have a question, or slip, or the boat sinks, they need me. Until then, I'm just a faceless automaton to them.

Ready to serve them, to care about them, if *they* needed somebody.

And that was why I was out here in the surprising chill, out on the stern with my neck stuck out a mile, trying to prevent a suicide I *knew* would happen, *knew* because I'd seen it three times before.

I was needed.

That was the measure of a human being's true worth, I felt sure. Not how many people ministered to your needs, but how many people you can help.

That girl—she had been brutalized, somehow, by society. Now I was to provide some counterbalance.

It was the surety of this that kept me from blowing myself up with the old Delaware ferry, or jumping off that stern rail myself.

I glanced uneasily around and looked ahead. There was Shipshead light, tall and proud this time in the darkness, the way I liked it. I thought I could almost make out the marker buoys already. I started to get nervous.

I was certain she'd jump. It'd happened every time before that we'd known. Maybe, just maybe, I thought, in this existence she won't.

I had no more than gotten the thought through my head when she came around the corner of the deck housing and stood in the starboard corner, looking down.

She certainly looked different this time. Her long hair was blond, not dark, and braided in large pigtails that drooped almost to her waist. She wore only the string bikini and transparent cape the Vinlanders liked in summer, and she had several gold rings on each arm, welded loosely there, I knew, and a marriage ring around her neck.

That was interesting, I thought.

Her friend, as thin and underdeveloped as she was stout, was with her. The friend had darker hair and had it twisted high atop her head, and had no marriage ring.

I eased over slowly, but not sneakily. Like I said, nobody notices the crewman on a vessel; he's a part of it.

"Luok, are yu sooure yu don' vant to halve a drink or zumpin'?" the friend asked in that curious accent the Vinlanders had developed through cultural pollution with the dominant English and French.

"Naye, I yust vant to smell da zee-spray," the girl replied. "Go on. I vill be alonk before ze zhip iz docking."

The friend was hesitant; I could see it in her manner. But I could also see she would go, partly because she was chilly, partly because she felt she had to show trust to the girl.

She walked off. I looked busy checking the stairway supports to the second deck, and she paid me no mind whatsoever.

There were a few others on deck, but most had gone forward to see us come in, and the couple dressed completely in black sitting there on the bench were invisible to the girl as she was to them. She peered down at the black water and started to edge more to the starboard side engine wake, then a little past, almost to the center. Her upper torso didn't move, but I saw a bare, dirty foot go up on the lower rail.

I walked over, casually. She heard, and turned slightly to see if it was anyone she need be bothered with.

I went up to her and stood beside her.

"Don't do it," I said softly, not looking directly at her. "It's too damned selfish a way to go."

She gave a small gasp and turned to look at me in wonder.

"How—how didt yu—?" she managed.

"I'm an old hand at suicides," I told her, and that was no lie. Joanna, then almost me, then this girl three other times.

"I vouldn't really haff—" she began, but I cut her off.

"Yes you would. You know it and I know it. The only thing you know and I don't is *why*."

We were inside Shipshead light now. If I could keep her talking just a few more minutes we'd clear the channel markers, and slow for the turn and docking. The turn and the slowdown would make it impossible for her to be caught in propwash, and, I felt, the cycle would be broken, at least for her.

"Vy du yu care?" she asked, turning again to look at the dark sea, only slightly illuminated by the rapidly receding light.

"Well, partly because it's my ship, and I don't like things like that to happen on my ship," I told her. "Partly because I've been there myself, and I know how brutal a suicide is."

She looked at me strangely. "Dat's a fonny t'ing tu zay," she responded. "Jost vun qvick jomp and *pszzt!* All ofer."

"You're wrong," I said. "Besides, why would anyone so young want to end it?"

She had a dreamy quality to her face and voice. She was starting to blur, and I was worried that I might somehow translate into a different world-level as we neared shore.

"My 'usbahnd," she responded. "Goldier vas hiss name." She fingered the marriage ring around her neck. "Zo yong, so 'andzum." She turned her head quickly and looked up at me. "Do yu know vat it iz to be fat und ugly und 'alf bloind and haff ze best uv all men zuddenly pay attenzion to yu, vant to *marry* yu?"

I admitted I didn't, but didn't mention my own experiences.

"What happened? He leave you?" I asked.

There were tears in her eyes. "Ya, in a vay, ya. Goldier he jomped out a tvventy-story building, he did. Und itz my own fault, yu know. I shud haff been dere. Or, maybe I didn't giff him vat he needed. I dunno."

"Then you of all people know how brutal suicide really is," I retorted. "Look at what it did to you. You have friends, like your friend here. They care. It will hurt them as your husband's hurt you. This girl with you—she'll carry guilt for leaving you alone the whole rest of her life." She was shaking now, not really from the chill, and I put my arm around her. Where the hell were those marker lights?

"Do you see how cruel it is? What suicide does to others? It leaves a legacy of guilty, much of it false guilt. And you might be needed by someone else, sometime, to help them. Somebody else might die because you weren't there."

She looked up at me, then seemed to dissolve, collapse into a crescendo of tears, and sat down on the deck. I looked up and saw the red and green markers astern, felt the engines slow, felt the *Orcas* turn.

"*Ghetta!*" The voice was a piercing scream in the night. I looked up and saw her friend running to us from coming down the stairway. Anxiety and concern was in her stricken face, and there were tears in her eyes. She bent down to the still sobbing girl. "I shud nefer haff left yu!" she sobbed, and hugged the girl.

I sighed. The *Orcas* was making its dock approach now, the ringing of the bells said that Caldwell had managed to raise the bow without crashing us into the dock.

"My Gott!" the friend swore, then looked up at me. "Yu stopped her? How can I effer—?"

But they both already had that ethreal, unnatural double image about them, both fading into a different existence than mine.

"Just remember there's a million Ghettas out there," I told them both. "And you can make them or break them."

I turned and walked away as I heard the satisfying thump and felt the slight jerk of the ferry fitting into the ramp. I stopped and glanced back at the stern, but I could see no one. Nobody was there.

Who were the ghosts? I mused. Those women, or the crew of the *Orcas?* How many times did hundreds of people from different worlds coexist on this ship without knowing it?"

How many times did people in the *same* world coexist without knowing each other, or caring about each other, for that matter?

"Mr. Dalton!" snapped a voice in my walkie-talkie.

"Sir?" I responded.

"Well?" the captain promised.

"No screams this time, Captain," I told him, satisfaction in my voice. "One young woman will live."

There was a long pause, and, for a moment, I thought he might actually be human. Then he snapped, "There's eighty-six assorted vehicles still waiting to be off-loaded, and might I remind you we're short-handed and on a strict schedule?"

I sighed and broke into a trot. Business was business, and I had a whole world to throw out of the car deck so I could run another one in.

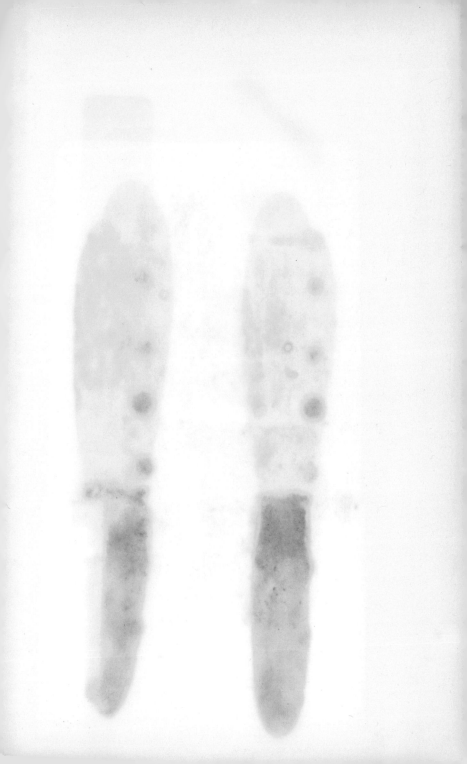